PRAISE FOR ED KURTZ

"*The Rib From Which I Remake the World* isn't only the best book I've read this year, it is Ed Kurtz's best book yet. While it echoes with the shadowy threatening of Bradbury's *Something Wicked This Way Comes* and the religious dread of Hjortsberg's *Falling Angel*, the clearest voice here is Kurtz's own cry into the existential abyss. This is a haunting story of seeing through illusion and the terrifying reality of what it means to meet your maker."

—Bracken MacLeod, author of *Mountain Home* and *Stranded*

"*A Wind of Knives* dusts off the classic western's most enduring motifs and gives them a shine. With no lack of gunplay and bloodshed, the book also has heart and intelligence. In short, Kurtz delivers an intense, gritty, and moving story that takes a new look at the Old West."

—Lee Thomas, Bram Stoker Award and Lambda Literary Award-winning author of *The German* and *Ash Street*

"[*Nausea* is] a gritty, hard-edged tale with just the right amount of feeling, making this one hell of a story. All of Ed's gifts are on display here: fast pacing, memorable characters and brutal action that aren't easy to forget, but make for great reading."

—Terrence McCauley, author of *Sympathy for the Devil*, *Prohibition*, and *Slow Burn*

D0288883

FIRST EDITION

The Rib From Which I Remake the World © 2016 by Ed Kurtz
Cover artwork © 2016 by Erik Mohr
Cover and interior design © 2016 by Samantha Beiko

Distributed in Canada by
Publishers Group Canada
76 Stafford Street, Unit 300
Toronto, Ontario, M6J 2S1
Toll Free: 800-747-8147
e-mail: info@pgcbooks.ca

Distributed in the U.S. by
Consortium Book Sales & Distribution
34 Thirteenth Avenue, NE, Suite 101
Minneapolis, MN 55413
Phone: (612) 746-2600
e-mail: sales.orders@cbsd.com

Library and Archives Canada Cataloguing in Publication

Kurtz, Ed, 1977-, author

The rib from which I remake the world / Ed Kurtz.

Issued in print and electronic formats.

ISBN 978-1-77148-390-2 (paperback).--ISBN 978-1-77148-391-9 (pdf)

I. Title.

PS3611.U775R53 2016   813'.6   C2016-901768-0

                                                            C2016-901769-9

Shelfie

A **free** eBook edition is available
with the purchase of this print book.

CHIZINE PUBLICATIONS
Peterborough, Canada
www.chizinepub.com
info@chizinepub.com

Edited by Samantha Beiko
Proofread by Leigh Teetzel

CLEARLY PRINT YOUR NAME ABOVE IN UPPER CASE

Instructions to claim your free eBook edition:
1. Download the Shelfie app for Android or iOS
2. Write your name in **UPPER CASE** above
3. Use the Shelfie app to submit a photo
4. Download your eBook to any device

Canada Council   Conseil des arts
for the Arts   du Canada

We acknowledge the support of the Canada Council for the Arts which last year invested $20.1 million in writing and publishing throughout Canada.

ONTARIO ARTS COUNCIL
CONSEIL DES ARTS DE L'ONTARIO

an Ontario government agency
un organisme du gouvernement de l'Ontario

Published with the generous assistance of the Ontario Arts Council.

Printed in Canada

THE RIB

FROM WHICH

I REMAKE

THE WORLD

ChiZine Publications

ED KURTZ

THE RIB
FROM WHICH
I REMAKE
THE WORLD

"He was a monster that nature had made."

—Clark Ashton Smith, "Monsters in the Night"

"Sure there's a hell . . ." I could hear him saying it now, now, as I lay here in bed with her breath in my face, and her body squashed against me . . . "It is the drab desert where the sun sheds neither warmth nor light and Habit force-feeds senile Desire. It is the place where mortal Want dwells within immortal Necessity, and the night becomes hideous with the groans of one and the ecstatic shrieks of the other. Yes, there is a hell, my boy, and you do not have to dig for it . . ."

—Jim Thompson, *Savage Night*

PROLOGUE

The hurdy-gurdy to the left of him and the shrill calliope to the right competed for dominance—the result being a deafening cacophony of noise without order. The fellow with the former instrument played mainly for an audience of one, the fez-topped monkey at his feet that chattered and danced to the delight of every child, and not a few adults, who passed by. Tim Davis was less impressed; he'd listened to the leathery old gypsy's abominable wheel fiddle for days on end now, and with each day that passed it sounded worse than the day before. Two days earlier, Tim gave the gypsy a look, one that said *I don't much like you*, but the old man just flashed a largely toothless smile underneath that stringy black moustache of his and said, "Is good, yes? Monkey likes."

Traipsing away now, his feet shuffling through dirt and sawdust, Tim revisited the notion he'd had the night before, the idea that by killing that damned monkey he'd never have to listen to the gypsy's hurdy-gurdy again. The calliope alone he could handle. Besides, it could hardly be called a proper circus without one. Monkeys were good for circuses, too, but monkeys were easier to come by than calliopes. Tim figured he could find a monkey within a day if he really wanted to. Even here, clear out in the middle of Nowhere, Arkansas.

He must have had a scowl on his face, because halfway between the calliope and the makeshift fence cordoning off the sideshow grounds, Lion Jack materialized like a spectre from thin air and roared, "Why the long face?"

It was sort of joke: Tim had a squat, round face. His scowl deepened. The strongman paused, patient as ever, rubbed the back of his freshly shaven head. He looked perfectly ridiculous in the spotted fur tunic he wore, but Tim couldn't begrudge him that—it was part of the act, just like the chrome dome. Jack had probably just come from lifting something stupendous to the delight and amazement of a tent full of gawp-mouthed local yokels. It beat the hell out of dumping sawdust on vomit, a task Tim performed a dozen or more times a day. Christ, but how those rotten kids puked.

The strongman said, "Minerva, again?"

Minerva, the Snake Lady—not the original Snake Lady, who suffered from some terrible skin disease that made her flesh scaly and hard, but rather a snake charmer who was really quite nice looking—had rebuffed the young carny time and again to the point of steering clear of Tim in fear of harassment. Sometimes Tim sulked for hours thinking about it. Sometimes he spied on her through the window in her little wooden trailer, watched her roll around with whatever rough-and-ready country boy she'd hooked that day. She liked them tall, lean, and dumber than dirt. Tim could play dumb, but he was doomed to be short and bony and not at all handsome. Even surrounded by freaks and monsters and not a few fugitives, Tim Davis was never a handsome man.

"No, not that."

He shouldered past the colossal strongman and continued on to the gate in the fence. He unlatched it, shut it behind him, and sauntered over to the periphery of the Ten-in-One tent. The afternoon sun was sinking, a slower process than usual with close to nothing on the terrain for it to hide behind. Hal White, the Human Skeleton, was lingering outside the flaps with a cigarette dangling from his white lips and a detective magazine in his bony, translucent hands. Per usual, he was naked to the waist, proudly displaying his startlingly gaunt, colourless torso.

"Show over?" Tim asked him.

"Yeah. Not such a good night."

"Small crowd?"

Hal nodded. "The wolf boy wouldn't stop crying and the geek passed out drunk."

Tim shook his head. Hal shrugged.

"I expect it takes a good bit of firewater to wash down all that chicken blood."

The skeleton jammed one of his pitch cards into the magazine to mark his place, his own hollow face peering sorrowfully over the pages as he closed it and took the cigarette from his mouth. The card had his life story printed on the back, not one word of it true.

"Minerva's gone to town," he said.

"What town?"

Hal shrugged some more. Every time he did it, the bones in his shoulders jutted out so sharply it was a wonder his skin could take it.

"Besides, I don't care about her. I want to see Harry."

The skeleton stabbed the air with a wretchedly thin thumb.

"Over yonder," he said. "In the woods again."

Tim knitted his brow and stared off into the distant woods before he had to watch Hal shrug again. Somewhere out there, beyond the tree line and among the scrubby, naked elms and hackberries, was the one-and-only Black Harry Ashford. Tim gestured his thanks to the emaciated man and made a beeline for the woods.

)(

Though he was absolutely certain he'd seen it, out there amongst the shadows cast by the thicker branches and brambles, Harry could not see it if he looked at it directly. Only from the corners of his eyes, in his peripheral vision, could he make out the dark, shapeless form loping in the woods, and only barely. At once it was decidedly human, a man, and now something like a dog, perhaps a goat. Harry could not be sure, not without peering intently at the form, at which point it vanished entirely. The whole business was frustrating in the extreme.

The figure came in the gloaming, as it had the night before and the night before that. The first night, Harry reckoned he'd summoned it. He had the grimoire; he'd said the words.

"*Lucifero, Ouyar, Chameron, Aliseon, Mandousin . . .*

"*Premy, Oreit, Naydrus, Esmony, Eparineson, Estiot . . .*

"*Dumosson, Danochar, Casmiel, Hayras . . .*

"*Fabelleronthon, Sodirno, Peatham . . .*

"Come Lucifer, come."

Seven times. Light the black candle.

Complete rubbish.

He was a magician, but corny parlour tricks were his bag, despite the convoluted and irrefutably false genealogy he provided his audiences at the commencement of every performance—son of an endless line of black magick practitioners, all that garbage. Without fail, he always managed to elicit some terrified expressions, usually children and old women, but then he launched right into sleight of hand and card tricks and that hackneyed fake mindreading bit with the "volunteer" from the audience, lately young Tim Davis when he wasn't cleaning up sick. Yet if anyone thought his act was a mountain of horse shit . . .

Utter nonsense, this book and all its babbling idiocy.

But still—the figure . . .

He saw it again, cantering in the falling twilight, and this time Harry was careful not to turn his head, to keep the amorphous form just in sight. Instead, he kept his eyes centred on the sigil in the loam at his knees, the sign from the grimoire, carved with the tip of a dagger:

Dime store Merlin, he thought.

Black Harry, indeed. Earlier, in the Ten-in-One, some hillbilly from the heath called out, "He ain't no black!" Not in any sense, no. Yet he would say the stupid words again, and scratch the sigil in a hundred forests, because what else could he do? And what could it possibly hurt?

A slight breeze picked up, disturbing the denuded grey and black branches which clawed at one another with witches' fingers. Gentle at first, but cold—and when it gathered momentum it blew the sigil apart, leaving nothing but the broken loam.

And out in the darkening recesses of the woods, the figure danced at the outermost edge of Harry's vision, changed shape, invited the building wind.

Come Lucifer, come.

)(

Tim sensed the form, too, but he dismissed it as some woodland animal, maybe a deer. For a moment he stiffened, wondering if there could be anything more aggressive in the sticks of Arkansas, a boar or a bear, but the figure was quick and skittish—not a threat. A minute later he'd forgotten all about it. His mind was set on Harry.

The magician sat cross legged on the ground, rotted detritus surrounding him so that it looked like a man rising from his own grave. His eyes were closed and the tattered leather-bound book in his lap lay open. Tim supposed the older man was asleep. He weighed the pros and cons of waking him up.

Then Harry's eyes opened, so quickly that it seemed as though his eyelids had simply evaporated. Tim's back leapt and he let out a little yelp.

"Harry?"

The magician's lips parted, only slightly at first, but as his jaw unhinged the mouth formed a gaping black pit. Tim stared into the opening. He could see no teeth.

"Harry, it's me. It's Tim."

Harry groaned softly. The sound was barely audible beneath the greater groan of the gathering wind. Somewhere behind Tim, something rustled the ankle-deep carpet of decaying leaves. He turned instinctively to investigate, and for a fraction of an instant he thought he saw somebody crouching behind the trunk of diseased-looking hackberry tree. But no one was there.

For some irrational reason he could not quite pinpoint, Tim got the idea that the monkey had followed him out there. He grinned at the ludicrous thought. It was impossible, of course. Stupid. He turned back to Harry.

And he gasped. Harry's eyes were pus-yellow, the irises washed over with the jaundiced coating. His mouth was open to an impossible degree, his chin digging into his throat. *A trick*, Tim thought. *The old bastard's trying to scare me.*

The old bastard was doing an exemplary job of it.

Tim made a tight knit of his brow and said, "Cut it out, Harry—the tent's over there and all the rubes went home, anyhow."

He'd barely finished speaking before Harry was up and upon him, all gaping, moaning mouth and clawing fingers. Tim screamed, staggered backward. His heel jammed up against a knotted root hidden by the leaves. He collapsed to the ground, and Harry went down with him.

It was over before either of them knew it.

※

Tim Davis went back to spreading sawdust on puke and cleaning up animal shit. He did not often speak to anyone, and he never bothered Minerva again. For the most part, the circus folks—carnies, freaks, and performers alike—steered clear of the strange, silent fellow who lurched gloomily among them. And since he kept to himself, everyone was satisfied with the arrangement.

Black Harry Ashford never came out of the woods. People came and went from circuses all the time, running away to join and then running back home when things got rough. No one much bothered to wonder what had become of the magician.

The show went on.

PART 1

You Gotta Tell 'Em to Sell 'Em

CHAPTER ONE

Jojo fished the matchbook out of his wallet, knocking his receipt tickets from the racetrack out on the floor. He tore one of the cardboard matches free and dragged the red bulb across the sandpaper strip. It crumbled without a spark. He sighed heavily, the exhalation making the Old Gold between his lips wobble. The matches were damp from the sweat seeping through the fabric of his trousers, his shirt, even his hat. *It's gonna be a hot one*, the day clerk had chirped when Jojo arrived for his shift. *No shit*, he'd fired back. But the kid was right—half past seven in the evening and there was nothing for the heat. Between jobs, after the force and just before the war, Jojo might have been tempted to take in a show at the Palace as he often did in those down-and-out days. The picture didn't matter (usually it was a woman's picture or some dopey monster show), but he'd take it all in, cartoons and all, just for the air-conditioning. He saw a lot of pictures over the course of that terrible year, all kinds, so that he got to where he could discuss them at great length with the girls who worked at the Starlight who dreamed, dumbly, of becoming starlets themselves. The only ones he ever made a point of skipping were the ones that starred Irene Dunne. She looked too much like Beth, and that only made him that much sorer at the lousy shape of things. He sat through the first fifteen minutes of *Penny Serenade* back in '41 before stamping out of the theatre in a huff. Couldn't help but feel like the screen was mocking him, daring him to do something about it. Then last year there was that girl from the drugstore who wanted him to take her to *A Guy Named Joe*. Jojo gave the broad an earful and never talked to her again.

Fucking Irene Dunne.

He bent over and picked the race tickets up off the soiled carpet. Oaklawn had been a bust: he'd gone safe and bet on Mar-Kell and Ocean Wave to show. Neither did, and now the two pasteboard tickets were just taking up space. Superficially, he went to Oaklawn for the corned beef sandwiches. Realistically, he was infuriated that a couple of so-called sure bets couldn't even show. For no reason at all, he slipped the tickets back into the wallet.

Tipping his hat back on the crown of his head, Jojo withdrew the handkerchief from his coat pocket and mopped his brow. The little metal fan beside his cluttered desk stopped working weeks ago, though Mr. Hibbs, the skinflint night manager, was in no great hurry to get it replaced for him. Said there was a decent breeze on the south side of the hotel at night if he'd only open a window. Jojo opened the window. No breeze.

He opened up a drawer in his desk, fumbled his calloused fingers past the Smith & Wesson and the faded receipts and paystubs and, yes, ticket stubs from the Palace Theater, looking for another book of matches. He found none, slammed the drawer shut. The crystal cigarette lighter on top of his desk just sat there, covered in dust and devoid of a single drop of fuel.

"Son of a bitch," he groused.

He swung his legs around and stood up, ignoring the audible creak of his knees and the twinge in the small of his back. Cop complaints. But he wasn't a cop anymore.

The night clerk was lounging in the cashier's cage when Jojo emerged from the stuffy office, his club foot propped up on the safe. He was reading a crumpled paperback that he held about four inches from the tip of his crooked nose. Jojo rattled the mesh wire of the cage with his knuckles.

"Hey, Jake—you got a match?"

"The hell I need a match for?" Jake snapped back, never taking his eyes from the book. "I don't smoke, Jojo. You know that."

Jojo finally took the Old Gold out of his mouth and propped it behind his ear.

"You ought to get some eyeglasses, Jake," he said. "You're like to go blind that way."

"Yeah, sure. I've heard every hard luck story. Even mine."

Jake turned the page and Jojo snickered, wandering off across the lobby to the cigarette machine. More often than not, there were spare matches in the cup on top. Tonight there were not.

His eyes wandered lazily, angrily, over the narrow lobby, landing first on the yellow square on the wall above the cigarette machine. The square was a lighter yellow than the rest of the wall that surrounded it, having been exposed to the elements—the *funk* of constant human traffic, smoking and breathing and stinking through the place like Grand Central Station, it sometimes seemed to him—for a far shorter time. Time was there hung a cheap reproduction of a Thomas Hart Benton painting where that square now yawned at the world—*Study For a Slow Train Through Arkansas*, it was called. It had never been there during Jojo's tenure, not for years before he got there, but the badly-framed piece remained in the janitor's closet where he'd seen it a few dozen times. The painting had been purchased with the expressed intent to add some class to the proceedings, but it didn't work. Folks around here didn't want class, not when it came in the form of namby-pamby modern art that didn't really *look* like anything, at least not like anything you'd ever actually see. The conductor didn't have a face, for one thing, and the smoke from the locomotive coming up the tracks was all wrong—angled, like. People cast odd, sidelong glances at the thing, and eventually they started to complain. So, down it went—Mr. Hibbs' orders. All of this from Jake, the de facto curator of the hotel lobby, who said he'd asked if he could take the Benton home with him if they weren't going to hang it, but no, Hibbs sternly denied him, it was hotel property and it was to remain in the closet indefinitely.

From the empty yellow square Jojo's eyes traced a line diagonally down to the long, narrow table shoved up against the wall, across the lobby from the cashier's cage. On top of it sat a dusty orange planter, inside of which was nothing but dirt. There might have been a plant in it once upon a time, but not now and not for the last year or so. For all intents and purposes, it was just a decorative bowl of hard, dry dirt, though unlike the Benton nobody ever complained about that.

The oppressive emptiness of the place struck Jojo, though this was nothing new. Empty walls and an empty planter and the empty match cup on the cigarette machine. Even the front desk was empty, unmanned as ever. Jake did all his business from his cage, taking leave of it only when he was presented with the need to use the toilet. Most of the rooms upstairs were similarly empty, as was the cramped sitting area between the stairs and the elevator with all the ragged and mismatched furniture that sat on top of each other there. The whole skinny expanse of the shotgun lobby, from the front doors to the back wall behind the faded green divan was empty of motion and interest and life and the world.

Jojo frowned. He tried to drag on his cigarette, his reverie having shunted off the match problem, then frowned deeper yet when all he inhaled was more of the humid lobby's air. It felt like even the air was unchanged, old and empty like everything else. His shoulders slumped and he let out a small groan.

Presently the doors clattered open and Charles, the coloured bellhop, came struggling in with two cardboard suitcases held precariously together with twine. A couple emerged in his wake, pointedly ignoring him as though their luggage was hauling itself into the lobby. The man was fortyish, mostly bald save for some greasy, overlong strands of black hair combed over his sweaty skull in a ludicrous attempt to mask his baldness. His bulbous nose was riddled with gin blossoms and his droopy eyelids looked almost as black as his hair. Accompanying the man was a girl of indeterminate age, though Jojo didn't figure her for much older than eighteen, if that. She giggled and hiccupped, her brown curls bouncing around her head like coiled snakes. Both of them were stone cold drunk.

Charles gestured with his chin to the cashier's cage, where Jake groaned and tossed his paperback to the side. The couple staggered that way. Charles looked to Jojo and shrugged.

"You got a match?" Jojo asked the bellhop.

Charles shook his head. Jojo extended his lower lip and sauntered over to the couple at the cage.

"Say, buddy," he said, tapping the man on the shoulder.

The man flinched, turned around. His eyelids lifted, but only barely.

"Yeah?"

"Do you smoke?"

The man tilted his head to the side. "Sure," he said.

"Gimme a match, will you?"

A grin stretched across the man's red face and he let out a noisy, foul-smelling breath. He shoved a hand into his trouser pocket and came back with a box of wooden matches. Jojo took the box, struck one to flame and ignited the end of the Old Gold. The cigarette bloomed bright red as he drew the smoke deep into his lungs.

"Thanks, pal," Jojo said, handing the matches back. "Checking in?"

The grin depleted some. "Yeah."

"Mr. and Mrs. Smith, I presume?"

Jojo exhaled a blue stream and smiled. The man smiled back, though his compatriot turned a nervous stare at him.

"How'd you guess?"

"I'm a good guesser," Jojo said. "You got a marriage certificate?"

"Marriage certificate? Say, what is this?"

"Maybe not such a respectable establishment, but respectable enough. We're not the Piedmont, but we ain't exactly a flophouse, either."

The girl squeezed the man's arm. Mr. Smith knitted his brow and sneered.

"I didn't reckon joints like this had house *dicks*," he said.

"I work cheap. Now how about that licence?"

"I don't got no licence and you know it."

"Hmn," Jojo grunted as he sucked another drag. "I expect you're familiar with the Mann Act, Mr. Smith?"

"I'm over twenty-one," the girl piped up.

"Cross any state lines on your way here?"

Across the lobby Charles set the suitcases down with a thump and leaned up against the wall for the long haul. Jake reached for his paperback and flipped to where he left off.

"You know, I don't have to take this," the man protested.

"You sure don't," Jojo agreed. "It's still a free country, after all. And I guess there's still rooms in town that don't care if she's twenty-one or seventeen, if you look hard enough. If you start now, you might still be tight when you finally get her between the sheets."

Mr. Smith yanked his arm from the girl's grasp and puffed up his chest. In the span of a second he'd gone from happy drunk to mean drunk. Jojo let the cigarette drop to the cracked tiled floor where he ground it out with the heel of his shoe.

"You got no right," Mr. Smith began, jabbing a finger into Jojo's chest.

Jojo seized the man's wrist and twisted it one hundred eighty degrees, debilitating the arm as he folded it in half and jerked it behind the man's back. The man cried out in pain. The girl threw her hands to her face and gasped.

"Now, I don't care what you do or where you do it," Jojo said low and evenly, "just so long as it's not in this hotel. Transporting a minor on the interstate for immoral purposes is against the law in this country, Mr. Smith, and it makes us look mighty bad when said immoral purposes are enacted on these grounds. So I suggest you take your little hussy to one of the rat holes on the east side with the hourly rates. I am quite certain they will be more than happy to accommodate you."

The girl squeaked. "Henry!"

Henry groaned and pitched forward, trying to ease up the pain in his arm.

"Awright, awright," he whimpered.

Jojo bent over and looked him straight in the eye. There was no anger there, no resentment. Only regret that he'd ever set foot in the Litchfield Valley Hotel.

So he released the guy, who stood up and backed quickly away, tenderly rubbing his aching wrist. The girl hurried to his side and he grumbled, "Come on, Bea."

Henry and Bea Smith, Jojo thought. *Well, probably not.*

The couple went awkwardly back to the bellhop, who tried and failed to conceal a knowing grin as he followed them back out to the curb with their suitcases.

Jojo said, "And there go the only matches in the house."

Jake closed his book using his finger for a bookmark and arched an eyebrow at the house detective.

"Some show," he said.

"No show. Just work."

Which was all it was to him. Jojo took no particular pleasure in ejecting people like Henry and Bea from the premises; he didn't even hold their minor transgressions against them. And the irony was far from lost on the man who owed his present circumstances to moral transgressions of his own—namely infidelity not only with another woman, but a *coloured* woman. Jojo thought about it every time he threw some hooker and her john out on the sidewalk, or sternly informed a Negro that his money was no good there. Shit, johns needed a place to rut and coloured folks needed beds to sleep in at night, but rules were rules and Jojo got paid to enforce them. Not well, God knew, but he was lucky to get what he got when no one else in town was willing to take the great social risk hiring an outcast like George Walker entailed. Hibbs was an ass, no one could question that, but he'd been the only one to shrug it off, to nod and smack his flabby lips the way he did when he came to a conclusion and say, "Why the hell not?"

There were plenty of reasons why not, but none of them legally binding, not since the judge ruled a lack of *prima facie* evidence of *concubinage* between Jojo and Sarah, the only actual crime pertaining to miscegenation on the books. Sure, it was more than enough to justify a divorce, the loss of a good job with the police force, the near total destruction of the life he'd built and loved and known. But Jojo Walker was a tough son of a bitch (as everyone well knew), and as long as Hibbs signed the cheques and the roof over his cramped corner office didn't leak, he survived and didn't complain too much. He did his job, didn't question authority much, and always slept alone on the little cot behind his desk. There were women—it was a hotel, after all—but Jojo avoided them like live grenades, no matter the circumstances. He'd had his fill of trouble with women, whatever colour they were.

Charles appeared at Jojo's elbow like a ghost and said, "Maybe they *was* married, Mr. Walker."

Jojo took his hat off and wiped his forehead. The damned sweating never stopped, not in summertime. Not even after sunset.

"Maybe they were, Charles. But I doubt it. That girl wasn't hardly more than a kid. Either way, I got to protect the hotel's interests, don't I?"

"You sure do, Mr. Walker."

Jojo crammed the hat back on his head. "Jojo, Charles. Everybody calls me Jojo."

Instinctively he stabbed another Old Gold in his mouth, then grunted as he remembered the total dearth of matches.

"Damn it," he said under his breath. Then, to Jake: "I'm going over to the Starlight. Call over there if you need me."

"On shift, Jojo?"

"There ain't anything going on, and if there is, I'm only two blocks away."

"Well, you'd best run back fast if Mr. Hibbs comes looking for you."

Jojo tipped his hand, cigarette still hanging between his lips, and went out through the door Charles held open for him.

"Be careful, Mr. . . . uh, Jojo."

Jojo grinned. "Back in a jiffy, friend."

※

The Starlight Diner was situated on the corner of Denson and Main, its west side facing the Palace Theater across the street and its south side opposite to Wade McMahon's filling station. Jojo lumbered into the joint with an open, panting mouth, his suit hanging on him like a wet towel. The bottle blonde behind the counter smiled at him, scoring deep lines in her already deeply-lined face.

"Coffee on your table, Jojo?"

"Yeah, Betty," Jojo croaked. "Gotta hit the john first."

He made a beeline for the back while Betty poured thin, brown coffee into a mug.

Jojo locked the door and pissed in the toilet for what seemed like forever, then washed his hands and face and stared at himself in the smudged, cracked mirror. It was a completely ordinary face, he knew, just eyes and nose and mouth and ears, none of which stood out in any noticeable way if you ignored the multitude of white scars that turned it into a checkerboard. His eyes were brown and so was his hair, which hung flat in wet, ropy strands from all the sweating. In any other town, a mug like that would have warranted quick, furtive glances from startled onlookers who would look away the second they got caught. But here, in Litchfield, it was a face that got long stares. Mean ones, usually.

It was sort of a miracle that they even let him keep coming back to the Starlight, all things considered. Beth had been a waitress here, a long time ago. Some folks, Betty Overturf included, were around even then, and clearly remembered the hullabaloo, the whole ugly scandal. *Married to such a pretty girl, that lousy cop, and he sneaks around sticking it to nigger girls.*

"Just the one, actually," he reminded the reflection aloud.

He ran the tap again and splashed more water on his marred face. It was room temperature and smelled like rusty copper, but it felt like a Canadian stream in contrast to the heavy, hot air. He patted his face dry with his tie and went back out to his table; the same one every time, by the west-facing window.

Jojo's coffee was waiting for him as promised, and he sipped it while knocking a cigarette out of the package. A fresh book of matches sat in the glass ashtray on the table. He smiled at it. His night was improving.

He lit the smoke and surreptitiously withdrew a small steel flask from the inside pocket of his coat. He unscrewed the cap and dribbled a bit of the amber fluid into the coffee. Betty came *tsking* at him, her veiny fists planted matronly on her broad hips.

"Aw Jojo, don't go Irishin' that up in here. We don't got a licence for it."

"Can't be helped, I'm half Irish myself," he remarked. "Besides, I've had it up to here with licences tonight."

"Gun, dog, or marriage?"

"Guns and dogs ain't allowed in the Litchfield Valley, Betty."

She smirked, and he knew why. She knew damn well he carried, and she also knew half the reason he was called Jojo. But his was the only gun permitted in the hotel, and him the only dog.

He downed a hearty gulp and gasped with satisfaction. The bourbon burned its way down his throat, warmed his belly. Betty screwed her mouth up to one side and shook her head.

"Good for what ails ya," Jojo said.

"Ain't you supposed to be working?"

"I am working."

"So I can see. You want a sandwich or something?"

"Coffee's fine, Betty," he said. "Thanks."

Betty shrugged and stalked off to her place behind the counter where an old man in a bus driver's uniform ignored his hash and eggs and opted to stare at Jojo instead. Jojo raised his eyebrows at him and blew rings of blue-grey smoke into the air that separated them. The man frowned and turned back to his plate.

Jojo breathed a sigh of relief. The guy hadn't started anything. If he had . . .

He dismissed it and killed the coffee. He pulled another Old Gold out of the pack and lit it with the last one. And as his weary eyes drifted out over the dark, vacant street outside, Jojo perked up at the sight of six or seven people milling about the front of the Palace Theater.

His eyes darted to the plastic clock on the greasy tiled wall: 11:43— much too late for a picture, not in this little town. The Palace marquee had its black block letters arranged to spell out a double feature of *Sweet Rosie O'Grady* and *Coney Island*, though one of the small throng in front was perched on a ladder, removing the letters one at a time. Someone else was hauling a sandwich board out of the back of the black sedan parked at the curb. This he unfolded and set carefully on the sidewalk. From where he sat, Jojo couldn't make out what it said.

But he could guess once the fellow on the ladder got through rearranging the letters on the jutting, angular marquee. Jojo watched him work, feeling like he was playing a game of hangman as the phrase came together, tile by tile. When at last the man was done and he climbed back down to earth, Jojo narrowed his eyes and studied the finished work.

BARKER DAVIS PRESENTS

MOTHERHOOD TOO SOON!

ONE WEEK ONLY—ADULTS ONLY

"Say, Betty," he said, keeping his eyes on the action across the street.

"What's that, honey?"

She wobbled back to the floor. Jojo jammed a thumb at the window.

"Any idea what these jokers are about?"

"It's Wednesday, darlin'. They always set up for the new shows on Wednesday."

"At midnight?"

Betty pursed her lips and thought on that.

"No," she said, "no, I don't reckon so."

"And that one don't exactly look like Betty Grable's in it, either."

"Ah, she was in last week's show, anyhow."

With that she took the coffee pot in her hand across the floor to another table, where a weary looking woman sat hunched over an empty cup. Jojo stabbed his cigarette out in the ashtray and continued his vigil, watching the people setting up in front of the Palace. He wondered which of them was Barker Davis. There was no way to tell. From his distance, through the dirty window and the darkness of Denson Street, they all looked more or less the same. All, except for the one man wearing the stark white lab coat.

A doctor?

Strange.

"You get to the pictures much these days?"

Betty startled him, appearing beside him like Charles had done earlier. He shivered, cursed himself for getting so jumpy, imperceptive.

"No, not really. I sleep when the matinees are on."

Which was true, though not the complete truth. Jojo *did* normally sleep through the day, since he normally worked through the night, but even when time and finances permitted he almost never set foot in the Palace Theater anymore. This was, of course, Irene Dunne's fault. And by proxy, Beth's fault. But the full truth of the matter was that it was Jojo's fault, like all his hard luck was, and the picture shows did nothing but reinforce that ugly fact in his already guilt-ridden mind. Beth hadn't been so bad, as wives go, though Jojo never really was the marrying kind. She never fussed much and she was a swell-looking babe, a hell of a woman to be honest, which was a great deal more than most cops could ask for in a mate. She was, in fact, the ideal woman for him. Every piece fit perfectly into place when it came to Beth. All the more reason he did everything in his power to forget all about her, and that goddamned Palace sure as hell wasn't going to help with that.

"That's too bad," Betty went on, dissolving his reverie. "They had this show the other week, *The Outlaw*, it was called. Boy, you shoulda seen it. But the real show was Russ Cavanaugh's old lady—man, was she hot he showed that picture! You know that Jane Russell practically shows her—"

The telephone on the wall by the pie display jangled, cutting her off to Jojo's great satisfaction. Betty rolled her eyes and stamped off to get it while he lit yet another cigarette. His pack was getting low; he reminded himself to ask Betty for a fresh one before heading back to the hotel.

She came back round, her teeth bared in an embarrassed grimace.

"How 'bout a package of Old Golds for the road, kid?"

"That was Jake on the horn, Jojo. Says you'd better get back."

"Christ."

He grabbed his hat and smashed it on his head as he slid out from the table. Betty scrambled to the back for a second and then came huffing back with a pack of smokes that she jammed in his hand.

"Pay me later, Jo," she said. "You'd best get."

Jojo got.

✕

The woman sitting cross-legged in the threadbare lobby chair was closely examining her fingernails and otherwise looked bored. Jake was anything but bored, enraptured as he was by her long legs and criminally plunging neckline. If the woman noticed his wolfen gaze she didn't let on. She just kept eyeballing her nails and giving the occasional sigh.

She'd come in with a group of six, all the rest men, who apologetically wanted to know if the hotel could spare three or four rooms at that dreadfully late hour. Jake felt like being ornery about it, sat back in his chair like he was the boss of the place and said he didn't really know, it *was* awful late, and how long were they planning on staying, anyhow? Then the lady came in—floated in, more like—right by the cashier's cage and straight to the beat up chair like she'd been sitting in it all her life. She lifted her right leg like a preying spider and angled it down over her left. She hadn't said a word to anyone, but Jake could tell she was part of the late crowd.

That changed things significantly.

"Two bucks . . . er, dollars a night, sir," he now stammered. "Three and fifty if there's two to a room."

He wondered about the woman, whether she'd be bunking with any of these men. Jojo would want to know about that. His eyes widened and he excused himself to go place that call.

Jake spoke to some waitress with a long drawl and had barely returned the receiver to the hooks before Jojo came plodding into the lobby. He looked tired and damp. Jake gestured to the circle of men in the middle of the lobby and noticed for the first time that one of them was dressed like a surgeon with the white coat and the little Van Dyke beard and everything. Jojo's face registered shock and perhaps a touch of dismay. He went slowly over to the cashier's cage and leaned in close.

"Just saw these clowns over at the Palace."

"I thought you went to the Starlight."

"It's right across the street, genius. Listen: did they mention anything about what they're doing? I mean why they're in town."

"They just asked for rooms. Four of 'em. The tall drink of water, the one with the tweed jacket, he's the one did the asking. And man, did you see the girl yet?"

Jake grinned and licked his lips.

"Forget about that," Jojo said sharply. "Get him to sign the register and make sure he fills in the bit about occupation, all right? Can you manage that, kid?"

Jake frowned but nodded.

Jojo sauntered over to the group and surveyed their faces, their clothes, the suitcases at their feet. Charles was lingering anxiously nearby, unsure of how to handle them. Jojo presumed they'd carried their own luggage in, which must have irked Charles to no end. Easy way to get out of a tip. *Strike one*, Jojo thought.

He put on his best fake smile and insinuated himself into the circle, making direct eye contact with the man in the tweed jacket.

"Welcome to the Litchfield Valley Hotel."

The man knitted his brow and drew in a long breath.

"I gather that we are in Litchfield," he said at length, "but where exactly is the valley?"

"There isn't one," Jojo admitted. "Used to be called Litchfield Palms. No palm trees, either."

The man stared for a moment. So did everyone else, apart from the woman in the chair. She just leaned back and rubbed her temples in tiny circles with the tips of her fingers.

"I see," he ultimately answered. "Are you the manager? When will our rooms be ready?"

"I'm not the manager, no, but your rooms will be ready as soon as you sign the register up front and pay the kid in the cage." Jojo stuck a cigarette in his mouth and patted himself down, searching for the matches he'd left on the table back at the diner. "Listen, though—before you do that, let me ask you—are you the folks setting up over at the Palace?"

The one in the doctor's getup darted his glance between Jojo and the guy in the tweed jacket. The latter smiled slightly and bounced on the balls of his feet.

"That's right. We're doing a roadshow, see? Town to town, like."

"Sure," Jojo said. "Saw *Birth of a Nation* that way when I was a kid. What sort of picture are ya'll bringing to Litchfield?"

"Say, you're starting to sound like the law," the man said. "I hope there isn't a problem."

"Nope, no problem at all. Not as far I can see, anyway. I'm just crazy for the pictures, that's all. Figured I might catch yours, if it's up my alley."

"Well, then," the guy said in a drawn out sort of way. His smile broadened and he shot a knowing look to the doctor. "It's a hygiene picture, as a matter of fact. Educational."

"Is that a fact?"

"It is, yes. See, we tour the heartland and spread the gospel, as it were. Our boss wants the young people to know the facts of life, the best ways to keep their noses clean. That sort of thing."

"Clean noses. I like 'em, too."

Jojo fiddled anxiously with the unlit cigarette in his hand and scratched his cheek.

"I guess I'd better let you folks get registered, then. It's awful late for an interview."

"That it is, detective."

"Just Jojo," he corrected the man. "Two questions before you go, though."

The fellow raised his eyebrows circumspectly and awaited them.

"That boss of yours, would that be Barker Davis?"

For a moment, the inquiry seemed to suck all the air out of the lobby. The men exchanged anxious glances. Even the woman in the chair looked up. Jojo betrayed no thoughts on the subject, just waited for an answer.

"Why, yes," said the man. "You've heard of him?"

"Only from the announcement on the Palace marquee. Hard to miss."

"Ah, of course," the man said with a peculiar shiver. "I hadn't realized you'd seen it yet."

"*Motherhood Too Soon*," Jojo said. "With an exclamation mark."

"Like I said, *Jojo*, it is a hygiene picture."

"Like you said. Fair warning to you, to all of you—Litchfield doesn't have a League of Decency contingent, but if there's anything remotely objectionable about your little hygiene film you can expect a visit from Reverend Shannon before too long."

"The local clergyman, I take it."

"He is."

"Nothing we haven't dealt with before, I assure you. There are many men whose views remain locked in the dark ages, who would rather their impressionable young people learn life's harsh lessons the hard way. We are here to ease that burden."

"You know, I saw a *hygiene* picture some years back, in St. Louie. All about white slavers and that jazz. The folks what put that one on were selling the same bill of goods, that it was all for the public good, but I'll be damned if it wasn't just old fashioned bunco. This ain't a wild town, mister—we don't got but population twelve hundred and eighty—but I expect you'll fill some seats all the same."

"Clean noses, Mr. Jojo," the man responded with a mask of indifference.

"Right," Jojo said. "Go on and get registered. I'm sure I'll see you all around."

With a limp salute from the brim of his hat, Jojo turned on his heel and headed back for his office.

"Oh, Mr. Jojo?" the man called to him.

Jojo paused and turned back.

"You said you had two questions. What was the other?"

"Almost forgot," Jojo said. He held up the cigarette, now crumpled from the constant handling, pinched between his forefinger and thumb. "Any of you got any matches?"

The man displayed the palms of his hands in a gesture of helpless apology.

"I'm afraid not. None of us smoke."

"Natch," Jojo said grouchily.

He tramped to the back and disappeared into his office.

CHAPTER TWO

As softly as the front door closed and the latch turned, Theodora heard it and sat up in bed. She had not yet fallen asleep, despite the late hour. Theodora never slept when Russ wasn't at home.

Downstairs, her husband shuffled around in the dark, knocked something over, cursed quietly. Theodora sat back against the headboard and wove her fingers together. She wondered if Russ had been drinking, though she recognized how little it mattered in the larger picture. She was almost certain he'd been with Lana, the cigarette girl at the theatre.

She hadn't much to go on, no solid or substantial evidence to back up her anxiety, but it only made sense given the widening distance between them these last few months. More and more Russ stayed at the Palace long past the end of the last feature, much too long to explain away with counting receipts and getting the theatre in order for the next business day. Towns far larger than Litchfield might have had regular midnight shows on the weekends, but the Palace could never convince people to stay up that late for a picture. The last reel always reached its end before midnight. Three in the morning just didn't make any sense, not unless . . .

Russ wasn't coming up, so Theodora got out of bed and slipped into her robe. Now that her blood was moving again, she felt hot immediately.

She padded out to the hall and went quietly down the steps. Halfway down, she heard Russ's voice, floating sonorously from the kitchen.

"Who, Jim Shannon? Sure, I know him—why, who told you that? Oh, well Christ, he can make a fuss all he wants . . . it's not like he can go to the law about it or anything. But then again, I had that Jane Russell show not too long ago and I was sure I'd hear about . . . turns out only my old lady wanted to piss and moan about it."

Theodora bristled on the steps, squeezed her lips into a wrinkled frown. She'd reckoned *that* discussion was long over and done with. All she'd ever meant was that the picture might make the theatre look bad, anyway—Litchfield was a small town with small town values. *Folks might not want to spend their money at a place that exhibits trash like that*, she'd told him. *Duxom isn't but an hour away, and they could just as easily make day trip of it just to show you how distasteful they find it.* It was them she was thinking of, she and Russ, their standing and their reputation and, of course, the state of their already shaky finances. She never meant to *fuss*, and she certainly wasn't judging her husband by the types of pictures he chose to exhibit. Russ was free to do as he liked. He wore the pants, didn't he?

She crept down to the landing and paused there, listening.

"You ever see that Garbo picture, *Two Faced Woman?* Hell's bells, I almost lost my shirt over that one, and Shannon led the party to take it off my back. Glorified adultery, he said. Violated God's will, or some such poppycock. Now that was two years ago, and I told him in no uncertain terms then that the next time he tried to make trouble for me I aimed to make plenty of trouble right back . . . well, yes, Mr. Winston. No, Mr. Winston, I don't suppose anyone ought to give him hell before he does anything. I'm just saying . . . sure, of course. I guess I'm a leading businessman in this community—I don't figure on stirring up a hornet's nest, but the Palace ain't what it used to be. . . ."

Russ went quiet except for a few punctuated grunts and the occasional click of his tongue, and Theodora took it as her cue to come silently into the kitchen as though she hadn't heard a word of it. Her husband flashed a startled grimace at her and turned away, toward the sink, nodding and saying *uh-huh* and *sure, sure* and *yes, Mr. Winston.*

Theodora poured a glass of water from the tap and sat down at the kitchen table, sipping it methodically until her husband finished his call at last. He returned the receiver to its hooks and emitted a heavy sigh.

"Is everything all right?" she asked as cheerily as possible.

"Long day, that's all."

"You want I should make you something to eat? I can whip up some scrambled eggs. . . ."

"No, no I don't want any eggs."

He loosened his tie and unbuttoned his collar, gasping as though it had been choking him to death.

"You know, I rather liked that Garbo picture," Theodora said. She immediately wished she hadn't.

Russ's face bloomed red and his shoulders rose and fell with heavy breaths.

"Can't you mind your own business?" he barked. "A man works a fifteen hour day—*fifteen hours*, Theodora—and he's got to come home to a nosy woman who can't mind her own business? Is that fair?"

"I didn't mean to be meddlesome. . . ."

"Then don't be, for Christ's sake. That was a business call, you hear? My business, not yours."

"I'm only taking an interest, dear. . . ."

"An interest," he mocked as he lumbered out into the living room. "Sure, sure. An *interest*."

He switched on the lamp and opened up the liquor cabinet by the bookshelves, from which he extracted a bottle of rye and a chipped crystal glass. Theodora mousily followed behind as he poured three fingers, downed it in a single gulp, and then poured three more. She lingered behind the divan and twiddled her thumbs while he drank.

"Who's Mr. Winston?"

Russ emitted a gravelly gasp from the liquor.

"An exhibitor," he said. "One of the folks come down with the new picture."

"What sort of picture is it?"

"Christ, Theodora . . ."

"I'm only asking."

"It's a sex hygiene picture, if you must know. The sort of garbage they sell as socially relevant, but all it is is pure exploitation."

"Oh."

"They got this fellow in a doctor's getup, and he does a spiel before each showing. Sells some books they got printed up. Then the show, it's all about some girl who goes and gets knocked up by a kid on his way to the war, see? Says he'll come home and marry her, then I guess they get the letter says he's been killed and the girl, she's stuck with the bun in the oven."

Russ tipped the mouth of the bottle against the lip of the glass, poured two more fingers. He paused for a moment like he was really thinking it over, then poured two more.

"Thing is, the last reel is a real whopper."

"That so?"

Theodora was loosening up a bit now that Russ was, too. He was getting drunk, and fast, but at least he was speaking to her.

"Live birth," he said with some disgust. "I haven't seen it—don't want to, really—but that's what it's got, right at the end. A real honest-to-Christ childbirth just as plain as the nose on your face."

Theodora blushed, her eyes bulged.

"But, Russell . . ."

"Yeah, I know. Jim Shannon's gonna get wind of it and bring half of Heaven's Christian soldiers down to give me hell about it. But Winston, he's not worried about it, see? Tells me it happens in nearly every town, and it don't but help sell tickets in the end. It's the young people, mostly, and in towns like this where nobody tells them anything . . . well, I guess they just want to see it for themselves. I don't reckon it can hurt."

"But do they . . ."

"What, Theodora? Spit it out: do they *what?*"

"Goodness, Russ—do they show, you know, *it?*"

"Why do I have to guess at what you're driving at? Are you talking about the *vagina?* Is that what you can't say? For Pete's sake, she's got one and she can't even say the damn word."

Russ laughed, a harsh, short snort, and dumped the remainder of the glass down his gullet. For her part, Theodora was embarrassed. For him, and for herself. He did not normally talk like this, not even when he was in his cups like now. He could be a bit crass, she knew—she'd heard plenty of crude male talk whenever he played cards with the boys from the lodge—but never like this, never to her.

Not since their awful, awkward wedding night, at any rate.

Hot Springs, Arkansas was the place, a little rundown hotel on East Grand with a view of the Ouachita Mountains and a lukewarm bottle of cheap champagne resting in a dented metal bucket with no ice in it. They heard children stomping up and down the hallway all night and into the wee hours, unattended little shits Russ had called them, but Theodora didn't agree or disagree since she was still hoarse from all the crying she'd done. It'll be *fine*, he'd told her, perhaps a bit condescendingly, you don't have to holler so goddamn much, it's just a bit of fun, for crissakes.

He couldn't see why she was making such a big sorry deal out of the whole stupid affair and she couldn't understand why her new husband would want to poke his ugly thing into her rear end in the first place, and they never did see eye-to-eye on the issue and not another word was ever spoken of it.

They had no children, she and Russ, and no intimacy or secrets between them, or love. Once in a rather great while, maybe twice a year, Theodora got it into her head to take him into her mouth, though she felt relatively certain that this, too, counted among the sins of Sodom. Pastor Shannon never said as much, not that detail specifically, but how was he supposed to? You didn't talk about things like *that*, and that went double under the roof of God's own house. She just knew, or at least strongly suspected, that she was doing something terribly, inevitably wrong, but the little wife figured it was better to burn in the lake of fire than to never again feel a kind touch from her own husband. Even if he did close his eyes and tip back his head every time, never once acknowledging who is was doing the filthy, shame-making deed down there.

And boy howdy would her ears burn the next few times she'd see the Good Reverend James Shannon, sure in her heart that he knew, that he could see it in her downcast eyes.

Life was funny. Took you places you'd never think it would, or could. Or should. Papas built dollhouses and mamas used them to instruct little girls about how life was supposed to function in God's Jesus-green world. Theodora laughed a little just thinking about it.

"What's so goddamn funny?"

"Nothing," she said.

"Christ, but you chap my hide sometimes, woman."

"I know," she whispered. "I'm sorry."

"A man tries to make a living," he began, trailing off. It was a familiar enough sentiment to both of them; further elaboration was unnecessary.

Russ screwed the cap onto the bottle's mouth and jammed it back in its place in the liquor cabinet. Ten years had crawled sluggishly by since Roosevelt overturned Volstead; before that Russ kept his hooch in the cellar. The day the Twenty-First Amendment swallowed up the Eighteenth, he'd hauled every bottle up by armloads from the dank cellar to the cabinet in the front room, carelessly emptying it of every bit of her mother's china and replacing it all with whiskey and rye and gin and every other drop of the devil's water he'd kept hidden since nineteen hundred and twenty. Theodora could not say where the china was now. She supposed it didn't much matter, not really.

"I've still got paperwork needs doing," Russ grumbled as the wiped the inside of the tumbler with his shirttail. "You go on back to bed now."

Theodora knitted her brow and lingered for a moment, mindlessly worrying the fringe of her robe. Russ carefully returned the glass to its place in the cabinet and slowly turned his head to lay a dark, startlingly sober glare on her.

"Now, Theodora," he said.

A faint, quivering smile tugged at the corners of her mouth and she swallowed noisily before turning on her heels and heading straight for the stairs. She climbed and felt the thin fabric of the robe cling wetly to her hot skin on the way up. Up to the lonely bedroom, to the pain that made her eyeballs ache whenever she shut them.

Now, Theodora.

"Yes, Russell," she said out loud as she crawled back beneath the hot, damp bed sheet.

※

Russ spread the promotional materials out on the kitchen table like a fan. There was the pressbook and the glossy stills and half a dozen handbills that were miniaturized versions of the one-sheet now hanging in front of the Palace.

FIRST INTERNATIONAL TOUR!
BOLD! CRUCIAL!
2 HOURS OF WHITE HOT TRUTH!

The words *white* and *hot* were designed to look as though they were aflame. It even promised an All-Star Hollywood Cast, which couldn't be farther from the truth. Who the hell was Jim S. Dawson, anyway? He sure as hell wasn't Randolph Scott, that much was certain.

He took up the pressbook and absently flipped through it.

"Puerile stuff," Russ groused.

Secrets of a Happy and Healthy Young Adulthood, the header on page five practically screamed at him. Page six introduced the esteemed Dr. Elliot Freeman (*On Stage! In Person! The Famous Hygiene Expert!*) whose photograph naturally did not appear since the good doctor changed appearance from one region to the next. For the Palace's purposes, it was Mountain Home native Peter Chappell who was to don the lab coat of authority and spout the memorized speech probably conceived by the head man himself. Then would come the business of selling Dr. Freeman's critically important book, from which Russ was not to see a single red cent, per the conditions of his contract. His take on the box office wasn't exactly spectacular, either, but these were hard times. Anymore Russ could only hope to see half-decent receipts from women's pictures since half his male audience was on the other side of the world killing Germans and Japs and getting killed in return. And even the women didn't come as often as they used to. There just weren't the resources, not when everything was rationed and their meagre incomes from whatever lunch counter or secretarial desk went to groceries and light bills first. No, the Palace needed something different, something *really* different, to coax his friends and neighbours out to the picture show again. Something new. Something maybe a bit dangerous.

The Outlaw sure as hell didn't do the trick, Jane Russell's criminal cleavage notwithstanding.

But then came the loud, fast-talking little man from Wilmington, Ohio with the pomaded hair parted in dead centre and the smart bowtie big enough to touch his chin. *You gotta tell 'em to sell 'em, Cavanaugh*, he barked, which was how he always spoke—a bark—which made perfect sense to Russ once he learned the excitable fellow's handle: Barker Davis.

He'd just come down for the afternoon from Mountain Home in a shiny black coupe with a stack of pressbooks and a picture to sell—going town to town, he said; a roadshow, he said. Maybe folks in Litchfield didn't see the advantage in spending their well-pinched pennies on whatever melodramas or hackneyed jungle adventure shows Russ had been projecting on the Palace's screen (Barker Davis intimated), but by Christ, give them something they haven't ever seen before, and damnit, do it with a guarantee they can't turn down, sell it to them *hard*, Cavanaugh, and you'll flip your goddamn wig when you see the receipts, pardon my Latin.

Russ Cavanaugh was dubious then, worried about the noisy proclamations on the pressbook cover, and he hadn't even seen the one-sheet yet, but more than that he was uncomfortable with the way this boisterous little stranger seemed to waltz right in like he owned the joint. Telling Russ how to run his business. Discussing his questionable little medicine show as though it was already a done deal, the ink dry on the papers. But then, of course, the ink *did* dry, and fast. Theodora's *tsking* over the subject matter of Davis's film probably had as much to do with it as anything—the only thing worse than a complete stranger telling him what to do with his own movie house was goddamn Theodora doing it. *I don't know, Russell; it seems a bit sordid, Russell; Reverend Shannon won't like it, Russell.* Russ couldn't sign fast enough after *that* round of henpecking hell.

So it was a done deal. A week's limited engagement, three shows a day at Litchfield's own Palace Theater: *Women and Hi-School Girls Only at 2, Men and Hi-School Boys Only at 7,* and the mildly precarious desegregated nine o'clock show for anyone with the half-dollar price of admission (up from thirty-five cents that past March). Tomorrow's two o'clock show was the first run, and although Russ had been assured that Davis' team would be beating the proverbial bushes for a gross that would knock him on his rear-end, he did not feel so sure looking over the loud materials on the table before him.

BOLD! SHOCKING!
VITALLY IMPORTANT!
SEE THE TRUTH & LEARN THE FACTS
A PICTURE YOU WILL NEVER FORGET

Emblazoned across the middle of the handbill like a too-tight belt was the question: *Are the boys and girls of today JUST PLAIN BAD?*

"Who cares?" Russ asked back. "So long as they're paying."

His mind then flashed on little Nancy Campbell, she of the bottled blonde hair and obscenely dimpled chipmunk cheeks, and how quickly her grandparents shunted her away last winter when her formerly table-flat stomach began to suspiciously distend. As far as Russ knew, no one asked whether she was bad or not, at least not aloud. No one talked about Nancy Campbell at all—she was a phantom, a forgotten spectre of an ugly moment that only happened in bigger towns and cities, but not Litchfield, never here. Russ wondered if he shouldn't resurrect that ugly moment, speak the girl's name aloud and recall her sinful predicament in the name of social betterment and moral fortitude and fat coffers. *Remember Nancy Campbell? Your daughter could be next!*

Anxiety was always the best sales pitch, he knew. It had worked for the churches since time immemorial, after all—why not the Palace, too?

Russ grinned, stood up to locate a pencil from the cup on the counter just below the massive black phone on the wall. He took the dull stub back to the table and made a note on the margin of the handbill: *Nancy Campbell.*

You gotta tell 'em to sell 'em, Cavanaugh.

Shrewd fellow, that Barker Davis. Obnoxious as all hell and a Yankee to boot (damn him) but a shrewd businessman who was priming the pump for the Palace to finally escape its slump.

To hell with Jane goddamn Russell, Russ thought. *If tits don't pack them in, fear will.*

They're all out to getcha: the Jerries and the Japs, the Devil his own self and, now, even the nice young man next door. He's got the Serpent in his trousers fixing to slither into the Garden when the angels aren't looking—*Christ this is good*; he made more notes in the margin—and you had best learn the facts, every mother's son of you, lest *it happen to you.*

"Fear," he said aloud as the flat lead nub scratched away, filling up what little white space remained on the handbill's edges. "That's the thing. *That's* the thing."

Russ chuckled a little and failed to notice the bruise-purple horizon on the other side of the kitchen window, inspiring a pair of chattering birds and signalling the start of a new day. He was still too enraptured with thoughts of his neighbour's lucrative terror.

CHAPTER THREE

Pain shocked Jojo's brain and he snapped awake in his chair as the smouldering end of his cigarette dropped from his freshly burned fingers.

"Shit," he rasped. The single syllable kicked up the gummy saliva in his mouth. He didn't much care for the taste.

Jojo turned in the chair and extended his leg to stomp on the butt, grinding it into the rug and into extinction. One more black pock mark hardly mattered. The rug was riddled with them like a long-forgotten World War I minefield. No one ever complained. Nobody ever came back there apart from him and the rare visit from Mr. Hibbs.

He leaned back in the chair, which creaked while he groaned. From the inside pocket of his coat he withdrew his little flask, from which he took a quick shot that he swished around in his mouth before swallowing. He made a face and groaned some more. His temples throbbed and the small of his back felt like it was making a tight fist he couldn't unclench.

"Shit," he said again. *Once more with feeling,* he thought.

Sucking on the rapidly developing blisters on his index and middle fingers, Jojo reached for the package of Old Golds on the desk and stuck one in his mouth. He knew he'd used his last match—he just wanted to lip the thing for a while. And while he lipped the cigarette from one corner of his mouth and kissed his blisters with the other, Jojo turned the knob on the white Coronado radio and closed his eyes. Al Dexter was warbling across the airwaves, a familiar tune to Jojo Walker.

Lay that pistol down, babe, lay that pistol down. Pistol packin' mama, lay that pistol down.

The tune was familiar, but so was the sentiment. He'd known a few pistol packin' mamas in his own time, too, his late bride among them. Good old steady Beth, looking like Irene Dunne at the tail-end of a weeklong bender, her wiry chalk-white arm trembling with a Mossberg Brownie gawping at the end of it. Just a tiny little thing, even in such a small, delicate hand, but Jojo didn't make a Federal case out of it. She who holds the .22 makes the rules, he figured, and the rule was shut up and don't move. So he was silent and still, and he watched as she screamed and the tears ran down and her nose bubbled with snot and she said things like, *Now you know I ain't prejudiced but for God's sake, George, a Negro girl?* As if the stepping out in and of itself was not enough. He'd had to go and twist the knife, too.

Drinkin' beer in a cabaret, was I havin' fun! Until one night she caught me right, and now I'm on the run. . . .

His foot tapped under the desk until he became aware of it and stopped. The electric fan hummed. Outside, a car horn sounded. Probably a guest honking for the bellboy, whoever it was that took Charles' place at that ungodly hour of the morning. Jojo wasn't very familiar with the day-shift crew.

He felt like a vampire, like Bela Lugosi repulsed by the sober, revealing sunlight that invaded his small private space through any chink in his Venetian window armour it could find. Under ideal circumstances, he would have been asleep on the cot by now, stripped down to his shorts with his green wool blanket draped half on him and half off. Instead he languished in his desk chair, an unlit and unlightable cigarette dangling from his lips, the heat in the room indicating temperatures rising to deep south of heaven. The goddamn fan just wasn't going to fix itself, not when he could feel the sweat running in streams down his sides from the endless springs in his armpits. So he took another hit from the flask, switched off the Coronado and crammed his hat back on his head to head out for cooler pastures.

The rest of the song followed him, inside his head, through the lobby and past the roughneck in the cashier's cage, all the way out onto the sweltering street. Jojo boiled in his damp, rumpled suit, but he was already out and going so grinned and bore it, hold the grin.

He walked toward the Starlight, though he did not plan on going there specifically. Time was he'd spend the day in the Palace, and after about fifteen minutes had melted by, the theatre's familiar edifice and stark white marquee came shimmering into view.

Barker Davis Presents . . .

Jojo had nearly forgotten all about that.

He squinted against the glare of the marquee and turned onto Franklin, away from the theatre, in a beeline for the drugstore with a mortar and pestle on the left side of its shingle and an ice cream cone on the right. In the middle, tall gold-painted capital letters spelled out FINN'S. The place was nearly vacant—too early for the bobbysoxers and too late for the white-haired crowd who lingered over coffee when they went to collect their sundries. Jojo flinched a little at the tiny brass bell that jingled above him when he opened the door. Sleeplessness, he decided. Made him jumpy.

Before the counter, all but one of the five red padded stools stood unused. The fifth from the front sank beneath the weight of an enormous man with his sleeves rolled up to his elbows and sweat roiling from his vast pink face. The fat man was pouring Coca-Cola down his gullet as though his life depended on it, and when he noticed Jojo his wet, fraught face moulded itself into a panting smile.

"Hi-de-ho, Jojo!" he called out in a wet, fraught sort of way. "What d'ya know?"

"Not much more than I ever did, Finn."

Finn patted the stool beside him.

"Get off them stompers and have a visit," he said.

Always with the hep talk, Finn. Jojo reckoned he picked it up from the kids who made his joint their second home during the summer—the active duties and share crops, he called them. The kids laughed at him and the adults found it crass, but Jojo liked the guy. He was an okay bird, a buddy from way back. And he was one of the very elite few who hadn't turned their backs on him when the soup hit the fan. When some of his own colleagues at the station were still calling him darkie-lover to his face, Finn just shrugged and said, "Y'ain't nothing but a man, Jojo."

At the time, Jojo figured it was the nicest thing anyone had ever said to him.

Jojo squatted over a stool and sat down with a sigh. Finn snapped his fingers at the jerk behind the counter, who looked up with lazy, heavily-lidded eyes beneath a jauntily cocked paper hat.

"Get Mr. Walker a soda, would ya?"

"Thanks," Jojo said.

"Or would ya rather an egg cream? D'ya know what that is? Stu here, he's been up north. Tell him about your egg cream, Stu."

Stu lifted one eyebrow and sucked in a deep breath, but Jojo waved a hand to cut him off.

"Soda's fine, Stu."

Stu yanked a clean glass from beneath the counter and filled it to the top at the fountain. Finn squeezed Jojo's shoulder with his massive hand.

"The simple things, am I right?"

"Sure, Finn."

"That's what them goddamn Germans don't get, you ask me. It's about the simple things. Hell, even them Yankee fucks don't get *that*. Pardon my language, Stu."

Stu pursed his lips and shrugged.

"They don't, though. You ever been to the city, Jojo?"

"I bet on the horses at Oaklawn once in a while."

"Well, okay—but I mean a big city. A *real* city. I mean St. Louie or, hell, or *Chicago*."

"Nope," Jojo answered, nodding his thanks to Stu as his soda materialized on the counter. "Can't say that I have."

"Shee-it, boy. Folks run around like motorized freckles in places like that, always on the run like the hounds of hell was nippin' at their heels. Now, that's no way to live, is it?"

"I reckon not," Jojo said. He tipped the glass to his mouth and drank greedily. The sugar shocked his system, but it felt good.

"The simple things," Finn said again. "Yes, sir."

"Say," Jojo began, wiping his mouth on the back of his hand. "When were you ever in Chicago, Finn?"

"Well, I wasn't ever. But I seen a hundred pictures at the Palace, haven't I?"

"Yeah, sure," Jojo said with a smirk. "I saw *Roxie Hart* myself a couple of times."

"Sure, sure," Finn said with a broad grin and a snicker.

"How about what they've got going now?"

"Who, the Palace?"

"Yeah. Something called *Motherhood Too Soon*. They say it's a roadshow."

"Sounds . . . licentious."

"News to you?"

"News to me, my friend."

Jojo finished off his soda and popped a cigarette in his mouth. Finn was quick with a match to light it. He lit his own off the same flame.

"Bunch of them checked into the hotel last night. *Late* last night. Odd folks. One of them dressed like a doctor, and a leggy gal looked like she's got ice water instead of blood."

"Got yourself a circus, sounds like."

"All three rings of it."

"Gunna give 'em the boot?"

"Got no reason to. Not yet, anyhow."

"Life of a hotel copper," Finn said.

Jojo nodded and groaned. "Not a cop anymore, Finn."

"Same difference, ya ask me. You just don't get tossed out for hitting the whiz now like you woulda been under Ernie."

Jojo wrinkled his nose at that. Ernie Rich was a tough boss all right—a lot of folks called him Chief S.O.B. when he wasn't in the room, since the B rhymed with his given name—but hooch had nothing to do with Jojo's dismissal, or anything else for that matter. He found himself resenting Finn for bringing it up.

For his part, Finn just chuckled and slapped Jojo on the back. He nearly drove Jojo right over the counter with the force of it.

"Boy howdy, do you worry too much! The *face* on you!"

"Yeah, sure," Jojo grumbled. "I know—Jojo the dog-faced boy."

"We-ell . . ." Finn drawled. "You know that ain't what I meant. . . ."

"Hell, Finn . . . it don't mean nothing."

"Well, I didn't mean . . ."

"Skip it," Jojo half-growled. "I just came by for the air, but I don't reckon it's any cooler in here than it is out in the sun. Guess I'd better dig into a better foxhole."

Finn wiped his face with the sleeve of his shirt and turned a nasty grimace on Stu, who seemed to be sleeping standing up.

"Damn your eyes, Stu—how come that fan ain't on?"

Stu snapped his head up and mumbled a protracted "*Hu-uh-uhn?*"

Jojo rose from the stool and smoothed his suit down the front with his hands. It didn't do much good.

"Ah, now, you're leaving sore," Finn complained.

"Do me a favour," Jojo said, ignoring the rest of it. "You see or hear anything from them roadshow people, drop in on me and let me know about it, huh?"

"Sure, Jo. I'll do that."

"Keep it under your hat—"

"—of course, of course—"

"—but keep your ear to the ground."

"I'll send ya a smoke signal," Finn offered with a wet grin. "Me good brave."

"Just be a discrete brave, savvy?"

"Natch."

Jojo gave a weak salute and headed for the door. The jangling bell overhead and the rush of hot, stagnant air in his face drowned out the sound of Finn bawling out poor Stu over the fan some more. The only shade to be seen was the tiny dark square on the sidewalk, the wobbling shadow of the shingle above. Everything else was hit hard by the late morning sun, bright and hot and unforgiving. Jojo blinked the sweat out of his eyes and touched the tips of his fingers to his face, suddenly self-conscious that he hadn't shaved yet that morning. He didn't think it showed, but he could practically feel the shadow forming over his face, darkening his otherwise pallid Scotch-Irish skin. He gritted his teeth and shook it off—like a dog shakes off water.

"Christ on a crutch," he muttered, just loud enough to be heard by a passing woman with blue hair and a shrivelled face. She shot a remonstrative look at Jojo, who presented an exaggerated smile and removed his hat in response.

"Good *morning*, ma'am."

The shrivelled woman grunted a *hurumph* in reply and tottered on by. Again, Jojo ran his fingers over his face, his cheeks and chin, his forehead and temples and the sides of his nose.

Woof, woof, he thought bitterly.

Jojo slogged on, up Franklin to Main, where the glaring bright Palace marquee reappeared, still shimmering in the liquid heat like a mirage in the Sahara. The black block letters remained unchanged, and as Jojo drew nearer—almost involuntarily, as if drawn by unseen forces—he became aware of the developing throng of people under the theatre's triangular awning, forming a jagged, misshapen sort of queue that extended the length of the white brick edifice. Jojo paused diagonal from the box office on the other side of the street. He didn't try to count the heads, but he guessed there must have been thirty-five or forty people milling up in front of the place. And it was a good two hours before the first show, according the obnoxious sandwich board by the curb.

For a low-rent hygiene picture?

He drifted up the sidewalk until he was directly across from the crowd, squinting in the brightness at the sweating faces floating along the line. He recognized quite a lot of them—one didn't serve on a small town's police force for as long as he did without getting familiar with the citizenry. And they were all women, or girls, from the first in line to the last. At first, Jojo assumed it was because of the war, but there was no dearth of serviceable young men in Litchfield. The only one Jojo could think of who had left to enlist was Eddie Manning, and that would still leave a few Toms, Dicks, and Harrys for the Wednesday matinee.

Then he took a more measured gander at the sandwich board and realized what was up—women and "hi-school" girls only, it said. He saw plenty of both: Tammy Hoff and Maggie Parker and Maggie's sister Lula (or was it Lola?) who'd caused so much trouble between the Barnes boys back in '39, trouble that ended up with a shooting and only three legs between both brothers. Jojo guessed Maggie's sister already knew plenty about the shocking facts of life, yet here she was alongside so many other anxious and mildly distressed-looking women, waiting for her turn to come inside and see what the hubbub was all about.

Curious.

Jojo noted the time for the next show—the men's show—and continued down Main for several blocks more until he reached the intersection with Lynch Street, where he hung a left and kept walking.

Tuck Arnold's hardware shop wasn't far. And Georgia May Bagby was about due for her lunch hour any minute now.

✖

Georgia lay on her side with her legs angled up, fanning herself with a tattered magazine that had Clark Gable on the front. Her chest sparkled in the shafts of sunlight spilling in through the blinds, each bead of sweat a tiny diamond to accent the ample cleavage swelling out from the top of her baby blue slip.

For his part, Jojo sat in the wicker chair by the dresser, smoking one of Georgia's cigarettes—Debs, which each came with a slightly emasculating rose tip. He'd taken off his coat and hat, but remained otherwise dressed, watching the fulsome blonde with detached semi-interest like a sleepy insurance salesman watching a stag film at a convention.

"You didn't come for me, then," she said. It wasn't a question.

"Sure, I did."

"But not for . . . *that*. This, I mean."

She swept the magazine along the length of her body, straightening her legs as she did so, as though she were the latest luxurious model on the showroom floor. Jojo grinned.

"No, I'm afraid not."

"Hot, though," she said, resuming her fanning. "Glad I took off the dress all the same. I don't know how you stand that awful suit this time of year."

"It's the uniform."

"Everyone's got one, haven't they?"

"More or less. Like belly buttons and assholes."

Georgia's face flushed pink and she frowned.

"But I'll bet you wore a suit when you were a little boy. I'll bet you were born in a damn suit. No short pants for wee little Jojo, nossir."

He just sucked at the red-filtered cigarette in lieu of response. It was nearly done, and he was already considering firing up another.

"You got anything to drink around here?"

"Rotgut," she said with disdain. "A guy left it here a month ago, untouched. Brought it in a brown paper bag, figuring on getting tight, but he was so nervous I guess he forgot all about it."

"Nothing else?"

Georgia shrugged.

In the kitchen, she brought out a pair of dusty-looking rocks glasses and set them on either side of the bottle. Crab Orchard whiskey, according to the label. Jojo screwed his mouth up to one side and filled the glasses.

"No, honey," Georgia objected. "None for me."

"Two for me, then."

After his first swallow he noticed the lipstick on the edge of the glass. He didn't mind, not much. He had another swallow and made a face. It was awful stuff.

"Told you," she gloated.

"If he'd been a gent, he'd have brought something nicer."

"Sure, or flowers. And told me I reminded him of his dear old mother."

"I'd like to meet the mother who reminds anyone of you."

"Play nice," she warned with a wagging finger, "or mama spank."

Jojo snickered. He'd never been on the receiving end of a Georgia May spanking, but he'd done plenty else with the girl who sported the worst reputation in Litchfield. Most folks, when they spoke in low, conspiratorial tones about her, freely called Georgia a whore—even the fabled Whore of Babylon, once or twice within Jojo's earshot—but he'd never seen any hard evidence of that. When at last the time had come for Sheriff Rice to appease the bible-beating busybodies and introduce a formal investigation into the matter, it was Deputy George Walker who drove out to the dilapidated Bagby house four and half miles south of town on Jackson Hole Road. The lady hadn't been pleased to find a policeman at her door and unleashed a blue streak of curses that would make a sailor blush to hear them, and yet they weren't long in getting into bed and dampening the dirty sheets with enough sweat for eight hours of vicious lovemaking rather than the thirty minutes it took them.

No charge, deputy, she'd snarled afterwards, and Jojo didn't think he'd ever laughed so hard in all his life. He told her when he left she was like an old mountain road, and when she gave him a puzzled look he explained how they both had dangerous curves. Then they both laughed. And Jojo was back within a week, and many times more besides.

It got old, but never sour. It just stopped in a natural sort of way. He'd met Sarah, who was substantially more than a turn in the sheets, and who would soon be the locus of the unravelling of his life. But through it all Georgia remained constant, a brick. They never screwed anymore, but Jojo was glad for what turned into something considerably better—a fellow outsider, a friend in sin. And also the first person since Beth to learn of Jojo's terrible, shame-making secret, the primary source of his lifelong self-loathing, half of the handle he'd carried since childhood when he began sprouting thick chestnut-coloured hair from the top of his head to the toes on his feet.

"Well, you're not saying much, and you didn't come for a poke." Georgia changed her mind and tipped the fuller glass against her full bottom lip. "Were you wanting to try the sugar treatment again?"

"Nah," he said, absently rubbing his forehead. "I could use a fresh shave, though."

"That'll have to be on your own time, sweets," she said. "I still need to get back to Tuck's. It's not as though anybody else would take me on if he tossed me into the street, you know."

"I've told you before I could get you on at the hotel."

"And I've told you a hotel is the last place for a girl with appetites like mine. I'd be tarred and feathered inside a month."

"You should leave for greener pastures. A bigger town."

"Sure, a place I could disappear into, like the invisible man. And then what? I'd forget myself, be dead before I was dead. And where would you be? How many friends you got left, Jo?"

"Hell, maybe I'd go with you."

"Yeah, and we'd open a restaurant together. You'd run the kitchen while I took orders."

"Christ," Jojo rasped, lighting another of her smokes. "That doesn't sound half bad."

"Sounds like a dream, because that's what it is. You shoulda left the day the walls started coming down around you, and me? Well, shit . . . I shoulda never come here in the first damn place. But it's too late for old-timers like us, Jojo. We're part of the foundations now. The town whore and the washed-up drunk ex-cop who stuck it to a . . ."

She trailed off, her lips still fighting to form the word but no breath the push it out. Jojo sighed heavily and finished off the glass.

"She wasn't such a bad kid," he said at length, *sotto voce*.

"I didn't mean . . ."

"Forget it."

"Hell, I never met even met her. And you know I ain't prejudiced."

"Sounds like the hit record this week. I keep hearing it everywhere I go."

"Who's a whore got to hate? I'm lower than them."

"I said forget it."

They were both quiet for a spell, just breathing and smoking and listening to the clock tick. After a while, Georgia rose from the rickety kitchen table and vanished into the back room to get dressed. She looked a bit rumpled to Jojo, but he guessed she usually did. They were a rumpled pair, she and him.

"You go on ahead," he said while he refilled his glass. "I'd better catch some shut-eye. Taking in a picture before work tonight."

"What, that garbage Russ Cavanaugh's got showing this week? Doesn't seem like something you'd enjoy."

"It's air conditioned," he answered. Then, after a moment: "And Irene Dunne's not in it."

"I'd hope not, for her sake."

"The hell with her. Listen, you get on to work. Just see that I'm up by half past six, will you?"

"Aye, aye, captain."

He gave a mock salute and drank deeply of the rotgut whiskey. Georgia opened the door, and she paused halfway through.

"Oh, and Jojo? There's a razor and some shaving soap in the washroom. You're starting to show a little."

With a sad, knowing smile, she went out and shut the door. Jojo listened to her steps crossing the short distance of the front porch, tapping down the stairs and diminishing into silence before he heard the roar of her engine. He killed the glass and groaned in disgust, at the foul hooch and at himself.

He rose, found himself a bit dizzy, and decided to sleep it off before shaving. He wouldn't want to demolish his hairline, which was always the toughest part. Besides, his face sported enough white marks from the nicks and slices he'd given himself over the years from shaving cold sober, including the long pink line that ran the length of the left side of his nose. Knife-fight, he always explained. You should see the other guy.

With a grunt and a warm flash of shame, Jojo staggered into Georgia's bedroom and was asleep in his clothes almost as soon as his head touched the pillow.

It smelled like her.

CHAPTER FOUR

By early evening, the world had been cooking in the heat of the day on high, and though the worst of the sun's punishment was past for now, the result lingered on.

And though the kitchen was by far the hottest room in the house, at least in summertime, Theodora found herself standing over the stove all the same, getting hotter by the minute. She'd drawn nearly every curtain in the house and switched off all the lights so that only what remained of the late afternoon light illumined her work, which was enough for now. Miracle of miracles, the pilot light kept on for a change—she hadn't had to relight it even once—and the potatoes were bouncing in the roiling water. In the oven, the ham spewed a nutty aroma from the peanut butter glaze she'd slathered on it, something new she opted to try from a list of low-point recipes printed in last weekend's Sunday paper. Rationing was tough, but she was getting better all the time at making the most of it. She only hoped Russ wouldn't scoff at her efforts. After all, everybody had to do their part. There was a war on.

Theodora pulled open a drawer and extracted a long fork with which to test the potatoes, but the jangling telephone on the wall had other ideas about that. She set the fork on the counter and hurried over to catch it before the caller gave up. She picked up on the fourth ring.

She barely got through the quick two syllables of *hello* before a throaty voice with a high Southern twang cut right into it.

"Gimme Russell Cavanaugh and do it quick," the man on the line said breathlessly. "It's an emergency, and I ain't kiddin' about that, neither."

Theodora frowned, taken off guard by the rudeness of it, and gave a little laugh.

"Why, Mr. Cavanaugh isn't at home. You'll just have to call back later."

"Dang, but I got to talk to him. I mean now."

"Like I just told you . . ."

"Listen, lady—you don't know me and neither does Cavanaugh, but I happen to know he's got some folks runnin' a show at his picture house and he don't know what they're all about. They're bad news, do you get me? Real bad news."

Theodora lowered her eyelids, unaware until then how wide her eyes had gotten, and cocked her hips to one side. She knew where this was going. It was Reverend Shannon's people, making their first salvo to shut down the picture Russ had going this week. She'd expected as much.

"Look," she said impatiently, "if it's a moral problem you've got in mind, you can pray about until you're blue in the face. And if you reckon Mr. Cavanaugh ain't got the right to show the picture, well then we've got a perfectly competent sheriff here in town you can go tell all about it. But what I will not have, Mr. Whatever-your-name-is, is harassing calls to my home when I've got supper on the stove and nothing at all to do with my husband's business, *which*, by and by, is a highly respected one in the town of Litchfield. Do *you* get *me?*"

"Lady, you've got me all wrong—I ain't never been to Litchfield and don't give two hoots about the moral or legal gobblety-gook you're yammerin' on about. I'm talkin' about real trouble, here. This don't got a thing to do with your husband's business. This here is the *Devil's* business."

Gritting her teeth, Theodora tried to will her heart to stop hammering against her ribs. Her hackles were up and she could feel the heat in her face getting hotter than summer could make it—it was a mad heat, and she could feel the fire building.

"I don't guess the Devil is in the picture business," she said with as much restraint as she could muster. "And even if he was, I certainly don't reckon he'd do it by way of educational shows like the one . . . never you mind. This is done, sir. Good-bye."

And with that, she slammed the receiver back on its hooks and let out an animalistic snarl at the temerity of the stranger on the line. Almost instantly, the bells atop the phone box jangled again. Theodora let out a startled yelp.

"Goodness," she said to herself. "My goodness."

She had no intention of answering it, not this time, so she returned to the stove and resumed her work, scooping up the potatoes and piercing them with the prongs of the fork to test how well cooked they were. They needed a few more minutes, and before they ticked by, the telephone went silent again. It stayed that way.

But Theodora's mind lingered over it the way the midday heat lingered in the air. Something the man said struck a chord with her, and not a pleasant one. *The Devil's business*, he'd said—a favourite turn of phrase often spoken in hushed tones by her nanny, Anne, all those years ago.

How come them men is killing each other in France?

Hush, chile—that the Devil's business.

Of course, now men were killing each other in France once again, and near everywhere else besides, but that was not what the man on the telephone was talking about. Nothing so monumental as a worldwide war . . . no, only a picture show. A lousy picture show.

What in the world could possibly be so devilish about that?

She wiped her face with the hem of her apron and gazed out over the darkening horizon through the kitchen window. It was looking more and more as though Russ would not be home for supper, which was hardly a surprise, but remained a bitter disappointment. Her mama (God rest her soul) would have *tsked* and reminded her that her husband knows best, just as she always said her papa did even when the powder couldn't hide the purple shiner grabbing her eye or the dark marks that hard, angry fingers made on the pale, flabby flesh of her arms. *Your father knows best, Theodora, don't you fuss.* But that, too, was the Devil's business in Anne's estimation.

Women ain't treated right and neither is coloured folks, and maybe that a cross your mama and ol' Anne got to bear, chile, but that don't make nothin' right. You find you a good man when the time is right, and not no man up to the Devil's business.

Like Papa, she meant, but did not say.

Your father knows best.

Russell knows best.

The Devil's business.

"Shoot!" she suddenly shouted.

The potatoes were coming apart in the water.

Theodora rushed to lift the pot off the flame before the damage could worsen, but in her hurry to minimize the catastrophe she forgot the oven mitts—the iron handles on opposite ends of the pot burned her hands, and she gasped, and she let go of the pain-inducing handles which dropped like a rock, pot and all, to the floor. The pot clanged loudly against the tiles—several of which cracked and broke—and hot water, just boiling, rose up and out like a wave. The overcooked potatoes swam out in pieces. Theodora leapt back to avoid getting splashed by the water and slammed up against the kitchen table, which slid back to the wall from the push of her weight. A wooden cross on the wall came loose from its nail and fell, crashing against the tabletop and splitting in two.

Steam rose in white circlets from the floor in front of her, from the mush of the ruined potatoes and the broad puddle of hot water that now pooled at her feet. Theodora staggered to one side and collapsed into one of the kitchen chairs. She was shaking all over, her heart pounding a tattoo in her chest.

When the tears came, she did not bother to wipe her eyes. And later, when the ham began to burn and the oven started smoking, she merely turned the knob to kill the flame and retired to the sitting room. She'd lost any semblance of an appetite anyway, and Russ wasn't coming home.

Before Theodora knew it, the room was dark.

But she did not get up from where she sat. Not for a long while.

CHAPTER FIVE

"Gentlemen! Gentlemen, if you please."

The auditorium—if such a small assortment of hard red chairs, bolted to the floor in twenty-five rows of fifteen, could be called that—softened its distinctly male roar to some degree, though not completely. A slight fellow stood on the dais beneath the screen, his hands raised up and out like a revival tent preacher, his face a mask of stone. He wore a long white coat, the familiar uniform of a medical professional. Beside him stood a plump young woman, also dressed in medicinal white, a stack of pamphlets cradled in her thick arms.

"Gentlemen, direct your attention to me, please. It is now time to begin."

The nurse—for indeed every fellow in the audience had to agree that was what she was—smiled in a decidedly phony way and tried to look interested in what the man in the white coat had to say. The roar softened some more, devolving to a dull murmur, then a whisper and, finally, silence.

The man grinned.

"I am Dr. Elliot Freeman," he announced. "I am a licenced sexologist."

Titters erupted from several clusters of young men in the audience. The doctor frowned.

"Ours is a nation in crisis," Freeman continued, a bit louder now. "Because of men like Hitler and Tojo, yes, but I mean here, in our blessed small towns, right in the heartland of America. In your *homes*, gentlemen!"

The tittering ceased. A few cleared throats, but that was all. Freeman had them now.

"I am talking about your sons and your daughters, about all the young people in your community. I am talking about the very future of—"

Here Dr. Freeman paused momentarily, his mouth hanging open and drawing a slow breath before at last his memory kicked in a beat too late to hide the lapse.

"—of Litchfield, my friends."

His eyes scanned the crowd, taking in the faces of the men, many of whom raised their eyebrows in anticipation for what was yet to come. Most of the seats were filled—only a dozen or so were vacant—and a second nurse wandered lazily up and down the aisles. She too had an armload of pamphlets. Unlike the one up on the dais with Dr. Freeman, this nurse seemed to have a perpetual scowl tugging at her face.

"Folks," the doctor resumed, "we live in an eminently modern era. Things have changed. Things are still changing. But some things, my friends, never change—even when they really ought to. Let me ask you—all *ya'll*—a question. When the criminals in our society get smarter, don't you want the lawmen to get smarter, too?"

Murmurs of assent arose from the audience.

"Of course you do—the question answers itself. So, when our young people get smarter about sex—come on, now, that's why we're here—when they get wise to the facts of life, don't you reckon we, their guardians, their caretakers, need to get wise as well? And wiser!"

Yeah, said a few voices; *That's right*, said one in particular. Several others grunted and hummed. A third of the heads nodded at least once.

"But here's the thing, here's the *crisis*, men! They—your young 'uns, I mean—they only know half the facts. They know all the rewards but none of the risks! Do you? You sir, in front—do you know all the facts you need to know to protect your little Susie or Lula Mae? I'm talking about the most vitally important facts, men. Do you? Can you be sure she won't end up like poor, unfortunate Barbara in the motion picture you're about to see?"

Ж

Jojo maintained a vice-like grip on the box of licorice in his hand, self-conscious about opening it up when no one else in the theatre appeared to have any concessions. Was it uncouth to bring candy into a picture like this? He felt like it was, despite the fact that they were selling the damn stuff right out in the lobby, though he did feel queer about being the only customer at the counter. Now he squeezed the sealed box like it contained state secrets, wishing he'd never bought it in the first place. If only he weren't so hungry.

He'd awakened with a start, certain that it was the result of his brain telling him he was late, he was going to miss the show and he couldn't make the next one on account of work. He sat up, staring wide-eyed but unseeing at an only marginally familiar room strewn with feminine chaos, and the female in question looking down at him from the doorway. She cooed something about waking the prince with a kiss and he responded by barking a question about the time. He wasn't late, as it turned out, and yet there wasn't time enough for supper if he wanted to make the picture, which he did. So Jojo settled for black licorice, his favourite, and all but crushed it in his hand for his anxiety concerning the propriety of eating it just then.

Instead, he gazed at the strange man on the dais and half-listened as he prattled on about the dawning of a grand new age when frank speech about human sexuality would be accepted as science, and reason became mankind's saviour—though the doctor was careful to couch his language in faux religious terms, lest the multitude of holy-rollers in the crowd get rowdy about it. They didn't, thanks in no small part to the lecturer's well-selected words, and by the end of his speech he appeared to have the men in the palm of his hand. He had, Jojo realized, scared the holy Moses out of them with all that talk about the sanctity of their daughters' virtue, after all. They would have been fools—or very terrible fathers and brothers—not to give the esteemed sexual hygiene commentator their full and undivided attention.

Privately, he regarded the whole performance as a lot of ballyhoo, just a lot of the same preposterous fire and brimstone twaddlecock you could get for free at any church you liked.

At length—finally—the doctor, who Jojo figured wasn't really a doctor at all, wrapped it up and gave it over to the unseen projectionist, who dimmed the lights and rolled the first reel. Flourishing orchestral strings crackled and a type crawl made its way up the flickering grey screen.

FOREWORD (it read)

Our story is uncomplicated, and much too common. Our story is yours! It unravels in every American town, in your own backyard! You will meet Barbara Blake, as demure and innocent a girl you shall ever know—unfortified against this new time in which we live!

This vague, fear-mongering assertion was quickly followed by a proclamation in bold, capital letters that filled the screen as the music turned low and sinister: IGNORANCE IS A SIN—KNOWLEDGE IS POWER.

Jojo smirked in the darkness. *Jim Shannon's going to have a heart attack if he sees this garbage,* he thought.

But at least it's air conditioned.

⚔

The film itself was perfectly unremarkable in every respect. Poor Barbara Blake, played drowsily by some unknown actress whose name Jojo forgot almost as soon as it vanished from the title cards, lurched stupidly through the first act, falling in desperate love with the grocer's son and, ultimately, ending up in the family way. Naturally she struggled through the shameful secrecy of the thing for most of the second act and found herself a pariah by the start of the third. Her screen time fluctuated between lethargic pouting and wild histrionics. She even had a fainting scene that elicited a few stifled chuckles from the audience.

By the end of it, Barbara's too-soon-motherhood came to a terrible, tragic end when her beau got tight and all but kidnapped her in the dead of night to secret her away to a new life in the Big City, only to slam his coupe into a massive oak tree. He died, she lived, but the baby was lost. And somewhere in the high-toned narration that concluded the whole sordid affair was the strong implication that fate decreed such awful calamity for those who did not properly learn the FACTS and abide by them.

Then, once the melodrama had finished, the last reel came to befuddle and astonish every walleyed, stony-faced man in his seat with a tacked-on bit of honest-to-Christ real live childbirth. Jojo directed as much of his attention to his fellow audience members as he did to the horrors on the screen, amused by their terror and intrigued to discover how much he could tell about each man's personal experience based on the degree of discomfort his face registered. The youngest of them turned a greenish-white. Conversely, one old-timer with a scraggly grey beard just grinned and shook his head. The miracle of life held no surprises for him.

Explicit though it was, Jojo remained largely unaffected and unimpressed. When the lights came back up, Dr. Freeman stood to the side of the dais and surveyed the audience, presumably measuring the mood of the room before launching into the next phase of his attack. Flanking him were the two nurses, their respective stacks of pamphlets at the ready.

"For the price of twenty-five cents, I hardly see how you can afford *not* to peruse the powerful information contained in these little volumes," said the doctor.

There were two from which to choose, as it happened, one from each nurse: *Motherhood Too Soon*, of course, but also its companion volume, *Fatherhood Too Soon*. Freeman liberally recommended interested parties pay the half dollar for both.

Jojo purchased neither, judging his own knowledge on the subject sufficient. When the more pleasant of the two women drew near to where he sat, he smiled and wagged a discouraging finger at her. She merely shrugged and tried her luck with the next schlub in line.

The other nurse kept her distance. They made eye contact once and only once, she and Jojo, and the mutual recognition was evident. She looked better in the black stockings she'd worn in the hotel lobby the night before, Jojo opined, but the tight-fitting nurse outfit (no doubt acquired from some costume shop someplace) fit her just fine. He guessed nurses did not normally wear so much make-up on the clock, but she was no nurse anyway. Like the esteemed Dr. Elliot Freeman, who was also among the Litchfield Valley Hotel's new guests, she was clearly nothing more than a latter-day Vaudevillian, earning her bread playing a corny part.

The nurses made two rounds each, trying every man who declined their offer a second time. Jojo pursed his lips at the woman when she reappeared near him, and she gave a nervous giggle in reply. There was a time, he realized . . . but no, not anymore. She continued on, sold a few more books, and Jojo made his way back to the lobby and out into the street. A pale-faced little man with a shock of white-blond hair stood just out of the streetlamp's range, furiously flipping through his copy of *Motherhood Too Soon*, his face pinched into a wild-eyed scowl as he searched the pages for whatever licentious material he hoped to find. As he reached the back cover, he uttered a frustrated growl and tossed the pamphlet into the street. The little man stalked off, and Jojo sauntered over to claim the disowned book.

One man's trash, he thought.

He rolled the booklet into a tube and stuffed it in his pocket. He checked his wristwatch, realized he wasn't wearing one, and then headed up to the hotel.

There was nothing to see here, as he'd so often informed any number of looky-loos back in his cop days.

And as he strolled along Main, Jojo finally opened up the box of licorice and had himself a walking supper.

※

Jake's eyes were a pair of silver dollars, shining bright at the ample bosom of the nurse bending at the waist to address him. She was a dish, all right, and mightily intimidating on top of it with her sleepily lidded eyes and the enigmatic line she made of her ruby red mouth. She presented a copy of *Motherhood Too Soon* like it was the offering plate at church and raised one eyebrow, an unspoken question.

Only a quarter, the eyebrow reminded him.

Jake grinned and tittered in much the same way he'd been doing all evening, part embarrassed but mostly a little tight. He'd put back a few beers with his brother-in-law and his boys—all of them about ready to move to Memphis and make their mark on Country and Western music—and as usual one became two, and two became four, and before he knew it he was staggering up to the Palace with the world doing cartwheels all around his head. Inside it, too.

He saw Jojo in the audience when he came in, but he avoided making himself known to the house dick, taking care to sit well behind him at the back of the theatre. He wasn't sure who it would make more uncomfortable, their meeting up under the circumstances, but experience taught Jake to generally avoid the man anywhere outside of the Litchfield Valley Hotel. Once, some months back, he'd taken lunch at the Starlight with some skirt he knew from school, a dizzy bitch called Caroline who never stopped smiling and yet always looked like she was about to cry. Halfway through his hamburger, in walked Jojo Walker, and here Jake thought he was running into a friend from work, a colleague, a pal. *Well, howdy there, Jojo, what do you say? Rest your rump and sit a spell, we won't mind.* Which was the God's honest truth, since the entire conversation thus far had come from his mouth and his only while poor, dumb Caroline just showed her crooked teeth and stared at him with wide, wet eyes. He might as well have said something awful about the man's mother for the way he got treated, all crumpled brow and eyes like a couple of mad hornets about to launch right out of their sockets.

All he said was *no thanks* before retiring to a booth by the window and chain smoking in surly silence while his coffee went cold, the lout. Couldn't have been ruder if he tried.

So when Jake caught a glimpse of old Scarface himself in the dead centre of the theatre, he was quick to sit and drop his head, hoping not to be recognized. The truth was he didn't much care for Jojo, not since that day in the diner—here was a guy with no friends to speak of, an outcast, practically an exile except that he stayed in town, and Jake had tried to rise above all that with a bit of common decency, but what did he get for it?

The hell with Jojo Walker. As far as Jake was concerned, the guy deserved what he got, and then some.

Whether or not Jake deserved this brunette beauty's attention, he couldn't say. Probably not, but he wasn't about to tell her that. Instead, he dug a quarter out of his pocket and pressed it into the woman's waiting palm. She managed to smile with just her eyes without moving her lips at all—dangerous eyes, he thought. Like bottomless pools. He could have dived right into them.

"Coming back for the midnight show?"

Her voice was a whisper, almost too low to hear, which was strange given how far her mouth was from his ears. Still, he heard her, though he did not quite get her meaning.

"I'm not . . . well, no," he stammered. "I mean—there's a *midnight* show? I thought the mixed one, you know . . ."

This time the stunning nurse did lean in close, her breath warm on Jake's cheek.

"That's just for this picture," she said. "The one at midnight, well it's different. Not advertised. Invite only."

Jake sucked in a sharp breath, unsure of what to make of the exclusive invitation, but vaguely thrilled to have received it. Vague, because she had not yet said what, precisely, the invitation was for.

"I—I have to work," he squeaked.

"No you don't," said the nurse. "Not really. Not if you don't want to miss the surprise."

She pronounced the last word slowly and seductively, stretching her plump mouth from a bright red bud to an opening almost wide enough to remind him of the awkward bit at the end of *Motherhood Too Soon*. And that begged the question: what sort of woman came onto a guy like this, a total stranger, after something like that?

This one, apparently. And Jake wasn't exactly complaining.

But Jesus, Mr. Hibbs—and what if Jojo *had* seen him? He didn't think he had, but the guy was a policeman for a hundred years, probably had eagle eyes in that cut-up mug of his. Getting out of his shift wasn't going to be the easiest task of his life, nor the wisest, but . . .

"It's not like everyone gets to go, you know," she said sullenly, her gaping mouth melting into a girlish pout. "Come, or don't. It's a free country, gorgeous."

She gave him a wink and moved on, harassing some of the other remaining men with her books and her bosom and her puzzling, impenetrable, voodoo eyes. Jake was relatively certain her nurse's outfit was just a size too small for her build, and was careful to study the motion of the fabric as it strained against her curves to make absolutely sure.

To hell with Jojo Walker, he thought again, *and to hell with Mr. Mitchell Hibbs*.

It was right at nine o'clock now, and even if he ran he'd be at least a few minutes late. But he had a paperback in his back pocket and enough money for a slice of pie at the Starlight, so why the hell not? They had a phone in the back there, he'd call and complain of a sour stomach, and who were they to make a stink about it?

Jake felt like the master of his own destiny. And destiny was wiggling through the aisles, selling cheap sex books and, he thought, casting the occasional surreptitious glance his way. He stood, edged his way into the aisle, and marched out to the lobby like he owned the place. Like he owned the whole damn town. By the time he was halfway through *Seven Steps to Satan* and mostly finished with the peach pie on the table in front of him, Jake's ego had swelled to majestic proportions. She had chosen him, hadn't she? He certainly hadn't seen her spend that much time—nor get so close—with any other swinging dick in the joint.

And speaking of dicks and swelling . . .

Whoa there, Tex, he warned himself, *there's plenty of time for that.*

He sipped his coffee and jabbed a forkful of pie into his mouth, and as he chewed, Jake closed his eyes and smiled, thinking of all the things he would do to that broad.

Whatever her name was.

)(

The cage was empty. Jojo wandered over to it, peered inside like a kid looking for a sleeping tiger at the zoo. No tiger, and no Jake, either.

He'd been at the Palace, though Jojo was sure he didn't know he'd been spotted. For the next fifteen minutes or so, Jojo guessed Jake would be along any minute now. Then Hibbs came into the lobby, his face drawn and hollow, his bald head gleaming with sweat. Charles all but leapt out of the boss man's way when he came through. Jojo leaned up against the front desk and waited to be addressed.

"Sick," Hibbs grunted, jabbing a thumb toward the vacant cashier's cage.

"So?" Jojo did not so much as consider giving the kid away. Even when he was a deputy he hated a stoolie, any kind of man who could turn over on an ally like he was combing his hair.

"So, no one to sit in the cage, 'less you care to do it."

"Can't say as I do."

"I didn't much reckon you would."

"Have I got a choice?"

"'Course you have. You're white and over twenty-one. You can march right through them doors over there if you've got a mind to."

"And if I like having a job?"

"Then you'll sit in the goddamned cage."

Jojo glanced over at the cashier's cage, and then back at Hibbs. He grinned.

"Just so long as nobody throws the switch that makes me fall in the water."

"Throws the—? Oh, I see. Carny humour."

"Right."

"Well, this ain't no carnival, it's a respectable hotel, so I expect you're on double duty tonight."

"I can't man the cage and patrol the floors at the same time."

"Since when do you ever patrol the floors? Just sit still and keep your eyes and ears open. That really isn't so tough, is it Walker?"

"And if something should happen?"

Hibbs frowned and cocked his head to one side. Jojo never thought of it before, but his boss kind of looked like a giant baby when he assumed that expression of his.

"Take care of it. That's what you're paid to do."

"Check," Jojo said.

"Thatta boy," Hibbs said patronizingly, patting Jojo on the shoulder. "Got a group coming in from Little Rock tomorrow—something to do with the Daughters of the Confederacy. I think they're putting on a barn dance or some such thing. War bonds, I guess. I don't reckon they'll arrive before you leave—er, turn in—at seven, but just so you know . . ."

"Double check."

"Right. Good. Anything else?"

"I dunno," Jojo said, shrugging his shoulders. "Is there?"

"Charles holding up all right? Doing his job?"

"Sure. Charles is niftic."

"He's a good boy," Hibbs agreed.

Jojo said, "He's thirty-seven."

"What's that?"

"Nothing."

Hibbs looked nonplussed, but recovered quickly enough. He turned and started off, then paused and looked back to Jojo.

"Oh, and one more thing," he added. "Those movie people came through last night—keep a close eye on 'em, would you? I'm not suggesting they're trouble, necessarily. . . ."

"I understand," Jojo said.

". . . and I'm sure they checked out, that they're not, you know, doing anything *wrong* or anything like that . . ."

"I'm on it, boss."

Hibbs smiled and clasped his hands together.

"I knew I could count on you, Walker. Yessir, folks might say—"

He cut himself off.

"Yeah? What do folks say?"

"Well, you know how people are. All I mean to say is that you do all right by me, regardless. I guess a man ought to mind his own business. . . ."

"Yeah," Jojo said through clenched teeth. "I guess he ought to."

"That's right," Hibbs said. "That's all I mean."

The two men exchanged an awkward glance, and then Hibbs smacked his lips and rubbed his hands together.

"If there's nothing else . . ."

"I think I've got it covered."

"There's a good fellow."

Jojo retired to the cage and within minutes decided he knew exactly how the tigers felt. He scanned the tight area for any reading material Jake might have left behind, but there was none to be found apart from a tattered brochure denoting some of the northwestern part of the state's natural wonders. It was a long time since they'd stopped handing those out, not since a pair of newlywed campers decided to take their honeymoon in the Ozarks and never came back out. Jojo wondered if whatever moon-shining hillbillies who no doubt killed them first trapped them in a cage like this.

But then hadn't he been trapped all along, for the last year and some change, in a cage of his own making? He could have left, gone elsewhere, to another town or another state or, hell, to Mexico for all it mattered. A fresh start, maybe even a new name to go along with it. Anything that couldn't be perverted into Jojo or any other carny freak moniker. Start scrimping and saving until he could afford electrolysis from some quack doctor in some shifty little border town with a skyline made of giant radio towers instead of skyscrapers. No more Jojo the Dog-Faced Boy. No more goddamned Ambras Syndrome. No more George Walker at all.

Then again, maybe *he* was the cage—his own self, his skull. His mind: nothing corporeal, but a cage all the same, and one of his own making. Cheat on your old lady one too many times . . . but it wasn't the quantity, it was the *quality*, in this case being the quality of *black*, which counted as miscegenation in the minds of everyone within a five hundred mile radius if not strictly according to law. And then you lose your old lady and your job and what little standing you ever had in the community, and even though no one really knows that you're a freak, that you're a real live fucking *werewolf*, it doesn't much matter because now you're something much worse and that's prison for you, George Walker, life sentence with no option for parole, in the impregnable cage you built with your own two furry hands.

Mexico, Jojo silently mused.

Wouldn't that be nice.

Jojo grimaced, kicked his feet up on the counter, and waited for the time to pass. It did, but slowly.

✕

He sat in the booth long enough to watch tables turn over as much as eight times, but the night seemed to speed on as though the clock on the wall was busted. He finished his pie, finished his book, and went through enough cups of mud to kill a small horse, and all the while Jake had only one thing on his mind—that fabulous nurse and her unbelievable figure.

It was half past eleven before he knew it. Time to stop fantasizing and get real. He left a dollar on the table, left the paperback too, and got out of the Starlight like the place was on fire.

✕

She knew something was wrong, something so ambiguous she couldn't name it, but it hung heavy in the air like fog. A substantial part of it was her own sustained sorrow, this much she knew, for she had cried for a long time and the world always seemed denser and more difficult to navigate after a deep, mournful cry. That, however, was far from a mystery to an old hand like Theodora, who spent more lonely nights in tears than not, and she knew the heaviness was something else, something more than humidity and regret. Perhaps her husband's cold distance was a part of it—though Russ was never a *warm* man, and his attitude toward married life went largely unchanged since day one—or, more specifically, the strange doings at his theatre.

The strange *man* at the theatre.

She'd only seen him once, and in passing, like a ghost. Entirely unremarkable in every manner, from his perfectly average height to his ordinary seersucker suit to the face he wore like a mask of every American male between the ages of forty and fifty she'd ever seen in her life. His hair was oiled and parted in the middle, a bowtie at his throat, the colour of which she could not recall. His voice was a trifle high, perhaps even on the effeminate side, but by no means gentle— he spoke too loudly and much too quickly, a northerner if she'd ever heard one. Theodora had nothing against Yankees, despite her father and grandfather's harsh contempt for them (her great-grandfather was one of only five Confederates to die at the Battle of Lynchburg), but they were as much a mystery to her as any Chinaman.

It was not just his foreignness that perturbed her, though. It was the peculiar glint in his eye and the almost immediate sway he seemed to hold over her normally fiercely independent husband. It was the strangeness of this whole "roadshow" business and the cruel manner with which Russ discussed Reverend Shannon on the telephone the other night. And it was the chilling smile that man flashed her in the brief moment she saw him, his head whipping to the side to catch her as if she was sneaking about, his small, thick-lipped mouth spreading open to reveal flat, white teeth in a grin that could just as easily have been described as a snarl.

So what was wrong, exactly? Theodora couldn't say. This "Barker" Davis certainly was wrong—what sort of first name was *Barker*, anyway?—and his sordid little picture show that was sure to scandalize the whole town if it hadn't already. He reminded her of the old medicine showmen; that, or the carny people who usually dragged along in the circus' wake like vultures after a dying animal. He reminded her of the sideshow her father took her to, a lifetime ago, which Anne didn't like at all and would have forbidden her from going if she had been in any position to forbid anything.

It was, of course, the Devil's business.

And if Anne had overreacted to every other thing that ever earned that designation in her view, Theodora came to learn that in this case, she had not. Not in the least.

Snatches of remembered images—faces and lights and the sawdust-and-vomit smell of the carnival—overcame her senses as she rose to finally switch on the light and try to make sense of the connection her mind wanted to make between that long ago time and the anxiety that presently gnawed at her. The shouting men and crying babies and the sad, strange people she couldn't feel right about staring at. . . .

She's just fat, Papa, it isn't so nice. . . .

Theodora knitted her brow and focused on the present, on the room and the house and all the picking up that needed doing. She arranged the magazines on the coffee table into a neat stack and wiped down the little bar with a dust rag. Next, she moved into the kitchen to eradicate all evidence of the earlier disaster, and she even found herself humming a little tune before she was done with it. It was "Nine Little Miles From Ten-Ten-Tennessee," but she only knew the refrain, which was what she part-hummed, part-whistled over and over again. It reminded her of infrequent visits to Memphis in her childhood, passing over the Mississippi on a rickety bridge and marvelling at the possibility of a town larger than Little Rock. *Heck, lil' miss* (said her father in a rare

THE RIB FROM WHICH I REMAKE THE WORLD

moment of warmth), *there's towns ten times bigger'n' this'un.* Theodora couldn't imagine. Anymore, she did not care to. Litchfield was quite big enough, thank you very kindly, and what's more, if you can't get it in Litchfield, then you don't really need it. She greatly doubted she would ever lay eyes on Ten-Ten-Tennessee again as long as she lived, and that was just fine and Jim Dandy with Theodora Cavanaugh.

She was fine right here.

Finishing with the kitchen, Theodora moved back through the front room to the foyer—such as it was—where she found Russ' coat and hat hanging haphazardly on the doorknob of the coat closet door. She couldn't begin to guess why the coat was out at all, this being the heart of July, but she deigned to open up the closet and return the smoky old thing to its hook in there, when something shifted in one of the outer pockets, poked out, fell to the floor.

Theodora bent at the waist and paused to examine the object before picking it up. It looked like a small purse of some sort, at least upon first glance, just faded blue cloth stitched up the sides. But it did not take the simple, rectangular shape of a purse, but rather the crude form of a man. Torso, arms and legs, and a round little head that jutted out on top. Buttons—small, opalescent—for eyes. No yarn for hair, as she might have considered adding, nor extra stitches to represent a mouth. No tiny garments for the doll (for that was what it was, surely—a doll). As crude and simplistic as it could possibly be, Theodora decided the thing must be some poor child's dolly. Probably she made it herself from whatever abandoned materials she could find and collect. *A regular little Frankenstein.*

The explanation sufficed, but did nothing toward illuminating how it got into Russ's coat pocket. Though this, too, was as plain as the nose that wasn't on the little dolly's face.

Russ's latest hussy—whoever she was—was somebody's mother.

"God damn you, Russell Cavanaugh," Theodora rasped, snatching the figure from the floor and squeezing it tightly in her fist. "God *damn* you."

She squeezed the doll so hard that the stitching at one shoulder popped. A heady aroma, spicy and sharp, erupted from the opening. Theodora narrowed her eyes and brought the figure close to her face. She sniffed at it, taking in the scent of cinnamon and cloves, and was that cedar?

Strange stuffing for a doll.

Some little girl's doll, she reminded herself. *Some little girl who calls him Uncle Russell and listens in the dark while he gives it to the woman in the next room.*

Theodora shook the doll and green seeds rained down from the tear in the shoulder. Fennel, she imagined. Stranger still.

She was infertile, of course, wholly unable to be a mother in the physical sense, which never bothered Russ in the least. He'd never wanted children, anyway. At his worst, she could only imagine what sort of a nightmare he'd be to a daughter or son, no better than her own father (God rest his soul). But still, the pain of it . . .

And now this.

Her lips curled back, receded from her clenched teeth as she seized the dolly with both hands, curled her fingers around an arm and its opposite leg. She pulled, and the stitches snapped, unravelled; the spices and shavings and seeds within exploding out of the body in a dusty, sweet-smelling cloud.

You are a naughty little girl, she faintly recalled Papa seething, foam frothing at his wrinkled mouth—*naughty, naughty, and naughty children get no playthings.* Sweat mixed with tears on her cheeks as the limbs came off and the doll dropped to the floor. Theodora choked on a sob and dropped the dismembered limbs, bent over and retrieved the body. She then repeated the procedure, tearing away the remaining extremities. Next, the head.

The limp pocket of cloth left over—the dolly's torso—drooped in her grasp, spilling its remaining contents on the floor. The air was pungent with its ambrosial entrails. It was done.

Theodora wiped her eyes with the back of her hand, smearing her vision until she could blink them clear again. The blurriness ebbed, and her eyes refocused on the mess on the floor. Torn blue fabric and brown shavings, greenish seeds, and something else. She squatted, sifting through the chaos with the tip of her index finger. The grey-white fragments that protruded from the herbal muddle . . .

They were bones. Tiny, broken joints, the fingers (or were they toes? no, definitely fingers) of a small child.

A babe's hand.

Theodora gasped and stumbled backward, losing her balance and crashing onto her rump. She whispered her husband's name as though it were a forbidden word. She laughed helplessly at the absurdity of her grisly discovery, though her titters soon dissolved to tears. And when she was finished with that, Theodora hefted herself up from the floor, retrieved the broom and dustpan from the closet, and swept it all up.

She dumped the contents of the dustpan in the kitchen trash, spices, bones and all. Just another phase of her late night cleaning project, nothing more. Nothing a stiff drink wouldn't dull down, at any rate.

"Funny," she said to herself, pouring a splash of Russ's gin into a tumbler. "I don't even drink."

She swallowed the drink, gasped from the heat of it. Then she poured another. When she finished that one off, Theodora stamped up the steps to see about the laundry.

CHAPTER SIX

Jojo smacked himself on the forehead with the heel of his palm.

"Idiot," he remonstrated himself.

He had *books*—he had scads of damn books, and his quarters were just a thin, peeling wall away from where he presently sat in Jake's cage. Here he'd sat, rotting, for the last hour and a half, chain smoking and staring through the mesh like a mental case, all for the want of something to read. *Idiot.*

Sleeplessness, he rationalized. That, and the brain-melting dullness of that lousy picture at the Palace. He'd already thumbed through the thin volume he picked up off the street, but a lousier assortment of regurgitated nonsense he'd never seen—all half-truths and licentious sensationalism. It was no wonder the reedy little guy had tossed it in the street.

Now his mind rattled past the sundry books in his room, stacked slapdash on a length of pine supported by two concrete blocks beside his cot. He had a Rex Stout and a couple of Raymond Chandlers, he had Hilton's latest—*Random Harvest*—and a fair-sized stack of story magazines with spacemen on the covers. There was Hemmingway and Greene, and even some scary stuff from the likes of Clark Ashton Smith and Arthur Machen. None of which appealed to Jojo at the immediate present.

No one was likely to peg the rumpled, scruffy, scar-faced house dick for much of a reader, and that was just fine with Jojo Walker. He learned quite prematurely that folks almost never looked beneath the surface of things: beneath the fur, beneath the scored flesh, to the soul that might dwell inside. Too much trouble, he'd long assumed, with so many people out in the world to choose from. So he fit a *type*, but that suited him; it provided him with a sort of blissful anonymity he'd never known until the day he melted into the scenery, became a caricature, started anew in this quiet, lonesome way. There were bright young things in town with beaming mugs and pink faces anyone might like to know, or try to know—enough of them that no one bothered with a dour, ugly fellow like Jojo Walker, even if they didn't know every nasty detail, which they did.

Fine.

He had his books, and his cot. A job that never asked much and, God help him, still a few friends about, even if they were pariahs like him.

He felt a little like Koestler, maybe—there was something about Rubashov in *Darkness at Noon* that was starting to remind him of himself in a decidedly self-pitying sort of way—so Jojo got out of the cage and whistled shrilly across the lobby at Charles.

"Yeah, boss?"

"I ain't your boss, Charles."

Charles smirked.

"I'm going to step into my office for a minute—keep a look out, would you?"

Charles offered a mock salute in affirmation. Jojo shut the cage door and went through his own. His copy of the Koestler book remained where he'd left it, between Eliot's *Four Quartets* and Smith's *Out of Space and Time* on the knotty pine plank, as did the strip of newspaper he used for a bookmark. He cracked open the book and his eyes drifted to the last sentence he remembered reading, the one that had kept him awake a lot longer than he would have liked, just thinking about it.

Satan, on the contrary (Koestler wrote), *is thin, ascetic, and a fanatical devotee of logic.*

Good old logical Satan.

Jojo returned the newsprint strip and closed the book, and his hand had only barely brushed the doorknob when he heard the shriek ripping through the lobby.

The volume sailed across the room. Jojo was already out and rushing headlong into the lobby before it landed anywhere.

Charles stood by the cigarette machine, slightly hunched over with his feet planted three feet apart. He was supporting a swooning woman Jojo recognized as one of the nurses from the sex picture—the cute one, the one who could smile. She was still in her nurse's uniform, though her cap and stockings were absent and her blouse was unbuttoned to her sternum.

She was absolutely spattered with blood.

"Mr. Walker!" Charles cried, his face a mask of horror. "Mr. Walker, come quick!"

He did not need to be told. Jojo instinctively reached for his side as he ran, fumbling for a gun that wasn't there. He reached Charles, empty-handed, and cradled the woman's head. Her eyes rolled around in their sockets, her mouth hanging open. She moaned plaintively.

"Let's get her to the couch," Jojo said.

Charles nodded, and together they carried the blood-soaked nurse to the cramped sitting area where they lay her across the couch. She trembled violently, and just when she seemed about to pass out, her body went rigid and she let loose another shrill scream.

"It's all right, lady," Charles assured her. "He's ugly, but he won't do you no harm."

Jojo shot a glance at the bellboy, who shrugged apologetically.

"Are you hurt?" Jojo asked. She resumed her silent tremors, working her mouth but not saying anything. "Charles, you'd better call for Dr. Hornor."

"Right," Charles said, scrambling for the front desk.

"And Sheriff Rich, too," Jojo called after him. He hated the idea of having Ernie Rich on what little area of authority he commanded, but it couldn't be helped. There was so much blood. . . .

But none of it appeared to be hers.

"Miss," Jojo called to her, lightly smacking her bloody cheeks with the back of his hand. "Miss—miss, snap out of it. You've got to tell me what happened."

"I called the doctor, Mr. Walker," Charles shouted across the lobby. "I'll call the police now."

Jojo nodded and continued to slap at the hysterical woman's face.

She gibbered incoherently.

"Christ," Jojo muttered. "This broad is gone."

Charles came scampering back from the front desk, his eyes wide and sweat glistening on his face.

"They all on the way, Mr. Walker."

"It's Jojo, Charles. I've told you—"

The woman screamed again, startling Jojo and Charles into silence.

"I'd better go up," Jojo said with a deep sigh.

"Oh, I don't know," Charles countered. "Maybe you best wait for the police. I don't 'spect Sheriff Rich would much like—"

"I don't give a damn what Ernie Rich likes or doesn't like. I want to see this for myself, *before* that blowhard gets here."

Jojo stood up and regarded the quivering woman on the couch, wondered if she would ever get over whatever happened to her.

"Well, what about me?" Charles asked, panic rising in his tremulous voice. "You can't just leave me alone down here."

"She won't *bite*, man."

"I don't mean her, Mr. Wa—Jojo. I mean the cage; I can't sit in there."

"You're going to have to. I'm the house detective, for crying out loud. I have to check this out."

"But Jojo! If I set foot in that cage Mr. Hibbs will put me on the street!"

Jojo frowned and planted his fists on his hips.

"All right, then how about *you* go see where all this blood came from?"

Charles furrowed his brow.

"You wouldn't be callin' me a coward now, would you, Jojo?"

"Wouldn't dream of it, pal. Look, just hang around the lobby. See the doc and the local constabulary in when they get here. Me, I'm going up."

He pointed at the staircase and raised his eyebrows.

"We ain't got but nine rooms occupied," Charles offered.

"It's got to be one of 'em," Jojo said.

Charles dropped his head and groaned. Jojo went back to his office, grabbed his gun from the desk drawer and went directly to the stairs when he came back out.

"And keep an eye on her, too," he said as he passed the bellboy.

Charles groaned again and said, "Lord, help."

※

Jojo drew his gun halfway up the steps to the second floor. At the top, he met a man in a silk robe and house shoes who gasped upon sight of the weapon and dropped his pipe.

"It's okay," Jojo assured him. "I'm the house detective."

"Sweet Jesus, you gave me a fright. There was a scream. . . ."

"I'm not holding this peashooter because my hand is lonesome."

Taken aback, the man stepped to the side. Jojo brushed past him into the narrow hall.

It was dim and dingy, the well-trodden carpet was brown when once it was orange, and of the fifteen lights strung along the length of the ceiling, only nine worked. A pair of shoes rested just outside the door to room 203—a guest with presumptions of staying in a classier hotel. Jojo heard the distant sounding drone of a radio emanating from 206.

He gripped the gun tighter, his palm beginning to sweat, and frowned at a curious thought nagging at his brain: *that gun won't do you any good.*

The roadshow people occupied the rooms at the far end of the hall—213, 214 and 216, respectively. 215 remained unoccupied in perpetuity out of respect for the former owner, whose late wife hung herself in that room one October morning. None of the current management even had a key for it, though Jojo supposed his skeleton key would more than likely do the job. He'd never tried it.

From his perspective in the muted light of the hallway, Jojo could detect nothing out of place—everything seemed to be precisely as he last saw it, warts and all. Everything, he noted with a rigid spine and widening eyes, apart from the dark crimson smears on the door, knob, and frame of Room 214, matched by splotches of the same sanguine colour marring the carpet just below. Jojo swallowed, hard, and dragged a deep, ragged breath into his lungs; he tasted the stale tobacco smoke and accumulated dust of decades.

※

George Walker had seen blood before: plenty of it.

He had seen blood, for instance, when he was a sheriff's deputy—

—Agatha Dinwiddie, John Dinwiddie's second wife and half his age, in the "wayout," as Ernie Rich called it: the far outlying planters' homes that were only part of Litchfield on paper. Dinwiddie's like the rest (sagging tarpaper roof, grease paper windows, dirt on the floor if dirt wasn't the floor itself) and who could say why Agatha shacked up with the likes of him? In the end, no one, because only Agatha could answer that question, and she'd been slashed from stem to stern, which was to say her husband inserted the blade just under her taut belly and wrenched it upward until it got stuck in her sternum. The result was an awful mess, and Rich said to Deputy Walker he'd have made John Dinwiddie clean it all up if he hadn't gone and blown most of his own head off with his dad-gum blunderbuss.

And he had seen blood even here, in the Litchfield Valley Hotel—

—Jane Smith, the name she gave on the register, though she was later identified as Caroline Atkinson of Bullfrog Valley, who stopped at the first town to come along when the labour pains made driving impossible. The baby, the deputies and Dr. Hornor were not particularly surprised to discover, was mulatto—it was also dead, as was Ms. Smith/Atkinson, who bled to death on the narrow twin bed in Room 303 hours before anyone smelled the strange and unpleasant odour wafting from beneath the door into the hall. Her corpse still held onto the corpse of her child. Both of them were bathed in blood.

. . . and then, naturally, there was Sarah. And Beth, too, later. Then, the blood was comparatively minimal; barely any at all, in fact. There really wasn't much a little .22 like that could do.

He'd seen plenty of blood, none of it anything less than tragically spilled, enough of it that a raging red sea of the stuff didn't seem likely to elicit much of a response from him.

But then he opened the door to Room 214.

)(

Worse than Agatha Dinwiddie, her murderous husband John, Caroline Atkinson and her stillborn child, Sarah and Beth combined—when Jojo switched on the ceiling lamp in Room 214, he found himself facing the goriest tableau that side of a minefield.

Indeed, that was the first conclusion he reached: that some manner of incendiary device had been detonated, blowing the body apart and painting the small room with his blood and entrails. But no, that couldn't be—he would have heard the explosion. And besides, there was nothing in evidence to suggest a blast of any kind. The remains of the room's occupant were all that was disturbed. . . .

Disturbed, he thought with a disgusted sneer. *Slaughtered, more like.*

On the floor at the foot of the bed was the torso, half-wrapped in a terrycloth robe. Unattached and scattered hodgepodge around the room were the arms (one atop the dresser, the other beneath the heater), the legs (one on top of the other, forming a grotesque cross by the window) and the unfortunate fellow's head (gaping, dripping, on the middle of the bed). Blood spattered everything. On first glance alone, Jojo could see that these were no clean cuts; this man had been *torn* apart.

But by whom?

Or what . . .

The girl couldn't have done it. A dozen of her couldn't have done it.

Jojo braced himself in the doorway and surveyed the carnage. The very walls dripped with blood and gore. His nostrils were filled with the sickly-sweet, slightly metallic odour of so much blood, which only marginally masked the gut-churning scent of the shit smeared on the floor beneath the dismembered torso. He took a single step forward, into the room, but stopped there. White spots danced before his eyes and the entire hotel shifted around him at crazy angles.

Jojo's head swam. He staggered out to the hall and vomited. He retched long and loudly, prompting a few curious faces to peek out of cracked doors. Jojo swatted at the air, shooing them off.

"Stay inside," he gasped wetly. "Stay in your rooms."

"What's doing out there?" barked a bleary-eyed traveller from the doorway to Room 208.

"Just . . . stay," Jojo demanded. "Please. The police are on their way."

He spit on the floor. The damage was already done, carpet-wise.

His stomach lurched again, leapt inside him, contracting, but there was nothing left for him to puke. Instead, he dry heaved. When he finally stopped, Jojo realized he was hunched over and looking at a pair of black-stockinged feet in the doorway directly across from him. One of them fussed at the carpet with small, painted toes. Jojo spit again, wiped his face on his sleeve and straightened up to look the other nurse, the grave, lethal looking one, in her baby browns.

She crossed her arms over her breasts and cocked an eyebrow at him.

"You look like hell," she said.

"You should stay in your room," Jojo said. "For now."

"You want a bromo?" She angled a thumb to point behind her, into her room.

"No, I don't want a bromo. I want you to go back into your room and shut the door."

She smiled, if only slightly. It sent a queer shiver up Jojo's spine.

"Are you going to make me?"

"I won't, but when the sheriff's men get here . . ."

"All right, all right—cool your barrels, cowboy. I'll play nice."

"Good," he grunted.

"But I'll still have that bromo if you decide you want it."

"Thanks."

"See you later, cowboy," she rasped as she gently shut the door.

Jojo stood stunned for a moment, then slowly turned to see that the door to the horrible abattoir behind him remained wide open—the crazy skirt couldn't have missed it. Yet she sure as hell acted as though she hadn't. Or as if it really didn't bother her in the least.

Footsteps pounded heavily up the steps at the mouth of the hall. Jojo directed his attention toward them as Ernie Rich emerged like a ghost.

"Jojo Walker, goddamnit!" he hollered as he stomped up the hall. "What in the hell do you 'spect you're doing, traipsing all over this mess? You ain't no deputy no more, in case you went and forgot."

"No, sir," Jojo grumbled reflexively. He stepped back from the door and gestured at the room with his chin. "I guess you'd best have a look in there, boss."

"And I ain't your boss neither, thank the Lord on high—"

The sheriff's words were choked off the second he saw the first long smear of blood on the floor. As he sidled up to the doorway, Ernie Rich removed the wide-brimmed felt hat from his grey head and gawped at the nightmarish scene in 214.

"Oh, my sweet Jesus," he whispered.

"Ernie . . ."

Rich whipped around, snakelike, and snarled at Jojo: "What kind of hotel are you runnin' here, anyhow? That poor son of a bitch been ripped apart, for chrissakes!"

"You don't say."

"Don't you patronize me, Jojo Walker—this . . . *this!*" Rich pointed a trembling finger at the gore-soaked room. "That don't happen in Litchfield, do you hear? It just don't!"

"Actually, boss, it *did.*"

"Put that iron away, would you?"

Jojo flushed and jabbed the gun back into its holster.

"And stop calling me boss, you goddamn idiot!"

Arching an eyebrow and flaring his nostrils, Jojo leaped forward and stabbed a forefinger into the startled sheriff's chest.

"Look, *Ernie*—this here is *my* hotel, understand? When I'm here, I'm responsible for it and everybody in it. That's what they pay me to do, by God, and that's what I'm doing up here same as you: trying to sort out what in the hell went on in that fucking room."

"If you was really responsible for it," the sheriff seethed through clenched teeth, "this terrible thing wouldn't of happened in the first place."

Jojo's brow scrunched up and his face darkened considerably. He could feel his fist tightening at his side, almost beyond his control, revving up like an engine to haul back and knock the top lawman in Litchfield on his ass. But before he could, the last door on the left groaned open and the tweed-jacketed man from the night before stepped sleepily into the hall, *sans* tweed jacket. He rubbed his eyes with the tips of his fingers, yawned dramatically and shuffled down the carpet toward the tense, angry men in front of 214.

"Say, what it this?" he grumbled. "It's the middle of the night, you know."

Jojo uncurled his fist and took a deep breath. Ernie Rich offered one last remonstrative look at him and spun around to address the sleepy man.

"There's been a murder, sir."

"A murder!"

"We don't know that yet," Jojo said.

"Oh, for the love a' . . . what do you reckon, Walker—a grizzly bear came in through the window? Or do you 'spose it was a gorilla?"

"A gorilla?" the sleepy man asked, confused and not a little irritated.

"No, sir," the sheriff said, "there weren't no gorilla. There's a fella been killed in here, I'm sorry to say, but don't you worry. I'm the sheriff here in town, and I got one of my deputies downstairs right this minute. Nothin' to be alarmed about—just go on back to your room and let us do our job."

"But . . . but that's Pete's room."

The sleepy man suddenly wasn't so sleepy anymore. He was wide awake, and shocked to all hell. He lunged forward, shouldering the sheriff out of the way to get a view of the gruesome scene in the room—a veritable slaughterhouse.

"Oh," the man moaned, "oh, *Christ!*"

Rich took a hold of the man's shoulders and swung him away from the door.

"Please, fella," he begged, "don't do that to yourself. You don't want to see that mess."

"Pete . . . oh Jesus, that's Pete."

Was Pete, Jojo silently corrected him. *Now Pete's just meat.*

Still holding onto the shaken man, Ernie Rich craned his neck to look at Jojo.

"These here them movie people?" he asked.

Jojo nodded. "Six of 'em. Er—five, now. A woman and four men."

Rich frowned. To the man, he asked, "And what's your handle, anyhow?"

"Muh—my handle? Oh, you mean my name."

"Well, you got one, ain't ya?"

"It's Phil. Phil Gossell."

"All right, Mr. Gossell: why'nt you get on back to your room and sit tight. I reckon I'll have a passel of questions for you folks, but first things first. Just sit tight, you got it?'"

"Sure," Gossell said. "God in Heaven, this is . . . well, it's just terrible. Terrible."

He kept muttering *terrible, terrible* all the way back to his room. After the door creaked shut, the bolt crunched home.

"Sounds like a Yankee," the sheriff commented, half to himself. "Or a foreigner, maybe."

"Maybe he's been taking elocution lessons," Jojo suggested.

"You always was a funny guy, Walker. Real funny."

"Sure, I'm a regular Bob Hope."

"Get downstairs," the sheriff commanded. "I'll have questions for you, too."

"Wouldn't it be easier to get everyone you want to question in the same place?"

"You tellin' me how to do my job?"

"Heavens, no."

Rich grimaced.

"Get!" he barked.

Jojo got.

※

The questions were all predictable, conventional cop stuff, and he answered most of them with the same simple statement: "I don't know."

In fact, nobody knew anything. Everyone heard the scream, but that was all they heard. Nobody saw a thing—nobody apart from the young blonde "nurse" whose statement didn't make any sense at all. She'd seen the whole awful affair, she said, but it wasn't a murder, it couldn't have been, because there was no murderer. The poor bastard just came apart at the seams, as it were. Dr. Hornor insisted on taking her home for observation, an insistence to which Ernie Rich only begrudgingly relented. The general consensus then and there was that the poor woman—she said her name was Elaine Weiss, and no, she wasn't really a nurse—had seen something too terrible to bear and paid for it with her sanity. Rich feared he'd never get any clear leads from her. Hornor told him he was probably right.

By the time the doc took off with Elaine Weiss and Deputy Mortimer took off with the various parts of the late Pete Chappell in six plastic bags, every guest had been thoroughly interrogated and each of them was as thoroughly unhelpful as the next. One of them, the man Jojo identified as the world-renowned sexologist Dr. Elliot Freeman, said he assumed it to be a scream of "erotic passion" (his words). Another fellow who described his role in the roadshow as pasting notices around town advertising the picture, claimed he hadn't heard anything at all; he'd drank himself into a stupor and could hardly hold his head up during the questioning.

The woman, a raven-haired beauty an inch taller than Ernie Rich in her heels, left the sheriff speechless and sputtering. She maintained a bemused smile throughout the interview. She told him when you stay in enough hotels and motel lodges, you learn to ignore little things like blood-curdling shrieks of terror. Like the rest of them, Rich asked her how well she knew the deceased. And like the rest of them, she responded that she barely knew him at all—of the entire entourage, Pete Chappell was the newest recruit, having only come aboard in Kansas City last May.

"Seemed like a nice enough boy," she added with an indifferent shrug. "I'm sure someone will miss him."

With only one witness, and her completely unreliable to the point of utter futility—"She'll be in the bughouse before this is done," Rich said—the Sheriff's Department was at an impasse. The window latch had not only been locked from the inside, but the whole frame was painted shut ages ago. And naturally, no one could say they saw anyone come down the stairs or elevator either before or after the incident.

"So either one of them up there did it," Jojo said to his former boss before the latter made his exit from the hotel, "or the crazy girl ain't so crazy."

"She's nuts all right, and not like no fox, neither. No sirree, it's *got* to be one of them Yankee sons of bitches up there."

"Which one of them looked like he could pull a man's head off with his bare hands to you, boss?"

Ernie Rich narrowed his eyes by way of response and stormed through the front doors. As they swung outward, a shock of orange daylight shot into the lobby, blinding Jojo. He threw an arm up to protect his eyes from the fast approaching morning, feeling as always a little bit like a vampire from a horror picture.

Once the authorities were gone, Mr. Hibbs—who had been lurking in corners, mopping his great bald head and twitching like a morphine addict in intense silence all night—emerged from the sitting area and reasserted his domain. He scolded Charles for coming within spitting distance of the cashier's cage, sternly informed the incoming maid that she had her work cut out for her in Room 214 (her last hour on the job, as it turned out, before she quit without notice), and demanded to know why he bothered to pay a house dick to keep the hotel in moral order when the guests were just going to end up dismembered in their rooms anyway?

It was all bluster, Jojo knew, and he successfully talked his way out of it, citing the fact that he had done everything according to policy and that not every awful thing could be prevented, no matter the precautions taken. Hibbs sulked, Charles went home, and the day crew came shuffling in to the terrible news. At a quarter to eight, Jojo retrieved the key to one of the vacant rooms on the third floor and stamped up the steps, careful to avoid looking down the dreaded second floor corridor on his way up.

In Room 301, he stepped into the shower, the water hot, and washed off the sweat. As soon as he got out again and towelled off, he immediately began to sweat anew, his pores leaking like a billion faulty faucets. With an exasperated groan he stepped back into the stall and ran the shower a second time, this round ice cold. But he still sweat.

And under the cold spray, he puzzled over the unseen Barker Davis, the name on the Palace marquee, and why his face remained unseen and unquestioned throughout the whole bloody affair. Jojo did not believe for one minute that any of the strange people on the second floor were really running the show—none of them seemed competent enough for the job, save for the woman, whose name he never quite caught. No, this fellow Davis—this *phantom*—was somewhere about, yet as far as Jojo could tell he'd never set foot in the Litchfield Valley Hotel. So what gave? And why hadn't Ernie Rich inquired into this gaping piece of mystery?

Why hadn't Jojo?

He redressed, locked the room up and made his way back down to his office. The whispers among the day crew were in full swing, replete with shocked gasps and hands covering trembling mouths. Jojo ignored them all, avoided their eyes, and secluded himself in the hot darkness of his quarters, where he laid out on the cot and sweated out the morning and early afternoon through a fitful sleep loaded with ominous nightmares.

CHAPTER SEVEN

She dreamed of an open field, razed farmland, stained brick-red with blood and covered with corpses, most of them arranged like crosses. She walked among them, her movement impeded as though she were in water, careful to step around the largely incomplete bodies, their severed parts made cruciform with gory spines and dripping crossbars. In places the ruptured bodies steamed in the heat, and black swarms of flies descended en masse to feed on the putrid mess and leave their yellow eggs. She hurried past them, deeper into the grue, her bare feet slapping at the hot earth sticky with blood. In the near distance, a church loomed big at the field's edge, ringed with sickly looking pines, its façade peeling from white to grey. A silhouetted figure emerged from the double doors, a man whose arms rose slowly until he too resembled the cross: the Revered Shannon, she realized—someone familiar, someone safe. She quickened her pace, splashing through the deepening putrescence towards her saviour.

All but wading through the gore, she twisted past the thickening filth, the sun rapidly descending behind the pines, a thumping panic developing in her breast, beating a harsh rhythm that insisted she reach the church before darkness fell. Only God in Heaven could help her now, and she somehow knew for the first time that God was only to be found within the peeling, rotting walls of his musty house of worship, that there was no help and no hope beyond the confines of the church. And despite the alarming hot wind that poured out of the dilapidated structure, hotter even than the stifling, rancid air that swamped the field, she pressed on, practically swimming now, desperate to reach Reverend Shannon before the death-imbued darkness overtook her.

Yet when she came near enough to see that it was not the Reverend Jim Shannon waiting to welcome her, but rather a man entirely strange to her, it was much too late—the hot wind had become a vacuum, drawing her in, directly into the waiting arms of the man with the jaunty little bowtie and the pockmarked face. He grinned, his teeth yellow and blunt, and opened up his white coat to reveal a startling display of tiny bones dangling over his chest, hundreds of them, babies' bones, held together with wire and clacking in the noisy wind.

"Welcome home, Theodora," he said, and she tumbled through the air into his grasp.

After that, Theodora knew only darkness with no air.

And she awoke gasping, clawing at the bed sheets, certain that she was buried in the ground with the remains of a thousand infants, among them her own lost son.

PART 2

The End of the Way

CHAPTER EIGHT

Jim Shannon had heard quite enough. His hollow face reddened and his concave chest expanded with deep, angry breaths. He felt downright medieval: like a minor lord whose small dominion was overrun by infidels, heretics, savages intent on raping the daughters of his realm and laying waste to the goodness his hegemony had bestowed to the faithful under his tutelage. Such threats were nothing new—the Devil never tired, even if his adversaries quite often did—but this newest menace to Litchfield, as described in shocking detail by plump Mrs. Hutchins who got apoplectic in the telling of it, was surely the worst yet.

At the centre of it, as usual, was that blasted Russell Cavanaugh.

Always pushing his luck, that one. Orgies of sex and violence, half-naked women and glorified murder gracing his appalling little screen every other week. It was disgusting—and made all the more disgusting when Shannon considered how easily seduced God's children tended to be. They weren't bad people, most of them, but putty in Lucifer's hands, oh yes! Not every member of his flock—real or hoped for—could maintain the consistent moral and spiritual fortitude of Emma Hutchins. This much was perfectly clear.

At least, that was how he presented the case to her. The truth of it was Jim Shannon could not get his hackles up about these sorts of trivial complaints anymore. It had stopped making sense ages ago, along with most of everything else around him. Be it dirty films, or Barry Malarkey's place serving whiskey and hops now, or that old deputy he and his congregation had helped to shame right out of his livelihood for running around with that coloured girl—none of it seemed to be his place anymore. None of it much seemed to matter at all. But still, the good Reverend Jim Shannon had a part to play, and he played it well. If ever Litchfield decided to establish a summer stock company, Shannon figured he'd be a shoe-in. He'd been acting his heart out for years, now.

So Mrs. Hutchins came to the reverend with hat in hand, her ruddy face stern and her voice clear in the way it got when matters could not possibly be more serious. She spoke not of things she didn't fully understand, because she had actually *seen* the whole shocking mess and she would have given that Cavanaugh an earful had he been around to receive it. Instead, she went directly to church. And Shannon heard the whole of it, from the first reel to the horrible last, so that he need never be subjected to its depravity himself.

"Yes, of course we will organize a picket," he told the exasperated old woman. "I'll get on the telephone straight away, and you might call some of the ladies in your sewing circle while we're at it, Mrs. Hutchins."

"But will it do any good? I remember when we came down on that awful place like a swarm of locusts, just a couple of years gone now, I reckon. It was that adultery picture then, you remember?"

The reverend nodded gravely. He remembered.

"I 'spect there must've been thirty of us in front of that picture house, all a' hollerin' scripture and demanding he stop running that nasty stuff, but he didn't pay us a bit of mind, Reverend Shannon—not one bit!"

"Let us not be weary in well-doing, Mrs. Hutchins," Shannon said, adopting holy writ to suit his point. "For in due season we shall reap, if we faint not."

"Oh, oh yes, reverend—you're so right. As usual, you're so absolutely right."

Shannon smiled sagely and patted the fat woman's knee, reassuring her as he might a frustrated child. With his other hand, he pointed at the ceiling.

"It's our great God who is right, you'll remember," he said.

Emma Hutchins smiled with trembling jelly lips and watery eyes. Yet again, Jim Shannon felt as though he had tamed a great beast.

With effusive thanks and an austere pledge to get her entire sewing circle behind this most important cause, Mrs. Hutchins took leave of the church, leaving Shannon to the blessed silence of his increasingly rare solitude.

"He that endureth to the end," he muttered to himself while he fumbled through the sundry items cluttering his desk in search of a cigarette. He found one, lit it, and emptied his thoughts as he enjoyed the simple pleasure of a quiet smoke. It was over much too soon.

For within hours, he knew he would find himself at the forefront of yet another angry mob, all torches and pitchforks in the figurative sense, demanding changes that deep down in the core of his being he couldn't possibly care less about. So there was a randy movie playing the Palace? So what? In a town where every able-bodied man and woman was fully expected to get hitched and make babies as soon as they're able, what was the harm in showing folks what they've already seen or what they'll be seeing before long? *Childbirth, reverend!* Old Hutchins had practically spat at him. *It's too disgusting to imagine!* This from a woman who'd birthed seven children of her own. Shannon shook his head and stabbed out his smoke.

He had a passel of calls to make.

XX

And while he begrudgingly made his calls, Jim Shannon's daughter put aside her dull social studies book to see who was tossing pebbles at her window.

"Margie!" Scooter shouted from the garden below. He was trampling the petunias.

"Scooter Carew, you ninny! You're standing on daddy's flowers, for Pete's sake."

Scooter, a reedy red-haired boy of seventeen, looked dumbly at the obliterated petunias beneath his huge, clumsy feet.

"Aw, gee," he moaned, stepping back from the irretrievably dead flowers.

Margie could not help but smile at his awkwardness. It was adorable, in its way.

"I hope you was plenty careful getting over here," she said.

"I came in through the woods," Scooter said. "Didn't even see the church, so he can't have seen me."

"You'd best hope not," she warned. "I'll be out in a shake."

Margie shut the window, checked herself over in the vanity mirror. Her curls were buoyant, her navy swing skirt dress crisp and clean. She considered adding a dab of colour to her lips from the secret make-up stash in her closet, but *God*—if anyone saw her! She dismissed the idea and hurried down to the front door. Scooter hung back behind a thick elm in the yard, putting the tree between himself and the church on the hill. He was *persona non grata* on Shannon property, even if he was more or less welcome inside the church. The church belonged to Litchfield, whereas the elm behind which Scooter nervously hid belonged to a man who would skin his hide if he ever found the boy snooping around his daughter.

"I don't hardly see why you can't just meet me at Finn's," Margie complained as she crept from the house to the vast elm tree.

"I feel like Romeo," he said, blushing. "You know, like in that play."

"I *know* the play, Scooter. And they both die in the end, remember?"

"They do? Hell, that's a dumb way to end a play."

Margie rolled her eyes and sighed.

"Besides," he added sheepishly, "I sorta wanted to talk to you in private first."

"Private?" she asked, narrowing her eyes. "You ain't about to propose to me, are you, Scooter Carew? Because I'm not aiming to be no lonesome war bride after you run off with the Army."

If Scooter's cheeks were pink before, they burned blood red now. He wiped his forehead and shifted his weight from one foot to the other.

"Pr—pruh—propose? Why, no, Margie!"

"Oh, I see," she said with a playful grimace. "You've got some other gal in mind for that privilege."

"That's not so, Margie," he protested. "There ain't no other gal. Why, I was just gonna ask you to the barn dance on Saturday, that's all."

"Oh, is that all? Sakes alive, Scooter—you act like it's a life or death question. Of course I'll go to the barn dance, you dummy. I'd have gone one way or the other, and I expect it might as well be with you."

"You mean . . ."

"Well, that Albert Sommer's been sniffin' around a little bit, you know. . . ."

"Albert Sommer! That—that fat turkey?"

"Oh, Scooter," Margie cooed, "that's not very nice, is it? I don't think

Albert's so fat, and he sure ain't no *turkey*. I heard he'll be an officer by the time he gets to Europe."

"Yeah, sure," Scooter whined, "one of them ninety-day wonders, I guess. I could do that too, you know."

Margie burst out laughing and landed a punch on the pouting boy's shoulder.

"God a'mighty, I'm just pulling your leg anyhow, Scooter."

Scooter pulled his brow into a tight knit and glowered past Margie, over the open grassland and into the dense conifers behind the church.

"Well, I don't guess it's very funny," he said. "I come to ask you a serious question. . . ."

"It's just a barn dance, Scooter," she interjected. "Don't be so glum, chum. Come on."

She grabbed his hand and gave his arm a tug. Looking perplexed and perhaps a bit injured, Scooter relented, allowed himself to be dragged from the relative safety of the elm to the perilous line of fire between the church and the house. He wasn't there long—Margie pulled at him and hurried around the side of the house. In a moment, they were once more blocked from her father's view. From this vantage point, they crouched alongside the rotting picket fence (a source of humour for Margie, given her father's penchant for pickets) and scrambled along the periphery until they reached the narrow dirt road to town.

✕

"We'll have to sneak in," she whispered conspiratorially between sucks at the straw in her chocolate malt. "Today's the day—Daddy's coming."

"To the Palace?"

Scooter's face drained white.

"He was gonna picket the stupid thing sooner or later, and like I said: today's the day. Him and every stuffy old crow who loves him more n' anybody but Jesus himself."

"Aw, cripes," he groaned.

"It's no big deal," she said. "We just go in through the back. He'll never see us."

"You mean without paying?"

"They don't got a box office in the back, dummy."

He gazed wide-eyed at the flat soda pop in his glass. He felt like he was planning out some sort of big heist, which never went well for the heisters in any story he'd ever seen.

"Ain't that the same as stealing?" he wondered aloud.

"You're missing the point, boy. It's not about the tickets, it's about getting in without being seen. If it helps you sleep better, leave a quarter on your seat after."

He shot a cockeyed glance at her and groaned.

"I don't hardly see what's so interesting about this picture, anyway. Ain't nobody I've ever heard of in it. Lester Keaveny saw it yesterday; he told me all about it. Les says the only reason anybody would want to see it is on account of the dirty stuff at the end. . . ."

"Real live birth, I heard."

". . . that's what Les said, too—except Les said it was *awful*. I mean, real flip-your-stomach sort of stuff."

She smacked her lips on the straw, drew a massive mouthful of malt in and swallowed it noisily.

"Yeah, I reckon."

"Then why bother with it? I bet Mr. Cavanaugh's got something better next week. And there's still the dance . . ."

"Good grief, you and that damn dance!" Margie exclaimed.

Scooter shot up straight, stunned.

"Look, forget about the dance, and forget about *Motherhood Too Soon*—that's not even the real reason to get in there."

"It ain't?"

"No, it ain't. Listen—"

She leaned across the table, sliding her malted out of the way as she gestured for him to follow suit. Once they were virtually nose to nose, she continued:

"You know Phyllis Gates?"

He nodded that he did.

"Well, she went last night, to the one for both boys and girls. She said just the same as your friend Lester, except there was something else."

"What else?"

"Another picture, *after* the one they got going. One that ain't advertised, like. Invite only."

"You don't say. . . ."

"That's right."

"Well . . . what's it about?"

Margie smiled and leaned back on her side of the booth. Scooter's eyes bulged, primed to pop.

"She didn't say."

"Didn't say? Didn't you ask her?"

"Of *course* I asked her, you lunkhead. She just . . ." Margie shrugged. ". . . didn't say."

Scooter frowned and made a scoffing nose. *Pfft.*

"Phyllis Gates," he said derisively.

"I don't think she *could* say, Scooter."

"What do you mean?"

"I mean, if you want to know what goes on at the midnight show, you got to go to the midnight show. Invite only. It's a *secret.*"

"A secret," he repeated in a whisper.

"Ain't that what I said? Now you're curious, right?"

He said, "Hmn," and rubbed his chin. He was curious, but he recognized the fact that he was curious about a great many things he had sense enough not to investigate too closely. He was curious what it felt like to fly, but he wasn't aiming to leap off a cliff to try it out.

"Could be anything, I reckon," he said.

"She says it's worth it."

"Who? Oh, Phyllis."

"Try to keep up, dummy."

"Sorry."

"At first, I thought maybe it was just some nasty stag film—you know about those?"

Scooter shook his head.

"Well . . ." Margie looked around, made sure no one was too close to hear. "It's like a sex picture."

"That's what *Motherhood Too Soon* is."

"Not exactly what I mean—that one is *about* sex, sure, but a stag film . . . well, don't you get it?"

He shook his head again, more puzzled than ever.

"Good grief, are you dense. It actually *shows* it, knothead. People, you know, doing it."

He scrunched his brow for a moment, mulling it over, and when it hit him all the blood drained out of his face in an instant.

"No!"

"You know Bill Lott? Mr. Lott's littlest with the missing thumb?"

"Mr. Lott at the filling station."

"Yeah, that's him. Bill's older brother moved on to St. Louis, sells insurance there. Well, Larry—that's the brother—he told Bill all about these films. Said they have these crazy conventions all the time, all over, in different cities. Just these insurance fellows, and they drink like fish and tear the place up, and a lot of the time—this is what Larry told Bill—a lot of the time, they end up with these filthy shows projected up on a wall in some room or another. You know, they all got them funny Shriner hats on and their neckties around their heads like Indians, and they hoot and holler at the picture on the wall, which is all folks with no clothes on."

"And they're . . . ?"

"Like rabbits."

"Gee."

"Which is how come I ain't never getting married, by the by."

"Huh? I don't follow."

"I know you don't—you're a *man* and men are just plain nasty. Didn't you hear what I just told you?"

"Well . . ."

"But I don't think that's what it is, anyway."

"What *what* is?"

"The midnight show, stupid. You know, I don't think you listen too good."

"I'm listening," he pouted.

"I reckon if it was just some old stag film, Phyllis wouldn't have stuck around, and she sure wouldn't have suggested I go, too."

"She said you should go?"

"She said I *have* to go."

Scotter half-closed one eye and screwed his mouth up to one side.

"Maybe she's putting you on."

Margie furrowed her brow. "What for?"

"I dunno. Maybe she wants to make a fool out of you. Maybe there's something that happens at midnight, something you're really not gonna like. I just dunno, Margie. Sounds . . . well, it sounds fishy to me."

Pursing her lips like a disappointed mother, Margie sat back and regarded him with something bordering on contempt. The look froze him, his fingers perched on the straw in his soda.

"Now, why in the world would Phyllis Gates do something like that?"

"People do all sorts of terrible things. They do 'em all the time, really."

"Yeah, sure," she said, dubious and aloof. "It's just a mean old world."

"That what I read in the papers, anyway."

"You're such a nimrod sometimes, Scooter Carew."

He sucked at his straw and exhaled loudly.

"I know," he said.

"A real screwball."

"I know."

The bright plastic clock on the wall behind the counter (*drink Nehi!* it read around the rim) clicked over to a quarter to seven on the dot. Someone inserted a nickel in the jukebox, selected a Rudy Vallee record. "Life is a Bowl of Cherries." Scooter smirked.

The truth of the matter was he was deeply, stupidly, hopelessly in love with Margie Shannon, had been for nearly as long as he could remember. The nature of the love changed and developed over the years, changed how he looked at her and what he dreamed about at night, and of course how the Reverend Shannon felt about him. And she had changed, too: not just physically (though boy, had she ever), but personally, too. Gone was the shy preacher's daughter in pigtails with the downcast eyes, long since replaced by a hawkish young woman with a razor sharp tongue and a fixed gaze that could melt a fellow like candle wax. Scooter did not figure *he* had done much changing, apart from shooting up like a wild reed to his present six feet, since those halcyon days on the Mount Sinai Bible School playground. Back then, he and the other more rambunctious kids would scrabble up the jungle gym like wild little monkeys while little Margaret sequestered herself in the shade of an imposing oak in the middle distance, munching on a bologna sandwich and avoiding eye contact at all costs. Occasionally, her father would come traipsing up to her, gesture toward the other children, get a stern shake of the head in response. Sometime he brought her a bible to study while she sulked in her solitude. Scooter never took his eyes off her, even when he was hanging from the scabby metal bars by his feet.

He had since learned the wisdom in looking away once in a while. Now, however, he turned his gaze back to her and managed something approaching a smile.

"I 'spect we best get to moving if we're gonna do this," he said.

"Back door's never locked," she answered like someone who knew what she was talking about. Scooter guessed that she did.

He slid out from the booth and dropped three quarters on the table. Rudy Vallee's optimism pervaded the drugstore, and some of it seemed to rub off on Scooter. With a grin and a mock salute, he bid fat old Finn goodbye and escorted Margie to the door. Finn smiled broadly, his thick hands rapidly working at a large soda glass.

"Nice kids," he said to no one in particular.

X

The sign was getting a little worn, frayed around the edges, but the words were still both legible and relevant to the proceedings at hand. NO FILTH IN LITCHFIELD. It was vague enough to suit countless pickets and protests. A hundred uses in one. Jim Shannon sighed.

On the other side of his office door was the chapel, and in the chapel were a dozen people—most of them women, all of them over fifty—who had come to get organized before marching directly to Russ Cavanaugh's Palace Theater to demand he pull the degenerative monstrosity boldly advertised on his marquee as *Motherhood Too Soon*. Among them was Mrs. Hutchins, increasingly agitated, and several charter members of the Litchfield Busybodies Association, Shannon's private name for her sewing circle. Two of these old crows had managed to browbeat their husbands into joining the good fight, men who gave up arguing a lifetime ago and just sat in the pews with sleepy, surrendered eyes while they waited to be told what to do. As the reverend emerged from his office and spotted the defeated old men, he realized how much he had in common with them. He, too, was at the mercy the LBA. His chosen profession, such as it was, largely depended upon their continued support. And, he bitterly suspected, their gullibility. He might have asked himself who was controlling whom in this relationship, but he simply hadn't the energy to care enough to address the matter. Things were what they were. Best not to stir the pot.

"Agatha and Mercy Durfee didn't come," Mrs. Hutchins said with a fierce scowl. "They told me they'd come, but they're not here. Those sisters are gonna get an earful from this old soul."

Shannon was sure they would. He did not envy them.

"We have twelve," he offered sympathetically. "Thirteen with me."

"Lucky thirteen," John Martin piped up from his pew. He looked sad.

"I've chosen a hymn," Mrs. Hutchins declared. "We will sing it as we come up the block. It's 'When I Get to the End of the Way.'"

"All right," Shannon said.

"You know it." It was a statement rather than a question—something of a challenge, the reverend thought.

"Yes," he said. "I know it."

"Well, I brought songsheets for those who might not. Though they ought to; we've sung it enough in this old house of the Lord."

"Good. That's good."

"Alice wanted 'Shall We Gather at the River,' but we did that one last time."

"Yes, we did."

"I thought it best not to repeat ourselves—they might not take us seriously enough."

"That's wise."

Alice Maxwell lingered half-invisible in front of the rostrum, staring at her shoes in the dominant shadow of Emma Hutchins. Suggestions always welcome, but never applied.

"We must be at our best and brightest," Mrs. Hutchins said. "Now, I propose we rehearse the song before we go."

"Oh, I'm sure we all know . . ."

"I'll lead us off. You don't mind if I use the rostrum, do you, Reverend Shannon?"

"Well, no . . ."

She turned on her heels and raised her great, flabby arms to the other eleven: a rotund, feminine Moses to her small band of wanderers. As she rounded them up and absorbed their full attention, Shannon considered an aphorism a Texan great-uncle often used when he was a boy: all hat, no cattle. That described him perfectly at that moment, he thought, whereas Emma Hutchins had both. The hat was his; the cattle maybe never really were.

He was just a cowhand at the Litchfield H.

CHAPTER NINE

"Put that damned thing away," Georgia said.

Jojo regarded the revolver in his hand as though it was the gun, and not the girl, who had said it.

"The way you're getting on with that gin, you're liable to blow your own pecker off."

"Doesn't do me that much good anyhow," he said.

He had already removed every round from every chamber, examined them, and pushed them back in, one by one. Now he was repeating the routine like some sort of sacred ritual.

"You've been playing with that thing for twenty minutes. It ain't a Daisy, you know."

"I know."

He loaded the last round, spun the chamber and closed it with a click. This he followed with a healthy gulp of gin from the jelly jar on the table, which he punctuated with a satisfied gasp.

"I'm waiting for you get tight enough to start shooting up the place," she said. "You don't want me to get the sheriff on you, do you?"

"Certainly not."

"Then how about letting me in on whatever's rattling around that ginned-up brain of yours?"

"Chekov," Jojo said.

"Chekov."

"That's right."

"Some Russkie?"

"A pretty important one, I guess."

"He running the Eastern Front or something?"

"Naw—he's dead. Been dead for forty years."

Georgia frowned. "Eventually this story's going to get interesting. I just know it."

"He wrote plays," Jojo explained.

"Well, that's nice."

"And he had this idea, see? He said if you're going to go and whip out a gun in the first act, then the damn thing had better go off sometime in the third."

"Fascinating." She sashayed over to the table and finished off his gin for him. "So what's it to you?"

"I'm waiting for the third act," Jojo said.

Her mouth screwed up to one side, she seized the bottle and filled the jelly jar. "Life's got plot holes," she said after a while.

"That's true."

She took a slug and passed the glass to him. He took his and lit a cigarette.

"Plus it's a police matter now. Ernie's problem, not yours."

"Happened in one of my rooms."

"In one of Hibbs' rooms," she corrected.

"I was responsible."

"You're a house dick, not a lifeguard. Folks bring all sorts of baggage to a hotel, some of it not the variety a bellboy can lug up the steps for them."

"We got an elevator."

"Yeah, but it hardly ever works."

"That's true, too."

"My old man killed himself in a motor lodge outside of Scottsdale, Arizona. Thumbed his way out there to do something he could have done anyplace. I guess he always wanted to see the Great Southwest."

"That's a sad story."

"You don't say," Georgia jeered. "Point is, only man accountable was his own stupid self."

"I don't think the victim in this case ripped himself apart."

"That's not what I'm . . . ripped apart?"

"Forget it."

She narrowed her eyes and plucked the cigarette from Jojo's lips, dragged on it and exhaled a long blue stream.

"Nope," she said, "you can't do that."

"The hooch loosened my lips. Loose lips sink ships."

"Listen," she lectured, pointing his own cigarette at him, "you're the one who brought it up. First act, third act—Chekowsky's rules, not mine."

"Chekov."

"Whichever. Spill, brother."

With a heavy, dramatic sigh, he fired up a fresh Old Gold, drank deeply from the jelly jar, and told her.

And after that, both Georgia and Jojo were silent for what seemed like a long time.

X

He'd come to sleep somewhere other than the cot in his office, never intending to get half lit so early in the day, but Georgia had to get back to the hardware store so Jojo shaved with her razor and hit the sack. He slept for an hour, then woke up for no reason at all and he couldn't do a thing about it.

He found a dirty skillet on the cluttered kitchen counter, wiped it down with a rag, and helped himself to a couple of eggs in the icebox. While they sizzled on the stovetop, he went into a kind of trance, going over the events of the night before, searching his muddled subconscious for some seemingly insignificant detail he might have neglected to fully understand. Nothing came to mind, and the eggs ended up burning. He ate them anyway, washing them down with what was left of Georgia's gin, and washed the skillet in the sink when he was done.

She was entirely correct, of course, when she said it was a police matter now, Ernie Rich's problem to solve and not his, not the ex-deputy with no authority or jurisdiction or any hand in a murder case at all—if indeed it was a murder. Which it was. He knew it as sure as he knew his stomach was churning from the burnt eggs and booze roiling in it. And he was curious, if nothing else: a man had been pulled apart like a tender Thanksgiving turkey, a feat no one could possibly achieve on their own, or with several of their strongest friends. It just couldn't be done, not as far as Jojo was concerned. He'd heard of people being drawn and quartered in the old days, but that particularly nasty method of execution required a team of horses. He was fairly certain he would have noticed had someone managed to smuggle four horses into Room 214 of the Litchfield Valley Hotel. Besides, he considered with a grin, they would never have fit in there, anyway.

The full-colour memory of the carnage in the room, however, made quick work of the grin. He glanced at the clock and decided that the roadshow people—the *survivors*, he thought grimly—would be gearing up for their second show before long. In the intervening time, he had a long, hot walk back to town and enough time to cool off in the Starlight before heading into the theatre to commence his casual investigation.

Or, he considered a few hundred feet up the dirt road from Georgia's place, in Earl's tavern, which had air conditioning where the Starlight did not. It certainly wasn't the truest reason Jojo changed his mind with regard to destination, but it was the one he went with.

X

The icebox was bereft of milk and John Fields wouldn't be around with a fresh bottle for another day, so Theodora spent the requisite time putting herself together for a trip into town. Russ had the car, his cherished Continental, which meant she was to walk the two miles in, heat be damned. Accordingly, she took the umbrella from the closet to provide walking shade, and set off as the waning afternoon sun hung low in the distance.

Theodora did not much like leaving the relative safety of her home. It was not that she deemed the rest of the world to be particularly hazardous, nor that she suspected anyone in town meant her harm. She simply wasn't comfortable in the world, and although she wasn't terribly comfortable in her own skin wherever she was, the typical loneliness of home was her sanctuary, her personal temple wherein she needn't worry about anything that wasn't directly in front of her and demanding her immediate attention—housework, largely. She could iron or sweep or dust without much anxiety if she only let her mind slow to a crawl with just enough power to focus on the task at hand and nothing else. Too much thought was an anathema to her, a terror she knew well from experience and which she avoided at all costs. Too much introspection was worse than the worst nightmare, a *living* nightmare of hopelessness and fatigue that scared her more than death itself. And when life seemed worse than death . . .

A dull-red truck rumbled in the distance, shimmering in the dancing heat and kicking up a dust storm in its wake. Theodora stiffened and clumsily stepped into the irrigation ditch, sliding on loose rocks and only barely managing to remain upright. The truck crunched over the loose pebbles and quartz and sediment of the unpaved road, and as it came near Theodora could see the mountain of corn in its bed. When it came up beside her, it slowed and a farmer in a battered straw hat waved as he passed by.

She was perplexed. There was nothing unusual about a truck farmer returning from town in the late afternoon, but why in the world did he still have his whole crop with him? She turned to watch the truck rock down the road, diminishing in size until it vanished in a brown puff of road dust. A flock of blackbirds took flight from the ruckus the truck made, crying out in their escape, and Theodora watched them. Her eyes followed them over the intermittent copses of lush hackberries and elms until Leroy Dunn's freshly-painted red barn came into view. And unless Dunn had gone and moved his barn a mile or so closer to town, Theodora recognized the fact that she'd gone the wrong way down the road.

It was a road she had travelled all her life. To the west, it led to town. To the east, it made a straight shot to the outlying farms and, further out, the shacks populated by Negroes and poor whites. There was absolutely no mystery about it: she went left to go to town. She never went right, had no reason to. But today, Theodora went boldly east, and there was no telling how much farther she might have walked had her muddied thoughts not been interrupted by the truck and the blackbirds and Leroy Dunn's bright red barn.

Her shoulders slumped and she gave a weak sigh. Holding her umbrella aloft, she stepped up on the mild rise between the ditch and the road, whereupon the rocks gave way and her foot flew forward. As her shoe sailed up and onto the road, Theodora dropped like a stone to the ground below, landing at an awkward angle with her left foot twisting underneath her until something snapped. She cried out—a pitiful, animal cry—but the only reply came from some of the blackbirds, which screeched as they fled yet again from impending disaster.

The pain shot up her leg en route to her brain, increasing the heat that was already baking her, and she gritted her teeth. She shifted a few inches, tried to lift her backside to move her injured ankle, but her body protested. She wasn't going anywhere.

Her eyes welled up with fear and frustration. She didn't want to cry:

the wracking sobs building in her breast only exacerbated the pain. But she couldn't help herself. The tears and gasping breaths came on whether she liked it or not. Had she gone the right way in the first place, this might never have happened, but even if it had there was a much greater likelihood of someone coming along to find and rescue her. As things stood, she was down and out on a little-used farm road, farther from town than her house, which wasn't particularly close. The red truck heading to town (not away from it) was something of a fluke, an uncommon apparition, particularly at this time of day. The possibility of another farmer passing by was so remote it wasn't worth considering.

Theodora wept at the bleakness of her prospects. One wet, sobbing breath later, she began to laugh at the absurdity of it.

If only she'd had her head on straight, if only she'd been capable of finding her way to town as she'd done thousands of times before without incident.

If only.

Still, she laughed.

Jojo went for another cigarette only to find the pack was empty.

"Damn."

He tossed the empty package on the side of the road and kept walking. The afternoon was segueing to evening, but at that time of the year it was much too hot at one in the morning. He reckoned that after a given point, hot was just hot, and a few degrees in either direction didn't make much difference. Halfway between Georgia's house and the edge of town, he was already planning out the rest of the evening and into the night in terms of which spaces were best air conditioned, which didn't leave much. There was Earl's, and the Palace, and the meat department inside the farmer's market had a walk-in freezer he could happily nap in if they'd let him. Most places had fans, but they only turned the thick, stagnant air into something of a sirocco, an over-exaggerated version of that blast you got when you opened up a hot oven. Any way he sliced it, relief was scarce and temporary. He wished he was in Antarctica, like some hoary old explorer, plunging himself and his crew deeper and deeper into the ice and snow and frost. It was a childish fantasy, and he knew it, but it helped shave off some of the heat, at least in his imagination.

It was like the yellowing Red Cross poster in the post office said: every little bit helps.

On the north side of the road, in the middle distance, Dunn's old barn appeared through the heat-haze. It was startlingly red—freshly painted, Jojo imagined—the colour close to that of the gruesome tableau he saw the night before. The bending of the image from the shimmering air complimented the comparison, creating the illusion that the colour was sliding, dripping, bleeding into the earth. He shuddered, shook it off, kept walking.

No sense crying over spilt milk, he figured. Or blood.

When he first heard the laughter coming from the irrigation ditch, he decided he was probably hallucinating. Heat stroke. Not good, so far from town.

He slowed his pace and ran the palm of his hand up his forehead and over his slick hair, sluicing the sweat back with it. The closer he got to the laughter, the louder it sounded, and as he came to be parallel to it, Jojo considered the possibility that it was not a hallucination, that there really was somebody madly cackling in the irrigation ditch. The way things had been going, it wasn't the oddest thing he could imagine happening.

So he stepped cautiously over to the ditch and looked down. There lay the woman, dressed in her best going-to-meeting clothes, all twisted up like the hand of God had plucked her up and dropped her there. And sure enough, she was laughing so hard she was crying, as though her predicament was the funniest damn joke she ever heard.

Jojo licked his salty lips and squinted at her.

"Um," he began. "Ma'am?"

The laughter cut off with a sucking gasp. Now that they were both startled and confused, she and Jojo regarded one another in silence for a long moment. It was he who eventually broke the awkward quiet.

"You look like you could use some help."

"Took a spill," she said, breathless from the laughing. "I think maybe I broke my ankle."

"I don't get it."

She wrinkled her nose. "I fell, I landed on my ankle, and I think a bone is broken," she said sternly.

"That I get. It's the good time you were having of it that escapes me."

"I don't guess I can explain it," she said.

"Well."

"But maybe while you're thinking it over, you might think about giving a lady a hand?"

Flushing pink, he straightened up and nodded dumbly. "Oh, right. Right."

He came to the edge of the dirt road, right up to where it dipped sharply into the ditch.

"Careful," she said, "wouldn't be too good if we both ended up mangled down here."

"I guess not."

He slid down, his arms extended for balance, and crouched beside her. She made a face he found difficult to interpret, but Jojo found women to be generally difficult in that way.

"I think we should get you straightened out first."

"All right."

"I reckon it's going to hurt pretty good."

"Wonderful."

"Here, wrap your arms around me."

He bent over and she smiled nervously.

"It's okay," he said, "I'm just going leverage you up, so you can get that leg out."

"Good grief."

She extended her arms like a child looking for a motherly hug and tightened them around his neck. With a mild grunt, he leaned back, lifting her as he hooked a foot under her calf and slowly pulled it out. The woman cried out, but she did nothing to impede him. Once the leg was cleared, he lowered her back down and knelt in the ditch to examine the injury.

"I don't . . . I don't suppose you happen to be a doctor?"

"No, ma'am—but I used to be a sheriff's deputy. I know a thing or two."

"A deputy? Oh . . ."

She might have meant to say more, but Jojo was using both hands to extend her leg to its full length, which elicited a startled yelp from her.

He said, "Sorry."

"Is it broken?"

"I'm looking now."

"Sweet Lord, I hope it's not broken."

"My daddy always used to say, 'Hope in one hand and crap in the other, and see which one fills up first.'"

"That's not very nice," she said, frowning.

"Yeah, I guess not."

"True enough, but not at all nice."

Jojo smiled. She smiled back.

Gently, he moved the pad of his thumb along every contour and crevice in and around her swollen ankle, feeling for evidence of a fracture. Apart from the swelling and darkening of the skin, he found nothing.

"If there's a break, it's where I can't feel it."

"Oh, no. . . ."

"It's not so bad. That means it's not broken clear through. The bones are still set, which is a hell of a lot better than the alternative."

"Will I be able to walk?"

"Eventually, sure—but I wouldn't recommend it for at least a week or so."

"Are you the deputy that got mixed up with that coloured girl?"

His eyes popped wide as his head jerked back.

"That was unexpected," he said matter-of-factly.

"I . . . I am sorry."

"Don't be."

"I am. That was . . . uncouth."

"It's fine."

She pinched the bridge of her nose between her index finger and thumb and groaned.

"I'm gonna need to find somebody with a car," he said, staring off into the unmoving distance.

"Don't mind me," she said with some strain in her voice. "I'll just have nice little nap."

"I don't think I can carry you two miles."

"No, I expect not."

Jojo stood up and stretched his arms. The sun still hung just over the horizon as if the gears had gotten stuck. He considered lying down on the road and putting his ear to the ground like the Indians always did in the oaters, but he decided it probably wouldn't work and he'd just end up looking ridiculous. Instead, he peered down one end of the road for a while, and then the other, holding his breath all the while and listening to the stillness of the outcropping country.

No one was coming.

While he weighed his options—which were limited to leaving her in the irrigation ditch while going for help and staying with her for indefinite period of time—Jojo's sun-blinded eyes fell upon the blood-red barn across the way.

"How about some shade?"

"Going to hold my umbrella over me?"

"I'm going to carry you to Leroy Dunn's barn over there."

"The dance isn't until Saturday," she remarked, "and besides—I don't think I'm much for the Lindy hop just yet."

"Well, I don't know about any dance, but I figure you'll be a lot less hot in there, and a lot less likely to get flattened by some farmer's son who's drunker than Cooter Brown and roaming the county in his papa's one-and-a-half-tonne stakebed."

She didn't need long to think it over. He went back down into the ditch, picked her up and carried her up to the road.

"Besides," he grunted, taking careful steps to the field on the other side, "maybe Leroy's poking around here someplace."

"And if not?"

Jojo's shoulders tensed as he balanced her weight and descended into the opposite ditch.

"Then we wait."

⋊

Although the ever-present scent of horse manure lingered still in the stifling air, the inside of the barn was already set up for the forthcoming festivities. It was one big open space, the floor covered with scattered hay, and the bales were stacked ten feet high in some places against the walls. A podium had been set up at the far end from the doors, and a pair of scored wooden tables were lined up for whatever refreshments the Daughters of the Confederacy had in mind. Jojo took it all in with some modicum of awe; he'd seen quite a few houses that weren't as livable at this barn.

He found a row of hay bales suitable enough for a temporary bed, upon which he gingerly laid his distressed damsel, who crinkled her face with discomfort but didn't say anything to let on about it. She sucked in a deep breath and blew it out like it was fire. Jojo examined every corner of the barn, then went back to the open doors and peered out in all directions.

"There's no one around."

"Figures," she said.

"Some places you can't ever be alone," he mused. "Like big cities, I mean. Even if you're in a room by yourself, there's someone right on the other side of the wall. You're ever in trouble, I guess you could just knock on the wall, say, 'Hey in there, I need some help.'"

The woman laughed a little and said, "I'm Theodora. Theodora Cavanaugh."

He turned back into the barn and took his hat off to scratch his scalp.

"The movie fella's wife?"

"That's right."

"I'll be damned," he said. "That's where I was heading."

"You don't mean you wanted to see that awful picture. . . ."

"Well, no—I already saw it, but no. Just something I'm wanting to look into."

"I thought you weren't a deputy anymore."

"Old habits, I guess."

"You don't suppose Russ is in some kind of trouble, do you?"

"I don't suppose much. Just some strange stuff going on, that's all. Makes me curious, and I can't sleep too good when I get all curious like that."

Theodora smiled thinly and Jojo patted himself down, absently looking for the smokes he didn't have.

"Hell," he grumbled. "I don't guess you've got any cigarettes on you?"

"Sorry. I don't smoke."

"Hell."

"It's probably just as well. You'd probably burn the barn down with all this dry hay in here."

"I still say hell."

"You're a rough one, aren't you?"

"Rough how?" he asked, half-closing one eye.

"I don't know. Seems like maybe life's giving you more knocks that a man usually gets."

"Sounds about right. I'm not complaining, though."

"See, I can recall the scandal—if you don't mind my calling it that—but I can't quite remember your name."

"Jojo," he said.

"I'd have remembered that."

"It's George Walker, but everybody calls me Jojo."

"Whatever for?"

"Well, there's two stories there."

She spread her hands out and dramatically surveyed the barn. "Plenty of time," she said.

"I'll give you one of 'em."

"Fair enough."

"My little sister, when we were kids, she had this speech problem. She couldn't figure out how to say a lot of words, so in the end she sort of had her own language, words she said her own way and if you didn't know her, you'd never figure out what she was talking about."

"Like what?" she asked, interested.

"Well, let me think—there was 'base-nip,' for basement, and instead of blanket she called it a 'bock-bock.' Things like that."

"That's cute."

"Some folks reckoned it was."

"And you?"

"I thought it was goddamned adorable."

She smiled.

"Anyhow, one of the words she couldn't say was my name. The poor kid couldn't say George."

"But she could pronounce Jojo."

He made a pistol with his forefinger and thumb, cocked it and fired away. "You got it."

"You're right: adorable."

He nodded and fanned his neck with his hat.

"What's her name?" she asked.

"Lilly."

"Did she ever get over it? The speech problem, I mean."

"Naw," Jojo said dismissively. "She died when she was eight."

"Oh."

"I was . . . thirteen, I guess. Yep, woulda had to've been."

"That's very sad."

"That's life," he said. "Nasty, brutish and short."

"You're quoting out of context, sir."

"Come again?" He cranked his head to one side, puzzled but intrigued.

"That's Hobbes, isn't it? From *Leviathan*? Because he wasn't talking about life in general, but life during wartime."

"Impressive," he said. "Except we happen to be in wartime, in case you've forgotten."

"There's no war in Litchfield."

He shrugged. "I wonder."

"The war at home?"

"Something like that. Listen—do you know much about the folks associated with that sex picture your husband is showing? These roadshow people?"

Theodora arched an eyebrow. "Old habits?"

"Yeah, that's right."

"Not much," she said, letting her eyes wander as she dipped into her thoughts. "Nothing, really. I know I don't like them, or what they're doing, anyway."

"Did you see the picture?"

"No, and I don't want to, thank you very much."

"Have you spoken to any of them?"

"Not directly, no. It's Russ's business—I haven't much to do with it."

"So you haven't met this Barker Davis fellow."

"I've seen him. Regular enough looking fellow, apart from his eyes."

"His eyes?"

"Hmm." She furrowed her brow and stared intently at the musty beams that held the roof up. "Have you ever been stared at by a snake, Mr. Walker?"

"Jojo, please."

"All right, but have you?"

"I can't say that I have."

"Cold and hot at the same time."

"I don't follow."

"It's hard to describe," she said. "I've never tried before. Where we live, Russ and I, we get a fair amount of varmints coming 'round the house—all sort of critters, from possums and coons to spiders almost as big as my hand—and snakes, too. Rattlers and copperheads, mostly, though I recall a time when I came out the back door to find myself standing not two feet from a big black cottonmouth with the cruellest looking eyes I'd ever seen on any of God's creatures. They were round and yellow, and . . ." Here she trailed off, squinting her eyes and screwing her mouth up to one side. "Now, I know Reverend Shannon says only people have souls, but I've never been very sure about that. I don't know if you've ever had a dog or a horse or anything like that, but I grew up with a lot of animals, and I called some of them friends. The way I see it, if I've got anything in me like a soul, then they sure did, too. So, if I'm to accept that animals can have souls the same as people, then I reckon I can be awfully startled by how utterly soulless that snake's eyes were."

"And this Davis fellow has eyes like that?"

"Cold and hot," she reiterated, "at the same time."

CHAPTER TEN

At the top of her powerful lungs, Mrs. Hutchins sang:

> *"When the last, feeble step has been taken,*
> *and the gates of that city appear,*
> *and the beautiful songs of the angels*
> *float out to my listening ear . . ."*

Everyone else sang, too—all but Rory Allmond, who could barely speak above a whisper as it was—though none of them matched the aggressive intensity of their de facto leader's vocal assault.

> *"When all that now seems so mysterious,*
> *will be bright and as clear as the day,*
> *then the toils of the road will seem nothing,*
> *when I get to the end of the way."*

Jim Shannon had trouble imagining where she got the power from, what with the heat and her age and weight. He supposed he was in fairly good shape and a good twenty years the old woman's junior, yet he was already drenched with sweat and feeling weak from her death march to the Palace Theater. Twice already he'd allowed his arms to drop, which resulted in his sign banging against the person in front of him, which resulted in a dirty look. This embarrassed the reverend, who felt vaguely humiliated as it was that Emma Hutchins was leading this silly little crusade rather than him. It was not as though he felt strongly enough about the issue to take command, but with her around to set these sorts of things in motion, who needed a preacher? He felt like a puppet leader, which was precisely what he was. At this realization, he dropped his head rather than his arms.

As the hymn reached its conclusion and the Palace marquee shimmered into sight in the middle distance, Shannon felt his stomach make a fist. He thought, and very nearly said aloud, *I've gotten to the end of the way.*

✗

Jojo stepped out onto the yellow-green grass and squinted in the fading sun, which threw blinding spears of light over the horizon in a last-ditch effort to win the battle it waged. He'd told Theodora he aimed to walk up to the big house—Leroy Dunn's two-story farmhouse—to see if anyone was around to help. He cocked his hat to one side to block the sun and set off.

Halfway across the fallow field, it hit him.

"Theodora," he muttered with a bitter laugh. "Fucking *Theodora Goes Wild.*"

He saw that picture way back in his early deputy days, '36 or '37 if he recalled correctly, and of course it starred the one and only world-famous Beth Walker lookalike Irene goddamn Dunne.

"Son of a bitch."

He walked on, cresting the mild hill that hid the big house from the barn, certain that the nice lady with the busted flipper was ruined to him now.

✗

"You look fine," she said, puckering her shiny, cherry-red lips and looking him over with her drowsy brown eyes.

He shrugged into the white coat and tightened the knot at his throat.

He had always hated wearing neckties but for some reason it didn't seem to bother him much now.

"Yeah?"

"Real professional like," she added. "A real doctor."

"Yeah," he agreed.

"Don't forget this."

She pressed a twice-folded sheet of typing paper into his hand. He regarded it quizzically.

"Your spiel," she reminded him. "You'd better know your lines."

"My lines. Yes."

"You don't have to pass a medical board review or anything, but most of those rubes want to believe you're Dr. Elliot Freeman, get it? So make 'em believe it."

"Yeah."

"Hey." She snapped her fingers an inch from his eyes. He blinked. "Get with it or get packing. You're with us now, baby. You do your job right and, well, everything's jake, Jake."

She grinned a lupine grin and flicked a long, thin cigarette into her mouth. Jake smiled back, though he had trouble understanding why. All he could really wrap his mind around was the performance, the most crucial act of his life, his defining moment. Do the job, say the words, be convincing.

Make Daddy Barker proud.

X

Scooter felt like Edward G. Robinson in *Little Caesar*, stealing into the alley (which wasn't so much an alley as the broad, open space between the theatre and the Rotary Club) and slinking against the brick façade with his moll in tow. Or maybe George Raft. Either way, he felt a tremendous surge in his chest like his torso was a hot water heater. He had to suppress an excited laugh as he held onto Margie's hand and turned to face the back door.

The door was open no more than an inch and half from the jamb. Scooter's eyes trailed down the drafty crack to the half-empty popcorn bag that someone had jammed there to keep it from latching shut.

"You got somebody working the inside?" he asked, maintaining his private gangster fantasy.

"I guess you could say that," she answered with a coquettish smile.

He arched an eyebrow and leaned over to peer through the crack. A tantalizingly cool stream of refrigerated air washed over his face, chilling the beads of sweat that dappled his cheeks and brow.

"What do you see?" she asked.

"Not much. Some boxes and a bare bulb in the ceiling. Looks like they just store stuff back here."

"Then the coast is clear?"

He swallowed, smiled, nodded.

"No time like the present," he said, parroting a phrase he'd heard in a movie somewhere.

He slid his hand into the crack, pulled the heavy door open and let Margie slip inside. He followed, and as the door closed behind them they found themselves sunblind in the dimness of the hall. Ahead of them the hall opened up into the main lobby, where a cacophony of voices came together to form an unintelligible roar.

Margie said, "Are you ready?"

Scooter felt bold. He playfully patted her rump with the flat of his hand and answered, "Let's go."

҂

Russ was hunched over the desk in his private office, the fingers of one hand curled around a chipped glass with a splash of brandy left in the bottom. Poking out between two fingers on the other hand was an unlit cigarette. He'd mostly forgotten about both the drink and the smoke. All he could really seem to think about was the sleep he wasn't getting.

Atop the desk was a small calendar, propped up by a cardboard tab. The top page was labelled JULY in bold, red letters, and MCMAHON'S FILLING STATION was stamped to the left of that. The main body of the small rectangular page was comprised of five rows of squares, thirty-one of which marked the days of the month. And written across each row were the titles of the features planned for that week with lines to mark their respective runs from Wednesday to Tuesday: scrawled in Russ's hand on the top row was *Riding High* and *The Outlaw*, and the second row showed *Destination Tokyo* and *Bataan*. Starting on the square for the Wednesday of the third week, Russ had written just one word: ROADSHOW. And though he booked a pair of horror pictures—*I Walked With a Zombie* and *The Mad Ghoul*—for the last week of July several weeks earlier, for whatever reason he never bothered to enter these features on the calendar. In fact, he hadn't written anything at all anywhere in the desk calendar after the present week, despite bookings leading well into September. He simply failed to see any point in maintaining the calendar, though staring at it now he equally failed to understand why he should feel that way.

As it happened, the movie exhibition business was booming in spite of rationing and shortages and all the sacrifices the government imposed upon the whole of the country—indeed, it was the war itself that turned him such a tidy profit. People wanted escape, even if that meant a double bill of war pictures like he'd shown the week before, and Russ never saw his auditorium so consistently crowded weekend after weekend, no matter what he threw up on the screen. It was a hell of a time to be in the picture racket, and a smart man would spend every free moment he had devising ways to make it even better, more lucrative—a second screen maybe, or big revival shows of old favourites during the week.

Russell Cavanaugh *was* a smart man, or at least a shrewd one. Yet he could not find the spirit to worry much about the next engagement, much less to take full advantage of the boon afforded to him by the war. In the main, he just wanted to be left alone. And to sleep. He reckoned he could sleep a month straight through, if only he could be let alone for the duration.

Of course, Barker Davis would never allow that.

That slick son of a bitch rolled into town like a forest fire and the heat was starting to get to Russ. He'd never hosted a roadshow before— this was his first rodeo—but his understanding was that they typically rented the joint out, more or less, and ran it their own way. Not so with Barker and Co. Not only did this bunch design to include the owner and operator of the Palace Theater in their engagement, they insisted upon it. Now he was far past merely run ragged and well into severe exhaustion. The booze didn't help, but he did not believe he could cope without it. Thinking of it now, his watery, bloodshot eyes darted down to the glass in his hand, which he tipped up to his lips and finished off. He then lit his cigarette and gritted his teeth, wishing he could blot out the growing furor in the lobby beyond his office door.

The wishing did him no good; instead, someone elected to add to the clamour by knocking at the door. He could feel each knock as though they were striking his skull from the inside.

"It's open," he groused.

The door squealed open and Lana poked into the room.

"Muh . . . Mr. Cavanaugh?"

"Jesus Christ," he muttered. "Shut the door, Lana."

She obliged. Russ rubbed his face with the palm of his hand and then poured another splash of brandy into his glass, followed by two more as an afterthought.

"I've seen you without any clothes on, Lana. It's a bit kooky to keep on calling me Mr. Cavanaugh at this point, don't you think?"

"I . . . I guess I didn't really think about it," she said quietly.

"I mean in private, of course."

She nodded, her eyes huge and glassy.

"Out there—" He gestured ambiguously at the door "—you should still call me Mr. Cavanaugh. For appearances, like. Understand?"

"Yes, Mr. . . . ah, Russell."

"Just Russ is fine."

Lana smiled and her cheeks flushed with colour.

"*Russ*," she cooed.

He knitted his brow and drew deeply on the cigarette. "Okay, fine. Great. Now, what do you want, Lana?"

"Oh, it's Mr. Davis . . . say, should I still call him Mr. Davis?"

"Crissakes, yes—unless you're schtupping him too, but that's your business."

"Schtupping, Mr. . . . ?"

"Forget it. Jesus H., forget it. What does *he* want, then? Davis, I mean."

"Why, to talk to you, I reckon."

He narrowed his eyes in the blue-grey haze of his own smoke. "He forget where my office is?"

"Forget? That'd been pretty hard to forget, Mr. . . . . ah, Russ . . ."

Groaning, he cut her off. "Where is he?"

"In the projection booth."

"Wonderful. Take a hike."

"What?" Her eyes glistened, welled up.

"I've got work to do, woman—and so do you. Go sell some goddamn cigarettes, will you?"

For a moment, she looked as though a torrent of tears was seconds away, but she composed herself and, wiping the corners of her eyes, opened the door.

"Yes, Mr. Cavanaugh," she spat on her way out.

The door slammed shut, startling him into dropping the cigarette on the desk. He picked it back up and stabbed it out in the ashtray like he was committing murder.

X

Jojo was still thinking about Irene Dunne, which in turn darkened his thoughts with awful memories of Beth, when he climbed the three short steps leading up to Leroy Dunn's sprawling front porch. It was only the second time he had ever stood on those decaying boards, the first occurring years earlier when Jackson Bondy broke into the place to see about a rumour concerning thousands of dollars in a steel safe. Jojo never determined the veracity of the safe story, but when he walked into the farmhouse early that morning he found Bondy spread out on the well-trod entryway rug with a hole in the back of his head big enough to put a fist through. By and large, folks cottoned to Leroy pretty well, but it typically paid not to cross the old coot. Jackson Bondy learned that lesson the hardest way possible.

He knocked firmly on the door, loud enough for a hard-of-hearing old man to hear, and a minute later received the expected response.

"Dance ain't 'til Saturday! And it ain't in the house, it's in the barn!"

"Mr. Dunn, it's George Walker."

"I don't much care if it's the King of Spain, the dance still ain't 'til Saturday."

Jojo smiled in spite of himself. He wondered how the Daughters of the Confederacy ever talked an irascible old bastard like Leroy Dunn into hosting a barn dance of all things.

"It's Deputy Walker, Mr. Dunn," he tried. "Do you remember me?"

"Deputy?" came the scratchy voice beyond the door. "You that fella with the cut up face?"

"That's right."

"Hell's bells, son—whyn't you just say so?"

A series of locks and latches clicked and cranked, and the door swung open to reveal a stooped, elderly man with a stark white beard and bright blue eyes.

"I ain't shot nobody lately, deputy," he said with a devilish grin.

"I'm glad to hear that, sir, though truth be told I'm not a deputy anymore."

"What d'ya mean, you're not a deputy? That godless little fool Ernie Rich get a thorn in his paw about something?"

"I suppose you could say that, yes."

Dunn scowled and tugged at his beard.

"I've voted for him twice, but I never did like him much. Next time I'll vote for the other fella."

"Not on my account, I hope."

"Bless, no. I just don't care for the man and don't know why he ever got my vote the first two times."

Jojo made a show of looking over both shoulders, conspiratorially.

"Just between you and me, Mr. Dunn, I never voted for him, either."

For a moment Dunn stared with piercing eyes and parted lips. Then he burst into raucous laughter, his small, frail body convulsing with every powerful guffaw.

"I guess you best come inside outta that heat," he said with gasping breaths.

Dunn turned to totter down the entryway and Jojo followed behind. He was not particularly surprised to discover that it was just as hot inside the house as outside, and perhaps a few degrees hotter yet. The old farmer moved into a dingy kitchen with dirty plates and pots littering the counters. Nearly everywhere Jojo looked there were white wax candles of various lengths—the innovation of electricity had largely passed old man Dunn right on by.

Dunn cleared his throat wetly and waddled to an open cupboard. He pulled two bottles of beer from a cluttered shelf and handed one to Jojo.

"Don't got an icebox."

"This is fine."

One at a time, they pried the bottle caps off with the black iron bottle opener screwed into the wall. The bottle opener bid its user to drink Atlas Beer. The beers they drank were Schlitz, and tasted hot enough to cook with.

"You still got that roadster pickup, Mr. Dunn?"

"That ole bucket? Sure I do. How come you to ask?"

Jojo swallowed a mouthful of hot Schlitz and made a face. "I got a lady in your barn with a busted wheel, if you can believe it."

"What's that?" The old man hunched over and stared intently at Jojo. "What on God's Jesus-green earth're you doin' with a *lady* in *my* barn, son?"

Smiling a little, Jojo said, "She just fell off the road, Mr. Dunn . . . right down into the irrigation ditch. I guess she probably broke her ankle, and you know as well as me there ain't many vehicles come along this way, not on a Thursday evening."

"Farm to town, sure, sure. That's Saturday. And what with that dern dance—shoot. We may have Litchfield's first ever traffic jam, you think?"

Jojo laughed and took another swig from the bottle, which only got worse from the heat of his hand. He shivered from the unpleasantness of it and set the bottle down on the nearest counter.

"I 'spect you'll be wantin' to drive her into town, then," Dunn said at some length.

"We were both headed that way, anyhow. Just a little hitch in our plans, I guess."

"Who is she, anyhow? That your little wife in there? What's her name . . . Beth, isn't it?"

"I'm afraid Beth passed on about a year back, Mr. Dunn. No, it's just a lady I found in a ditch."

"Widowers both, us," Dunn said sorrowfully, shaking his head. "I reckon a house needs a woman in it. Ain't been no woman in this'un for nigh twenty years. And that ain't no kind of house at all."

"No," Jojo agreed. "I suppose not."

"Truck's out back," said Dunn. "Go on ahead and get you another beer for the road, if'n you want to."

✕

Theodora lay on the hay bed, occasionally swatting at flies, and thought about the former deputy with the sad, scarred face.

Story was that he'd stepped out on his wife, which was fairly bad enough in and of itself, but to compound the scandal the man's mistress was a Negro girl from the Shacks. Theodora could not recall the girl's name (if she ever knew it) but seemed to remember she worked in town, cleaning houses and running errands for the white folk. Whether or not she cleaned the Walker house she didn't know either, but some way or another Jojo Walker became acquainted with her and must have wasted little time climbing into bed with the girl.

Pretty bad, she thought. She figured a man could get away with something like that if he was in Paris or someplace similar, but in Litchfield it was a severe kind of social death. Not many folks wanted much to do with a man like that, and it all seemed to go underground for a spell until it burned back up again and left two bodies in the wreckage. That was the first she'd heard of it, when a woman named Beth Walker saw the coloured girl enter a neighbour's house to work and followed her inside with her husband's revolver. It was by all accounts a nasty scene that came to a head when Beth squeezed off three shots in rapid succession that all but annihilated the other woman's skull. The sheriff's department was called out—by the murderess, no less—and when the senior deputy arrived at the scene he found himself enmeshed in an armed showdown with his own wife.

Theodora imagined the horror of it, put herself in Jojo Walker's shoes. She envisioned herself standing in her own living room, a few feet away from a grief-maddened Russ who waved his own gun around in a teary, screaming panic. Jojo would have begged with Beth, pleaded and made a hundred promises, anything to disarm her and save her life—but would she? Could she even be bothered to speak as Russ raised the gun and pressed its barrel up against his temple?

She shuddered, suddenly disgusted with herself. Disgusted and, she thought, perhaps a little frightened. Poor, loveless Russell with his own infidelities and quiet, simmering rage. What was it about men's wives, she wondered, that imprisoned them so? Was Holy Matrimony always such a terrible burden on men like Russ and Jojo and, she figured, damn near every other fellow with a wandering eye and a hole where his heart used to be?

Was everybody truly so utterly, irremediably alone?

She felt wet warmth on her cheeks and at the same time heard the distant thunder of a rumbling motor. As it drew nearer and grew louder, her thoughts shifted to the eerie doll and its macabre innards, and she knew in that moment she had always been alone.

)(

The crowd subsumed them like drops of water falling into the river, or minor stars in a clear night sky. A hollow-faced man in a tweed jacket stood at the doors beside the box office, taking tickets, which meant they were home free. Margie heard a door slam above the din of the crowd and glanced over to see Mr. Cavanaugh storming through the lobby, parting the densely packed assembly like Moses and the Red Sea. He disappeared behind another door marked PROJECTION BOOTH and she promptly forgot all about it. Scooter looked down at her and grinned anxiously.

"In like Flynn," he said.

People milled everywhere, all shoulders and elbows as they squeezed past one another to snake toward the concession counter or the toilets or some person they recognized. Margie saw a man's face brighten as he called out, "Why, Jason Agee, you old so-and-so," and she was suddenly quite apprehensive that *she* might be recognized, too. It went without saying that it was a small town—she could hardly go anyplace without somebody nosing into her life or asking after her father or, worst of all, expressing their condolences even after all that time—and it certainly wasn't unthinkable that half the people in there recognized the egregiously misplaced preacher's daughter. When she felt a hand on her shoulder she leapt with surprise. Her heart flew up into her throat and stayed there even as she realized it was only Scooter.

"Say, I need to hit the head."

"The head?"

"Navy talk, Margie. It means the toilet."

Since when did he know anything about Navy talk? Maybe, she considered, he'd gone off to join and just hadn't told anyone yet. She felt the tiniest bit ashamed of herself that she didn't much care one way or another.

"Don't be long," she instructed him. "I'm getting nervous."

"Here," he said, pressing a crumpled dollar bill into her sweaty hand. "Go get a Coke or something. I'll just be a minute."

He had barely finished speaking before the crowd reabsorbed him. She tightened her fist around the dollar. Someone behind her, a woman, began to complain loudly about the lack of moral turpitude on the part of Mr. Cavanaugh for exhibiting "this trash," as she called it. Margie wrinkled her nose, wishing she could give the busybody what for, to tell her nobody forced her to come get a ticket, for crying out loud. She let her mind drift into a daydream in which she did just that when a big, bearded face appeared in her line of sight and called out: "Margie Shannon?"

Mr. Mixon, she saw with no little terror, was coming right for her. He shouldered his way through the throng, taking his hat off as he came and twisting his face into an expression that was part shock and part fatherly concern.

Peter Mixon sometimes played the battered old piano in her father's church on days when Mrs. Penney felt unwell, which was more and more common these days. Their eyes locked, she and Mr. Mixon, and Margie thought of a joke she'd heard about Baptists running into one another at a tavern, or something like that. Except, the way the joke went, the Baptists acted as though they didn't know each other. In this nightmare version happening to her now, the other party was racing toward her like a monster in a horror picture.

She smiled and made a break for it, feeling for all the world like a criminal on the run from the law. She ducked and she turned this way and that, worming her way through the crowd until she reached a dead end at the long glass window that stretched across the front of the lobby. There was another dozen people on the sidewalk outside, and Margie wondered if they'd come for the picture, too—and then she saw the picket signs, and she saw awful old Mrs. Hutchins, and she saw her own father emerging from the procession, his mouth stretched wide in song.

"Oh, no," she squeaked.

X

The supply room was cold, which was odd considering the lack of ventilation and the erstwhile crippling heat. Still, he felt a chill enough to raise goose pimples on his flesh, though none rose. It crept up his back and gripped him by the back of the neck. His ears burned from it. Stranger still, when he took up the faux spectacles—part of the costume—the metal frames he fully expected to sting with their own inherent coldness were, conversely, perfectly warm.

This nonplussed the young man. But of course, today everything did, ever since . . .

"Fix your tie," she said.

He pulled his eyebrows together into a downward point and studied the brown necktie dangling from his throat. He wondered what was wrong with it. As if reading his thoughts, she said, "It's all crooked, you dolt. And the knot's all wrong. It's almost time, so fix it."

Cold, trembling hands went up to the hollow of his neck, absurdly threatening as though they weren't his own hands, under his complete control. His eyes narrowed to slits and his jaw hung slack; this seemed too much of a challenge, so what of the rest of it? He had a performance to do, a lecture to give. There was the film he was to introduce and then all those pamphlets she told him to sell. And Christ knew if she'd instructed him to cut his own throat before throwing himself into the Arkansas River . . .

. . . well.

With fingers like frozen sausages he fumbled at the knot, digging into the folds and unraveling the tie. Concentrating, he failed to wrap his mind around the concept of retying it. Seeing this, she slid a warm hand between his arm and ribs, gave a gentle squeeze and said, "Let go, Jake. Just let go. Then it's all smooth, like cream."

Which it was.

)X(

The hymn wound down as the congregation reached their destination, and Shannon realized he'd only been moving his lips without actually singing at all. Through the glass, and despite the blinding burnt orange glare of the setting sun, he could see that the lobby was positively packed with people. He thought, *And this is only Thursday.*

Their voices sputtering out, Emma Hutchins was the last to belt out the hymn's closing refrain before immediately launching into a strident announcement. Shannon felt his ears burn, humiliated as he was that she, and not he, led this futile little crusade.

"Sisters and brothers," she pompously shouted, "*friends*, we have come to the end of the way."

Fluffy white heads nodded. The reverend glanced over at Rory Allmond, who appeared to be asleep standing up. Shannon envied him his escape.

"This is not the first time we have gathered here before this wretched temple of sin," Mrs. Hutchins blathered on, fairly rolling the R in *wretched* as though she came from upper crust New England stock (which she most certainly did not). "Indeed, I do doubt it will be the last. I believe, however—mark my words, friends and brethren—I believe, from what I know to be true, that we have never been more needed to speak out against Russell Cavanaugh and his wickedness than we are today. We are called to this. *Called.*

"Our presence should embarrass our neighbours in there," she continued. "We must shame them back into the fold. We must show them how wrong they are to listen to the Devil's sweet-sounding song instead of righteous hymns of praise."

The reverend made a severe face, jutting out his lower lip, though he fought the urge to roll his eyes. Someone said, "Amen," but he couldn't tell who it was. Quickly, he nodded in assent and parroted the sentiment: "Amen."

The second syllable had barely escaped his lips when his eyes lit on the strangely illuminated form of his daughter through the glass fronting the theatre. For a moment, he considered the possibility that it was merely an illusion, a trick of the light. The figure was haloed by the glare of evening sun; it was not unthinkable that he was looking at some other young woman, perhaps a total stranger, who was either made to resemble Margie or who did not look like her at all, but rather his tortured mind was creating the effect.

After all, he reasoned, Margie was safe at home.

And besides, she wouldn't be caught dead at that appalling picture show, not knowing what it would do to her father, how it would make him look. . . .

The face brightened, eyes wide and mouth agape. The face that looked like Margie's. That looked like hers because it was.

"Lord," he whispered.

"Raise up your signs and sing to the heavens," Mrs. Hutchins bellowed like a pious foghorn. "Fill your lungs and blast this place with your voices."

And then Margie was gone, melted back into the undulating horde as the glare broke and Emma Hutchins' chosen hymn returned with a furious vengeance.

"When the last, feeble step has been taken,
and the gates of that city appear,
and the beautiful songs of the angels
float out to my listening ear . . ."

It was a warning, Jim Shannon knew. Through the words of the hymn, Mrs. Hutchins was notifying the patrons of the Palace Theater that the gates of that golden city would *not* open for them as it would for her—that quite the opposite awaited those who failed to heed and repent. For *their* listening ears there would come only screams of anguish, among them their own.

The reverend frowned as his breath momentarily hitched in his chest. An unanticipated defensiveness boiled within him, rooted in the notion that this loud, nosy woman at the head of his flock *wanted* his little Margie to burn in Satan's lake of fire.

The bitch!

The vile thought rocked his body and he half-convulsed, dropping his sign in the process.

"Reverend Shannon, you all right?"

That from Alice Maxwell, who looked aggrieved to have to ask, or so Shannon judged. He squinted one eye and looked from her face to the ground, where the sign he carried all the way from the church—from *his* church—screamed up at him: NO FILTH IN LITCHFIELD.

"Reverend?"

He shook his head and retrieved the sign, as much as he wanted to leave it underfoot.

"I'm fine."

"Are we just gunna sing, or are we gunna . . . do something?"

For half a minute he regarded her quizzically, and then he turned his attention back to the broad glass window through which he had seen Margie. His daughter had not returned, but in her place stood a stocky little man with a pockmarked face and his hair parted in the middle the way some men did two generations earlier. (All he needed was a jaunty bowtie and garters on his sleeves, and Shannon would have sworn he was looking at an Old West bartender.) The man's arms hung limp at his sides and his small, black eyes all but burned through the glass at the reverend. All around him the crowd ebbed and flowed, pressing up against one another like slaughterhouse cattle, but somehow avoiding contact with the man altogether.

He was like a ghost.

Shannon gawped at him, unsure and curious about everybody else's reaction to his stoic, cadaverous poise, when Mrs. Hutchins began singing again from the start of the hymn:

"The sands have been washed in the footprints
of the stranger on Galilee's shore,
and the voice that subdued the rough billows,
will be heard in Judea no more."

Her voice—not especially melodious to begin with—grew hoarse and deep. Frog-like. Even her eyes seemed to bulge as her jowls trounced up and down, giving the reverend the distinct impression that she might actually be transforming into an enormous frog.

"But the path of that lone Galilean (ribbit),

with joy I will follow today (croak);
and the toils of the road will seem nothing (RIB-BIT),
when I get to the end of the way (crooooak)."

A schoolboy grin played at the corners of his mouth. He caught the short man in the window in his peripheral vision, turned to see him—he too grinned boyishly, and he nodded encouragingly.

Yes, that's right. Go ahead and laugh. It's funny, the froggy lady. Froggy lady is funny.

Laugh, Jimmy. Laugh.

He did. It came in short, snorting bursts at first but descended rapidly into a raucous fit of noisy hysterics. Alice Maxwell and John Martin gaped at him. Emma Hutchins' gravel road voice skidded into a ditch. Her face bruised red with the heat of angry blood, which only made the chortling reverend laugh harder.

"Frog . . . froggy," he gasped, tears streaming from his eyes and hands tight against his midsection.

"What!" Mrs. Hutchins croaked.

Shannon dropped from the sidewalk to the pavement like a sack of apples, quivering and cackling and sobbing all at once. His left elbow struck the macadam; skin peeled away to reveal raw, pink flesh beading red. Two skeletally thin old widows to the back of the congregation lowered their signs and stepped away like birds, back the way they came. Jim Shannon screamed with laughter as he watched them go.

Now several theatregoers pressed themselves against the glass to observe the bizarre scene in the street outside. Shannon recognized a few of his own among them, and he laughed at their faces. Heads shook. Others turned away in disgust.

Standing at their nucleus was the pockmarked man, whose brow rose solicitously as he stepped through the glass. The window shattered all around him, falling in a glittering cloudburst to the sidewalk, and as he passed through and away from it, Jim Shannon watched with wild amusement as every shard, both knife-like and microscopic, came back into place in the now unbroken glass. No one seemed to notice—all eyes were on the reverend, and not upon the man. They paid him no attention at all.

"Quite a trick!" Shannon hollered, his lips dripping with froth.

The man smirked and extended his hands, palms up. *It was nothing,* his gesture seemed to say. Shannon reasoned that it must have been nothing indeed, since no one else batted an eye. At his thought, the man shrugged.

Behind him, through the miraculously unbroken glass, the throng in the theatre lobby milled more anxiously, like a swarm of bees.

They cannot see things as they really are, the man intimated to the trembling reverend on the macadam.

"They can't?" Shannon asked, still gasping from the stitches in his sides. "Why not?"

I have not shown them.

"How can they see?"

In there.

The man jerked his cratered chin back at the lobby, where the crowd was gradually draining out, into the auditorium, like dirty bathwater down a pipe. Shannon squashed his face into a mask of incredulity and giggled.

"What, the *sex film?*"

No. Not that. Something else. Later.

"Something else? Something . . . *worse?*"

Much. You will see. Not now, but you will see. Now I will show you.

"Show me? Show me what?"

Things as they are, of course.

Ж

Dean Mortimer felt the crush of the surging crowd and grunted as he was pushed along with it. The muscles in his back tensed and he made fists of both his hands. He gritted his teeth and sucked deep breaths in through his nose. It was all he could do to fight the slowly building anger he harboured at the obstinate crowd and the disgusting film he was about to see and, of course, at Sheriff Rich for making him do this.

It had everything to do with the quartered stiff in that dump hotel, naturally, though neither Rich nor Mortimer expected anything at the Palace to shed much light on the subject. All Ernie Rich wanted was a bit of reconnaissance, for the young deputy to get the lay of the land with regard to these shifty roadshow people in their own element. It might turn up squat, but at the very least the police presence would surely make them sweat a little. On this last count, Mortimer wondered if he should have shown up in uniform, give his attendance a more official—and by proxy threatening—bent. As things stood, hardly anyone paid him any mind at all. Only one person bothered to say hello, and that with patent embarrassment. Practically everyone in town wanted to be there, it seemed, but no one wanted to be *seen* there. Deputy Mortimer did not blame them for the latter, though he remained largely puzzled by the former.

Didn't anyone in Litchfield have any common decency anymore?

Ahead, the two ornate doors to the auditorium swung open and outward, each of them attended by a member of the roadshow company. Mortimer studied their faces: he had personally interviewed one of them and eavesdropped on Ernie while he put the clamps on the other. Both cool characters. Barely even knew the cat, the one said—that was what he called the victim, *cat*. Mortimer grimaced now at the memory. He did not have much of a problem with Negroes, but he could not abide by whites who elected to speak like them. It made no sense to him. But little about these crafty out-of-towners did.

The doorman on the left smiled on one side of his mouth and Mortimer thought the man winked at him. This was the one he'd interviewed at the hotel the night before. His grimace deepened.

"We picked him up in Missouri," the man had said. "That was just three weeks ago. Why, I don't even know the cat's last name."

A cool character, all right.

And the accent sounded vaguely uppity, despite the jazzy Negro talk. Northern to be sure, possibly New England. The list of reasons to dislike the man went on. Someone behind the deputy gave him a gentle push in the small of the back.

"Go on," said a peevish voice. "We're movin', pal."

Mortimer grunted and stepped forward, keeping his eyes on the left side doorman. When they were parallel, the man gave a single, sharp nod and said, "Enjoy the show, deputy."

Hell.

He was ushered into the soundproof auditorium, the air thick with shouting voices, where he could not hear the scream from the street.

⋉

"Hopefully Doc Hornor can see to your ankle before long," Jojo said.

"How many emergencies can there be at one time?"

"Just one big one I know about. There was a . . . an *incident*. At my hotel."

They were just under a mile from where the farm road went abruptly from dirt to pavement, having passed Theodora's house and the half-rotted grain silo a few hundred yards west of it. In the Thirties it was decided to paint WELCOME TO LITCHFIELD on the side of the silo that faced the road; now it only said OME TO LITCH.

Farmer Dunn hadn't wanted to go into town, it not being a Saturday. He had not been to town on any other day of the week in more than a decade and explained that he saw no reason to bust up a perfectly good tradition now. Accordingly, he turned the rumbling heap over to Jojo and instructed him to take care of it before jamming a corncob pipe between his teeth and sauntering back to the big house.

"An incident?" Theodora asked.

"Somebody died."

"Oh," she said, staring dreamily through the windshield. "Was it that bad?"

"How do you mean?"

"Well, if a dead person is going to take up so much of the doctor's time that he might not get to see me, I reckon it must be pretty bad."

Jojo snorted and jerked the gearshift. The road gave way to deep pits and dips that jostled them both to the point of nausea.

"Yeah. It was bad, all right."

"A killing," she inferred.

"I don't know—maybe. Hard to say." He reached over her lap to pop the glove box, took a quick look and then shut it again. "Sorry. Looking for cigarettes."

"Don't look at me," she said. "I don't smoke."

"Story of my life," he said with a bitter grin. The world jolted underneath them; they'd reached smooth macadam. "Hornor's essentially the medical examiner for whenever the sheriff's department needs one, and today they need one. I don't want to get you upset or anything, but it was a damned gruesome scene."

Theodora pressed her lips together and sighed through her nose. Her thoughts wandered, but not far: only as far as her own gruesome scene with the doll stuffed with tiny bones. The doll she found in her husband's coat pocket. Somehow she'd nearly forgotten about it. Now she couldn't get it out her mind.

"What's your hotel?" she asked, snatching at anything to change the subject.

"Come again?"

"You said, 'my hotel.'"

"Oh. I'm a house detective at the Litchfield Valley. It's not really mine, I just work there."

"I never could understand why they called it that," she said. "There aren't any valleys in Litchfield."

"There's not much of anything in Litchfield," he countered. "I guess they had to call it something, and Litchfield Valley was as good as anything."

Theodora said, "Hmn," and resumed staring through the windscreen. A dragonfly exploded against it in the next second, and she flinched. The insect's gooey yellow entrails formed a starburst on the dusty glass. It was not, however, quite dead—rather, the dragonfly's spindly legs and curling green tail twitched against the wind as the life slowly drained out of it. She thought it was a terrible way to die, though she supposed she could imagine worse.

"What happened?" she asked suddenly.

"Hmm? What do you mean?"

"The person who died in your hotel," she explained. "How did he die? Or was it a she?"

"It was a man. I don't know if you know about these people showing a picture up at the Palace this week. . . ."

"The Palace? My husband owns it."

Jojo's eyes widened and he stammered for a moment. "You don't say."

"There's a roadshow company in town," she added. "I guess Russ is . . . helping them."

"I see."

"Was the deceased one of those people?"

"Yes, he was."

"Was it Barker Davis?"

Again, he was at a loss for words. He shot a glance at her; she was still carefully studying the exploded dragonfly. It was not moving anymore.

"Do you know this Davis fellow?"

She shook her head. "No, I don't, and who's asking the questions here, anyway?"

"I'm sorry. You asked how he died?"

"That's right."

"Truth be told, I don't really know. But some folks heard the fellow scream, and there was even a witness—a young lady—who claims he just came apart at the joints like horses were pulling him in all directions. Anyone would believe that's just what happened, too, except it was in a cramped hotel room with no one else in it apart from the girl and the vic."

"Vic?"

"Victim, sorry."

"Victim of what, though?"

Jojo shrugged his shoulders. "No one knows. Mayhap Doc Hornor's got something figured out. All me and anybody with the department knows is that the poor son of a bitch got his arms, legs and head torn clean off, but none of us can figure on how it was done."

The blood drained from Theodora's face, leaving her pallid and trembling like a kitten. "Oh my God," she rasped.

"Hell, I'm sorry," he said. "Me and my dirty mouth. I've gotten unaccustomed to being around nice ladies."

"It can't be. . . ."

"It can't—wait, are we still talking about my profanity?"

"Go back."

"Say, what's going on here?"

"Please, Mr. Walker—turn around and go back to my house!"

"But why?"

"Mr. Walker," she said, her eyes half-shut and her face slick with new sweat, "I think I'm going to be sick."

"I'll stop the truck, then."

"And I think I need to show you something," she added. "At my house."

Jojo creased his brow at her even as he slowed the truck to turn back down the way they came.

※

Everything behind the glass went dark and a bank of grey-black clouds swarmed in the early evening sky.

Someone croaked, "There's a storm a'comin'," and Shannon saw that it was Emma Hutchins, whose green face bubbled with boils and warts.

"Say, why ain't you singin' no more, rev?" she roared at him. She punctuated the question with a wet belch. One of her huge yellow eyes bulged. "You got to sing. We come to sing, and you got to do what you told."

Jim Shannon could not understand why the typically prim woman was suddenly speaking in the strange patois, but it occurred to him that this creature was not Mrs. Hutchins at all. Whoever or whatever she was, he could only presume that the staring, pockmarked man on the sidewalk had everything to do with the sudden transformation. He watched the unfolding proceedings with detached gravity, an impartial observer with genuine interest in where it would all lead.

"Sing, Jimmy," croaked froggy Mrs. Hutchins. "Jimmy, sing."

Her flabby jowls quivered and expanded; her throat blew up like a greasy green-white balloon. And she sang:

"I an' Satan had a race—
Hal-le-lu! Hal-le-lu!
I an' Satan had a race—
Hal-le-lu! Hal-le-lu!"

Here Alice Maxwell joined in, throwing her spindly arms into the air and convulsing as a woman possessed. *"Hal-le-lu! Hal-le-lu!"* she cried. In contrast to Mrs. Hutchins' green marbled countenance, Alice's flesh was turning a sickly, jaundiced yellow.

The frog-thing that was Mrs. Hutchins—but wasn't—continued:

"Win de race agin' de course—
Hal-le-lu! Hal-le-lu!
Win de race agin' de course—
Hal-le-lu! Hal-le-lu!"

"*Hal-le-lu!*" Alice screeched. "*Hal-le-loooo!*" John Martin abruptly repeated.

Now the whole of the congregation joined the wild song, all of them jerking and taking on a different verse each, though all at the same time.

Sue Casey bellowed, "*Satan tell me to my face!*" even as Rory Allmond warbled, "*He will break my kingdom down,*" and Rose McKendrick cried, "*Satan mount de iron grey.*" Alice Maxwell, the colour of pus, could hardly catch a breath between desperate screams of "*Hal-le-lu, Hal-le-lu!*"

"*Hal-le-loooooooo!*" John Martin shrieked as tears spilled from his bursting red eyes.

Why do you not sing, Jimmy Shannon? the pockmarked man asked somewhere in the reverend's muddled mind. *Unburden yourself—it is good for the soul.*

He glanced down at Shannon from the sidewalk, indifferent, his arms still dangling lifelessly at his sides.

"It isn't funny anymore," the reverend squeaked.

The comedy portion of our program is finished. Now: the time for song.

Shannon scooted back on the rough pavement and moaned as he hoisted himself up to his knees. His elbow was pitted with chunks of gravel and hard bits of tar. He felt like a penitent kneeling before some high priest and his chorus of madmen and madwomen, the twelve of which continued to screech and hiccup their way through the eerie, unfamiliar tune.

Hal-le-lee, hal-le-la, hal-le-lu!

"And then?" Shannon dared to ask, fighting against the tremors that rocked his weary frame. "What comes after the time for song?"

You did not read the program for tonight's performance, Jimmy Shannon. Every performance must have a program, and every member of the audience is expected to study the program to prevent inane questions such as you ask.

The man jerked his head to one side, ruffling the bowtie at his throat that now seemed several times larger than it should have been.

First comes the time for comedy. You laugh. Then comes the time for song. You sing. Next is the time for dreams, peppered with the time for terror. You float, you scream. Then you bleed, and then you die, but only until the denouement. There is, of course, an encore—the audience always demands one—and it is a real corker, believe you me.

Have you come for the special midnight show? Can you stand its secrets, its delights? Do you know the power of magic, true magic, the law of things as they really are?

In that instant, the man's face leapt through the rapidly darkening space between him and Shannon until the tips of their noses were but an inch apart. Shannon gasped.

The man roared: "DO YOU KNOW WHO I AM?"

The sky cracked open and the thunder roared. The jumbled chorus of hal-le-lus devolved into wordless grunting. Shannon's eyes darted to the congregation despite his terror of the man looming over him; his twelve congregants convulsed and contorted impossibly on the sidewalk and in the street. Mrs. Hutchin's flouncy summer dress fell away from her twisted, leathery body, revealing a wholly devastated landscape of swampy green pustules. When the clouds opened up and the oily, black rain began falling in greasy dollops, the insane congregants became aggravated and screamed at the heavens.

Reverend Jim Shannon watched them and wept.

"Things as they really are, Jimmy Shannon," the man with the pitted face hissed in his ear.

"No," he protested lamely. "A trick."

"If you like."

Shannon fell back and scrambled away from the man, slipping in the pooling puddles of slippery black rain.

"Mount your milk-white horse and go home, preacher man," said the pockmarked man. "You are not invited to partake of my peculiar amusements."

The reverend rose to his feet and shielded his eyes from the noxious rain with his hand. The congregants were gone. There was nothing but the man, the awful black rain, and himself.

He turned in a pool of the thick, viscous stuff, up to his ankles in it, and slogged away from the focus of his terror as fast as he could.

※

The murmuring deafened him; every chin wagging.

Nervous glances, wide eyes.

The nurse worked the room, gliding up and down the aisles; her delicate, high-heeled feet barely touched the carpet. He watched her like an ornithologist watches some bird he's waited all his life to see in the wild. She caught his hungry eyes and threw a look right back at him. He smiled, she nodded.

It was time to begin.

"LADIES AND GENTLEMEN: IF YOU PLEASE."

His heart sang—he was better at this than the other guy was. He had not wondered what happened to him.

"I am Dr. Elliot Freeman," Jake announced. "I am a licenced sexologist."

※

"It's here, somewhere."

She was rooting through the garbage bin, tossing bits of food and chicken bones on the floor to get at whatever mysterious treasure lay within.

Jojo watched, incredulous.

"I'm not crazy," she said, picking up a wad of newspaper dripping with something pink. "You'll see. Just give me a minute."

"Sure," he said. "Take all the time you want."

She went on digging in the trash, and he wandered from the kitchen to the sitting room, wondering if she really was crazy. The place fairly reeked of cigarette smoke, so he scanned the room until he saw the cherrywood box on the bar. He went to it, opened it up—sure enough, it was full of cigarettes. Jojo breathed a sigh of relief and helped himself to one. As he lit it, he glanced over the ample supply of half- and quarter-full bottles on and behind the bar: rye, whisky, rum, brandy. There was even a bottle of mezcal back there, with the worm in it and everything. Jojo sucked at the cigarette and reached for a glass.

He selected the rye.

She really wasn't a bad looking broad, as far as married women with a propensity for falling in ditches went. He kept his eyes to himself for the most part, but though Jojo lived a more or less ascetic life since the death of his wife, he was not dead himself. He had to admit it: the woman was a looker. He had absolutely no intention of doing anything about it—hell, if he wanted a roll in the hay Georgia wouldn't kick him out of bed for eating crackers—but there it was.

"It's gone!" Theodora suddenly shouted from the kitchen. "I don't know how, but it's gone!"

Jojo exhaled a stream of smoke and asked, "What's gone?"

"The . . . the bones!"

"Bones?"

He downed the rye, thinking he'd need it. When he returned to the kitchen and saw Theodora's wide, haunted eyes, he decided he was right—he did need it. And how.

"Maybe you'd best start at the beginning," he suggested.

She staggered backward, nearly toppling over. Jojo lunged to steady her, but she found a kitchen chair on her own and collapsed into it. Jojo wanted another drink.

"Last night," she began, her gaze vague and unfocused, "I found something in my husband's coat pocket. A doll . . ."

※

Deputy Mortimer was so bored he had to fight to keep awake. The speaker—a phony doctor with a young face he dimly recognized—was dynamic, but everything he said was pure bunkum, and the guy had a queer look in his eyes that would freeze water. After that, a hot twist in a snug nurse outfit sashayed around the joint, passing out dumb hygiene books to whoever was sucker enough to part with his jack just to see her smile—Mortimer was not among them. He watched her smile for free, and though she was something else, she was cooler than the cool character on the stage. No thanks.

Of course, she spent a little extra time with the real suckers, the ones who ponied up for both booklets and then fumbled blindly in their wallets while keeping their wet eyes on her bursting cleavage. Jackasses. Mortimer recognized a few of them: married guys, mostly. What did they expect to happen? Or was a quick gawk and a whiff of her pungent perfume really worth it for them? The deputy shook his head, failing to understand them.

When she arrived in front of him, he only smirked and drew the edge of his hand across his neck. She smirked back, twice as hard.

"Not interested?" she asked, her voice low and breathy.

"No, ma'am. Actually, I'm here in an official capacity." He emphasized the O in official, drawling it out long and importantly.

"Is that right? Are you a married man, officer?"

"*Deputy*, ma'am. And I don't reckon that's none of your business."

The nurse laughed, exposed big, bright teeth that were framed perfectly by her blood red lips.

"My apologies. *Deputy*."

She dipped a slender hand into a tight pocket at her hip and came back with a small orange square of pasteboard. She regarded it for a moment like it was really something worth looking at, then flipped it between two fingers at Mortimer like a magician performing a card trick.

"What's this? I said I didn't want . . ."

"Why, it's an invitation, handsome. Not everybody gets one. But you do."

He creased the skin at the bridge of his nose and snorted. The nurse did not relent; she remained in position, extending the pasteboard invitation between her paper white fingers. The deputy could not help but notice the shiny, lacquered fingernails and how remarkably smooth the skin at her knuckles was. His, he knew, looked like cracked leather.

Evidence, he told himself as he took the card. It was a ticket. On its face, in simple bold typeface, it read: SPECIAL MIDNIGHT SHOW—ADMIT ONE.

It did not say what the show was. Mortimer frowned at it.

"See you then," the nurse said. She went on her way to the next rube, a fat man who grinned stupidly like he was in love.

Deputy Mortimer slipped the ticket in his shirt pocket and laced his fingers together as the auditorium lights began to dim.

X

Jojo killed the bottle. It was rude as hell, finishing off another man's hooch like that, but under the circumstances he didn't feel guilty about it. Theodora had finished her story, including enough details about her failed marriage to make her eyes well up and her cheeks burn hot. Jojo got the picture, and he pitied this put-upon woman with a bum for a husband. He'd been a bum, too, but he'd never gone around collecting creepy fetishes with baby's bones in them. It was hearsay, of course—as a sheriff's deputy, his first thought would have been to question her veracity and, necessarily, her sanity. After all, there was no proof. The bones, if indeed there ever had been any, were gone with the rest of the doll. It was a hell of a story he'd told himself, a shocker if ever there'd been one with all the blood and nastiness of it. Maybe the lady was the victim of a fragile psyche, just waiting for something to put her over the edge and his nightmarish tale of death and dismemberment at the Litchfield Valley Hotel was the proverbial straw that broke the nutjob's back. The idea wasn't exactly far-fetched. He'd seen it before.

He could not remember her name, which was unusual. What he did remember was that she called the sheriff's department complaining that her old man was wailing on her, that she thought she might have a broken rib, and that if they didn't send somebody over to pick him up soon they were going to have to carry him out in pieces. She had a butcher knife, she calmly explained over the phone, and had no qualms carving the man up if it came down to it. So Jojo drove out to the sticks—well past the silo on the old farm road—and discovered to his horror a haggard, wild-eyed woman holding a terrified man at knifepoint in her bedroom. The man was not her husband; he was selling brooms. The woman's husband, it turned out, ran out on her six months earlier, whereabouts unknown. No one knew about it because she'd acted as though everything was perfectly normal up until that afternoon when she nearly murdered a stranger. Last Jojo ever heard of it, she was sent up to St. Louis and juiced with enough electroshock therapy to keep the raving to a bare minimum.

People under pressure snapped sometimes. Probably it happened every day.

What did not happen every day was voodoo fetish dolls deciding the gruesome fate of a guy four miles away in a closed hotel room, as Theodora was suggesting to him. That was plain crazy. That was fodder for the juice in St. Louis.

It was bullshit. It was batshit crazy.

Theodora goes wild, he thought.

But then there was the matter of the telephone call. Somebody had rung her up to warn her about the strange people at the Palace, or at least so she claimed. It could very well have been all part and parcel of the same harebrained delusion that led her to believe she accidentally dismembered a man with a magic doll, but Jojo had to admit that there was plenty about those damned roadshow people to make him more than just uncomfortable. They rubbed him wrong from the start, well before one of them got ripped apart by force or forces unknown and seemingly unknowable. The whole damn thing was fishy, and the theatre owner's beleaguered wife only made it fishier.

"I think I'd like to talk to your husband," he said at some length. The words tasted astringent from the booze.

"He's at the theatre," she said. "He almost always is."

"Funny thing. That's where I was heading when I ran into you."

She arched an eyebrow. Jojo studied her face: she didn't look a thing like Irene Dunne. She looked more like Ann Southern.

"Let me get a glass of water," she said, rising from her chair. "I'll go with you."

She crossed the kitchen to the sink and Jojo made the beginning sound of protest when something crunched noisily beneath her shoe. She leapt away from it, startled, and they both peered attentively at the small, broken bone on the tiles.

The chair under him toppled over when he jumped up from it. He paid it no mind, lunging for the bone on the floor. He picked it up gingerly and gawped open mouthed for a full minute before whispering, "That ain't no chicken bone."

Theodora said, "I'll get my hat."

X

Neither Margie nor Scooter received an invitation. They were not aware of anyone who did. They had only the word of Margie's friend that the special show even existed, in addition to the earnest hope that it was true. If it wasn't, they each privately feared their risk would be for nothing—the film they were watching was boring as hell.

Scooter waited for the screen to brighten enough to check his wristwatch, and when he did he saw it was a quarter to ten. Two hours to the fabled midnight show, which was much longer than *Motherhood Too Soon* could possibly run. He worried about what they could do to kill that much time and remain inside the Palace. It was an eternity to hide out in the men's room, but he couldn't think of anything else. He puzzled over the quandary as the film meandered on, minute by uninteresting minute.

Margie let her mind drift, thinking about other, better pictures she had seen on that same screen over the years. The Laurel and Hardy pictures and Our Gang shorts she grew up with stood out, and she tried to replay the best of them in her memory. Alfalfa's antics were immensely more entertaining than the stuttering and moralizing amateur actors flickering ahead of her, even if they were all only half-remembered.

Scooter nudged her in the ribs with his elbow, leaned in close and whispered, "What do we do when it's over?"

"I dunno," she whispered back, looking a little annoyed to have been pulled out of the picture show in her head. "Hide out 'til it's time, I guess."

"That'll be more than an hour, though."

"Well, you can go on home if you want to, Scooter Carew. I aim to see what the fuss is about."

She would think him a coward if he left. He had to stay, there was no two ways about it. Maybe if he had brought a comic book to read in the stall for the duration, he thought, it wouldn't be so bad. There was an issue of USA Comics on the trunk at the foot of his bed at that very moment; it had Captain America on the cover, jumping on the wing of some Jap's warplane. He wanted to kick himself for not bringing it along. He just hoped to God it would all be worth the trouble and the danger and relentless boredom.

He swallowed hard and leaned over again to tell her it was all right, he would stay with her, but the hand on his shoulder put that kibosh on that.

"No talking during the performance, please."

"I'm sorry," he whimpered. He looked up at the ghostly white face of the beautiful nurse, how it seemed to fade in and out of existence in the changing light from the big screen.

"If you have something to say," she reprimanded him, "you can come out to the lobby and say it to me."

She smiled cruelly. Scooter withered.

"It won't happen again, ma'am," he croaked. "I'm sorry."

The hand on his shoulder squeezed hard enough to hurt.

"Give me your hand," she said. He gaped, wondering if Margie was watching this, why she wasn't saying or doing anything. He held out his hand, palm up, and the nurse pressed a pair of stiff pasteboard squares into it.

"If I catch you gabbing again, I'll take them away," she warned.

And with that, she vanished back into the darkness of the auditorium.

Again, Scooter waited a moment for the screen to brighten up, at which point he examined the strange artifacts in his hand.

They were tickets to the midnight show.

※

They passed the bank a block away from the Palace Theater. The clock jutting from the brickwork claimed it was half past ten. Jojo parked on the street and flicked one of Russ's cigarettes out of the window. Theodora looked at him, her face failing miserably at masking her apprehension. He got out and slammed the door. She followed suit.

"Where does he normally go when the picture's on?" he asked.

"I don't really know. His office, I suppose. He certainly doesn't come home."

He glanced across the street at the Starlight. Betty was making the rounds with a pot of sludgy coffee, the spring in her step long gone after several hours on shift. He didn't see Russ Cavanaugh in there.

"Let's check his office, then."

Side by side they approached the doors, and Jojo yanked on one of the big brass handles. It did not budge. A girl with a gaudy updo that had big curls and loose bangs smoked a cigarette by the concession counter, a cigarette tray with straps unloaded beside her. He banged on the glass and she exhaled lazily in lieu of reply.

"Ugh," Theodora moaned. "I can't quite recall her name, but that's the little hussy Russ . . . well, you know."

Jojo cranked his mouth to one side—he could believe it. The cigarette girl couldn't have been a day over twenty-one and she wasn't exactly hard on the eyes, her attention-grabbing hairdo notwithstanding. He banged on the glass again.

"No more shows, buster," the girl called out. "Come back tomorrow."

"We're not here for the show, we're here to see your boss."

The girl laughed a blue-grey cloud. "That right? He expecting you?"

"This here's his wife, wise-ass."

Her eyes popped as she shot a hard look at Theodora. She tamped her smoke out in a hurry and rushed over to unlock the doors.

"Gee, I'm sorry Mrs. Cavanaugh. I didn't realize . . ."

"Can it," Theodora growled.

The girl shut up and Jojo grinned. He was glad to see the woman had some grit to her, after all. Theodora pointed across the lobby to a door marked MANAGER. He wondered if that was where the boss normally stuck it to the rude cigarette girl, or if they were brazen enough to get a room someplace, signing in as Mr. and Mrs. John Smith or some such jazz. He'd have tossed the old letch out on his ass if he tried that shit with him. He made a beeline for the office door with the boss's wife in tow.

"He's not in his office," the cigarette girl squeaked.

Jojo flipped around and stared her down.

"How about telling us where he is, then."

She stabbed a trembling finger at one of the two doors behind the snack counter, the one marked PROJECTION—EMPLOYEES ONLY.

"Hey," she said, her eyes getting wet. "Am I going to go to jail?"

"What for?"

"You're a cop, ain'tcha?"

"What if I was?"

The girl gave Theodora a pleading glance, and Jojo caught on: the poor little tramp thought the boss's old lady had gone and called the cops on an adultery charge.

"This is a . . . private matter," he added quickly, hoping to ease her up a little. The fact was he didn't want anything to do with marital squabbles. All Jojo Walker wanted was to figure out how a guy got impossibly killed and why nobody seemed anywhere near as bothered about it as he was. "Is it locked?"

The girl shook her head, and the motion shook loose the tears in her eyes. He studied her for a moment, thinking she wasn't Sarah, but she was in Sarah's shoes. The other woman. He hoped Theodora had the good sense to just up and leave the bastard, let the girl get on with her life and learn from her mistakes. Let everybody be bitter but not necessarily broken beyond repair. Or dead.

He twisted the doorknob and opened the door to reveal a dark stairwell going up.

"Anybody else up there?"

"The projectionist, of course. Chip's his name. And Mr. Davis, I think."

"*Barker* Davis, you mean?"

"Yes, sir."

Jojo had to laugh at the "sir." He never disabused her of the notion that he was a cop.

"Marvellous," he said. "It's about time I met this fella."

He subconsciously touched his side to feel the hard bulge under his jacket. To Theodora, he said, "Shall we?" She stuck close behind him as he climbed the steps, hoping to Christ he didn't walk into a dim projection booth painted with fresh blood and strewn with bits and pieces of Chip.

As it turned out, he did find Chip, though in one, fully functional piece. The kid was changing out a reel and didn't bother to look up to see who was invading his workspace. The room was hot and cramped with film canisters and sundry equipment that was utterly foreign to Jojo. The walls were papered with torn one-sheets from previous engagements, a few of which Jojo had attended. There was a cigarette burning in a glass ashtray in the little projection window.

No one else was in evidence. Jojo waited until Chip was finished with the reel before putting the lean on him.

"You must be Chip."

"That's what they call me." The kid popped the cigarette back in his mouth and looked up with bored disinterest.

"The girl downstairs said your boss was up here. Him and a certain Mr. Barker."

"The girl downstairs is mistaken."

"So they never came up here?"

"Did I say that? I thought I said they weren't here now."

"So you did."

"All right, then. So what's the problem?"

Everyone was being a smart-ass, Jojo noted. He frowned deeply and took a step forward. The ceiling was low and the sex picture in the auditorium murmured loudly below.

"Cavanaugh and Barker were here, then they left—is that is?"

"You got it, champ."

"My name's George Walker, and you can call me Mr. Walker," Jojo said acridly. "Call me champ again and I'll escort you down to the auditorium the hard way."

He jabbed a thumb at the window and Chip sat up straight. The kid got the point.

"I didn't mean nothing, Mr. Walker. Honest."

"That's better."

Theodora stepped out from Jojo's cover. "Where'd he go, Chip?"

"Muh . . . Mrs. Cavanaugh?"

"I'd answer the lady's question, *champ*."

Chip looked from Jojo to Theodora and then back to Jojo again.

"I think they went back to wherever Mr. Barker is staying."

"And where's that?"

"I don't know. Swear to God, I've no idea."

"Which leaves us no place," Theodora said.

"Look," Chip began, lowering his voice and adopting a mask of discomfort. "That man . . ."

"Who, Davis?"

"He's . . . well, he's queer."

"Queer how?"

"I'm not sure I know how to explain it. One thing is he's got some kind of grip on Mr. Cavanaugh. And not *just* him, neither—others, too. He says jump and they ask how high, that sort of thing. He's a real lively sort of fellow, but Mr. Cavanaugh don't jump for nobody."

"Except for Barker Davis," Jojo said.

"Except for him. Anybody would, I mean if Davis wanted it that way. I don't even look him in the eyes."

"Why's that? What's with his eyes?"

"It's when he looks at you—*really* looks at you. His eyes lock onto you, like. You ought to see that guy they've got doing the doctor spiel now. He's a real head case, this guy. All far away, like he can't see or hear anything around him until Davis—or that creepy nurse—tells him to. He does the bit better than the last guy . . ."

". . . who got dead in my hotel," Jojo interrupted.

"Yeah, I heard about that."

"Tell me about the nurse."

"A real knockout; I reckon she's a city girl. New York, maybe, or at least Memphis. Colder than a fish's belly in February, though. Half the fellas come in here crawl all over each other just to say hello to her, but they'd be smarter not to. That one's lethal, you ask me."

"Sounds about right," Jojo said to Theodora. "I've met this broad. She's staying at the hotel with the rest of them."

"Except Barker Davis," she corrected him.

"I talked to her right after I found the body. She seemed . . . inconvenienced by it. Talk about head cases."

"Far as I can tell," Chip continued, "she's his Man Friday. She's the one who gives the orders when Davis ain't around, and he really ain't around that much. She also works the room during the doctor's big speech, passing out tickets to the midnight show. She's cagey as hell about it, but you can see everything from up here."

"Who gets invited? What are the qualifications?"

"That I don't know. Young people, mostly. Not a whole lot of ladies, though some. Some older folks, too. If there's fifteen to a row? Let's see . . . I'd reckon about two to a row get the tickets from her."

"And I presume you've seen the secret show?"

Chip nodded.

"Stag film?" Jojo pressed.

"Not at all. As secretive as they are about it, you'd think that or worse, but the truth is it's just a hokey silent film about magic. It doesn't run but two reels, and it's nothing but some goofy looking magician with a black beard and a top hat doing a bunch of dumb stunts with camera tricks to make it look good."

Jojo and Theodora looked at one another questioningly. She said, "Curiouser and curiouser."

"What's Russ got to do with magic?" he asked her.

"Not a thing. Nothing I know of, at any rate."

"Nothing apart from voodoo dolls in his pocket, anyway."

She visibly shuddered.

"It's the same thing every night?" he asked Chip.

"It's only been the two nights so far, but yeah. To be honest, I was pretty damn curious last night—excuse my language, ma'am—but I checked out after about ten minutes. It was silly. Kids' stuff."

"So as far as you know it could be something else altogether after those first ten minutes."

"No, sir. I have to change the reel and then shut everything down. It'd be some coincidence if the film was only something crazy when I wasn't looking."

"I guess it would," Jojo agreed.

"I'm telling you, it's just organ music and some old timey magician pretending to raise the dead and float in the air, stuff like that."

Jojo ran his fingers across his brow to wipe the sweat away and felt the coarse stubble coming up there. He needed a shave in the worst way, but there wasn't time for that now.

"Anything with dolls that you saw?"

"Dolls?"

"Do you know what a voodoo doll is?"

"I think so. But no, nothing like that. Not that I saw."

"Fine. You did fine, Chip."

Chip smiled tentatively. "Sorry about the whole 'champ' thing, Mr. Walker."

"Forget it, kid. And call me Jojo."

He shook the projectionist's hand and ushered Theodora for the door to the stairs.

"Let's go see about that nurse."

※

They came out of the dark stairwell and into a bustling crowd. The audience was mostly breaking up and hitting the street, disappearing down both sides of the sidewalk or climbing into chrome jalopies. Jojo scanned the throng, looking for faces either familiar or strange. Most were familiar, all of them strange in their way. He didn't know what to look for. As far as he could tell, everybody looked off most of the time.

Taking Theodora by the hand, he made his way into the crowd. From the centre of the lobby he had a straight shot through the open doors leading to the auditorium. A dozen or so people remained sitting in their seat. Special ticket holders, he assumed.

The nurse moved among them.

He said, "Come on" and gave Theodora's arm a tug. Along the way, faces turned toward him, looks of recognition and looks of shock. *That's the guy*, some were telling themselves. *What's wrong with his face?* others wondered. He could practically read their minds, though he didn't have to. He ignored them all and pushed on to the auditorium.

A blast of cold air hit him as he passed the doors. He paused long enough to savour it when a man in a doctor's getup sidestepped him and droned, "Tickets?"

It was Jake. Jojo gaped.

"New job?" he asked.

"Tickets?"

"Normally a body lets his old boss know when he means to move onto another gig, you know. Mr. Hibbs is gonna give me an earful."

"Tickets?"

His brow descending into a dark shelf over his eyes, Jojo went quiet and looked the ex-clerk over. His heavily-lidded eyes were pink and unfocused, the skin on his face drawn and greyish. He looked to Jojo like a man who had been drinking for two days straight and sleeping none of it.

Someone else who asked Barker Davis "how high?"

"You don't look too good, pal," he told Jake.

Beside him, Theodora whispered, "Who is he, Jojo?"

"Used to sit in the cashier's cage at the hotel. Now I guess he's Davis' doctor." He swallowed and fixed his eyes on Jake's. "The last one ended up in five nasty pieces in his hotel room. You ready for that, Jake?"

Jake said, "Tickets?"

Jojo frowned. "Sure, pal."

He withdrew the wallet from his pocket and thumbed through it, pulling two pasteboard squares from within and depositing them in Jake's waiting palm.

Jake said, "Thank you please enjoy the show." All the words mashed together with little inflection and no sign that he knew what he was saying. After that, he just froze up like an automaton that had done its job and shut down for the night. Jojo nodded and escorted Theodora to the aisle.

"Where in the world did you get those tickets?" she whispered.

"Oaklawn," he said. "Mar-Kell and Ocean Wave."

"What are those?"

"A couple of slowpoke horses that got us in."

He could tell she didn't follow, but she let it go. Instead, she asked about Jake.

"What do you think happened to him?"

"I don't know. He's wiped out. I've seen guys on hard narcotics get like that, or guys who get shell-shocked, but not overnight."

"Something Barker Davis did," she inferred.

"All I know is the idea of a guy dying like Pete Chappell did because of a magic doll is seeming a little less nuts all the time."

He led the way to their seats—eighth row centre, the way he used to like it. Sitting two rows ahead of them and off to the left was Dean Mortimer. Jojo eyed the deputy, hoping he would go on being ignorant of Jojo's presence behind him. The guy was a firecracker with bad feelings toward the man whose job he took. Jojo couldn't see why— his fuck-up gave Dean a good position. He reckoned the deputy ought to be grateful, friendly even, but it just didn't work out that way. He slouched in his seat and scanned the rest of the sparse group. There was one other person he recognized, apart from Jake and the nurse, and that was Georgia May Bagby.

"The hell you doing here, Georgia?" he muttered under his breath.

"What?"

"Nothing."

The clamour from the lobby was petering out. No one among those seated spoke, not even so much as a whisper. Theodora squeezed Jojo's arm.

"I'm not so sure this is a good idea," she said.

"Maybe you should go," he said. "Take Dunn's truck and head on home."

"At the moment I feel safer here than at home. But that doesn't account for much."

"No, I guess it wouldn't."

"Still . . ."

"Still."

Behind them, at the open doors to the auditorium, Jake droned, "Tickets?"

"Indeed," came a much closer voice, low and breathy. "Where *are* your tickets?"

Jojo half-smiled and craned his neck to see the nurse hovering over them from the ninth row. She was not smiling at all.

"Your boy at the door has them," he told her.

"Doubtful, Mr. Walker. You see, this show is by invitation only. And I don't recall inviting you. Either of you."

"Must've been somebody else, then."

"More doubtful, still." The nurse pressed her long, slender fingers into Jojo's left shoulder and Theodora's right. Theodora gave a little yelp. "I believe Mr. Davis will see you now."

"Well, it's about goddamn time," Jojo said.

He rose from his seat and Theodora rose beside him, but the nurse wagged a scolding finger at her. "Not you, Mrs. Cavanaugh. Just him."

"Is my husband with this Davis person?" Theodora asked derisively.

"I don't tend to keep track of other women's husbands, Mrs. Cavanaugh," the nurse hissed back. Then, with a sneer: "Enjoy the show."

"What about the tickets?" Jojo asked.

"This is her husband's theatre, after all. She doesn't need a ticket."

With that, the nurse inched down the row toward the aisle, her rump moving seductively from side to side. Jojo noticed.

"Reckon I'd better follow," he said to Theodora. "Take the truck if you need to. Don't worry about me."

"I'll wait," she said. "I'll be right here."

Jojo looked at her and didn't say anything, even when she amended, "And Jojo? Be careful."

He went. And on his way back out to the lobby, Jake called after him, "Tickets?"

☀

"I'm Jojo," he said by way of introduction as he followed her across the now vacant lobby.

"I know."

"I didn't catch your name."

"I'm the nurse."

"Is that your Christian name?"

"This way, Mr. Walker."

She minced past the unattended concession stand to the manager's office at the opposite end of the building. When she reached the door, she waited for Jojo to catch up. She then smiled and said, "Mr. Davis will see you now."

"Is Cavanaugh in there with him?"

"Enjoy the show."

"Enjoy the show," he repeated. "Right."

The nurse took her leave of him and he raised his fist to knock on the door, but before he could he heard a clear, authoritative voice call out: "Come in, Mr. Walker."

He went in.

A man with slight shoulders sat behind a desk Jojo presumed belonged to Russell Cavanaugh, who was nowhere in sight. The man made a steeple with his laced fingers, the tip of which he tapped against his chin. A cigar burned in the ashtray; its ash was a few inches long, having gone unsmoked for a while. It burned very evenly, so much so that it impressed Jojo; he rarely smoked cigars, but when he did they always ended up burning fast down one side and slow on the other. The fellow continued to tap his chin rhythmically as he said, "Close the door, Mr. Walker."

The man behind the desk glared out from a stony, heavily-pitted face with steel grey eyes. His pomaded hair, parted dead centre, looked like a piece but Jojo could tell it wasn't. One thing that struck him particularly was the fellow's fingernails—they were frayed, chewed up. Practically mauled. For some reason it occurred to him that they looked like the fingernails of a man who had clawed his way out of a premature grave.

Jojo did as he was instructed and went directly to the nearest chair in front of the desk. He sat down and took one of Russ's cigarettes from his shirt pocket. He'd snatched several of them.

"I didn't ask you to have a seat."

Jojo crossed his legs and lit the cigarette. "You prefer I'd stand?"

"Tell me, Mr. Walker," the man said, knocking the ash from the cigar but not bringing it to his mouth. "What do you do for a living?"

"Don't you know?"

"Indulge me."

"All right. I'm a house dick."

"You mean detective."

Jojo nodded.

"For a hotel?"

"That's right."

"Which one?"

Jojo knitted his brow, wondering where this was going. "The Litchfield Valley," he said.

"Ah, yes—just up the street, isn't it?"

"Yes."

"I believe some of my crew are staying there for the duration of our engagement here."

"They are, yes."

"Nasty business there last night, I hear."

"Nasty as it gets," Jojo agreed. "I see you've got a new doctor, though."

"Oh, of course. Our Jake was your colleague, was he not?"

"He worked for the same hotel, if that's what you mean."

"But not anymore."

"I guess not. Where's all this leading, Mr. . . . Davis, isn't it?"

The man smiled. "You are not a patient man, are you, Mr. Walker?"

"Life's too damn short. And I'm late for work."

"Ah, but that's my point exactly—don't you see?"

Jojo drew a long drag on the cigarette and blew out a slow column of smoke.

"Can't say as I do, Mr. Davis."

"Your work, at the hotel. The hotel up the street. That's your business. That's your—well, I don't know that *jurisdiction* is quite the word, but for the lack of a better one . . ."

"Oh, I see now. You're telling me to quit playing policeman and to know my place, is that it?"

"Not in so many words, but more or less, yes."

Jojo said, "Hmn." He smoked quietly for a full minute and kept his eyes trained on Davis. If they were having a staring contest, they were due for a tie. Jojo thought he'd been in good shape if he'd bet for a quinella.

"So, are we in agreement then?" Davis said after a while.

"In agreement about what, exactly?"

"That a man ought to mind what's his and—well, let's say render unto Caesar what is Caesar's, yes?"

"Under normal circumstances I wouldn't be able to agree more to that, Davis," Jojo drawled as he leaned over the desk to put out his smoke. He smashed the ember against the cigar, effectively ruining the latter. "Thing is, I'm still working out what happened to a guest at my hotel, which happens to be mine to mind. I need to know the other guests are safe, which I can't guarantee if I don't know what happened to the poor bastard in the first place."

"I believe I can assure you that your guests are perfectly safe."

"Is that right?"

"You have my word."

"Hell, with that and a nickel I can cross the street for a cup of coffee, Mr. Davis."

Davis frowned.

"Here's the facts," Jojo went on. "Roadshow comes to town, all but one of whom stay at my hotel—that one would be you, Mr. Davis. One member of the aforementioned entourage dies in his room under very suspicious circumstances. Sheriff's Department investigates, but one Barker Davis isn't around to make a statement. Hotel dick—that would be me—investigates one Barker Davis, finds him to be suspiciously casual about the whole affair.

"Any argument so far?"

Davis slowly shook his head.

"Then there's one Russell Cavanaugh, owner and operator of the Palace Theater, in whose office we are currently seated."

"I do wish you would get to the point," Davis complained.

"It's a delicate issue," Jojo countered. "If it's tedious, then the tedium is absolutely necessary."

"Get on with it, then."

"Do you know anything about dolls, Mr. Davis?"

"Dolls."

"You *do* know what a doll is?"

"Naturally I do. But I do not understand what they have to do with me."

"Maybe nothing. But I think something. Let me tell you a strange story."

Davis sighed dramatically and leaned back in Russ's chair. The chair's groan seemed to echo Davis's own.

"Late last night, Peter Chappell was in his room—Room 214, for the record—with a young lady. At about that same time, Mrs. Russell Cavanaugh was at home, where she discovered an unusual item in her husband's coat pocket. She describes the item as a sort of doll, crudely made, sort of like a voodoo doll. You're a picture man, Mr. Barker; you ever seen *The Circus Queen Murder?*"

"I have not."

"Not a bad picture, really. It's got Adolphe Menjou in it. You don't see him as much as you used to . . . I wonder if it's harder for a fellow to get work these days if he happens to be called *Adolphe.*"

"What does this have to do with anything?" Davis barked impatiently.

"Oh, just that there was a voodoo doll in that picture, that's all. I thought if you'd seen it . . ."

"I know what a voodoo doll is."

"Well, that's about what it was, this doll Mrs. Cavanaugh found in her husband's pocket, I mean. Now, I know what you're thinking: what makes the difference between a regular doll and a voodoo doll? Not much, as it happens. Just that it was full of spices and bones, and that when the damn thing came apart, so did Pete Chappell. Now how d'you like them apples, Mr. Davis?"

"I think that's the most ridiculous thing I've ever heard."

"It's pretty damn crazy, I'll give you that. But then so was the murder—no, it hasn't been officially classified as a murder, but that's what it is—and so is a nice kid like Jake turning into a zombie after coming into contact with you people. It's a big damn crazy fruit salad, you ask me, and that's how come I don't seem to know my place so well lately."

"I see."

"Particularly when 'my place' gets so blurred. That bloody room back at the hotel is my responsibility, you know. And the bloody footprints, so to speak, all seem to lead right here."

For the first time, Davis took the cigar from the ashtray and sucked a mouthful of smoke from it, despite the damage inflicted by Jojo's cigarette. He held it in while he mulled things over, his eyes narrowing and rolling around blindly in their sockets. When at last he exhaled, there was no smoke.

"You were at the men's show last night, were you not?" he asked.

"I was," Jojo agreed.

"Are you an aficionado of motion pictures, Mr. Walker?"

"I used to be. I don't seem to take them in much anymore."

"How about the stage? I fear you haven't got a playhouse in your humble little hamlet."

"Spit it out, Davis."

The pockmarked man grinned, cigar still in hand.

"What, courage man!" he shouted abruptly, giving Jojo a start. "What though care killed a cat, thou hast mettle enough in thee to kill care."

"Believe me," Jojo said, "I care plenty."

"Not in this sense, Mr. Walker. Our Bard means *curiosity* when he says *care*."

"Oh, I'm hip. Curiosity killed the cat."

"That's right."

"Cute. Got any others like that one?"

Barker Davis returned the cigar to the ashtray and stood up from Russ's chair. He stared deeply at Jojo's face, taking in every scar.

"Helter skelter, hang sorrow," he intoned, "care will kill a cat, up-tails all, and a pox on the hangman!"

"More Billy Shakespeare?"

"Ben Jonson, actually. My preference, as it happens, when it comes to English Renaissance dramatists. What is yours, Mr. Walker?"

Again with the smarmy grin. Jojo pulled another cigarette from his pocket and fired it up.

"I'm a John Fletcher man, myself," he said matter-of-factly. "Care-charming Sleep, thou easer of all woes—"

"Brother to Death," Davis cut in, "sweetly thyself dispose."

"Do you always got to have the last word?"

"I'm a showman," Davis said, shrugging apologetically. "I can't help myself."

"Then you can understand how I feel about being a detective."

"A *hotel* detective."

Jojo did not argue.

"I've always been in show business, Mr. Walker," Davis said expansively as he began to pace behind the desk. "All my life. Before I was in the picture business, I was on the sawdust trail—do you know what that means?"

"Sure. You were a carny."

"At first, yes. Picking up peanut shells and elephant leavings; one must pay his dues. But I made friends in the Ten-in-One, a magician, particularly. Taught me many things, that sorcerer. A great many tricks. In a way, I took his place. In another way, he took mine."

"You're losing me, Davis."

"It is an entirely different world, the life of the travelling circus. A whole other universe with its own rules, its own laws and etiquette. I once knew a fellow who was probably the most handsome man I'd ever seen, and he was hopelessly in love with a woman we called Big Bertha. She weighed nearly six hundred pounds. Children laughed at her. But this fellow loved her more than life itself. Only in the circus, Walker. But I suppose you know that just as well as I do. After all, you are of the same . . . pedigree, might I say? Or is that touching too close to home?"

Jojo grimaced. "What's that supposed to mean?"

"Your coat is beginning to show, Jojo Walker."

"My coat . . . ?"

"You're in bad need of a shave."

"Listen—"

"I was never much of a comedian—that much I left to the clowns—but do you want to know what really strikes me as funny? That I'm the one called 'Barker' when you, Mr. Walker, are the dog-faced boy."

Jojo launched himself to his feet and slammed his fist against the top of the desk. The cigar leapt from the ashtray, rolled across the desk and fell down to the carpet.

"Now you listen to me, you son of a bitch," he growled, his fists clenched and shoulders trembling with rage. "You don't know a goddamned thing about me, hear? And if you call me that again, I swear to Christ I'll lay you out."

"It's only what was painted on the canvas, Jojo—or don't you remember?"

Jojo opened his mouth to retort, but no words escaped his throat. Instead, he froze in an angry pose, a statue of fury stopped in time. Barker Davis threw his head back and laughed as the office door creaked open and two members of his roadshow entourage came in. Jojo twisted at the waist to see them—the tall guy in the tweed jacket he'd seen at the hotel was one of them, but he was less sure about the little fireplug with the red beard beside him. He may have been there, too, but Jojo was reeling from the shock of what Barker Davis had said.

Painted on the canvas.

At the Ten-in-One. The sideshow.

The *freakshow.*

Davis reached down behind the desk and came back with a long, shiny black cane. He twirled it expertly and spread his legs in a dramatic fashion. Jojo braced for a beating, but instead the showman spread his arms and proclaimed:

"Laaaaaaadies and gentlemen—from the dense, wild forests that bank Russia's Volga River comes an untamed, uncivilized beast the likes of which you have never seen. It was hunters from Kostroma that found the little beast, tracked him and his father to their cave where they were captured *for your astonishment.*"

Jojo's head swam. He staggered backwards and would have fallen over had the two heavies not steadied him. The room grew hot very rapidly. The reek of sweat and popcorn and animal shit filled his nostrils.

"He is a savage who cannot be tamed! He is locked behind iron bars *for your safety!*"

The bars materialized all around him. He could not recall if they had been there the whole time. At his feet was a bed of hay and he had a strong sense of déjà vu he couldn't quite place.

"Ladies and gentlemen, this specimen is not for the faint of heart. Do not be ashamed if you must look away from . . . *Jojo the Dog-Faced Boy!*"

A heavy velvet curtain came away, taking the office walls with it. Hot late summer sun beat down through the bars of the cage and Jojo instinctively put his hand to his brow. He seized a fistful of long, course hair. A chorus of cries and gasps was followed by a spate of laughter. One of the men behind him, the fireplug, jabbed him in the ribs with a wooden pole. Jojo scrambled away from it to the opposite corner of the cage.

The man snarled, "Bark, you damn monster! Growl, goddamn you!"

"Bark, dog-boy," someone in the crowd cajoled.

"How come he don't bark?" cried someone else.

Again the pole flew at him, stabbing into the small of his back. Jojo let out a pitiful moan. He was surprised at the smallness of his own voice. It was the voice of a young boy.

"That's it," the fireplug seethed. "Growl, boy. *Growwwwwl.*"

The man bared his teeth cruelly and rattled the bars with the pole. Jojo whimpered, flattened himself against the bars and let out a shrill howl. The fireplug laughed. The crowd roared with applause and shouts of delight.

Jojo tried to say, *This is a trick. None of it's real.* But it all came out a series of rumbling barks, like a dog imitating human speech.

He threw his hands to his face and grabbed handfuls of the hair his Ambras Syndrome caused to sprout from his face and neck and every place else on the body he loathed. He ripped the hair out by the roots, but there was too much to tear out. It was like hacking through a primeval jungle with a butter knife—wherever he tore away a handful, the hair seemed just as thick as ever. Thicker.

"So savage it cannot even speak, ladies and gentleman," Barker Davis hollered. "His mother mauled by a pack of hounds when she was pregnant, and when time came to deliver the child into the world—*this* abomination was the horrifying result."

A different lie than the first, Jojo realized. The story changed all the time. He thought he could remember one about a flying saucer depositing him in a cornfield, abandoning him there. A sad, motherless boy with a shame-inducing cutaneous disorder made for a terrible tale at a circus sideshow, even if it was the truth. The barker could always come up with a better one.

And this one had his audience by their throats. Davis thrilled them with one fabrication after another, each one more improbable than the last, while his sneering abettors jabbed at Jojo the Dog-Faced Boy with their poles and spit in his dark, matted hair.

Then Barker Davis swept his arm over the crowd in a wide arc and they were gone. His stooges remained, but he called them off, shouting, "Enough!"

Gradually the walls came back, and then the rest of the office with them. Even so, Jojo could still smell the rich odours of the travelling sideshow, the menagerie of human oddities to which he belonged. A fraction of it was real: he had soiled himself.

"I'm a showman," Davis said as he had before, this time with evident derision. "I can't help myself."

Jojo croaked, afraid to hear himself bark again. But his voice came back to him.

"Wha—what did you do to me?"

"It's *your* nightmare, Mr. House Dick," the showman answered. "You tell me."

"Poison," Jojo weakly posited.

"No, Mr. Walker. Magic."

"Magic . . ."

"The best and strongest. Why, if you think *that* was good, you should see what they're seeing in there." He pointed at the door, but Jojo knew he meant the auditorium. The special midnight show.

"Theodora," he rasped. "Georgia."

"So many nice ladyfriends for the Wild Man of Kostroma. I would never have guessed."

"Mr. Davis," the man in the tweed jacket interrupted. "The show—it's nearly over."

"You're quite right, Abner. And tomorrow is Friday, after all. Best night at the pictures, Friday—but I suppose you already knew that, Jojo Walker."

"You . . ." he wheezed, short of breath. "Leave them alone."

"Good night, Jojo Walker," Davis said, strolling past the prone form on the floor as though he was no more than a kink in the carpet. "We show business people work late, and there's much to do."

He handed his cane to Abner and reached for the door.

"You know, perhaps I might leave you with some Fletcher, as you so seem to enjoy him—

"With as little feeling as I turn off a slave that is unfit to do me service, or a horse . . . or *dog* . . . that have out-lived their use, I shake thee off, to make thy peace with Heaven.

"Take him home, Ab."

The man called Abner in the checked tweed jacket removed a black leather sap from his coat pocket and lunged for Jojo. There was a burst of lightning and his head exploded.

After that, nothing.

X

Theodora crossed her legs and looked occasionally at the blonde woman Jojo couldn't keep his eyes off of. She didn't recognize her, but this was hardly surprising—though she had spent her entire life in Litchfield, her social experience had always been severely limited by the men who ruled over her life. First her father, and then his replacement in Russ. It was astonishing, now that she thought about it for the first time. It was such a small town, and yet she barely knew anyone in it. Even the people she did know she didn't know.

Her breath hitched in her throat and she realized that she'd been glaring at the back of the woman's head for quite a while. Quickly she averted her eyes, repositioning them on the big, empty screen ahead of her. The picture was about to begin, and she needed everything in her power to focus on that rather than the consuming sense of loneliness that washed over her.

A tear spilled out of her right eye and she moved swiftly to wipe it away. She didn't need to. The lights were dimming down.

PART 3

The Midnight Show

CHAPTER ELEVEN

Georgia May Bagby went rigid in her seat and shrieked.

It commenced with a soft sepia image of a tall, slender man in top hat and tails, his beard waxed to an impish point and his long fingers dancing menacingly over a table in the middle of a stage. From this the picture cut to a flickering title card that introduced him:

"BLACK" HARRY ASHFORD

MAGICIAN—ILLUSIONIST—ENTERTAINER

MASTER OF MYSTERY

Back on the stage, Ashford gazed intently at the table as a thin mist formed at its centre and rolled out in all directions. There was no sound and no music, only the hypnotic clicking of the projector above. From amidst the thickening vapour a reptilian column rose up and struck out—a viper. In a single deft motion, Ashford snatched the snake in one hand, just below the head, and began to stuff the entire length of the hissing creature into his fist with his other hand. In a matter of seconds, the viper was completely subsumed by the magician's hand, and when he uncurled his fist and spread out his fingers, the beast was gone. A sly, lupine grin spread across Ashford's gaunt, pallid face and the picture snapped to another title card.

ASHFORD LEARNT HIS UNFATHOMABLE DARK ARTS
FROM AN INDIAN FAKIR—
QALANDER AL'HAZRAD!

Now, stock footage, or so it seemed. Somewhere in the East—India, Georgia assumed—on a crowded market street hedged in on both sides by leaning shanties. In the middle of the street the multitude gave a wide berth to the half-naked man sitting cross-legged on a bed of nails. The man's head lolled from side to side, his simple white turban undisturbed by the motion. Apart from the turban, he wore nothing but a tattered loincloth; the remainder of his dusty, wrinkled flesh was exposed, and much of it pressed down against the sharp points of the nails beneath him.

QALANDER AL'HAZRAD—
FEARED AND RESPECTED BY HIS OWN PEOPLE—
PRIVY TO SECRETS NO MAN SHOULD KNOW!

Upon cutting back to the fakir, the screen was suddenly taken up by the startling image of the man convulsing on the nails, his limbs flailing against the sharp, ripping points. The crowd backed away even as the camera closed in on the spasming man. The nails shredded his skin wherever they touched it, and though none of them came near his chest, the flesh there seared and came apart in a confluence of deep, bleeding lines. The lines, drawn by some invisible blade, formed a puzzling symbol when completed:

That was when Georgia screamed, though she did not fully understand why. Naturally, the gruesome spectacle of the fakir in his aggrieved state was enough to unsettle any observer, but for some reason it was the symbol itself that struck her as particularly horrifying. She knew she had never seen it before. She had no idea what it signified. But for every second the sigil remained on screen, Georgia's scream became louder and her fear more pronounced.

CHAPTER TWELVE

But of course there was no sigil, no fakir, no market street somewhere in India. There was only Black Harry Ashford, alone in the mist, his sunken eyes almost transcending the divide between cinema and audience member in a very real way that made Theodora shift uncomfortably in her seat. She presumed that anyone, from any seat in the house, could have gotten the impression that magician was staring directly at them, not unlike some of those eerie portraitures old people sometimes hung in their stairwells. Yet somehow Theodora figured anyone would be wrong, that though it might have *seemed* as though Ashford's eyes were trained on them, it was *her* he was truly staring down. And though the idea was as terrifying as it was fantastic, she could not look away—

—not even when Jojo Walker's blonde friend let loose a shriek that would normally have made Theodora leap out of her skin.

"Shhh," said the magician, his voice echoing from the speakers positioned all around the auditorium. "Pay her no mind, Theodora. She does not like what she sees. Do you like what *you* see?"

A small, girlish smile turned up the corners of her mouth as her eyes widened to saucers and spilled over with warm, happy tears. For she most assuredly did like what she saw.

For here was daddy on a cool autumn morning, the square necktie he only wore on weekends dangling over his trim torso in the years before alcoholism and self-neglect caused him to balloon like a human zeppelin. He crouched to hold hands with a beaming child on a glossy gymnasium floor, a small girl in a white dress whose face belied the greatest happiness a child can know. *That's me*, Theodora thought. *Look how happy I am. I'm so happy.*

A knowing smile sliced across daddy's square, crew-cut head as he looked down at his darling daughter, showing her off to all the men in basketball jerseys who called him Coach and respected him like soldiers respected a four-star general. Then one of them, a hatchet-faced young man who held the ball between two gigantic hands, suggested they all call her Lil' Coach from then on, and they did. *When Coach ain't around, maybe you can fill in for him. I bet we'd be some team under you, Lil' Coach.*

Daddy laughs (though it is a laugh without sound), lets go of the small girl's hand so he can hold his stomach and rock his shoulders. Everyone is happy. The little girl is the centre of the world at that moment. No one even notices the tired-looking woman in the stands, her head canted to one side and the needlework on lap untouched.

A title card burst onto the screen, washing the moment away.

1912!
BEFORE THE WORLD KNOWS GLOBAL WARFARE!
SIMPLER TIMES! HAPPIER TIMES!

A close-up on a slightly older girl's drawn face, her mouth quivering and eyes dead. Some years later, she realized.

BUT YOU KNEW BETTER—
—DIDN'T YOU, THEODORA?

"Yes," she agreed aloud.

She knew much better, and the next scene—so nightmarishly familiar—did nothing more than prove her awful knowledge of that fact. The tired woman with her left eye swollen almost completely shut. The cowering fear, the misery hanging thick in the house like a fog. Midnight visits, daddy's breath hot and pregnant with drink and desire. Then:

SAINT LOUIS!
BUSTLING CITY OF MIRACLES AND SIGHTS UN-DREAMED OF!

Streetcars and horse-drawn carriages, a multitude of people numbering a hundred Litchfields, a thousand. She knew it well in memory and in too many dreams, this intimidating, threatening, wildly inviting metropolis to which she was spirited away, all those years ago. It was in St. Louis that she convalesced in that dirty little home for unwed mothers on the east side of town, it was here that they took her unholy progeny from her womb and spirited it away so fast she'd never even known its sex. The riverfront, the warehouses, the seedy wharf culture to which she ran with hopes and terror of never being herself again.

"Oh, but daddy found you, did he not, little Theodora?" said the devilish magician, Black Harry Ashford. "Look."

In one hand Ashford held a fan of cards, stark black on both sides. With the other he pointed a long-nailed index finger at the screen descending behind him at the back of the stage. A flicker of light and the film began: the film-within-the-film.

The young woman, her face a ghostly parody of pancake make-up and dark, black eyes, made a wide O of her mouth and pressed the back of her hand to her brow—the over-emotive performance of a Louise Brooks or a Theda Bara, though it was herself performing for the sorcerer's audience. It was Theodora On The Wharf.

Her fright came at the slavering, hunched form of daddy, his hands stretched out like vulture's claws, come to make a dishonest, ruined woman of her. Though of course it was much too late for that. She had only one option left to her now, with daddy on one side of her and the roiling Mississippi on the other. A tad dramatic, perhaps—but upon directing her enormous black eyes at the dark water she could have sworn the river opened up as though it had a mouth, inviting—no, *demanding*—that she come inside.

Come to daddy.

Swim into the pitch.

And though so clear a memory should not have surprised her, Theodora started in her seat when the tragic heroine on the screen in the screen made for the edge of the wharf and launched her frail body toward the yawning mouth of the river.

And, if only she hadn't been wearing so loose and flouncy a dress as was given to her at that filthy home, the huge wharf rat would never have been able to reach out with his great, apelike arm and snatch her back to safety.

Safety. She snorted.

Saved from the belly of the whale to be returned to the dragon's lair. Probably, Theodora thought, Louise Brooks or Theda Bara would have been rescued before it was too late. But it was too late for this suffering heroine before the picture ever started. The screen went grey and the magician frowned, clown-like. He removed his hat and pressed a hand to his chest, mournful and full of mock grief. When, a second later, a fluffy white rabbit poked its head out from inside the hat, Ashford could not contain his mirth. From sad clown to happy, he shook with laughter and dumped the rabbit into a small cage on the stage floor. A feminine arm crooked in from off-screen, passing a white tablecloth to him. This he accepted without acknowledging the assistant, and he spread it out with a showman's aplomb before draping it over the cage.

With a theatrical wave of a black wand, the magician worked his magic. He paused, pondering what he might have done, and then tossed the wand to the back of the stage and whisked the cloth away from the cage.

There was no more rabbit, naturally. In its place, a small, terrified boy—naked apart from the thick brown hair that covered every inch of his shivering, waifish body. The hair beneath his eyes was matted and wet with tears. Ashford spread his hands out and bowed to the audience, his face a ghoulish mask of wicked delight. The wolf-boy shrank into a corner of the cage and hugged his furry knees. Theodora's heart ached for him.

Ashford's mouth moved, his lips stretching comically to over-pronounce silent words. The next title card translated:

THIS ABOMINATION CANNOT HELP YOU

The magician smirked knowingly in the next scene, stepping back from a frame filled with his leering face to reveal the bright, dusty view of the circus unfolding behind him. Jerkily, the camera moved in a shaky arc to take in the carnies setting up the tents, the menagerie of exotic animals being led into the Big Top, the ashen-faced clowns practicing their juggling routines. And then: daddy, his countenance slack and without expression, holding a large placard upon which the traveling camera stopped to focus.

BARKER DAVIS PRESENTS:
THE DEVIL'S BUSINESS

A grotesque caricature of a simpering demon appeared in a bottom corner of the placard, approving of the title while keeping its dismal, soulless eyes directed forward, into the camera lens and through it, at Theodora.

Daddy turned the placard around, where a different demon leered and grinned at the list of players—

LIL' COACH—OL' ANNE THE NEGRO NANNY
& JO-JO THE HIDEOUS WOLF BOY OF KOSTROMA

Daddy let the placard droop in one hand and walked backwards until he vanished into the Big Top. A small crowd was forming: men in straw hats and women in thick, hot dresses and a mass of children leaping at their heels. Amidst the mob came a man in both "drag" and blackface; a great, fat man with floppy breasts sewn into his dress and his face done up with burnt cork after the manner of a minstrel singer. This ridiculous pickaninny Theodora understood to be "ol' Anne, the Negro nanny." Gripping Anne's hand was a small, wild-eyed girl with brown curls and a smear of caramelized sugar across one cheek, the remains of some infrequent confection.

She was Lil' Coach, Theodora herself.

Anne dragged the girl through the crowd, parting the milling people like a bulldozer and stopping when they came to a smaller tent on the outer fringe of the circus proper. An ornate, hand-painted sign hung from wire above the half-open tent flaps: HUMAN ODDITIES.

The drag Anne made a broad circle of her mouth, framed in white greasepaint, and wagged a finger at the child.

"LAWS, NO! DAT DERE AIN'T NO PLACE FOR A CHILE!"

(Theodora shifted in her seat, frowning. She had no recollection of her childhood nanny speaking or behaving in the exaggerated manner of the performer playing her part on screen.)

The child pouted and kicked up a tiny cloud of dust. Anne scowled at the kid and planted her huge hands on her broad hips. From the tent came a dwarf in a jester's costume, smoking a cigarette and regarding Anne and Lil' Coach warily. The dwarf was followed by a squat man with a pockmarked face that was stretched to form a rictus grin. He wore a striped band skimmer on his round head and tucked his thumbs into his suspenders while he bent back, bouncing on his heels as he spoke to the nanny and little girl.

"MADAM—THIS SHOW IS FOR ALL AGES,
RACES, CREEDS AND PEOPLE OF ANY FAITH.
COME INSIDE AND SEE WHAT WONDERS LIE WITHIN!"

The nanny shook her head zealously, her great, cork-blacked jowls shaking like a bloodhound's. As she did so, the child tugged at her nanny's skirts and pleaded with huge, glossy eyes. For his part, the barker grasped his sides and quaked with laughter. Neither the nanny nor the child could determine the source of his merriment—and for that matter, Theodora couldn't, either.

There came more jabbering from the barker and more head shaking from Anne to match, none of which was translated to title cards, but whatever spiel the experienced barker gave was successful in the end— the nanny relented and followed the man into the tent.

※

WHAT THEY SAW

The picture cut to the startling image of an enormously obese woman dressed in nothing more than a two-piece bathing suit. She sat on a bed of hay behind iron bars and shook herself with all her might, causing her great folds of fat to wiggle and flop.

(Theodora said out loud: "Big Bertha," because she remembered.)

Indeed, the title card that followed identified the gigantic woman as none other than BIG BERTHA, 450 LBS OF PURE WOMAN.

Now at the next specimen, also behind bars, as all of them would be—a sorrowful looking creature with cracked, plated skin and no hair on her reptilian head. THE CROCODILE WOMAN. Next came the gruesome spectacle of a table laden with half a dozen jars in which vaguely humanoid shapes floated within murky liquid—PICKLED PUNKS.

In quick succession the bizarre parade went on like this. A bearded lady in a ballet costume performed a pirouette; a pair of Siamese twins played a game of chess; the Lobster Boy sipped tea, perilously gripping the handle of the teacup between the two malformed digits that extended from his wrist. There was a shuddering pig with one bulbous black eye in the centre of its head and a deformed man with a jutting brow and tumorous jaw billed simply as APE OR MAN?

The penultimate freak on display was the armless fiddler, a small coloured man who played his fiddle with his feet—without the benefit of sound, his skill was unknowable.

At last the tour concluded with its *pièce de résistance*—

JO-JO THE DOG-FACED BOY!

SAVAGE ABOMINATION!

NATURE'S WORST MISTAKE!

Recoiling from his onlookers, the boy-thing masked his face with shaggy hands. He bared his teeth and seemed to growl even as he savagely snapped at the inquisitive camera that filmed him. It was a furious and terrified brute, worthy of both sympathy and horror.

A sharp cut shifted the focus to the spectators, among whom the drag and blacked-up Anne wailed and waved her arms over her head in a histrionic fit.

"LAWS, LAWS!

DAT AIN'T NATCHREL!

DAT BE DE DEBBIL'S BIDNISS!"

(Theodora groaned. She recalled the words and her nanny's reaction, but bristled at the silent picture's parody of it. Worse still, it was entirely out of context: as Theodora remembered it, it was not fear of the poor boy that ignited Anne's outrage, but rather the showman's treatment of him. But then the man on screen was not the barker she saw that day— the man on the herky-jerky, flickering screen, of course, was Barker Davis.)

The child largely ignored her nanny's hamming theatrics; she was too entranced with the hirsute boy in the cage. She gingerly approached the bars, equally ignored by the grown-ups, and reached a chubby pink arm between them. At first, the boy—Jo-Jo—did nothing but continue to cringe and growl. The girl did not understand he did this only to appease his handler, that he was in no way the savage abomination he was said to be. To her mind, this undreamed-of creature was every bit the brute the barker claimed, an understanding that only served to make her gesture so much more extraordinary. The dog-faced boy turned his huge brown eyes from the kind-faced girl to the barker and the nanny and the startled observers who observed one another, and not him. His growling tapered off. His heaving breaths slowed to gentler inhalations and exhalations. He looked deeply at the girl-child, the fortunate kid who had hair where hair was expected to be, who got to wear clothes and visit stinking roadside circuses only to peek and then go back home. He cocked his head to one side—unintentionally and comically dog-like— and let loose a whimper that elicited fresh tears from the girl on the other side of the bars.

A miracle happened then. In her empathy and grief, the girl swooned and dropped backward, still grasping the cold iron bars. . . .

And the cage door swung open with her.

The boy gasped and threw a hairy hand to his mouth to muffle the sound. Apart from the girl, no one seemed to notice; the grown-ups had directed Anne to the far opposite corner of the tent to sit her down and fan her face. The girl threw a quick glance in that direction. While her head was turned, the boy darted out of the cage, knocking over a bucket that slopped shit all over the hay in his wake. The bucket clanged against the hard ground underneath and the open bars, jarring the girl back to attention and alerting everyone else inside the tent. Anne screamed. The barker shouted a blue streak of profanity. The dog-faced boy shrieked like a banshee, scrabbling alongside the row of freaks on display.

The crocodile woman wept, her scaly face buried in her scaly hands, but the armless fiddler and Big Bertha raised a chorus of alarmed shouts to *catch him, catch him.* The girl gave chase, the adults close behind. The pounding ruckus of a dozen or more scrambling feet jarred the insubstantial cages, shook the pickled punks until one of the larger ones toppled over and smashed to pieces. (The smell was overwhelming; she remembered it so clearly she could very nearly smell it now. Rot and sewage; those damn things were *real*, for God's sake.)

Catch him, catch him.

They didn't. Despite his starved appearance and short legs, the little beast outran them all, clear out of the tent and into the dusty yellow sun. Stark naked and looking the way he did, there was no telling how far he might have gotten, where he may have gone—but it was a moot point. For what his keepers and unfortunate brethren failed to do was accomplished with seemingly effortless ease by a reedy man with a pointed beard in a wrinkled suit.

Black Harry Ashford swept the panicked youth up with one arm and whispered into his fur-hidden ear:

EACH OF US HAS HIS CAGE—
BE GRATEFUL FOR YOURS!

And after the pursuing mob caught up and Barker Davis commenced beating the Dog-Faced Boy and the little girl bellowed silently at her disinterested nanny, the picture cut abruptly to a wide shot of Theodora in her kitchen, weeping over a mess of overcooked potatoes on the floor.

The startling image was intercut with a new title:

THEODORA IN HER CAGE.

CHAPTER THIRTEEN

Deputy Dean Mortimer's midnight show was considerably less complex.

He saw the magician ("BLACK" HARRY ASHFORD; MAGICIAN—ILLUSIONIST—ENTERTAINER; MASTER OF MYSTERY) performing marvellous feats of sorcery upon his little stage, feats much more impressive than any magician he'd ever seen before. Mortimer had seen, for example, Earl Child's numerous card tricks many a night at Earl's tavern, and he'd seen a magician at the Litchfield Autumn Fair twist balloons into animal shapes and even make a farmer's wife disappear in a trick cabinet. Nothing the man on the Palace's screen did, however, could possibly have been a trick.

Mortimer understood the basic rudiments of special effects, that film producers were perfectly capable of making it look like the impossible was taking place before the audience's very eyes, and yet when Harry Ashford began yanking the long, writhing black snake from somewhere beneath his velvet coat, the deputy knew he was seeing something quite special. More special still was the moment the magician brought the thrashing head of the serpent up to his mouth and gobbled the head up, an exploit outdone only by the continued consumption of the squirming snake, all four feet of it, clear up to the tail. For a fleeting moment the tip of the tail, glinting like onyx, lashed between the magician's moving lips. Mortimer watched with equal parts horror and delight as Ashford's throat muscles worked, clamping down on the unhappy reptile and pushing in down, down into whatever devilish machinery Ashford had for guts. The tail vanished with a slurp and the magician grinned, sated.

All in one, unmoving shot. No trick.

Somewhere, distant hands came together in applause, though no one in the auditorium clapped and the noise did not originate from the speakers, which emitted only tinny organ music to accompany the silent picture. Mortimer presumed it was somebody in the lobby, beyond the red doors, and dismissed it entirely. They were not applauding Ashford, whoever *they* were, though the deputy figured they damn well ought to have been. He was fantastic, this silent film sorcerer, the real thing. It never even occurred to Mortimer that magic was illusion, by definition *unreal*; at least it was before he set foot in the Palace that night. That such a monumental change had occurred to the way he perceived the world around him was inconsequential to Dean Mortimer. Only Ashford's magic mattered.

Now the performer strutted back and forth on the little stage, searching his unseen audience with black eyes. He waved his arms expansively and spoke to the camera—

I shall now need a volunteer

Before he could absorb the ridiculousness of his response, Mortimer vaulted an arm into the air and waggled his fingers. He even let out a muted squeak in his excitement.

Ashford twisted his neck to take in one side of the screen and then swung his head around to the other side. His nostrils flared and his eyes rolled back before snapping back into a direct stare at the camera—at Mortimer.

You there, he mouthed.

Mortimer let out a tiny gasp and let his arm down slowly.

Come, the magician's lips said soundlessly. *Don't be afraid. Come on up, now.*

The deputy rose from his seat and stepped into the lighted, red-carpeted aisle. The seat sprang shut in his wake, slapping loudly as it folded up. He did not hear it as he moved guardedly toward the screen.

"That's right," Ashford said, curling an index finger at Mortimer.

Somehow the magician had found his voice, which sounded thin and crackly like paper. "Step right up."

The relative warmth of the auditorium abandoned Mortimer as he approached the screen and stepped up onto the stage. He did not feel cold; merely grey.

"Right this way."

"I—I'm nervous," Mortimer stammered.

"No need, my boy. No need. Here—" Ashford drew a long, thin knife from his coat and presented it to Mortimer "—take this."

He accepted the grey-silver knife by its black handle and regarded its winking edge and surprising heft. Ashford bowed slightly at the waist and showed grey teeth in a black mouth framed by a plaster white face. The sudden dearth of colour did not alarm Mortimer; rather, it comforted him, made things much simpler. He hoped at that moment to never see colour again. It was, more or less, how he had always viewed the world anyway.

"Now . . ." Ashford said, trailing off as he went hunched over to a long, narrow table at the edge of the stage.

Mortimer followed him, squinting in the stage lights at the curious symbols expertly carved into the surface of the table. None of them were remotely recognizable, though beautiful to look at, the centrepiece in particular—an upside-down triangle pointing at an ornate capital V, curlicues sweeping out on both sides and a pair of lines slicing through the shape on top.

"The Sigil of Lucifer," the magician explained. "But look."

He swept a dark sheet up from the floor and let it drift over the table, covering it completely. Mortimer shielded his eyes with his free hand and tightened his grip on the knife's handle with the other. This way, he could make out the shadowy forms of the people in the scant audience, the people in the dark theatre with whom he had been sitting only a moment before. He felt embarrassed, a little like being naked, but also vaguely superior.

Ashford made a dramatic show of opening up one side of his coat, the same side from which he'd taken first the snake and then the knife. From the bottomless inside pocket stitched into the lining, he drew out a long, thin wand of the type stage magicians nearly always used. Mortimer smiled childishly and cooed like a pigeon. With the deputy enthusiastically looking on, Ashford leaned over the table and drew a circle in the air with the wand, first clockwise and then counter-clockwise. Satisfied with this, he returned the wand to the pocket and spread his long, grey hands out over the sheet, which shifted and bulged like a bladder filling with water. In seconds the sheet took the general form of a human body, prone as a corpse. Mortimer gaped.

"Go ahead, Dean," Ashford said. "Lift the sheet and see what I have done."

The deputy hopped at the chance to oblige the magician; he grabbed handfuls of the sheet and yanked it away from the table as quickly as he could. The mischievous, boyish smile melted from his face when his foggy mind registered the face on the person beneath.

"Mama?"

His mother, two decades dead, lay in state just as she had on the day of her funeral, apart from the fact that she was utterly naked. Her skin was marbled and grey, her cheeks taut and receded to the point of her cheekbones protruding through. Though she had been divested of the lovely powder blue dress her sisters agonized over in the days leading up to the viewing, the late Mrs. Mortimer retained her pearl earrings and ruby red hummingbird brooch, which for lack of cloth was pinned to the dry, shrunken flesh of her breast.

Dean Mortimer sniffed, touched and not a little puzzled by the conjuration of his deceased mother.

"That . . . that's my mama," he said.

Ashford nodded and moved his lips, but he made no sound. Mortimer beetled his brow and shifted his eyes from his mother to the magician and back again. Now the corpse's lips were slightly parted and a weak, wheezing breath whistled out. The magician laid a gentle hand on Mortimer's shoulder and continued to speak without sound. Shaking his throbbing head, the deputy leaned in close, aimed his ear at Ashford's mouth which whispered almost inaudibly, "For her, Dean. Do it for Mama."

"What? Do what for her?"

Ashford covered his mouth with one hand and looked away, sad and ashamed. With a shuddering gasp, Mortimer jerked his head back around to see Sheriff Ernie Rich, his own nude flesh markedly white in contrast to Mrs. Mortimer's dull grey, pounding his rump up and down as he defiled the cadaver on the table. Mortimer screamed mournfully and shook like a drunk with the DTs for several seconds before he could persuade his body to take action.

"Not my mama," he moaned, launching himself at the slobbering man rutting his mother's body. "Not my mama, Ernie, goddamn you!"

"You must protect her," Ashford hissed. "You must protect mama."

Mortimer threw himself at Rich, piling into his boss's naked body and knocking him off the table. Rich groaned and slammed against the stage floor. He instinctively cupped his genitals with one hand and flailed the other, balled into a fist, at his deputy.

"What kinda man," Mortimer sobbed as he stamped around the table, "what kinda man . . ."

"She still looks good to me, Deano," Rich said breathlessly, his stark white lips curling back into a nasty grin. "You can have her, too. We all can."

"Kill you," Mortimer snarled. "Kill . . . you!"

"The knife, Dean," Ashford kindly reminded him.

He had forgotten all about it, but the blade still gleamed in his hand. Mortimer grunted and gripped the handle with both hands as he lunged for Ernie Rich. The sheriff screeched and recoiled on his side. Mortimer saw that the man's penis was still erect and glistening in the stage lights.

"You can't keep her buried, Dean," Rich sobbed.

Mortimer brought the blade down hard, driving it into the sheriff's side and pushing it through his ribs. Black blood bubbled up from wound, slid down in viscous rivulets across his back and belly. Rich coughed wetly, jerked in a single violent spasm, and disappeared.

"What is this?" Mortimer cried, leaping to his feet with the still dripping knife in his hand. "A trick?"

"I do not do tricks, Dean," Ashford said reproachfully.

Mortimer scanned the stage; his breath hitched when he saw that his mother was also gone. Now only the strange, indecipherable shapes remained on top of the table.

"I don't understand," he said.

"Isn't it time, Dean Mortimer? Isn't it time to finally assert yourself, to finally be a man? Why, your poor, dear mother lies in rest, unaware of the obscene intentions of men like Ernie Rich. And that is to say nothing of the Reverend Jim Shannon."

"Reverend Shannon? What's he got to do with anything?"

The magician laughed: an abrupt snort. "Only everything, Dean," he said with a flourishing gesture of his hands. "Only absolutely everything."

CHAPTER FOURTEEN

Margie and Scooter each had their own midnight shows, as well. In Scooter's, Captain America burst into Hitler's secret bunker with his shield in one hand and the severed, dripping head of a Japanese soldier in the other. The Führer's goons opened up with machine guns that went *rat-a-tat-tat-tat*, but their bullets were useless against the hero's impenetrable shield. Scooter gaped, utterly thrilled, as the colourful hero hurled the Jap's frowning head at the brown-uniformed Nazi guards and then set upon them with savage force, caving in one's skull with his great, gloved fist and crushing another's throat with the edge of his shield. In no time there was no one left in the bunker apart from hero and villain, a result at which Captain America laughed uproariously while Adolph Hitler wept with despair and fear.

Scooter laughed too when his hero tore Hitler's right arm out of the socket, leaving only dangling red strips of seeping tissue, and then repeated the procedure with the Nazi leader's other arm, and then both legs. Now merely a brown-coated torso with a shrieking, babbling head, Hitler begged for death. Except it was not Adolph Hitler at all, as Scooter previously thought, but Margie's father, the Reverend, who screeched at the hero, mad with pain and agony.

That's strange, Scooter thought. *I didn't know the rev was a Nazi. That ain't no good.*

And when Captain America removed his mask to stare down his nemesis during the latter's last moments of life, Scooter was pleased as punch to realize that the hero was himself.

Ж

Brimming with emotion, Margie Shannon fought back tears while she watched the story of her life performed by dolls. They were not at all like her old dolls in the attic, with frilly little dresses and pink cheeks and blonde curls; these dolls were ugly in their simplicity, poorly stitched together and entirely lacking any identifying features. Also unlike Margie's childhood playthings, the dolls on screen moved all on their own.

They reenacted key moments from her sixteen years in a pasteboard house. She saw a mama doll give birth to a baby doll (the shot vividly recalled the startling last scene of *Motherhood Too Soon*). There was a reverend doll speaking to a congregation of dolls, all packed awkwardly into pasteboard pews; the smallest doll was at the front, rapt with her father's fiery speech. Later, the reverend doll and little Margie doll stood shaking around a well made of paper—a trio of other dolls was straining to lift out the doll that had fallen to the bottom with a length of thread. They would never know if it was an accident or suicide.

From then on, Margie watched through blurry eyes as the reverend doll grew more and more restless and isolated in the wake of his wife's death; she saw her own avatar grow to the size of the other dolls and sneak furtive cigarettes behind the pasteboard church and drugstore; she forced herself to watch a greasy, fat doll called Marcus Nims flail on top of her doll on a Sunday afternoon after worship. All these things she remembered with bitter tears and quivering lips. What happened next, however, was wholly new to her.

Her father's doll, sitting cross legged on the church's cellar floor, a small hole dug out of the dirt there. He held something in his fingerless hand, some sort of charm or amulet. The amulet was caked with dirt and rusty with age and neglect, but its shape was discernible enough. The doll's faceless head turned one way and then another, taking in all sides of the strange artifact, before standing up and slipping into the open stitching in his side. He had something, Margie knew, something to change the way he perceived his world and the world beyond it. Something that made his status as Litchfield's resident clergyman a joke known only to him, a private joke at which he spent most of his time inwardly laughing even when he cried. And whenever he was alone with his secret talisman, he pressed it tightly to the side of his head and listened carefully to whatever it was only he could hear.

The sigil seemed to glow when the doll did this; its dull grey burned gold as though it lay directly in the sunlight. Margie could not hear what it told him, but for some reason unknown to her she imagined it was something like *Your life is a lie; you are praying to no one.*

Something she had always known, and hoped her father would never figure out.

Then, a curious scene: the doll representing Reverend Jim Shannon seated at a pasteboard table in what Margie took to be their kitchen, bending over a tangled nest of cloth and thread and dried herbs—the doll was constructing dolls, the latter doll-sized to him after the manner of Russian matryoshka figures. Upon stitching one up to completion, he produced the amulet, which he rubbed over the body of the doll like some mystic salve. Margie expected something incredible to follow—or something horrifying—but the reverend doll merely set the figure down on the paper table and began working on a new one. She could not make sense of it.

Not until, a moment later, he touched the sigil to this new doll as he had the first and then ripped the head clean off of it. The picture cut to the pasteboard drugstore, where the Margie doll surreptitiously dragged on a tiny toy cigarette and exhaled smoke made of cotton. She leaned up against the wall, one jointless leg curled back, and in an instant her head popped off, leaving a trail of bright red yarn dangling down from the open neck.

Margie yelped, and as if her cry caused it, the screen cut abruptly to a crackly old silent film, sepia in colour, of some magician performing hackneyed tricks on a ramshackle stage. She snapped back to reality, to the dark auditorium where Scooter sat beside her, hugging his knees and giggling like an infant. More alarming than this was the woman in the fourth row who was screaming her head off, something no one but Margie seemed to notice at all. The dark-haired woman behind the screaming lunatic was sobbing into her hands while the cop—she could not remember his name, but knew to avoid him—pounded the seats on either side of him with his fists and grunted every breath.

Others behaved erratically, as well; in fact, nearly all of the dozen or so people who freckled the theatre's seats either wept, yelled, or acted as though they were terribly frightened. As far as Margie could tell, Scooter was the only one having a good time. Despite the clamour made by the increasingly agitated audience, he kept on snickering and rocking back and forth on his seat. She furrowed her brow at the pressure building in her head and shook Scooter's knee.

"Scooter? Scoot?"

Without taking his eyes from the screen or altering his gleeful expression, Scooter slapped her hand away, even as he squealed with delight at the second-rate magician . . . or whatever it was he thought he was seeing. Because it occurred to her then that nobody else among the suddenly lunatic filmgoers around her would have seen the strange little melodrama of her life in dolls—only her. What *they* saw was something only each of them could say, their own private delight, in Scooter's case, or mind-destroying horror, as with the still shrieking woman in the fourth row.

Margie got to her feet and edged along the row until she reached the lighted aisle. From there she could take in the whole crazy scene, including the screaming woman who had stopped screaming but was now disrobing in front of her fellow lunatics.

She tried calling out to Scooter one last time, and as she expected he paid her no mind. Nobody in that theatre would have; they were each in their own private cells, trapped and isolated by what they saw, or thought they saw. Margie swallowed hard and ran for the doors.

She needed to get back home; she needed to know what her daddy had done.

CHAPTER FIFTEEN

The midnight show ended just before one o'clock in the morning, whereupon the screen went dark and the auditorium lights blinked back on. The audience, all but Margie Shannon, sat still and dazed for several minutes thereafter, groggy as if having just woken up, and eventually staggered out to the lobby, one by one, and then out to the dark, humid street. Dean Mortimer walked to the sheriff's office rather than going clear out to his house, where he slept in one of the two holding cells. Georgia May Bagby drove back to her house; she ran over a raccoon along the way, though she was not consciously aware of it, nor was she aware of the fact that she was stark naked. Scooter only vaguely wondered what became of his date during his long walk home—his thoughts were more focused on the notion that Litchfield may be in trouble, that the war in Europe might have spilled over and infected his own hometown. It occurred to him, hazily, that there was a conspiracy afoot that was rooted in Reverend Shannon and his bullshit church, but that is was much broader than that. It occurred to Scooter that probably his parents were deeply involved.

So Scooter went home, arriving just after two o'clock, and made a beeline for his father's gun cabinet. He mulled over his choices for a few minutes and settled upon the Browning Auto-5, which was the old man's preferred fowling weapon. He loaded it with three shells from the cabinet's bottom drawer, made sure one was in the chamber, and climbed the stairs to the second story. John and Mary Beth Carew were sound asleep in their queen-sized bed when he entered their bedroom and switched on the lamp. John did not stir, but Mary Beth cracked one eye open and mumbled something incomprehensible. Scooter figured it was probably German, which was enough to seal his mother's fate. He raised the shotgun, bracing the butt against the meat of his shoulder, and blew her head apart from three feet away. The headboard was spattered with red-black blood and lumps of skull and brain, some of which struck John on the side of his face. He was awake by then, scrambling out of the bed before he even knew what had been the source of the thunderous report. Then his bleary eyes found what remained of his wife and John Carew let loose a long, shrill scream. He turned to look upon his only son, who turned the shotgun upon him, and said, "Scoots?"

Scooter shot him in the gut, knocking his father back with a spray of buckshot and blood, and then calmly walked over to where the old man fell before expending the last shell, which obliterated John's neck and nearly severed the head completely. Sniffing the air, his nostrils stung from gunpowder and the tangy, faintly metallic odour of his parents' blood. He wiped his nose on his sleeve, laid the Browning down beside his father's mangled corpse, and went back down the hall to take a cold bath.

His skin shrank in the chilly water, budded with goose pimples. From the window above the tub, he heard a breeze pick up, rustling the leafy branches on the trees in the yard. Briefly, Scooter wondered if a storm was coming.

He dreamt that night of righteous vengeance.

CHAPTER SIXTEEN

Theodora stood in the middle of the street for a long time and cried. She felt both lost and trapped, as though contained in an invisible box, a showman's cage. She knew that she could move if she wanted, that there was nothing from which she needed to escape, but she knew just as well there was no place to escape to. Home was an anathema, a faraway place of hurt and lonesomeness, black magic and children's bones. Little ugly dolls that killed people when she touched them . . .

She was stumbling down the street before she realized it, moving east for no reason at all, struggling to get her thoughts in order. She felt drunk. Or brain damaged. Her ankle screamed at her, carrying waves of hot pain through the telegraph wire of her nervous system to her fluttering brain. Though she was less convinced now that the bones were broken, every ungainly step still agonized.

When the first blast of cold air arced down from above and chilled her, she figured she must have been mistaken, that she hadn't left the Palace at all—she was still smack in the middle of Barker Davis's midnight show. It was, after all, the middle of July, and the sweat was rapidly cooling on her brow. A dream, a chimera induced by the picture. She walked a little faster, more assured of herself, and braced herself for the next scene.

But nothing happened. Apart from the quickly dropping temperature, the street was silent and still, the singing insects the only sound she heard. Half a block ahead of her, the Litchfield Valley Hotel loomed sorrowfully, a mid-rate hotel on the fast track to a no-rate flophouse. Slowing her gait, she approached warily as if coming upon a haunted house. Somewhere in the back of her muddled mind she was aware that this was not only Jojo's hotel, but the place where that poor man died so horribly . . . where she had inadvertently killed him.

Though she strode slowly, Theodora approached the cracked, circular drive in front of the hotel a few minutes later. Saffron light glowed from the front doors like honey, intensifying when a young coloured man in a bellhop's uniform opened one of them and held it open as he fixed a kind gaze on her. She froze halfway up the drive and looked at him.

"You coming in, ma'am?" Charles asked.

"I—" she started, preparing to explain that she was merely passing by. In mid-thought, she realized that wasn't true; she was precisely where she needed to be. "Excuse me, but isn't this where . . . I mean, does a man named Jojo Walker work here?"

The bellhop smiled and laughed. "Work here? Why, he lives here."

The smile was a kind and easy-going one, but Theodora paused, her uncertainty about the world around her nagging at her, waiting for the bellhop to sprout fangs or transform into her father. These things did not happen. The young man only raised his eyebrows and let the smile melt a bit.

"Are you all right?"

"What? Oh, yes. Yes, I'm all right. I wonder if I might come in and see Mr. Walker."

"Of course you can come in," Charles answered, more than a little surprised at the woman's humility before him, "though I dunno if Jojo's 'round. I guess he's off tonight. Tell you the truth, I ain't seen him at all."

Theodora nodded and glided through the door Charles held open. A cold draft followed her into the stuffy lobby and she shivered. She asked him, "Do you feel that?"

"Feel what, ma'am?"

"Nothing."

He let the door swing shut and moved around her toward the cashier's cage. A dark, bearded man sat inside the cage, still as a mannequin.

"Say, Mr. Thomas? This here lady's looking for Jojo; you seen him 'round?"

The man Charles called Mr. Thomas leaned closer the mesh and studied Theodora. She watched him as he did so and felt mildly uncomfortable beneath his gaze, particularly when a phlegmy laugh spilled out from somewhere in his wiry black beard.

"Looks a might too pale for Jojo Walker, don't you reckon?"

Charles frowned and gazed down at his shoes, avoiding the look of shock that crossed over Theodora's face. It did not, however, last long. She was not entirely sure what drew her from the bizarre show at the Palace to this less than desirable hotel, but she knew it had everything to do with Jojo, which was enough for her to feel strangely protective of her new friend. Her brow creased and shoulders jumped as she stomped across the lobby to the cage. Startled, Charles stepped away and passively observed.

"Now you listen to me, you laughing hyena," she snarled. "I didn't come here to suffer slights about my propriety or Mr. Walker's private life, neither of which are any of your damn business. I happen to be a personal friend of his and I've come to see him about a private matter, and if you think you're going to have a nasty little laugh at either of our expenses, you're sorely mistaken, Mr. Thomas." She pronounced *mister* like it was the filthiest word in the language.

For his part, Mr. Thomas gaped and stuttered before he managed to collect himself enough to ask, "And just who might you be?"

"As it happens, I don't have to answer to you. That's why I'm standing out here and you're in that lousy little cage like that baboon you are. So shut your mouth unless you want to come on out here and say something directly to my face, you hear?"

Charles covered his mouth with his hand and turned toward the wall. Theodora saw this and decided that she liked him.

Mr. Thomas sighed heavily and jerked a thumb over his shoulder. "Door right over there. That's his office. Have at it, lady."

"Thank you," she said with a sardonic smile.

Taking leave of the ugly little man in the cage, Theodora went directly to the half-hidden door he'd indicated and looked to Charles, who nodded. She knocked. There was no answer. She knocked again and the results were the same.

"I didn't think he was in his office," Charles said. "On a night off, there ain't no telling where Jojo might be. Sometimes he goes all the way down to Hot Springs to bet on the horses."

She narrowed her eyes, remembering the tickets Jojo gave the moon-faced "doctor" at the Palace. "He's not in Hot Springs," she explained. "He was with me less than two hours ago. He went to . . . see a man. And he didn't come back."

"Maybe he's still with that man," the bellhop suggested.

"What's your name, young man?"

"Charles, ma'am."

"Charles, I think our Jojo is in trouble."

He stiffened up, his face registering concern and puzzlement. His eyes trailed from Theodora to Mr. Thomas and back again. A sheen of sweat glistened on his forehead, which Theodora could not understand for the life of her. She was chilled to the bone.

"Where were you?" he asked. "When Jojo went to see the man, I mean."

"The Palace Theater, just up the street."

"You think he's in real trouble?"

"Yes, I do."

Charles pursed his lips and swept the round red cap from his head.

"Mr. Thomas," he called out without turning around, "this nice lady needs some help and I aim to give it to her."

"Mind your place, Charles," Thomas warned.

"Mind your *ass*, Mr. Thomas," Charles said as he strutted over to the door to open it one last time.

Theodora's eyes popped wide as the former bellhop gestured toward the world outside and said, "After you, ma'am."

"I'm Theodora," she said on her way through the door. "Theodora Cavanaugh."

"Pleased to meet you, Ms. Cavanaugh."

"It's *missus*," she corrected, "but please call me Theodora."

Charles laughed.

"You must be good friends with Jojo," he explained. "You're the only two white folks in Litchfield that ever told me to use their first names."

He shook his head as he chuckled and dragged a sleeve across his face to divest it of sweat. Half-consciously Theodora touched her own face—it was tight and cold.

Charles led the way, and they walked side by side back to the Palace.

X

The theatre was dark and locked up. Under the cover of the triangular marquee, not even the moonlight illumined their faces. Charles cupped his hands on either side of his eyes and peered through the glass.

"I don't think there's no one in there."

"Russ never shut down this quick. There's a lot to do, I guess. Machines to shut off and receipts to tabulate. Cleaning up."

"Maybe they was in a hurry."

"A hurry for what? It's the middle of the night."

"I seen all sorts of crazy things people do in the middle of the night. You wouldn't believe it."

"I'd believe practically anything tonight."

"Let's go around back."

"What for?"

In lieu of answering, she limped around to the side of the theatre, the pain registering less and less, and vanished into the shadows. Charles followed.

Behind the building was pitch black night, and he had to feel along the rough brick wall to make his way. He heard a jarring crunch, metal against metal, and gasped.

"It's just me," Theodora said from the darkness. "Sometimes the back door gets stuck, doesn't lock. Kids sneak in all the time on account of it, though I doubt Russ ever caught onto that."

"Not tonight, though."

"No, not tonight."

Charles went cautiously forward, his hands out in front of him, until his foot struck something soft on the ground. He stopped, bent over to prod at it with his finger, felt cloth and stuffing. He picked it up and described its shape with his fingertips, which was vaguely like a person.

"Ms. . . . er, Theodora," he said, "if you don't much mind my asking, what sort of trouble are you and Jojo into here?"

He heard her exhale loudly while he absentmindedly played with the doll he found.

"I'm not really sure, Charles. Something bad, I think. Something my husband brought to our town, or at least allowed to stay." She followed his voice, touched him on the shoulder. "Come on."

Together they went back to the street where the weak moonlight fought a losing battle with the cloak of night. Still, they could make out one another's outlines, and Theodora could see the doll in Charles's hand.

She gave a frightened shout and swatted it out of his hand.

"Where did you find that?" she yelled.

"I . . . it was on the ground . . . back there, behind the theatre. Gee, I'm sorry. I didn't know—"

"No, you didn't. I apologize for sounding harsh, but . . ."

Her voice hitched into a soft sob and Charles shifted his weight from one foot to the other, at a total loss.

"What is it?" he asked, peering at the featureless doll on the pavement.

"It's . . ." She cut herself off, made a smacking sound with her lips. "Do you believe in magic, Charles?"

"Magic?" he said, punctuating it with a curt laugh.

"I do," came a small voice from the darkness.

Charles instinctively put himself between Theodora and the owner of the small voice. "Who's that?" he demanded to know.

"My name is Margie Shannon. I'm the pastor's daughter."

"Wha—what are you doing out so late, Margie?" Theodora asked, her tone oddly matronly.

"I saw you at the midnight show," Margie said. "What did you see?"

The cold air bit at Theodora's neck and she felt her spine shift in her back. She stepped away from Charles so that she could see Margie in the moonlight.

"My father," she said. "I saw my father."

Margie gave a sad, quiet laugh. "Funny. I saw mine, too."

Charles said, "Wait a second, what's going on here?"

Margie looked at him, and then at Theodora.

"I think you two better come with me," she said.

CHAPTER SEVENTEEN

Turning over in the damp, cool dark, Jojo's head sank into a hole in the dirt floor. Loose earth crumbled into his ears and nose, all loamy and warm and rich. He snuffled and coughed, jerked his shoulders to free himself from the hole, and sharp pain ignited in his skull, neck and back. He'd been worked over in more ways than one. The world tilted and he rolled with it, unable to determine up from down, just falling away from the hole into open space until he jammed up against something metal that clanged and smelled of gasoline. A quiet moan escaped his lips and he raised his hands to his aching face. It was, for the first time in years, a dog's face, concealed by coarse, matted hair. He moaned again, louder this time.

He wondered, somewhat desperately, how long he had been down there. More than a week would have had to have passed for his hair to grow so long, unless it was another one of the magician's tricks. Barker Davis, the showman, he remembered. He'd put him in that awful cage again. . . .

Again?

Jojo planted his palms on the dirt floor and heaved himself up to his knees. His head swam; his skull felt like it was full of sloshing fluid. An intense heat ignited in the pit of his stomach and he lurched, vomited into the hole in the floor. *Not my best moment*, he thought ruefully.

Get it together, Walker, he scolded himself. *Fucking* move.

He spit bile on the floor, wiped his face on his shirtsleeve (*Where's my jacket?*) and staggered up to a hunched, standing position. The floor canted and he spread his legs, anchoring his feet. Something jagged scraped against his head and he grabbed at it: a bare light bulb hanging from the ceiling, broken. He stumbled away from it, his hands out in the pitch. A dry and dusty shelf fell into his hands. He felt along the edge and surface of it, touched at the shapes of mason jars and rusty gardening tools. A burlap bag and a tangle of frayed twine. *A shed, or a garage*, he concluded. *Or a cellar*. The mystery was solved in the next moment when Jojo heard creaking steps a few feet above him—dust rained down from the ceiling wherever the footsteps fell. He ducked his head to keep the dust from his eyes and stabbed a hand into his trouser pocket. A soft laugh escaped his mouth: for once, he actually had a book of matches on him.

Striking one against the strip on the back of the book, Jojo pinched the end of the match and held the tiny, wavering flame up. It made only a tiny globe of light, and he was nervous about getting it too close to the smell of gasoline on the floor. Still, he got close enough to the shelves to see the mason jars and their murky contents—some ancient preserves, he guessed—along with a spade and a pair of gardening shears and all the other things he'd felt in the dark. He also saw a book, leather-bound, brown and cracked. The match singed his fingertips and he waved it out before striking another.

The book was a thin volume, the pages terraced from tears and substantial wear. The binding was solid, though, despite its apparent age. Jojo reached for it, took it from the shelf. Unlike everything else in the cellar, the volume was not coated in dust: it had seen recent use.

He was momentarily afraid it would crumble in his hands. It didn't. He held the match close as he examined the cover, which was bereft of any text or title—there was only a symbol, printed in chipped, fading gold. The symbol was meaningless to him. He jammed the book in his armpit and dropped the now dead match to the floor. With the next one he found the rickety-looking wooden steps, at the top of which was a closed door. A quick survey of the surrounding walls revealed no other means of egress. Jojo made for the steps and began to climb.

Halfway up he thought he could hear someone crying on the other side of the door. At the top he was sure of it. He tried the knob, which was as rusty as the tools down on the shelves, but it was frozen in position, locked. The crying went on; decidedly male, Jojo decided. He blew out the match and flicked it out into the darkness.

"Why?" the weeping man asked someone, or no one.

Jojo clenched his jaw, tightened his grasp on the book, and rammed his shoulder against the door as hard as he could. The wood splintered and the knob came away, banging noisily against the jamb as bright light flooded his eyes and blinded him.

Ж

Theodora and Margie talked about dolls as they walked west along Main. Charles did not understand half of what they said and he didn't believe the other half. Mostly he just wished they had a car. All the same, he kept up.

"Do you reckon your daddy made my Russ's doll?" Theodora asked. She had already explained to the girl everything that had happened with the strange artifact, including what she found inside of it and what she and Jojo suspected it may have done.

"I don't know," Margie answered. "For all I know, he never made any of 'em. What I saw on that movie screen was only what I was supposed to, ain't it? I mean, somebody wants me to think daddy made 'em, but that don't mean much."

"But it's the only lead we have."

"Lead? Well—ain't you the little junior detective, Mrs. Cavanaugh?"

"Call me Nora Charles."

"Fine, and you can call me Asta."

Both women laughed, the sort of laughter endemic to the exhausted and afraid. Theodora shot a glance back at Charles, whose mild smile was apparent in the moonlight. His face dripped sweat. He had taken his red jacket off and slung it over one arm; his shirt was darkened with patches of moisture. The women's playfulness calmed his otherwise frayed nerves to a degree, but he knew it belied a deeper apprehension on their part. Something dangerous awaited them, but he was not about to abandon Jojo's friends when they needed him.

It was a long way yet to the church, which gave Charles the

opportunity to steel himself—he was completely unprepared, however, for the sound of marching feet coming from Franklin Street. Theodora and Margie were still cutting up—gallows humour, he supposed—and did not see the silhouetted figures appear from the side street, moving in time like a military exercise. He opened his mouth and tried to speak, but only a scratchy squeak came out. His eyes fixed on the dozen or so approaching people, Charles lunged forth and touched Theodora on the shoulder.

She stopped talking mid-sentence and turned to see what he wanted; instantly she stopped, her attention fixed on the coming people.

"Who are they?" Charles asked.

Margie walked on a few more steps before she too stopped to see what was happening. A multitude of heads bobbed up and down as the gathering crowd drew nearer. A cloud shifted away and a shaft of white moonlight illumined some of their faces. Margie recognized Phyllis Gates among them, her high, pinned up hair a dead giveaway.

"Phyllis?"

The others saw familiar faces, as well: Charles was shocked to see Jake among the shambling throng, dressed in a surgeon's white coat, and Theodora yawped upon realizing it was her husband who appeared to lead the brigade. She leapt to the forefront of their three person phalanx and stared Russ down.

"Russell Cavanaugh," she boomed, shouting at her husband for the first time in over a decade. "What in the world are you doing wandering the streets at this hour with these people?"

"What did you see?" he seethed through clenched, grinning teeth.

"What did you see?" Phyllis parroted, her glassy eyes trained on Margie.

Charles stepped back, glaring at Jake.

"What did you see, Charles?" Jake asked.

"Hey man, I wasn't even *there*," Charles hollered as he curled his hands into fists.

Theodora stiffened, her face a mask of rage and fear combined. The entourage continued on, shuffling toward them, Russ ever at the head.

"What did you see?" he repeated, over and over. "What did you see?"

"Muh . . . Mrs. Cavanaugh," Margie stammered as she began to shake.

"Charles," Theodora snapped. "Go get the doll."

"The doll?"

"Just get it!"

Flustered, Charles sped back up the street from where they had come. As the night swallowed him up, Margie pressed in close to Theodora's back.

"What do they want?"

"I don't know," Theodora said. "And I don't think I want to know."

"Is it real?"

"Shhh."

She reached behind her, grabbed Margie by the waist and stepped backward several paces with her. By then the steadily approaching group was close enough for Theodora to clearly make out the bloodstains spattering nearly all of them.

"We're changing," said a fat man Margie recognized from the drugstore.

Russ regarded his wife quizzically, as though she were the one with blood on her clothes rather than him. He cocked his head to one side and his solid black eyes glinted in the weak light.

"We're changing, Theodora," he said softly. Several others repeated it in staccato fashion.

"Change, then," she barked back at him. "Just leave me out of it."

The girl Margie identified as Phyllis stepped out of line, walked quickly ahead of Russ and bared her teeth in a snarl meant to be a smile. To Margie, she said, "Look what I can do."

The high-haired girl had barely finished speaking before she threw both arms behind her back and jutted her bony shoulders forward; the rounded knobs of her shoulders cricked and popped loose, enabling her to twist her arms around almost three hundred and sixty degrees. She tied them behind her back like loose straps and lurched forward, pushing her ribs out and lifting one of her legs up and over her head at an impossible angle. To Margie she looked like she had been struck by a train, yet she hopped around in a circle like that, all twisted and broken.

Phyllis giggled—a shrill, high-pitched titter that made Margie's skin crawl.

Theodora's skin crawled too, though largely from the still dropping temperature. She hugged herself and backed up a little more, her eyes pinned on the contorting girl. She could not so much as look away even when she heard the slapping steps hurtling toward her from the right. Phyllis continued to twist and snap into increasingly gut-churning positions, but at least the others had stopped advancing to allow her the gruesome performance. Russ seemed to watch her more closely than anyone. A thin rope of saliva unfurled past his lips and dangled precipitously.

"Maybe we should run," Margie weakly suggested.

"We have to wait for Charles," Theodora reminded her.

"I'm here," he rasped, short of breath. "I got the doll."

He jabbed it at Theodora, who accepted it with evident distaste. It was identical to the one she found in Russ's pocket in every respect, at least externally. As to the fetish's internal contents, she had yet to see.

Accordingly, Theodora seized the doll tightly, a fist gripping each of its arms, and yanked with all of her strength. The coarse fabric limbs tore loose and the rest of the doll dropped to the street. At the same instant, Jake screamed.

)(

Wood scraped against tile and something crashed as the sob-wet voice cried out, "What in hell?"

Jojo rubbed his eyes with the knuckle of his thumb and groped blindly forward, anticipating a fight. Instead, the crying man scuttled away from him, knocking over every stick of furniture that got in his way in the process.

"Wha—what are you?" the man bawled.

"Can't you tell?" Jojo groaned. "I'm the goddamn wolfman."

The man whimpered. Jojo sighed.

"Christ, it's . . . I'm not the wolfman. Who's there, anyhow? Who are you?"

He fell back against a wall and skirted the periphery to where the light was not shining so directly at his face. His light blindness ebbed and he began to make out the form of the man cowering before him.

"Don't . . . don't," he blubbered.

"Look, I already told you. It was a joke, all right? It's a fucking congenital disorder, that's all. . . ."

The indistinct form collapsed in a heap on the floor as Jojo's eyes adjusted to the light. He rushed forward and knelt down beside the man.

"Say, aren't you the pastor?"

"I don't know why I did it," Shannon babbled. "I never thought—I mean, if God isn't real, then nothing is, right?"

"You're not making any sense, Rev," Jojo said, running a fur-backed hand over his shaggy face.

"Was it a test? Did he send you?"

"Did who send me?"

Shannon's eyes popped wide and tears spilled down his cheeks, dripping off his jaw in fat dollops. "The Devil," he said conspiratorially.

"Aw, Christ," Jojo said. "I don't suppose you've got any hooch in this shack, have you?"

Shannon wiped his face and shook his head. "I wouldn't put a thief in my mouth to steal my mind, demon."

"Swell," Jojo said.

Jake jerked and flew up into the air, several feet above the ground. His face twisted like his head was in a vice; he squeezed his eyes shut and screamed through clenched teeth. His arms stretched out on either side of him, pulled taut by an invisible force, and something cracked loudly like a gunshot. Margie cried out and Charles muttered a half-silent prayer. The man in the air emitted a deep, mournful moan as dark spots, black in the moonlight, bloomed on his erstwhile white coat. His body shuddered violently and his hands stretched far beyond the cuffs of his sleeves as he screamed louder and more horribly by the second. A moment later his arms shot off in either direction as though blown off by some great explosion, and he sank back to the street below, bleeding out into a great black puddle.

"Oh, oh," Charles moaned. "Oh, Jake."

"Forget it," Theodora reprimanded him sharply. "That wasn't Jake. Not anymore."

The others gathered around the dismembered body slumped on the macadam, forming a misshapen semicircle of mindless mourners. One by one they began to tremble, their shoulders rocking and hands jerking wildly. Theodora glanced down at the split remains of the doll at her feet, at the familiar innards of dry spices and bits of white bone. As if he was reading her mind, Russ snapped his head around and fixed his black gaze on her. He stretched his mouth open as wide as his jaw would permit and spewed a long, crackling groan. Foamy spittle formed on his lips as the groan went on for an impossibly long time, far past the point his lungs should have deflated. The contortionist, Phyllis Gates, straightened up and stared in the same direction as Russ, and she mimicked the same awful groan. In a matter of minutes—which, to the terrified trio in the street, seemed like hours—every one of the throng ended up facing them and groaning deep, low groans that seemed to come from someplace much deeper than their own trunks.

Margie squeezed Theodora's arm tight enough to bruise the flesh and squeaked, "We need to go, Mrs. Cavanaugh. We need to go right now."

"I'm not sure we can," she answered sullenly. "Not without a hell of a lot more dolls, anyway."

"We can run," Charles offered.

"So can they."

In fact, they were already advancing again, albeit slowly. Their horrible groaning kept on without break or pause, not even to take a breath. Whatever they were, whatever had happened to them or been done to them, Theodora was absolutely certain they could no longer be classified as human beings.

As far as she was concerned, she was a widow now. Russell Cavanaugh was dead.

"Just standing here don't make no sense," Charles said sternly, snapping her back to attention.

Theodora nodded rapidly, her chest rising and falling as if in anticipation of the hard run ahead of her. "Right," she said. "Let's go."

Margie led the way, wasting no time. She took off in a hard sprint, her shoes smacking the pavement, and both Charles and Theodora followed close behind. Russ bellowed angrily, flailed his arms and took off after them. The remaining members of his frightful entourage followed suit, leaving Jake behind in a pool of his own blood.

Theodora hadn't run far before her chest started to burn and feel much too tight, and she did not have to look back to know their pursuers were gaining ground. The pain in her ankle seemed to have spread out across the foot and up along her calf like poison moving slowly through her bloodstream. She bit her bottom lip and did her level best to ignore it. What air she managed to suck in with her short, desperate breaths was ice cold and stung her lungs like tiny needles. The chilled air burned her eyes and numbed her cheeks. Behind her, Russ moaned and screamed as he rapidly closed the distance between them. She knew she did not have long now, but she aimed to make what seconds were left to her count. Pumping her arms like pistons, she drove herself forward with her last ounces of energy, her final reserves. She never even heard the squealing tires or the roaring engine over the pulsing of her own blood in her ears.

Charles, conversely, twisted at the waist as he sped down the street and caught sight of the wildly swerving headlamps. He cried, "Look!"

The automobile careened toward them and when it was close enough for Charles to notice the bulbous roof light on top, he spread his arms and hooked Margie and Theodora around their waists to sweep them out of the speeding car's path. The police car jerked to the right as the three of them fell into a tumble on the grass beside the road and plowed purposefully into the scrambling horde. Bodies smashed against the grill, rolled up over the hood and windscreen, flew into the air with limp arms and legs. Blood washed over the headlamps so that they burned an angry red.

Half of the horde was sprawled out on the street, broken and twisted out of shape, when the police car growled down the street and abruptly spun around for a second pass. Theodora lifted herself up from the grass and watched Russ shake his arms like an enraged ape at the speeding automobile. He grunted and screeched, stamped his feet and screamed, *"You can't stop it! You can't stop HIM!"*

Less than a second later, the broad expanse of the police car's impenetrable Detroit steel pulverized Russ, collapsing his chest and driving him down and under the crushing tires. The car screeched to a halt, leaving a wide trail of slick black blood in its wake.

Margie broke into a fit of heaving sobs and Theodora squeezed her as though she was the girl's mother. The car idled where it stopped and the driver's side door opened. A few of the horde still loomed near, the fat man from the drugstore and Phyllis Gates among them. The first thing to come out of the police car was the barrel of a 10-gauge shotgun. Sheriff Ernie Rich followed, grasping the gun like a man on a mission with a snarling face to match. He turned the weapon on the fat man, who waddled rapidly toward him.

"Stop right there, Finn," Rich yelled. "If there's any part of you left in there, listen to me, man. I don't want to put you down but I'll do what I have to, you hear?"

Finn kept coming. He still wore the long white apron he usually wore at the drugstore, which was now spattered with the blood of his dead compatriots. He threw his head back and let loose an ear-splitting wail as he pin-wheeled his arms and came on twice as fast.

Ernie Rich proved himself to be a man of his word. With a shake of his head and a deeply furrowed brow, he drew a bead on Finn and blew a hole in the fat man's chest big enough to push a glazed ham through. No sooner than Finn slammed against the street, Phyllis was up and scrabbling madly toward the sheriff, shrieking and spitting, clawing furiously at the air. The next thunderous blast took off the left side of her head in a gruesome red-black burst. Rich did not bother to wait for the remaining two to come after him; with grim determination he ejected the spent shells and reloaded as he marched over the dead and dying and took aim at a reedy little man with wispy blonde hair and the complexion of a corpse. *Hershal*, he thought as he squeezed the trigger and sent the little man spinning. *His name was Hershal—sold me my shoes.*

The last of the horde was an older coloured man with stark white hair and stooped shoulders. He stood in Russ Cavanaugh's blood and viscera, staring sorrowfully at the approaching sheriff. Rich recognized this man, too: he had been a tenant farmer back in the day, before Sims Dailey sold off his land and hung himself in the attic. Briefly, the lawman wondered what became of the sharecropper and his kin when they lost the lease, but the reverie was short-lived. The old man raised his trembling hands and seized two handfuls of his own hair, which he tore out at the roots.

"You cain't stop 'im," the man said, grinning a toothless grin. "We seen things. We changin'."

Rich kept the 10-gauge trained on the old man and wished he could remember his name. He figured he'd have a better shot at keeping the old guy calm if he used his name, but it just wouldn't come to him—far too many years had passed since last they crossed paths.

"You fixing to run up on me, too?" he asked instead.

"It don't have to be like that," the old man said, still holding on to his handfuls of hair. "You can change too, if'n you want to. You just got to see. You want to see, Mr. Sheriff?"

"You ain't got nothing I want to see, fella. Whyn't you just show me the palms of your hands and keep real still, all right?"

"But he wants to *show* you, Sheriff. He wants you to *see*."

Rich's hands were slick with sweat despite the incredible cold snap, but he maintained a firm grasp on the shotgun. "Just do like I say, fella. Palms up."

The old man opened his mouth, stretching his lips to their utmost limit, and opened his hands. White tufts sprinkled down and floated away.

"Okay," Rich said, "Here's what we're gonna do—"

But he did not get to tell the old man what they were going to do. Instead, he was interrupted by the keening screech that erupted from the man's gaping mouth, an impossible, wholly inhuman siren. Startled, Rich jerked as the old man curled his hands into talon-like claws and fell into a stumbling run.

"Stop!" Rich yelled.

The old man did not stop. Rich gritted his teeth and fired. At six feet away, the old man's head came apart like an overripe melon. Rich turned away and squeezed his eyes shut. A shiver worked its way through his body that didn't come from the cold. When he opened his eyes again, a pair of figures stood up in the grass beside the road. Rich spun around and pointed the shotgun at them, suddenly nervous that there was only one shell and no time to reload if they both came screaming at him. Instead, both figures threw up their hands and a male voice cried, "Don't shoot!"

"Who's there?" the sheriff shouted. "Speak up!"

"Ch—Charles Day, sir! My name is Charles Day! And this here's Theodora Cavanaugh, Russell Cavanaugh's wife!"

Rich balked. "I just ran Russ Cavanaugh down," he called back. "Killed him. You aim to do something foolish, Mrs. Cavanaugh?"

"No, I don't," Theodora said. "I aim to thank you, Sheriff. Those . . . *people* . . . were like to have murdered us."

Gradually, Ernie Rich let the barrel of his shotgun down until it was even with his leg. He squinted into the dark and said, "Who all you got there with you?"

"Me, Charles, and Margie Shannon," Theodora said.

"The preacher's kid?"

"That's right," Margie said, standing up.

"I think I need to have a word with your daddy, Ms. Shannon," Rich told her.

Margie expelled a heavy sigh. "I think we all do," she said.

※

Jojo handed the shaken man a mug of coffee from his own cupboard. It was instant, but it was all Shannon had. The reverend accepted the steaming mug with a nod of thanks.

"Please excuse me," he said solemnly as Jojo sat down across the table from him. "It was not my intention to insult or offend you. I was already in a—well, a troubled state of mind."

Jojo sipped at his own cup and made a face of displeasure that he hoped, for once, was masked by the coat of hair covering his features. "It's all right," he said. "I guess it can be pretty startling. Normally I shave two or three times a day. It's been a strange day, though."

"You said it," Shannon agreed. He gulped at the sour coffee and didn't make a face.

Jojo asked, "Mind if I smoke?" even as he lit a cigarette. He raised his bushy brow and sucked deeply at the filter. "I guess we should start from the beginning," he said.

Jim Shannon killed his coffee and exhaled loudly. He drummed his fingers on the tabletop and after a while muttered, "It's all my fault."

"How's that?"

"I lost my faith. I think I'm being punished. I think we're all being punished for my sin."

"That doesn't . . . I mean, I don't buy that, rev. I'm not a believer myself, not really. If that's all it takes, it could just as well be my fault."

"No, you don't understand."

"Okay: make me understand."

Shannon smiled sourly and reached for the packet of Old Golds in front of Jojo.

"Do you mind?" he asked.

"Go right ahead."

The reverend stabbed one in his mouth and ignited it. He inhaled and turned a light shade of green and coughed like a man dying of tuberculosis.

"I don't really smoke," he apologized when his breath returned.

"Could've fooled me," Jojo said.

"Hell, I've fooled everybody. I've been doing it for years—spewing all this garbage from the pulpit and laughing at the absurdity of it down inside. I'm a liar, Mr. Walker. A fraud."

"Did you ever believe any of it?"

"Absolutely," Shannon said, taking another drag. He was starting to get used to it. "When I was a boy, I thought I saw the Devil once. Or I saw *something*, had a sort of experience, I suppose you could say, and later when I talked to my granddad about it he laid it all out for me. I had met Satan himself, and the mean old bastard drew a fork in the road for me. He said I could take the easy way or the hard way. I always thought I opted for the hard way, the Lord's way. These last couple of years, though . . ."

"Forgive me, rev, but you're sort of talking in circles."

"I know I am. I don't know how else to talk. Empty platitudes and reassurances, that's all that's come out of this mouth in twenty years or more. I'll tell you, if the good people of this town honestly need me to tell them not to kill each other and rape their neighbours, then there's no hope, Mr. Walker. There's no hope at all."

Jojo expelled twin streams of smoke through his nostrils and gazed at the oily surface of the coffee in his mug. A shimmering reflection of a hairy face he had not seen since a different lifetime stared back at him. A lifetime he had somehow managed to forget altogether until Barker Davis took it upon himself to make him remember. Jojo swallowed and rolled his shoulders, working out the cricks from laying so long on the cellar floor.

"Tell me about Barker Davis," he said at length.

"I'm not sure what to say about him. We haven't met, but I think he came here because of me. Because of what I've done, and what I haven't done."

"Circles, rev."

"I'm sorry. I'll try to be more clear."

"Just give me the facts; tell me a story in chronological order."

Shannon laughed. "That's right—you used to work for Ernie Rich, didn't you? I'd forgotten."

"I didn't look like a monster movie reject then."

Shannon shook his head.

"Let me think," he said. "I expect it started around the same time you and Rich had your falling out, really. That's been about a year now, hasn't it?"

Jojo quietly agreed that it had.

"Yes," Shannon said, "a bad time all around. You got it the worst, I suppose, but a great deal of people had rough going around then."

Jojo narrowed his eyes. "How do you mean?"

"Hmm—you probably wouldn't have noticed other people's problems, not with so much tragedy raining down on your own head. But I'll give you the scorecard version:

"Russell Cavanaugh, the fellow who runs the Palace Theater? I gather he started drinking around then. That, and wailing on his poor wife. They both stopped coming to church, but a pastor hears a lot.

"And there was Tuck Arnold, whose wife ran out. Tuck was allegedly having relations with his register girl. . . ."

"Georgia May," Jojo said, frowning. He hadn't known that.

"Yes, that's her. Mrs. Arnold found out about it and simply up and left one day. I don't believe they ever positively identified the body they found out in the northern woods as her, but Tuck knew. Everybody knew. That poor woman went out there to die.

"Of course, there's Eddie Manning, who went off to fight in the war, and nobody's heard hide nor hair of him since. His mama doesn't speak anymore, I've heard. And Bradley Finn."

"Drugstore Finn? I just saw him the other day. Seemed as jolly as ever."

"He's a generally optimistic type, Finn. And he's had a year to get used to sleeping at the drugstore since his house burned to the ground."

"God."

"God's another thing," Shannon added. "Sometimes I think God left Litchfield a year ago. That's when my faith dried up and died, practically overnight, and a whole mess of other people, too. I have a core group of faithful congregants, old ladies mostly, but nothing like it was before. Maybe they only lost faith in me, but I'm sure it's more than that. With everything else in this sad, pathetic place, it *has* to be more. A dark cloud settled over Litchfield and it never went away. If you were to ask me, I'd tell you it never will."

Jojo tamped his smoke out and immediately lit another. "Bleak perspective."

"Just the way I see it, my friend. Life goes on—it always goes on—but that oily, black sludge keeps on bubbling up in the flower beds, if you'll forgive the metaphor."

"So what has any of that got to do with you?"

The reverend made a taut line of his mouth and scrunched his brow.

"Before any of those catastrophes happened, I found something. Something unusual, to say the least. I had been trimming the hedges around the church that morning and brought the tools back here, to the house. I keep them down in the cellar."

"I saw."

"I had quite the armload, and I must have stumbled at the bottom of the steps. The whole load of tools I was carrying went sailing, and the shears stabbed the dirt right in the centre of the floor. They couldn't have been more than a couple of inches in, hardly enough to support the weight of the rest of them, but sure enough those shears were standing straight up like a dousing rod. I worked around them, picking up every other tool and depositing them on their places on the shelves, and then

I just sat down on the ground and waited."

"Waited? For what?"

"I'm really not sure. For something to happen, maybe. Perhaps I just wanted to see if the shears would fall, something to prove that it was just a freak thing. But they remained quite firm. A few minutes later I even discovered that it wasn't easy to dislodge them. It reminded me of Excalibur, the way I had to jerk my back and shoulders to free the damn things."

"But you did."

"Yes, and I took up a fair amount of the floor in the process."

"That hole down there?"

"I dug it out some more, after I saw the gleam of the metal."

"Something buried there."

"Something buried there," Shannon agreed.

"What?"

The reverend cleared his throat and rose from his chair. "It's probably better that I show you. I won't be a moment."

Shannon vanished down a dark hallway, leaving Jojo alone in the cold, quiet kitchen. The cold came as something of a surprise to him; he did not expect a reverend to have the wherewithal to pump expensive cold air into his house. A cursory glance at the curtained kitchen windows surprised him even more: the curtains danced and floated from the frigid air passing through the open windows. He screwed up his face and started to get up for a closer look when Shannon returned from the hall, a shiny metal sculpture in his hands.

Returning to his chair opposite Jojo, Shannon held onto the object a moment longer before gently setting it down on the table between them. Jojo gripped the edge of the tabletop and leaned over for a better look. An inverted triangle with a pair of slashes cutting through it, its point splitting into curving loops with an ornate V resting between them. The burnished metal shone almost gold in the kitchen light.

"Okay," Jojo said. "What is it?"

"It took me months to find out for myself," the reverend said, keeping his eyes on the mysterious cipher. "I'd never seen anything like it. Eventually I mustered the courage to write a letter to a fellow I know in Little Rock, another pastor with a peculiar interest in arcane matters like this." Running the tip of his index finger over the intersecting lines of the symbol, Shannon continued: "I drew the symbol in pencil as best as I could and asked my friend if he could tell me anything about it. I couldn't believe how quickly his response came."

He reached for his shirt pocket and extracted a red and blue envelope, folded in half. He unfolded it and withdrew the single sheet of paper from within, which he also unfolded and presented to Jojo. Scrawled there in hastily written capital letters were just two short sentences:

GET RID OF IT. I WILL NOT TELL YOU AGAIN.

There was no date and no signature.

"It frightened him," Jojo said.

"I should say so.

"Why? What did he know about it?"

"I wrote him back, lied and said I threw it in the Arkansas River. Only then did he tell me what it is, or what he thought it was. He called it Lucifer's Sigil."

"Lucifer? You mean like the Devil?"

"Not exactly, no. Of course, that's the typical connection you would make—it's what I thought, too. Here I was with the sigil in one hand and my friend's letter in the other, thinking 'Good God, I've stumbled onto something Satanic!' But no, it's nothing quite that prosaic.

"You see, Mr. Walker, *Lucifer* is a bastardized word that comes from the Latin phrase *lucern ferre*, which means light-bearer."

"Seems the opposite of what most folks would say about the Devil," Jojo surmised.

"It hasn't anything to do with that. It has to do with Venus."

"The goddess?"

"No, the planet. Upon seeing it in the dawn sky it was called the Morning Star, or *lucern ferre*, the Light Bearer. In Greek it's called *Heōsphoros*. There are myths associated with it, deities that personify the heavenly bodies and all that. Venus always captured the imaginations of the ancients because it is brighter than any of the stars, particularly when it takes the form of the Morning Star."

"I feel like I oughta be taking notes, Professor," Jojo said as he got another cigarette going. He wished he had something to Irish up the unpleasant instant coffee in front of him. "Maybe some of this claptrap might start to make a little sense if I did."

"Just *listen*," Shannon commanded. "The appearance of the Morning Star isn't an everyday occurrence; it only happens once every couple of years. Well, every five hundred and eighty four days, to be precise. On one day in every cycle it overtakes the Earth, becoming brightly visible at dawn—*lucern ferre*. The morning of Lucifer, if you like."

"No, I *don't* like, Shannon," Jojo growled. "I don't *like* at all. All I'm getting from you is an astronomy lesson when what I want to know is what the hell is going on my town, goddamnit!"

Reverend Shannon smiled sadly and placed his hands on the table, palms down.

"You're not a very patient man, Mr. Walker," he said.

"And for Chrissakes, call me Jojo, will you?"

Shannon smiled thinly.

"Do you know what a sigil is?"

"Tell me," Jojo said with a sigh.

"It's a symbol, obviously," Shannon said, touching the object again. "More than one symbol, really—an ordered series of symbols. It's a sort of code, or message, that translates to a particular magical purpose for the bearer. Medieval grimoires are full of them, as it happens: *Liber Razielis Archangeli, Sefer Raziel Ha-Malakh . . .*"

Jojo's eyes shifted to the leather book. Noticing the look, the reverend nodded. "Like that one, yes," he said. "That, Jojo, is the Lemegton. *The Lesser Key of Solomon.*"

"Where did you get it? Oh, wait . . ."

"Yes, you know. It was in the ground, in the cellar."

"With the sigil."

"Right. I figured out fairly quickly that the sigil was going to tell me something that was in that book, but which couldn't be read without it. Think of it like the *Little Orphan Annie* decoder ring."

Jojo chuckled. "Or the *Captain Midnight* pocket decoder, huh?"

"Basically, yes. You see, Lucifer's Sigil works like a map, but you have to know how to read it or it's pointless."

"And this book tells you how to do that?"

"Consider it a symbiotic relationship of sorts."

Jojo wrinkled his nose.

"For the purposes of our discussion, one cannot be understood without the other." The reverend drew in a deep breath and held it in his chest for a moment. When he exhaled, he gave Jojo a serious look and said, "I sense you might not believe a word I'm telling you. Magic isn't exactly something you can accept on face value."

"If this was yesterday I'd think you're a lunatic, rev. Today, I'm a lunatic, too."

"All right then, have a look at this."

Reverend Shannon dragged the volume toward him and gingerly opened it up.

"What we have here is little more than a collection of conjurations, in the middle of which is a list of the seventy-two chief spirits, or demons. They're broken into rank and seals, each subdivision associated with a particular planet. . . ."

"Planet," Jojo interjected. "Venus."

"Right. Naturally, it can't be too easy, and the entities associated with Venus just so happen to belong to the longest list." He found the pages containing the lists and ran a fingertip down to the line he wanted. "Twenty-three of them—more than a third of the whole list. They're sealed with copper and summoned by sandalwood. These are the infernal dukes, according to the text.

"I spent months going through them, cross-referencing with all the conjurations, sitting amidst piles of Latin and Greek and Hebrew texts that fill my little library now. Here's what I figured out: the spirit that concerns us is called Focalor. As far as the Lemegton is concerned, Focalor seems more or less indistinct from most of the other demons, but it's the name that I hit upon. The name is an anagram for *rofocal*, which refers to *Lucifuge Rofocale*, one of the Hell's three arch-demons. The name means 'he who flees from the light.'"

"The Light-Bearer and the Light-Fleer," Jojo muttered.

"Eternally opposing forces, sure. Like a pair of magnets with different polarizations, except that's science, and this is magic."

"So you thought it might be a good idea to bring them together."

"According to the sigils and their explanations in the book, Focalor's element is water and his direction in North. There is a stream in the woods back there, back behind the church. I went there—"

"—on the Morning Star," Jojo said.

"Yes. Venus was *radiant* at dawn, Jojo. I pointed the sigil north, across the stream, and recited the incantation for the summoning of Focalor."

"You went into the woods to summon a devil?"

"No, not at all—you're not listening to me. When I started all this, I thought it was about devils, too. I fell into it to prove to myself that there wasn't any such thing as the Devil. No Hell, no Heaven. I wanted to justify my complete loss of faith. But that isn't what this is about. This isn't theology, Jojo; it's magic. Magic operates on an entirely separate set of rules, it's all about symbolism and ciphers."

Nodding, Jojo sat back in his chair. "In other words, you can't just say, 'Hey magic, make a rabbit come out of this empty hat.' You have to say 'abracadabra' or it doesn't work."

"Now you're getting it. None of this has anything to do with demonology, or theology, or faith of any kind. This is sorcery, Jojo, plain and simple. My original intent was wiped away, no longer pertinent. But by then . . ."

"So what happened, rev? What did you do out there?"

"I conducted the result of my research. I went at the right time, to the right place. I arranged the sigil and read the conjuration aloud. *I do invoke and conjure thee, O Spirit Focalor*, and so forth."

"And?"

"And nothing. Absolutely nothing happened. The text says if the spirit doesn't come, to repeat the invocation, and to recite others as prescribed. I did all of that, but like I said . . ."

". . . magic never means what it says."

"That's about the size of it."

"Except something *did* happen, didn't it?"

"I couldn't have known it then, but yes, of course. And hell, maybe a devil did come through. After all, that's when Barker Davis came to town."

CHAPTER EIGHTEEN

"Fucking Mortimer," Sheriff Ernie Rich grouched as he stomped on the accelerator and sped away from the town centre. "Pardon my Polish, ladies," he added a moment after.

"He was at the show," Margie said quietly, almost apologetically, from the backseat. "The midnight picture show. He was there with us."

"I'd wager every one of those crazies back there saw it either tonight or last night," Theodora put in. "Maybe the Legion of Decency is onto something with these sex pictures. They really do warp minds."

"Hell's bells," Rich spat. "That dumb sumbitch Mortimer was crazy before he saw that picture. I don't reckon I ever rode with him driving when he didn't deliberately run down a possum."

"Then the show made him worse?" Margie asked.

"The show made him dead, if that's what done it," Rich said. "Came pounding at my door in the middle of the night, screaming his fool head off about his dead mama. Said some right nasty things that ain't fit to repeat, but I let him in to talk it through. I expect that makes me a fool, too."

"Did you . . . did you kill him, Mr. Rich?" Charles wanted to know.

"Yeah, Charles. I killed him, all right. But not before the bastard took to shooting up my living room with his sidearm. He came to put a bullet in my head—my own deputy! And he said there were more like him coming, that folks like him were going to have folks like us underground before a week was over and done. That's how come I jumped in my car and got to patrolling. Couldn't take the chance, you know."

"We're awful glad you did, Sheriff," Theodora said. "You really saved our hides back there."

"If I was to go and let people get killed by loonies in the streets, I'd have to go look for another job come election time. Folks tend to take a dim view of sheriffs who sleep through things like that."

He offered a sardonic smile, which Theodora returned.

"I don't understand," Charles said, looking to Margie beside him. "Didn't you and Mrs. Cavanaugh see that same picture too?"

"There was no 'same' picture," Theodora countered. "Not from what I can tell. Mine was all about my past, my personal history."

"Mine was about my daddy," Margie said.

"Damnit," Rich groused. "I sure as hell wish I knew what was going on around here."

"Hopefully that's what we're going to find out at the Shannon place," Theodora said.

Margie lowered her head and shrank into herself. She loved her father the way a daughter should, despite the claims insinuated by the midnight picture show. Still, she was being forced to confront a distance between them that had begun with her puberty and only widened ever since. She was pressed to admit that she hardly knew the man anymore, and to her that meant anything was possible. It was just as possible that the picture, or dream, or *psychic attack* if that's what it was, was lying to her. She could not imagine where those images came from, whether from her own mind or some kind of hypnosis performed by the stranger who brought all this misery to her home, but whatever the source, she had to know the truth behind them.

Rich tore off the smooth macadam and the police car jounced on the bumpy dirt road stretching endlessly away from the centre of town. It occurred to Theodora, as she peered farther down the road than the headlamps illuminated, that she had no idea how far the road went. It could have run clear to the ocean for all she knew, and she'd have believed it. Then again, Theodora had never actually seen the ocean except for scenes in films, and those were just films. Maybe the road abruptly ended someplace down the way, just stopped and dropped off into nothingness, pure dark, empty space. The end of the world.

She thought it would be just as well.

"What's your stake in this mess, Charles?" the sheriff piped up, shattering the women's respective reveries.

"I just want to see my friend's all right. I guess I only got the one, so it's important."

"You mean the reverend?"

"No, sir. I mean Jojo Walker."

Ernie Rich gave a long, low groan.

"I should've known *he* was mixed up in this shit," he said.

X

Jim Shannon rose and went over to the window to push it shut. He rubbed his hands against his arms and shivered.

"Cold in July," he said. "That's something new."

"What is he?" Jojo asked sharply.

"Who, Davis? I don't know, exactly. Just a man, would be my guess, but a man with access to extraordinary power."

"The projectionist at the Palace, this young kid, he told us the midnight show was just some old silent footage of a corny sideshow magician."

"Hang on," Shannon said, shaking his head. "What midnight show?"

"After the picture, that sex show, Davis has this midnight picture going. Strictly invite only, though who knows how they chose the invitees. He's got this fake nurse with him, a hot little number, and she's the one passes out the tickets."

"And you've seen this picture?"

"I'm just about the only one in town who hasn't. Davis *summoned* me to his office—well, Russ Cavanaugh's office—before the picture started. But the kid says it's nothing, just a guy in a ratty tux doing lame old card tricks."

"You've spoken to him!" Shannon exclaimed, leaning excitedly over the table at Jojo.

"Sure. Most regular looking guy in the world. Kind of short, bad skin. Funny old haircut."

"I've seen him. I was at the theatre tonight myself."

"To see the picture?"

Shannon laughed. "No, to picket it. It didn't work out so well—Davis appeared at the window and he . . . God, I don't know how to explain what he did."

"I think I know," Jojo said, scratching his shaggy cheek. "He got into your head, made you see things, nightmare versions of the way you see the world."

"I—yes. Yes, that's exactly what happened. How did you—?"

"Are you sure you haven't got any booze around here?"

"No . . . well, there's the wine for worship, but . . ."

"Get it. I want to tell you a story. And when that's done, we're going to finish this."

The reverend scurried away to the cupboard, fumbled through clanging tins and clinking glass until he found the bottle, half-filled with blood red liquid. He snatched a couple of water glasses from the kitchen and brought the lot back to the table, where he filled both glasses. Shannon swallowed his own in two massive gulps and immediately refilled his glass.

"I have a disease called Ambras Syndrome, or hypertrichosis. A little less flattering, some folks call it Werewolf Syndrome. There isn't much too it—I just grow too much hair, everywhere but the palms of my hands and the soles of my feet. I've been shaving my face and hands two or three times a day since I was a teenager. That's how come I've got so many scars, though I guess you can't see them now.

"Anyhow," Jojo went on, slurping at the too-sweet sacramental wine, "I don't really remember much about my early childhood. The disease is supposed to be hereditary, which means my old man probably had it too, but I don't know a thing about my old man. My mother threw herself into the river when I was a kid. I grew up in a house full of retarded kids run by a nasty old woman named Parsons. I ran away when I was fourteen, thinking if I got to a big city I could find a cure. There isn't a cure. I came back home and learned to shave and when Mrs. Parsons finally croaked, I pretended like I was a normal guy and ended up getting a gig as the sheriff's deputy."

Shannon slowed to sipping and watched Jojo over the edge of his glass.

"There's a point to this," Jojo said, reading the other man's face. "Up until a few hours ago, I never remembered where I was or what was happening before I ended up at the Parsons place. Maybe a head-shrinker could suss it out, but the thing is it just wasn't there—lost time. But Barker Davis found it, and worse than that he fucking *showed* it to me. I was a circus freak, reverend. Locked up in a cage in the Ten-in-One tent and called Jo-Jo the Dog-Faced Boy. Folks dropped a dime in the barker's hand to have a look, a shriek, a good laugh at my expense. That's where I was between the time my mother went in the drink and whenever I ended up among all the headcases at old lady Parsons' place."

"Then you remember now. You really remember."

"Oh, I remember, all right. I remember the filth and the whippings and sleeping in my own shit, and I also remember a magician there, a tall, pasty fella used to scare the shit out of me, and a nasty kid with a face like pumice stone who swept up when the rubes went home. Parted his hair right down the middle, that kid. Followed the magician around like a puppy and gave everyone else the evil eye."

"Barker Davis."

"Tim Davis in those days. One of those white trash bumpkins runs away with the circus when they came through town, you know? Then one day he was gone, ran back the other way. And now he's here, showing me the worst parts of my life. Now what do you make of that, Reverend Shannon?"

"He must have some connection to Litchfield, that's what I make of it. Maybe he's the one who buried the sigil and grimoire in my cellar."

"But why?"

"I don't know."

"And why now?"

"I don't know that either. But I think I may have brought him here."

"What, with your spell?" Jojo pronounced the last word with evident derision.

"Like a homing beacon, maybe. All the details were right for him to come back."

"To do what?"

"I can say 'I don't know' all night, Jojo."

Jojo frowned and downed the contents of the glass. He sighed and shivered, stood up and planted his hands on his hips. "I'm going to need two things," he said. "A gun and a razor."

"I've got a razor, but no gun. What's the razor for?"

"I need a shave," Jojo said.

The reverend smiled, but it melted away the instant the voices came alive in the yard beyond the window. There were people out there, in the dark, shouting at the house. Shannon leapt back. Jojo went to the window and tugged the curtain away to look through.

"Who's out there?" the reverend asked, his voice shaky.

"Don't know, but there's half a dozen of 'em."

"What do they want?"

As if they heard his question, one among them screamed back, "We want the monster! We want Jojo Walker!"

Jojo drew in a deep breath, his chest expanding like a balloon, and turned to face Shannon.

"Christ, I wish you had a gun," he said.

⋇

And there it stood, just like in her dream. Theodora let out a tiny squeak, something she tried and failed to suppress, and stared with bulging eyes through the sheriff's windscreen at the church of her nightmare. The chief difference laid in the fact that her nightmare littered the churchyard with bodies, whereas now the bodies lurched forth, toward the house, screaming at the tops of their voices.

She glanced from the people back to the clapboard church, but the church was no longer there—in its place rose a towering conglomerate of edged, knife-like spires cutting into the gathering dawn. The spires, black as onyx, pronounced martial power and spiritual invincibility for the angular structure from which they sprang: an impossibly immense byzantine coffin, an inverse church that would remain enshrouded in pitch even at the height of day.

Nearer, backlit dimly by the approach of purple daybreak, skeletal shapes jigged and goose-stepped and danced before the horizon, making jagged circles around a slow moving cart dragged by mules. Some of the shapes wore high, pointed caps while others were bald or had the flouncing tentacles of a jester's hood twisting around their heads. A hurdy-gurdy and a shrill calliope screamed jangling, dissonant tunes at one another—a deafening cacophony of noise without order. Cackling laughter added to the noisome chaos, and a chorus of falsetto voices cried out, "Jojo! Jojo! We want Jojo!"

Torches were lit, their explosive orange flames giving faces to the shadow skeletons. Theodora recognized those that were not caked with pancake make-up and grotesque red mouths: Russ's mistress Lana, a waitress from the Starlight Diner, Tuck Arnold. Over the deafening din of the jerky music and screaming voices, these three bellowed a cheerful song as they danced alongside the slow moving congregation—

"The Dog-Faced Boy
He growls and bites!
Growls and bites!
Growls and bites!
The Dog-Faced Boy
He growls and bites!
We've come to bite him back!"

Theodora whispered, "Jojo."

"I guess you see 'em too," Rich said. Theodora nodded slowly. "Well, at least I ain't crazy—or at least no more crazy than you are."

"What is this?" Charles asked, sitting up straight as a rod with fearful, staring eyes. "Is this like what ya'll saw at the movie theatre?"

"I don't think the show is over yet," Theodora said. "What we saw at the Palace was just the first act."

"Jeepers," Margie said, immediately embarrassed that the word had escaped her lips.

"Jeepers is right," Rich said, applying the brakes and slowing the police car to a halt. "Look at that."

The sheriff gestured with his head and all eyes in the car rotated to the house, a single story A-frame structure with healthy yellow light leaking from the windows. The front door swung open violently and a burst of bright light splashed into the early morning gloom. Someone stepped out from inside, brightly illumined from the indoor lights behind him and the sheriff's headlamps in front of him. Theodora gasped and Margie yelped.

Ernie Rich said, "Well, if that don't beat all. It's a goddamn werewolf."

X

"*We've come to bite you back!*" Betty Overturf screeched, her lips pulled up as if by invisible hooks, forming a skull's smile.

"Hi, Betty," Jojo said calmly. "Sorry to see you like this." He wasn't quite sure if he meant her awful state or his. Either way, it fit.

Betty chuckled: a low, throaty sound. Beside her, a white-faced clown opened his yellow eyes and joined her in laughter. Strapped to his torso was the hurdy-gurdy, which he cranked jerkily to fill the air with music like broken glass.

Inside the house, Shannon shouted, "Are you nuts? Get back in here and shut the door."

"It's not real," Jojo muttered. "Can't be."

"For Christ's sakes, it's magic," Shannon yelled. "Haven't you listened to a word I said? Get back in here!"

"Magic, he says."

He took a step back, wrapping the fingers of one hand around the edge of the door, when he spotted the automobile up a ways on the drive. The car's unmistakable green and white colouring was just barely visible in the emerging light. Jojo grinned and said, "Ernie fucking Rich."

He leapt out of the house and slammed the door behind him before falling into a sprint for the police car.

X

"Oh Jesus, here he comes," Theodora said, bracing herself and starting to breathe too rapidly.

Rich snatched up the 10-gauge from the floor.

"Next thing it'll be Dracula," he grunted as he kicked the door open and stepped out of the car. He pointed both barrels at the fast approaching apparition and bellowed, "Hold it right there, you! This is Sheriff Ernie Rich talking!"

"Get that damn blunderbuss out of my face and toss me a rod, Ernie," Jojo called back, nearly upon the car.

"Jojo? Is that you?"

"Of course it's me, you bloated old moron—now toss me that iron!"

"It's a trick," Margie blurted out, her voice rising and frantic. "It's a trick! Shoot him!"

"Be quiet, child!" Rich barked back.

Jojo skidded over loose dirt and gravel and stopped, gasping for air, where the sheriff could take in the startling sight of his former deputy's hair-covered face.

"Jesus Christ, Jojo," Rich said.

"Gun, Ernie."

A shrill scream erupted from the travelling circus as a clown with a high-peaked cap broke away from the group and came spinning wildly at the police car.

"*JojojojojojojoJOJOJOJO*," the clown cried crazily as he scrambled toward them.

Rich pumped his shotgun and blasted the clown, winging him. His flouncy white sleeve came apart in a red mist. It did not slow him down.

"JOJOJOJOJOJOJOJO!"

Jojo spun around and saw the revolver jammed beside the seat in the car. He snatched it up and pulled the hammer back with his thumb. He swung it up and the clown smashed his forehead against the barrel the moment Jojo squeezed the trigger. He expected blood, bits of skull and brain. Instead, the clown's head burst like a balloon filled with cream—a wet, white explosion and then it was gone, as if the clown had never been there at all.

Which Jojo presumed was more or less the truth.

"What in the *hell*," Rich said.

"I've got to get to that carriage," Jojo told him, flipping the cylinder to see how many cartridges were left. There were five. *Good man, Ernie,* he thought.

"Now hold on a minute, damnit," the sheriff protested. "We haven't got the slimmest damn clue as to what's going on around here—"

"I do." Jojo jammed the cylinder back in place and cocked the gun.

"Care to enlighten me, son?"

"We're cursed, Ernie. The whole rotten town is cursed. Started back in twenties when I was just a pup . . ." He laughed at his unintended joke. ". . . the last time the circus came to Litchfield."

Sheriff Rich yanked the hat from his head and rubbed his pink scalp. "I wish you'd make sense, man."

An automobile door slammed shut and Theodora rounded the car to where the two men stood, her face stolid and grim. She grabbed the sheriff's shoulder roughly and insinuated herself into the conversation with ease.

"I—I think he's right, Sheriff," she said, her eyes burning like coals. "I remember that circus. Don't you?"

"Hell, I never been one to go for that sort of thing."

"I was there," she went on. "I remember now. And I saw you, Jojo. You were . . ."

". . . in a cage," Jojo finished for her. "I tried to escape."

"The magician . . ."

"I think he might be in that carriage. He's come for me, because he thinks I belong to him. And for the reverend, too, since he's the one who brought the bastard back."

"Who is he?"

"Black Harry Ashford," Jojo said with a sneer.

"Wait a minute," Rich cut in. "I thought it was this Davis fella behind all of it."

"It is. They're one and the same. At least, I think so."

"You think so. Christ, Walker—this ain't right. This just ain't right!"

"You're telling me," Jojo said with an arched eyebrow.

He rolled his shoulders and crooked his neck so it popped, and started off across the churchyard toward the carriage and its dancing attendants. Rich grunted and jumped for him, seizing Jojo by the elbow.

"Hang on a damn minute, Jojo—I don't understand any of this. And what's more is you can't run around blasting holes in people in my town, much less with my peashooter. In case you forgot, you ain't no deputy no more, Jojo Walker."

"I recollect that being your call, Ernie," Jojo said plainly.

"Christ Jesus," the sheriff complained. "Do you know I killed Dean Mortimer tonight? And more, too. This poor woman's husband. Others. I think I'm going crazy."

He released Jojo's shoulder and put the hand to his forehead.

"I think I'm going crazy, kid," he said.

Jojo looked at his former boss and felt a stab in the heart. A long time had passed since the sheriff last called him *kid*, an affection from the older man who was as close as Jojo would ever have to a father. Then he met Sarah and the world came crashing down. It was still crashing, faster and harder now, and Ernie Rich was coming down with it. Jojo felt responsible, like he was the one who pulled the switch so clearly labelled *Do Not Pull*. He reached out and patted Rich on the chest, reversing the old roles.

"I'm gonna fix it," he said, not believing it for a minute. "Just stand back, Ernie. I'm gonna fix it."

As if whatever he was about to do could bring back Beth and see that he never met Sarah, and he'd go back to wearing tin on his shirt and breaking up brawls between drunk cousins and not remembering how they kept him in a cage full of his own shit and piss. Still, Ernie nodded and wiped a stray tear from one eye.

"I'd deputize you," he croaked, "but what's the point?"

"That's okay," Jojo said with a smile. "My facial hair ain't up to regulation anyhow."

"Fucking magic," Rich said, brushing a hand across Jojo's furry face. Jojo laughed.

"Naw," he said. "Just bad luck."

The circus procession was closing in on the house, their crazy, jerky music slowing even as the carriage wheels spun a little faster over the bumpy yard. Theodora moved around to the sheriff's side and wrapped her hands around the stock of his 10-gauge.

"You won't mind if I borrow this, will you?"

Rich released the shotgun to her, stunned.

"Miss, that blunderbuss will knock you on your pretty little rump the first time you shoot it," he said. "I reckon you and Jojo ought to trade."

"I'll take it," Charles said, claiming the gun for himself. "You take the rifle in the back of the sheriff's car, Theodora. That way we all armed."

"I think I got me a posse," Jojo said, equal parts shocked and impressed.

"A woman, a Negro, and a werewolf," Rich muttered, shaking his head. "Chrissakes, kid—I sure as shit hope you know what you're doing."

"Nope," Jojo answered. "Not a damn clue." Then, to his compadres: "Ready?"

Charles ejected the spent shells from the shotgun and replaced them with fresh ones, cracking it shut and assuming a fierce, steely gaze. Theodora returned from the backseat where she found a .22 rifle and a shell-shocked teenaged girl, to whom she whispered, "Sit tight, we're going to make this right."

"You're in the lead, boss," Charles said.

Without another word, Jojo set off in a rapid walk for the nightmare entourage, Theodora and Charles flanking him with weapons in their hands.

CHAPTER NINETEEN

"Well, you've really done it now, Jim," Shannon scolded himself, cupping his hands over his ears in a futile attempt to block out the horrible, jangling notes from outside the house. "I hope you're happy, you stupid old fool."

The sun was peeking over the edge of the land now, and though some small part of him hoped the light of day might burn up the terrors of the night, he knew it wouldn't happen. It didn't. He thought about the note from his friend in Little Rock—GET RID OF IT; I WILL NOT TELL YOU AGAIN—and wondered briefly if it was too late, if there was still time to be rid of the burnished sigil and everything it brought with it.

He knew it was.

Shannon bit his lower lips and shuddered at the song that rose above the choppy music: a chorus of wavering voices that sobbed the words even as they laughed them.

> "Jim an' Satan had a race—
> Hal-le-lu! Hal-le-lu!
> Jim an' Satan had a race—
> Hal-le-lu! Hal-le-lu!"

"Hal-le-lu," the reverend mumbled wetly. "Goddamnit it all to hell."

"No such place and no such entity to damn it," a small, calm voice said behind him.

Shannon pivoted on one heel to find a visitor standing in the middle of his kitchen like he belonged there, like he'd always been there. Barker Davis added, "I am surprised you haven't figured that out just yet. And perhaps a bit amused."

"Why are you here?" Shannon growled at him.

"Don't be rude, Jim. After all, you invited me."

"I—I was . . ."

"What? Trying to make a point? I'd say that you have. Nothing is real. Everything is perspective. Life is a dream. Have you learned these lessons yet?"

"Lies."

"All of it, yes."

Shannon slumped into a kitchen chair, his arms dangling lifelessly between his knees.

"But why here? What's Litchfield got to do with it?"

"I'd wager your friend out there could answer that question," Davis said, pointing at the window. Shannon looked and saw Jojo Walker marching pointedly toward the caravan, a silver gun gripped in one hand. A woman—Russell Cavanaugh's wife, he thought—and a black man followed close behind. "He thinks he's come to kill me. Like you, he thinks there are rules that cannot be broken. Like you, he will learn different."

"For God's sakes, I did it because I thought nothing would come of it," the reverend emotionally protested. "That's the only reason I bothered with it, with this damn book and this damn sigil. I was only trying to justify my faithlessness."

"Haven't you?"

Shannon shut his eyes and squeezed out a salty tear. "Yes. I suppose I have."

"And now you wish to rescind your invitation because *you didn't really mean it*. Did you know that was what Tuck Arnold said in the moments after he beat his wife to death?"

"Oh, no. Oh, oh, no," Shannon moaned.

"He took a wrench from his store—priced at twenty-five cents—and smashed her head in until he couldn't recognize her anymore. And he said, 'I'm sorry, Helen, I'm so sorry. I didn't mean it.' Now, do you suppose that made any difference to poor, dead Helen Arnold?"

Barker Davis split his pitted face into a toothy grin and laughed a low, gravelly laugh. Jim Shannon groaned and broke into a series of wrenching, breathless sobs. He thought, not for the first time, about ending his own life, and about the myriad ways one could go about it, but he was much too tired to act on any such impulses. Perhaps after a good sleep, he decided while his back convulsed and shoulders shook; a nice long rest. Then the crushing reality of life and death and nothing ever after could claim him and there would be no one to answer to, just as he had always secretly hoped would be the case. A sputtering sigh broke up the pattern of his sobs and grasped the sides of his head as though that was the only way to keep it from tumbling off his neck.

"Life's a funny thing, isn't it, Mr. Davis?"

"It's merely a dream," the showman assured him. "Why don't you go climb into bed and see where it leads?"

"Yes," Shannon agreed, smearing a hand across his wet face. "Yes, I think I should."

He stood up, stumbling a little, and staggered across the kitchen to the hall.

Davis said, "The last reel is about to begin. I think it's going to be good."

PART 4

The Last
Reel

CHAPTER TWENTY

Brightly painted in vibrant, living hues, the circus wagon was a work of art, decorated on all sides with intricate wood carvings and lying mirrors and gold leaf. An ornate, three dimensional Samson struggled with a snarling lion on one side, the long-haired fighter's jaw coming off in graphic detail, and David battled Goliath on the other side, the giant crushing the boy's ribcage with a single powerful grasp. Jojo noted the inverse stories the reliefs told: heroes undone. A glimmering gold face shone down from above a retractable section he took for a hidden door—it was the face of Barker Davis, realistically pitted and grinning like a devil, laughing at whoever came near enough to see it.

A pair of clowns with faces like cadavers cavorted in the dew-wet grass between Jojo and the wagon, leaping like apes and swinging their arms in practiced defensive motions. Tuck Arnold slapped his own face and screamed at Jojo as he stomped the earth like he wanted to shake it apart.

In one hand he gripped a huge wrench, dripping with blood.

"You can't have her, you rotten son of a bitch," Tuck yelled. "I killed my wife for her! What did you ever do?"

"I guess I killed mine, too," Jojo answered simply. Tuck looked momentarily stunned. "Get out of my way, Tuck."

As if under a spell—which Jojo assumed he probably was—the hardware man stepped back and away. The others followed suit, all but the two remaining clowns, who danced and jumped in the stark morning light, oblivious to everything around them. As Jojo passed them on his way to the wagon, he decided that they weren't wearing any make-up— their faces really were that white, their eyes the colour of pus. Abruptly one of them winked at him.

"Enjoy the show," he said in a child's voice.

Jojo gripped the splintery edge of the interlocking panel and gave it a hard yank, sliding it open. A blast of frigid air rushed out, stinging his, Charles's, and Theodora's faces. With it came the distinct odour of dirty animals, burnt popcorn, and shit. The interior of the wagon was completely dark and the jangly music echoed deep inside of it, deeper than the exterior of the wagon logically permitted. In the middle distance, beams of sunlight were sliced in half by the razor sharp spires of the black church at the forest's edge.

Jojo said, "Neither of you needs to come. Ya'll can go on back now."

"Lead the way, boss," Charles said.

Theodora patted Jojo gently on the back. He breathed in the cold, foul-smelling air and stepped up and into the waiting blackness.

※

The panel slammed shut behind them and Theodora yelped. She felt a hand at her elbow and jumped away from it, knocking against a wall and tumbling down to the floor. Someone said, "What is it?" She thought it was Charles but she wasn't sure. The question bounced around a broad, enclosed space.

"What is it?" the voice repeated. It was Charles, after all.

"I—I fell down. Where are we? Is this the inside of the wagon?"

"Can't be," Jojo said from a few feet away. His feet scuffled the floor a bit and then a clunk. Theodora listened, holding her breath. "A row of seats," he called out. "Jesus, we're in the theatre."

A rapid clicking sounded above, drawing all eyes to the burst of light from the tiny square in the wall there. The screen at the far end of the auditorium filled with white light and the speakers crackled all around them.

Charles said, "Look."

On screen was a familiar room: it could have been any of the rooms in the Litchfield Valley Hotel. Small and dim, though the picture was in full colour, though every colour was brown and muted. A man and woman sat on the edge of the bed—he with his shirt off and her in her brassiere and nothing else.

"What's this, a stag film?" Theodora asked.

Jojo turned to glance at her. "How would you know what a stag film is?"

"Heard it someplace," she answered without answering.

He returned his attention to the screen, to the man he'd only seen alive once and the pink-faced little blonde who would probably be afraid for the rest of her life. He knew what was coming next, so he said, "Don't watch."

It was too late. The man arched his back and cords popped thick and dark on his neck and forehead. He screamed the scream of the dying and twisted up and off the bed, red seams forming at his shoulders and around his throat. The seams widened and dark blood sprayed from the broadening gaps as the skin pulled apart. In a matter of seconds that seemed like long, torturous minutes, Peter Chappell was dismembered and beheaded in a fountain of blood that coated the floor and the walls and the poor, shrieking girl.

Theodora screamed, too.

Charles muttered, "Sweet Jesus. Sweet, sweet Jesus."

"I told ya'll not to watch, for Chrissakes," Jojo grumbled, fighting against his own trembling muscles.

The view of the room fell away as the picture shifted, through the door and down the hallway, at the end of which was an open door. The room beyond the door was identical in every respect to the blood-soaked one before, except for everything being in reverse. Sitting with her long, stockinged legs crossed in a chair by the window, the nurse adeptly threaded a needle in and out along the seam of a little cloth doll. Her bright red lips were moving rapidly, her voice a low drone. What she said could not be heard above the whimpering coming from the bed. There, a girl thrashed like a freshly-hooked fish, her arms and legs bound with torn up bedsheets. She was nude, her skin nearly as white as the clowns'. When the girl jerked her head to reveal her face, Theodora cried, "Margie!"

The nurse continued her inaudible muttering as she completed her stitching. She tied off the thread at the crook of the doll's neck and bit off the excess with her teeth. Pleased with her handiwork, the nurse smiled, showing lipsticked teeth. She then drove the point of the needle into the doll's left thigh and Margie screamed with agony. Thrashing more wildly now, a dark indent formed in the girl's thigh to correspond with that of the doll's. The skin snapped and blood boiled out. The nurse stood, leaving the needle stuck in the doll, and walked on her toes to the side of the bed.

"Poor baby," she taunted. "Does it hurt?"

"Please," Margie's agonized voice echoed from every speaker in the theatre. "Please stop."

The nurse puckered her full lips and shook her head, playing the part of the concerned medical assistant to the hilt. She gently set the doll down on the nightstand beside the bed and leaned over Margie, taking the girl's chin in her hand and bending over until their faces were only inches apart.

"Please," Margie moaned.

The nurse flicked out her tongue and ran it up the length of Margie's face, lapping up the girl's tears. Margie squeezed her eyes shut and tried to turn her head away from the nurse, but the woman held on tight, even as she moved her face down the length of the girl's body.

"Oh, God," Theodora groaned, looking away.

As the nurse fell upon the leaking wound in Margie's thigh she grunted with pleasure, sucking at the thick pulses of blood.

"Is it real?" Theodora asked, her face buried in her hands. "Is she there? Is she really there?"

"That's crazy," Charles said. "She was just way out at the church."

"So were we," Jojo reminded him.

"What about the sheriff, then?"

"I don't know, but we'd best get to the hotel."

"Isn't that just what she wants?" Theodora asked. "That, that awful woman?"

"Probably, yes. But I'm going."

Jojo stormed the auditorium doors and smashed against them. He might as well have thrown himself at a wall for all the good it did—they were locked up tight.

"Damnit!" he growled.

"They just want to torture us," Theodora said. "They want us to watch that girl die."

Jojo pounded on the doors and shouldered them with all his weight. They did not budge.

Charles wandered away from them, watching the screen as the camera backed out of the room and zipped down the hall, backwards down the stairs and into the lobby where it stopped. A man in a crumpled grey hat sauntered up to the cigarette machine and pushed a coin into the slot. Charles' bellhop cap remained where he'd left it on the floor. It looked for all intents and purposes like the most regular night in the world at the Litchfield Valley.

"Couldn't be," Charles whispered, scratching his chin.

"Maybe if we both hit them at the same time," Theodora suggested behind him.

Charles flipped around and hollered, "Hey, forget that. I know the way out."

"What?" Theodora said, puzzled.

"Where?" Jojo asked.

"Right there," Charles said, pointing at the screen. "All I need's a knife."

CHAPTER TWENTY-ONE

Ernie Rich never saw them take her; he merely looked into the backseat of his automobile and Margie Shannon was gone. He would have naturally assumed that she'd run into the house—she lived there, after all—except for the high-pitched scream that echoed in the distance, as though a giant bird had plucked her up in its talons and taken her to the clouds.

The sun shone bright over the hills, but the air was colder than ever. The sheriff blew a puff of warm mist and rubbed his arms with his hands. The circus wagon rested quietly on the grass, still as a coffin. He'd watched as the three went into it, then nothing. The clowns vanished and the remaining people—Tuck Arnold, Betty Overturf, and Lana Ashe—simply wandered away, their heads bowed and eyed hooded. Rich called out to them, singling Tuck out particularly, ordering him to stop. He had questions, but all three of them behaved as if they hadn't heard him. They staggered on, headed vaguely in the direction of town. Rich let them go.

Rubbing his temples with circular motions, Ernie Rich considered his options. He was the last of the law in Litchfield, which had gone from a force of two men to just him overnight. As far as he knew, his deputy remained where Rich cut him down, dead on the carpet. He thought about Jojo, about how much he trusted the man he was forced to shit-can a year earlier. He'd always liked Jojo, and never considered his former deputy's dalliance with the coloured maid to be any of his business, but there were elections to think of. In a small town with only two cops, he couldn't brook one of them being at the centre of such an outlandish scandal. It was a matter of the circumstances undoing them both, or just the one of them. Rich opted to save his own skin.

Now he felt like the entire world depended on Jojo Walker.

At the present, however, Sheriff Rich was on his own and damned curious about the freshly abandoned circus wagon into which Jojo and company went and from which no one had yet emerged. He drew his service revolver and steeled his nerves and walked determinedly over the cool, wet grass to the interlocking panels with their ornate, gilded patterns.

"Jojo? What's going on in there?"

The jarring music was gone with the departure of the wagon's attendants, so Rich pressed his ear to the panel in an effort to hear what was happening inside. He heard nothing, but smelled sweet wood smoke. Deciding that the wagon was aflame, he hurried away from it to a vantage point that revealed the wagon to be in fine condition. But the pastor's house was engulfed.

"Sweet Jesus," Rich mumbled.

Flames the colour of autumn leaves danced in the windows, which presently exploded from the intense heat. The kitchen and living room were wholly consumed by the fire, and the porch was going up fast. Rich stood stock still and watched dumbly, his revolver dangling at the end of his arm, completely powerless to act. There was no way he could enter the house without passing out from the smoke and perishing in flames. Whoever was in there was a goner, and he knew it.

As the fire roared to greater intensity, Rich scampered away from it. He scanned his immediate environs and discovered to his bewilderment that the wagon had vanished and the old clapboard church was back where it was supposed to be. If the magician's influence had left this place, he realized, then the fire was quite real. And that meant that the Reverend Jim Shannon was probably dead.

He kicked up a clod of earth and cursed under his breath.

※

In lieu of a knife, which no one had, Theodora offered a nail file. Charles stabbed the screen with it, six inches above his head, and dragged the file down to the stage to create a jagged, six foot tear. Light spilled out of the crevice. Jojo said, "You've got to be kidding."

Footsteps scuffed against tiles on the other side, their heels clacking loudly. Jojo grabbed one side of the gash in the screen and ripped it wide open to reveal the hotel lobby where an inebriated guest was staggering toward the staircase. He whistled and shook his head.

"If I don't ever see another trick like this again that'll be just fine by me," he said.

Charles looked to Theodora and shrugged.

She said, "Don't even think about saying 'ladies first.' It's your damn hole—you go through it."

Charles smiled and peered into the lobby. The drunk was gone, though he had begun to sing from somewhere on the second floor. Charles spotted his cap on the floor and snorted. He stepped through.

Theodora half expected something terrible to happen, for a bright light to flash and burn Charles up like a piece of tissue paper. Instead, he simply entered the lobby as though walking through any ordinary door. Jojo went next. The men stood side by side and looked back through the gash at her. She shrugged, let loose a small, nervous laugh. Then she too went impossibly from the Palace's auditorium to the hotel lobby.

"Them trolleys in St. Louie got nothing on that," Charles observed.

"Is this really the hotel, though?" Theodora wondered aloud. "I mean, how can we know for certain where we really are?"

"I don't reckon we can," Jojo said. "But that's not going to stop me from doing what I can for that girl."

"That woman . . ." Theodora said, glancing apprehensively at the stairs.

"I guess she's Davis's right-hand gal," Jojo said. "I think just about everyone else in his gang were probably recruited the same way they got Jake."

"Poor Jake," Charles said, shaking his head.

"Regular folks, more or less, and Barker Davis has a purpose for them. That nurse is different, though. I don't think he made her what she is. I think that's all her—cold as a snake."

"You can see it in my eyes," a deep, feminine voice said.

The nurse walked seductively from the cashier's cage, her round hips swaying like a pendulum. Her bare feet barely touched the tiles as she advanced, walking diagonally until Mr. Thomas was visible behind her. He was sprawled out on the floor, his face swollen and bluish. A massive black snake had its fangs deep in Thomas's neck, its body undulating in perpetual waves down the dying man's torso.

The nurse smiled, flicked her tongue and hissed. Jojo started; a sharp intake of breath.

"How did you forget so much, Jojo?" she seethed. She floated toward him, kicking at the floor with her toes like a dancer. "Was it so terrible, living with our little family?"

"Who is she?" Theodora whispered.

"I—I'm not sure . . ."

"Not sure, he says. The only mother he ever had and the kid says he's not sure. Jojo, I'm offended."

The woman pressed her breasts against Jojo's chest and ran her narrow fingers through the hair on his face. She closed her fist around it and ripped out a handful. Jojo snarled in pain.

"Stop it!" Theodora shouted, throwing herself at the nurse.

Unfazed, the nurse swung her arm in a wide arc and knocked Theodora to the floor as though she was swatting a gnat. Charles stared, his eyes wobbling in his skull, and tightened his grip on the shotgun which he sharply raised to take aim at the nurse. She turned her head to regard him, her expression registering mild annoyance.

"Are you going to kill me, *bellboy?*" she fumed. "Blow my fucking head off? Perhaps you'd like to fuck my corpse afterward, yes? I'll bet you've never had a white woman before, have you? And a dead one's just as good as anything you're likely to get—"

"Shut up!" Charles cried, shaken. "Shut up and get away from him!"

"You can do whatever you like when a girl's dead," she went on, her breasts rising and falling with her building excitement. "You stick it anyplace you choose—how can she object? Why, if you can take my head clean off, you can even fuck my neck."

"Shut up!" he screamed, tears roiling out of his glassy eyes. "Shut up, shut up!"

Her grin broadened, showing bright, flawless teeth. She stepped lightly toward him, arching her back to push her bosom forward. Charles jerked, keeping the gun trained on her. Slowly, she raised her hand and wrapped her fingers around the barrels, stroking them gently. She then guided them down until the shotgun was directed point blank at her crotch.

"Go ahead and shoot when you need to, honey. No sense in holding back on my account."

Charles trembled. Theodora nodded rapidly, mouthing the word, *Shoot.*

When the nurse swept the shotgun out of his hands, she did so without much effort. He just let it go.

She said, "There's a good boy."

The faint, warbling strains of "Danny Boy" echoed down the stairwell from the drunk on the second floor.

"You want to see the girl," the nurse said to him as she let the shotgun clatter against the floor. Theodora jumped, afraid it might go off.

"Yeah," Jojo answered.

The nurse held out her hand. "Then let's go see her."

Jojo eyeballed the hand for a minute, amazed at its whiteness, its lack of lines. She wiggled it, urging him to take it. He did.

She led the way, dragging Jojo behind her as she floated to the stairs. Theodora started after them, but the nurse stopped her with a sharp gesture and an icy stare.

"Not you. Just him."

"Jojo," Theodora said.

"It's okay. Wait here with Charles."

"But she's . . ." She trailed off, uncertain of which adjective to use. Crazy? Dangerous?

Beautiful?

"It's okay. Wait for me."

"I don't like it. It's not right."

"We're not in charge right now," he said, shrugging. "It's this or nothing."

She hung her head and sighed. "I'll wait right here."

"Good."

"Come back."

"I will."

Jojo blinked and turned back to the nurse and the stairs. She went up, lugging him along like a Pekinese on a leash. For the second time in her life, Theodora watched as a frighteningly evil person dragged the Dog-Faced Boy away.

※

"I always knew you were a sweet boy," the nurse cooed as they went down the hall together. It was dimmer than ever and one of the lights in the ceiling flickered incessantly. "He did a hell of a job getting all the rubes to think you were wild, but I knew better."

"Who are you?"

"Come, now. You'll hurt my feelings."

"I know the face, but I can't remember. I don't remember much from that time."

"I expect you don't. I had an uncle like that. Fought the Mexicans and saw some pretty awful things, I guess. Couldn't recall one damn thing from that war. Half the time he didn't even believe he'd been there."

"All right, but I was in the circus, not a war."

"Hmn," she said. "Maybe worse, then." She stopped in front of the last door on the left and carefully, gingerly touched the doorknob. "Here we are, champ."

She turned the knob and Jojo said, "Why don't you tell me who you are, huh? Short of a thump on the noodle I'm not planning on just magically remembering."

"Maybe a thump's the answer."

She pushed the door open and he saw the girl on the bed.

"Goddamnit, who are you?" he snarled.

"Knock it off, Jojo," complained the girl on the bed.

He stiffened at the realization that she wasn't Margie Shannon. He melted at the fact that she was Sarah, his long-dead mistress from the wrong side of the tracks.

"And take them damn shoes off before you track dirt all over this house. I spent all day cleaning up white folks' dirt; I ain't about to have to do it in my own house, too."

"Sarah," he whispered raggedly.

"And don't you dare argue with me, Jojo Walker," she went on with a knowing wink. "You can boss your own wife around, you want to lord over a woman, but *I'm* the head of this house and don't you forget it."

Her stern, pinched expression couldn't last—it never could. Her forehead smoothed and the full smile, the most genuine, guileless smile he'd ever seen told the truth about how she felt.

"My God," he said.

"Good grief, Jojo," she laughed, "why in the world do you look so shocked? I was only joking. You know me."

If her absence had made his memory of her richer, more beautiful, then Jojo decided that was what he was looking at: a memory. But people didn't interact with their memories. Memories were for when connections were dead and gone, contact forever done with. He sniffled and rubbed his chin, suddenly shocked back to the reality of the circumstances.

"Shit," he grouched. "My face."

"You *do* need a shave, wolf-boy."

Anyone else and he'd have been offended, but he accepted the pet name from Sarah early on. He accepted *anything* from Sarah.

She stood from the bed, smoothed out the wrinkles in her nightie, patted at her raven black hair with the palms of her hands. She was meticulous about straightening it with her pressing comb, despite Jojo's constant comments that she'd look pert near perfect if she was as bald as a cue ball.

"Come on," she instructed, hooking a finger at him as she crossed the room to a door that hadn't been there a moment before. "Let's get my boy all lathered up."

He took a step forward and froze. Sarah tilted her head playfully and snorted a laugh, shutting her eyes momentarily and fluttering her eyelashes. Jojo turned to look at the nurse, who remained standing behind him like a bodyguard.

"Why?" he asked.

"Go to her, you fool," the nurse said, suddenly bereft of all her menace. "She's the love of your life. Don't miss it."

"It's . . ."

"It's what? Not real?"

"It isn't."

"Does it matter?"

"I loved her."

"I know you did. You still do. Go. Love her now."

Sarah opened the door and dramatically planted a hand on her round hip.

"Are you coming or do I have to drag you?"

The nurse went back to the door, stepped out to the hall.

"Go," she said again, and then vanished from the room.

Jojo said, "I'm coming."

On his way to her, to the love of his life, he remembered the nurse's name like it was burned into his brain with a branding iron. *Minerva*, he thought.

"You get the water hot and I'll get your shaving kit together," Sarah said.

He followed her into the washroom feeling vaguely guilty for watching the way her buttocks moved beneath the sheer fabric of the nightie. He watched all the same.

"Sometimes I think we're the two biggest frauds in Litchfield, you and me," she said lightly, rummaging through the medicine cabinet.

Jojo twisted the knob above the faucet in the clawfoot bathtub. "What's that supposed to mean?"

"I'm a coloured woman who wants a white woman's hair, and you're a wolf-boy who wants to be hairless like everyone else."

She laughed again; a lilting, soulful laugh.

He said, "Everybody wants to fit in, not get stared at or treated like last week's garbage. That's not asking too much, is it?"

"I don't reckon so, but why's it all got to do with hair? Mine's too curly and yours is too damn much. Some's too red, or too grey, or too thin or not enough. Jumpin' Jesus, I expect if we all stayed bald the way we were born the world would be a lot better off."

"I suppose you'd blame the war on Hitler's moustache."

"Why not? His silly little moustache and Churchill's big, bald head."

Jojo erupted into peals of laughter, and Sarah joined him.

"By God, woman," he said, gasping, "you're in rare form today."

He touched the stream of water rushing from the faucet and it stung him with its heat.

"Well, I ought to be, *by God*," she answered.

She was unzipping the leather shaving kit and extracting the brush and straight razor. The soap and scissors she'd already taken out and set beside the bathtub. She sat down beside him on the tub's edge and started to unbutton his shirt. Thick brown hair puffed out along the way.

"Yeah?" he asked. "And why's that?"

"Because it's been so long, you big, hairy dummy."

Furrowing his brow, Jojo let his arms go limp as she pulled the shirt off. He was puzzled by what she meant. He wondered how long it could possibly have been, given the fact that they were never apart long, not between the first time he stole a kiss and the day she died. . . .

Sarah gently took his chin with one hand and snipped at the hair on his face with the scissors in the other. Brown clumps rained down on his lap. The faucet roared behind him, sounding for all the world like Niagara Falls.

"How . . . how long has it been?"

"Bless me, but you really *are* a dummy, Jojo Walker."

"I'm sorry."

Snip, snip.

"Don't be sorry—just be still, for crying out loud!"

Snip, snip, snip.

She leaned in close, taking extra care along his nose and around his eyes.

"How long, Sarah?" he whispered.

"It's been a long, long time, lover."

"You mean since . . ."

"That's right, baby. That's right." She cut faster now, making horizontal rows on his brow. "Since your wife killed me."

A shot rang out and with a dull, sickening *thud* a deep red-black hole appeared an inch above Sarah's left eye. Jojo jerked, startled, and the pointed tips of the scissors stabbed the skin at the hairline she was shaping for him.

"Now look what you made me do!" she complained, sitting back and giving him a disappointed mother look. Blood trickled out of the hole in her head, gathered in the fine hair of her eyebrow.

She pursed her lips and went for a wad of toilet paper to dab at the two dark beads welling up on his brow.

"You got to stay still," he scolded him, the blood oozing from the wound and falling in fat droplets above her eye. "This is why you got scars all over your face, you know."

"I know," he muttered, staring.

She patted with the tissue paper until the bleeding stopped, entirely oblivious to her own. She held the bristles of the shaving brush beneath the running water for a moment, then applied it to the cake of soap in the bottom of an old coffee mug. Working up a foamy lather, she smiled and started to hum softly. Her big brown eyes half-lidded, she did not seem to notice the red drops falling into the lather.

"Gonna get you all cleaned up," she said, half to herself. "Then maybe we'll get you all dirty again, what do you think about that?"

Sarah winked like she always did, the cheek below her winking eyes dimpling in a way that made Jojo's chest feel tight. She gathered a heady foam on the brush and set to soaping his face, twisting the soft bristles in circular motions until he was nothing but suds. Through the thin honeycomb haze of the soap bubbles, he watched as she unfolded the razor and red blood vessels burst in her eyes. The dark brown skin of her face was taking on a blue hue and her breathing was becoming laboured and heavy. She held up the razor until it glinted in the light and brought it down to scrape across Jojo's cheek. Her left eye clouded, rolled up into the socket until the iris disappeared.

"Steamy in here," she said.

She swiped at him with the razor and Jojo ducked back. Her depth perception was shot with the one eye out of commission.

"Oh," she said, touching her mouth. "I'm sorry."

Jojo frowned and reached for the razor. "Maybe I should—"

"I—I don't . . . feel . . ." Sarah moaned and dropped to the floor in a heap. Jojo smelled fresh excrement; her bowels had voided. He cried her name and threw himself at her, seizing her shoulders and shaking her madly. He was helpless in the face of the oozing, dime-sized hole in her brow, open-mouthed and eyes welling up.

"Sarah," he muttered. "Oh, Sarah."

White foam fell in sudsy blobs from his face and burst when they splashed against her body. The water continued to roar out of the faucet, but he was oblivious to it. His eyes burned from the soap and teared up, washing it all out. He fell into a squat beside the dead woman and whimpered, reached quivering fingers out to touch her cold, blue face. The skin retracted at his touch, tightened and broke apart, fragile as an egg yolk. Jojo gasped as he watched her face shrink against her skull and split wherever the angles of her face pressed through, turning her once smooth and perfect skin into melting mush. In moments, she came to look like what she truly was: a woman who had been dead over a year, left to the damp earth and its countless parasites and the ravages of time. A sheer blue nightie filled with bones and rot and useless, agonizing memories.

"I killed you, didn't I?" he asked of the decomposed remains. "Beth pulled the trigger, but I'm the one who killed you. Jesus Christ, I'm the one who killed you."

Sunken in the wretched puddle of rot that encompassed the bones of Sarah's right hand was the straight razor, still wet with soap and a thousand tiny brown hairs. The blade accused him, beckoned to him. Jojo heaved a laugh and the laugh became a sob. A year of self-pity and bitter regret had done the trick—he thought only of himself and his own pain, drank to dull it and managed to bury the sting of love. Love that rotted away to the putrescence he saw before him. It stung him now, and it hurt like hell.

"What a fucking world," he said as he plucked the razor from the fetid pap on the washroom tiles. He ran the razor under the steaming water in the tub, washing away the yellow-black gunk of dead flesh.

"I shoulda let you alone, darling."

He flicked his wrist and knocked water from the gleaming steel.

"Either that or Beth ought to've killed me, too."

Love, he knew now, was something for the pictures: another damn good reason he never went anymore. William Powell and Myrna Loy, or Fred Astaire and Ginger Rogers—fantasy couples who shared fantasy loves. In real life it was compromise and disappointment, wrong choices and deep societal limitations that reined a man in and lashed him into submission. You did what you were damn well supposed to do or you paid for it in blood and hate. And for a sub-human freak like Jojo Walker, you sure as shit took what you could get and didn't complain when you got it. He'd been lucky and he spit in luck's face. Then the spit turned into bullets and both his distant wife and impossible lover were spared the anguish he spent every hour kicking and screaming against, to no avail.

Jojo stood up and stepped over the liquid remains of Sarah to the small mirror on the opposite wall. He ran the heel of his hand up one side and down the other, wiping the condensation away to see the strange face that stared back at him: a monster's face, dripping with froth, two wavering red eyes embedded in the stubbly prickles of unwanted hair. He thought about what the reverend had told him, the implication that his incantations to the Morning Star were what brought upon the myriad miseries that afflicted the people of Litchfield, that he'd extended a foolish invitation that ignited a firestorm of despair as a forerunner to the coming of Barker Davis. He scowled at the werewolf in the mirror, whose personal responsibility he could not absolve no matter how many ancient words twisted the sleepy quietude of an unremarkable Southern town.

No sorcerer had forced his hand, made him fall for a girl he wasn't allowed to have. He clenched a fist and wrenched it back, ready to smash the monster's face in front of him, but the rage expired in heavy sigh.

"What a fucking world," he said.

He felt the spiny contours of his throat with one hand while he brought up the razor with the other.

CHAPTER TWENTY-TWO

"This ain't no good," Charles said, pacing the lobby. "We can't just leave him up there, not with *her*."

"He knows what he's doing," Theodora offered lamely.

Charles snorted. "Then I don't reckon you know too good. Now I love that man, he's my friend, but making good decisions ain't one of his best skills."

"I know a bit about that."

"You know the *white* side of it. Me, I know *both* sides. I'm telling you that man's lucky he didn't get strung up once on this side of town and then again on the other. And him a policeman at the time."

"Nice words for a good friend."

"It's the truth. As things went, he was lucky as all get-out; he didn't really break no laws and all he got for his trouble was fired by the sheriff."

"I'd say he got a lot more than that."

"That's true. But being an outcast is a sight better than swinging from a tree."

"You sure about that, Charles?"

Charles puckered his eyebrows and glanced away.

"From what I know," she continued, "that man has been a pariah all his life, since the day he was born. Now, I don't much cotton to an unfaithful man, but I expect love is love and when it hits you there isn't a whole hell of a lot anybody can do about it. You take your chances and place your bets, and maybe more often than not the bet's no good and the horse comes in last, but that's life, ain't it? Unless you have a crystal ball tells you how everything's going to work out, you just got to jump in feet first and hope for the best. Most of the time, anyway.

"I don't suppose I would have ever stepped out on my husband, God rest his wicked soul, but being married to him certainly didn't turn out the way I thought it would, and my guess is the same went for Jojo Walker. Maybe it ain't pretty to look at life that way, but I don't see it being any other way. He bet on the wrong horse the same as me."

"Then maybe he shoulda took his licks and gone on home like everybody else."

Theodora pressed her lips together until her mouth looked like a cut. Behind them something pounded from the cashier's cage. Charles frowned and looked that way.

Mr. Thomas threw himself against the mesh, snarling and clawing at the criss-crossing wires like a rabid animal in its cage. The mesh rattled and Thomas growled, then backed up and hurled himself at it again. Theodora caught a convulsive breath. Charles muttered, "The hell?"

"You're not supposed to be here," Thomas rasped, his voice like broken bones grinding together. "Get out, nigger! Get out, whore!"

"Oh, Jesus," Theodora groaned. "Here we go again."

Thomas collided with the mesh, his face scraping along the exposed wire ends which cut his skin and dragged it into open, jagged wounds. He pawed at the cage like a mad dog and screamed, though from pain or frenzy no one could tell.

"That bitch nurse took my shotgun," Charles said. "It's all you, lady."

"All me? But—I can't . . . I can't just . . ."

"Then give it here."

His eyes half-hooded and mouth turned down to a determined grimace, Charles reached for the rifle in her hands. She wrenched away, wide-eyed and afraid.

"It's not his fault. It's none of their fault, Charles! It's that, that man—the magician. Please . . ."

The front doors boomed open, slamming against the inside walls and sending a deafening echo across the lobby. Thomas screeched furiously and found the latch to the cage's door. Ernie Rich jerked in, revolver at the ready and looking very much like a man who had been to hell and back.

"Sheriff, wait," Theodora managed to say as Thomas broke free from the cashier's cage. He dropped to all fours and fell into a loping gait, growling and lashing his head from side to side.

Rich took aim at the rapidly approaching man and bellowed, "Hold it!"

"Get out, get out, GET OUT!" Thomas roared, coming on fast.

The sheriff squeezed the trigger and his revolver bucked as a black burst formed in Thomas's cheek and he went skidding back across the floor, leaving a broad swath of blood in his wake.

Theodora cried, "*No!*" and fell to her knees. "It wasn't him! Oh God, it's not any of them, can't you see? It—it's the *magic!*"

"Wouldn't have made much difference whose fault it was after he'd bitten my throat out, Miss," Rich said between heaving breaths.

"He's right," Charles agreed. "It's just like the war. They all just kids over there blasting away at each other, but it's that or get your head blowed off."

"It isn't though," Theodora wept, her face hidden in her hands. "It isn't a war."

"You're wrong about that, Miss," Rich said sternly. "It sure as hell is."

)(

Washing the last of his shame down the drain, Jojo snatched a towel from the side of the basin and wiped down his freshly-shaven face, neck, and hands. He blinked several times in succession and looked in the mirror. The werewolf was gone. And so was Sarah.

He went back through the door to the hotel room, unsurprised when he closed the door and it vanished completely. He wondered if there was anything left to surprise him at all.

The bed was unoccupied, though the sheets remained pressed into the vague, wrinkly shape of the slight young girl who recently lay there. *She* had taken Margie away again.

Minerva.

Jojo scowled at the vacant room and repulsed the shiver building at the base of his spine; a shiver born from the frigid air blasting through an open window and the savage anger reeling in his brain. He was making sense of something so utterly senseless that it defied his sanity. They had taken everything away from him, Barker Davis and Minerva, but making him believe he'd ever had anything to begin with.

His hands tightened to fists and the freshly shaven skin there burned. He knew now exactly what he had to do and why, and the cracking report that sounded from somewhere in the hotel only galvanized him to get to work.

You want chaos? he thought as he raced from the room and down the hall. *Well, you damn well got it.*

CHAPTER TWENTY-THREE

Some stars winked at Margie despite the smoky haze that filmed the sky, and she wondered why it was night. She was naked, on her back upon a bed of dead leaves and soft, loamy earth. The air was cold and the tree tops swayed gently in the breeze high above her. Her thigh stung, and she remembered the woman cutting into her, tasting her blood. She smelled the wood fire and worried for a moment that the forest was burning, but since she felt no heat she could think of no reason to move. If the air got warmer, she would. But for now she was quite comfortable.

Though she sensed movement in the middle distance among the trees, Margie still couldn't be bothered to raise her head. Someone was coming, their footsteps scuffing through the detritus—maybe more than one person. And they were dragging something, or at least that's what it sounded like to her. The closer they came, the more strongly she smelled the rich odour of upturned earth, no doubt dug out by whatever they were dragging. The haze was thickening but one star in particular shone brightly. She thought she recalled what it was, but the name escaped her. A gentle voice, much nearer than she expected, answered the question for her.

"It's Venus," he said. "Brightest thing in the night sky, apart from the moon. It's my lighthouse, this forest my harbour."

Margie raised her arms to cover her breasts and shifted her hips to conceal the dark patch of nakedness between her legs. The voice chuckled.

"Poor child. Saving your nakedness for that boy, Scooter, I imagine. Murdered his parents last night, you know. Brutal stuff."

Now the man was looming over her, his shape illumined vaguely in the starlight. She glared up at him and breathed out. Someone else moved behind him, just out of sight.

"They'll say I made him do it, but I didn't. I'm no hypnotist, and even if I were you should know that hypnotism is not an art to make people act beyond their natural capabilities. Scooter Carew killed his mother and father because he wanted to. It's not unusual, actually—not unusual at all. Youth always takes the place of its antithesis, just as life is required to make up for death. This place is positively marred by imperfections, in spite of my best intentions. There was only ever supposed to be one, my entry point in a way. An ugly door to a lovely house. Alas . . ."

"Who are you?" Margie squeaked.

The man smiled and turned to the person behind him. "Bring it up," he commanded. Then, to Margie: "Patience, child; that's what I've come to show you."

The nurse came into her field of vision, a tattered rope grasped in both hands which she pulled with all her strength. The rope's other end was affixed to a long wooden box, covered in loose dirt that fell off in clouds and clumps. A coffin.

"It had been a lot of years, of course," the man said almost apologetically. "I nearly forget where I'd buried it."

"Buried what?" Margie whispered.

"This, this right here," he said, clapping his hand against the old, dry wood of the coffin. "My body."

"Your . . . *body?*"

A grunt, then—a curt, impatient laugh.

"The author's characters can never comprehend his intentions, can they? Otherwise, Othello would surely have avoided Desdemona like the plague, had he understood the playwright's nasty little plans for them."

Margie wrinkled her nose and turned her gaze to the nurse, who relinquished the rope and stood up to her full height. She wiped the sweat from her brow and squinted at the haze.

"Will that damned house ever burn down?" she asked.

"It skipped a day," the man reminded her. "With the cat out of the bag so early on, I saw no reason to prolong the inevitable."

Margie shook her head and tried to sit up, but she felt as though a great weight was pressing her down. "Skipped a day? What does that mean?"

"It means that it's Friday night, child," he explained patiently. "The best night for a performance."

"What performance?"

The nurse hissed an angry sigh. "Will you shut her up?"

"Calm yourself, darling," he said to her.

"She's dancing on my last nerve."

"You must learn to be more tolerant."

Margie listened to them argue while she watched the man bend over the coffin, wiggling his fingers with uncontained excitement. He curled them under the lip of the lid and pulled. The wood groaned and something cracked. A strong, unpleasant musk escaped from within, sickly sweet and heavy like syrup. Margie gagged.

"Christ," the nurse groused. "What a stink."

"Thirty years," he responded cryptically as he lifted the lid the rest of the way and flung it off into the leaves. "Have a look, girl. Come on, you can get up now."

Margie sat up, the invisible weight gone, and pushed against the ground with one hand while keeping the other arm wrapped around her chest. She got to her knees, and then her feet, and stepped cautiously forward to look inside the coffin. A black, skeletal corpse rested there, its thin arms crossed over exposed ribcage. The jawbone was crooked and hair still sprouted from the top of the skull. She gasped and looked away, covering her face with her hand and stifling a small sob. The woman chuckled.

"You never looked better," she said.

"An extraordinary thing," he commented, "staring down at one's own corpse. I cannot say I recommend it, but still—extraordinary."

"What is this?" the child moaned. "What's it mean?"

"My poor girl," said the man, resting a hand on her shoulder. She jerked away. He shrugged. "These are the earthly remains of one Black Harry Ashford, magician extraordinaire, who died not five feet from where you are presently standing. He died because I killed him, smashed his head with a rock which accounts for the sad state of the dead man's jaw."

"God, but why?"

"Because I am Black Harry Ashford, Margie. And I hadn't any more use for those diseased old bones."

Margie stared, open mouthed, and forgot to keep covering her chest.

✕

Theodora heard the steps and spun around, her mind spinning wildly between flight or fight. When Jojo appeared from the staircase, she held her breath and felt tears spill down her face. He raised his brow and said, "Hiya, kid."

Sheriff Rich laughed. "'Bout time you shaved, Walker. You were looking pretty rough there for a spell."

"I guess I was."

"What about the girl?" Charles cut in. "Ain't she with you?"

"She wasn't there," Jojo said, sidling up to the trio and glancing around at their faces. "But I reckon I've got a good idea as to where we might find her. First I want us to split up into two pairs, though."

"What for?" Rich asked.

"Because I want to burn this goddamn town to the ground tonight," Jojo said.

CHAPTER TWENTY-FOUR

"Here's what I know," he began, facing the semi-circle of allies in front of the hotel. "I spent my early childhood in a circus freakshow, on account of my condition." He absently touched his smooth cheek when he said this. "I must've been nine or ten before I ran off, ended up in the home here in town. When I was little, there was a magician and a carnie, names of Harry Ashford and Tim Davis. Ashford died, and after that Davis came on strong and gradually took over the sideshow. I think he probably killed the magician and assumed whatever power the older man had, and he used that power to make a place for himself."

"Some power," Theodora said. "To place himself at the head of a sideshow."

"That's not what I mean," Jojo said. "The place he made for himself was this—he made Litchfield."

Theodora, Charles, and Sheriff Rich stared silently for a moment before Charles said, "Come again?"

"Yeah, all right, so it's not so easy to swallow. But hear me out. When Ashford died, the circus was camped out in the country, right at the edge of a forest. He'd been heading out into those woods every day, all alone, and staying out there until well into the night on some occasions. I know about it because it frightened a lot of the carnies, particularly when the guy started to get more and more introverted and less interested in performing parlour tricks. Looking back on it now, I think Ashford hit upon some *real* magic and he was going out there to practice."

He paused, reviewing everything the Reverend Shannon had told him about the spells and the astronomy and the summoning of Barker Davis. The picture was coming together even as he told it.

"Now this carnie, this kid Tim Davis, he heard about it too, only he wasn't scared. He was intrigued. I guess he followed the old sorcerer into the woods and tried to insinuate himself into the equation. The kid wanted some of that power for himself."

"So he killed the magician," Rich said skeptically.

"I don't think so."

"But you said—"

"I think Ashford killed Davis, more or less, but that Davis killed Ashford, too. Hang on, I'm getting myself mixed up. . . ."

"You and us, both," Theodora said.

Jojo found a bent cigarette in his pocket and lit it. He offered the pack around, but no one was interested.

"Okay," he went on, "here's the thing. Ashford used his magic to take over Tim Davis's body, and once he was in there, he killed his old self and came back alone."

He sucked at the end of cigarette and inhaled deeply. Ernie Rich scratched his head and narrowed his eyes.

He said, "You don't say."

"Maybe a day or two ago you'd lock me up and call the nearest bughouse, Ernie, but today—*now*—you know better. I was there . . . and so was she."

Jojo gestured with his head at Theodora, who gulped and nodded.

"You?" Rich asked, dumbfounded. "What in hell were you doing in a freakshow?"

"I wasn't in it, but I saw it. One hell of a coincidence, really."

"Except that it isn't one," Jojo countered. "Ashford did his magic and died in the woods behind the church, only there wasn't any church there at the time. . . ."

"Nonsense," Rich interrupted. "That church has stood there for five generations."

"Which church, Ernie? Shannon's crumbling old clapboard shack, or the towering black thing I know you saw out there yesterday?"

"I . . . well, I—"

"Some years later we returned to the same encampment, and that was when Theodora and her nanny came to see the circus."

"The first time we met," she said, her eyes wide with disbelief.

"I tried running away then, but I got caught. Later I tried again, and that time I made it. Or I thought I had."

"The home was a . . . a place keeper," Theodora said.

"Yes, but not just the home. What I'm telling you is that there wasn't anything here but open land and trees and scrub. There was no Litchfield. Ashford, or Barker, or whoever made it all up to keep me here. Waiting."

"Waiting for what?" Charles asked.

"For him to come back, when the time was right."

Rich snorted and made a face. "Right for what, Jojo? What's the point?"

"He's the God who went away," Jojo said, striking a puzzled look at his own wording. "He made a little world, this town, and let it come into its own over the last thirty years or so. I think I was the seed, in a way—Litchfield's own Adam. The link between the first world—the sideshow—and this one. Slowly, he sent others along, too; Theodora and her nanny, for example. I'm very sorry to tell you this," he said to her, "but I don't believe you ever went home again after that. You came here."

"But I'm *from* here," she argued, her face betraying her fright. "My daddy was from here. I can take you to his grave right now."

"A trick," he said sadly. "An illusion. This place is a lie, always has been. That son of a bitch collected people to fill it up until he was satisfied, then stopped to let it grow. Kids like Margie Shannon were born here, sure, but that doesn't make it any less the lie."

"And what about your wife? And that black girl . . ."

"Sarah," Jojo said. "Her name was Sarah."

"All right, Sarah. Was Sarah a lie, too?"

"I don't know. I hope not."

Ernie Rich grunted and stamped his foot on the pavement.

"Bullshit, Walker. Bullshit! This pavement, it's real. This . . . this hotel! It's fucking real!"

"As real as that black church was. Or the circus wagon and the clowns that vanished into thin air. Come on, Ernie—it's hard to accept, but look at the facts. We've been duped, all of us. Prisoners for thirty years." He dragged on the smoke and laughed. "We're all a bunch of goddamn rubes."

"But what's the point, Walker? What's the damn point?"

"Control, for one thing," Theodora calmly suggested. "It's like Jojo said: Davis got to be God, and that's no small thing."

"And even God destroyed the world he made that one time," Charles said.

Jojo flicked his butt into the street and watched the orange sparks burst when it hit the pavement. He smirked at the talk of God, an entity in whom he'd never believed, and he remembered the pastor's faithlessness and how it had seemed to set the maelstrom in motion. All Shannon had really done, Jojo thought, was toss out one deity and take on another. Now Barker Davis was God and Devil both, and he'd come back to the world he made to destroy it and everyone in it.

The sheriff asked what was the point. Jojo decided it was a good question.

"Look," he said to the group, "Davis never set foot in this hotel, so he must have been staying elsewhere. My guess is the woods where all this started."

"And that's where Margie is?" Charles asked.

"Maybe. I don't know. But unless one of you's got something better, that's where I'm heading."

"I'm going with you," Theodora announced.

"Fine," Jojo said. "That leaves Charles and Ernie with the other thing."

"You can't be serious," Rich said.

"As a heart attack, buddy."

"For Christ's sake, Jojo—you do realize you're instructing the elected sheriff of this town to set it on fire, don't you?"

"I hate to break it to you, but you're the elected sheriff of jack shit, pal. This is a dream, and half the folks in it are stark raving bug-fuck crazy. Now, I don't have the first clue what's to become of us once Litchfield is done and gone, or at least those of us who're still left. There's implications here that are far beyond me. All I know is that Davis is here to turn this place into a madhouse and I don't reckon you can destroy what's already burned to the ground."

"Scorched earth," Rich muttered. "That's what they call it in war. It's crazy."

"Fight fire with fire," Charles said.

"Right," Jojo agreed.

"Jesus jumped on Mary," the sheriff blasphemed, glaring at the night sky and the winking stars that filled it. "Say, how'd it get so dark so fast?"

Charles grinned and shook his head, taking Rich by the elbow. "Come on, Sheriff," he said. "We got a town to burn."

X

It did not take Jojo long to find a car with the key still in it. It was a Packard and the fender was all beat to hell, but it worked. He opened the passenger side door for Theodora, who half-curtsied before climbing in. He got in next to her on the other side and stood on the accelerator all the way out to the country. Along the way he gave her the digest version of his talk with Jim Shannon. She listened quietly and responded with silence.

"Something Charles said struck me," she said at some length. "He was talking about the Bible story, when God destroyed the world? Well, I guess he did that because he didn't like the way it turned out, right?"

"I can't say I know the Bible that well, but sure."

"It seems to me this might be similar, if reversed. Say Barker Davis wanted to create a little kingdom for himself—wouldn't it be a kingdom fit for its king? A sideshow world, populated by freaks and prisoners?"

"Sawdust and elephant shit."

"And misery, that's the key. I remember what it was like, what *you* were like. That's got to be how come you're the link. Forgive me for saying this, Jojo, but you're a particularly unhappy person, aren't you?"

Jojo jerked his head and threw a surprised glance at her.

"It's been a tough ride for you, and you haven't always reacted well, but really it's been tough from the beginning. The truly awful beginning."

"Big deal," he said, returning his gaze to the pitch black road. "Who's really happy with their lot, anyway? No one I've ever known."

"But that's not necessarily true. Some people are, even if they recognize the big, sometimes ugly sacrifices they're forced to make just to eke out a tiny little bit of happiness in their lives. And *that* is Davis's equivalent to the wickedness of man being great on the earth."

"So you're saying he expected us to develop into a parody of civil society? And that he's disappointed that we didn't?"

"Not even all the tragedy that started a year ago ruined us like he expected it to. It's his world and we're his puppets, maybe, but we're people, too. He can't decide how we feel or how we might react to those feelings. Jojo, I think he expected us to bring Litchfield down all by ourselves."

Jojo clicked his tongue against the roof his mouth and groaned.

"Knocked me down as low as I could go, but . . ."

"But you still got back up again," she finished for him. "That's what he couldn't have seen coming."

"And that's why he's back to finish the job himself."

"Yes, at least that's my best guess. Maybe he's planning on starting over, learning from his mistakes. One thing's for sure: he's a sadist in the extreme, and he needs a big sandbox to play in."

"Then let's go take it away from him."

The Packard lurched over the uneven road as he applied the brake to turn off, back toward the church and the sprawling woods behind it. The world remained enshrouded in night until, a few hundred feet down the side road, the treetops began to glow a dim orange. A little further still the lights came into view. The first light they saw derived from the leaping flames that consumed Shannon's house.

"Damn," Jojo said. "I hope he got out of there."

"Maybe he did," Theodora suggested.

He nodded, not believing it.

A minute later they saw the dozens of torches that lit the grounds of the encampment and its tents and numerous wagons. Shadowed figures moved about, some in groups. Many more sat still or leaned against tent poles, smoking cigarettes and juggling balls and engaging in impromptu wrestling matches. There were clowns and dwarves, men in battered hats barking orders and carnies, stripped to the waist, who obeyed them.

Jojo ground the car to a halt and switched off the headlamps.

"Looks like the circus is in town," Theodora said bitterly.

CHAPTER TWENTY-FIVE

He killed the engine and watched in silence, moving only when a fire-breather made him flinch. The flame leapt five feet from the bare-chested man's face, brightly revealing the ornate tattoos that covered his torso and snaked up his neck to the back of his shaven head. An obese woman applauded him: his only audience for the moment. Jojo thought the man looked vaguely familiar, and it occurred to him that a man wasn't likely to experience *déjà vu* with a heavily tattooed fire-breather unless he'd known one.

He had little doubt about it—this was the circus sideshow of his childhood.

He said, "Maybe you should wait in the car."

"Nuts to that," she said. "There's no telling what might happen down there."

"Exactly why you shouldn't come."

"Exactly why I should."

He frowned. "That isn't how I figure it."

She smiled. "I didn't ask how you figured it."

She pulled the handle, opened the door. "Come on," she said. "Let's go."

Slumping his shoulders and softly grunting, Jojo acquiesced and got out of the Packard. They each shut their respective doors gently and quietly, and they traipsed down the mild incline to the encampment at the forest's edge.

It was a muscular man with a handlebar moustache who noticed him first. Their eyes met, the strongman and Jojo, and the latter froze. A toothy grin spread out beneath the meticulously waxed whiskers and the huge man winked.

"Hey, kid," he said, his voice a resonant baritone. "Who let you out?"

The man's handle flashed in Jojo's mind—*Lion Jack*.

"We're looking for Davis," Jojo said. "Or maybe Ashford, the magician. You know where we might find either of them?"

"And who's the little lady?" Jack said, ignoring the question completely and bending over to display his teeth more closely. "Be careful, now: I know he's cute, but he's known to bite."

The strongman snapped his jaws at Theodora and roared with laughter. He then snatched a barbell up from the ground and carried it off, still shaking with laughter.

"What was that all about?" Theodora asked.

"Not really sure, but I guess they were all snowed. Even the kind ones believed I was everything they billed me as—a vicious little monster."

"That's what he saw, Jojo," she said, awed. "He saw you as a little boy, and me as a little girl."

"Hmn," he grunted. "I guess the show must go on."

"The hell it does," she said, her glowering face lit yellow by the torchlight.

He looked around, taking in all the hazy, ugly memories of the encampment from the rickety wagons to frayed canvas of the tents. One tent in particular interested him, and he pointed to it.

"There," he said. "Do you remember it?"

She followed the line from his finger to the tent and said, "Oh. Oh, yes."

It was the tent in which they first met, more than three decades before, and it was remarkably unchanged in every respect. The Ten-in-One.

Jojo took a moment to take it in, the unfeasibility of it, and then commenced a quick beeline straight for the open flaps. Theodora caught up with him before he ducked into the tent, squinting in the murkiness of the weak lantern light. Sawdust carpeted the ground inside. A sickly, yellow-skinned man crouched like a gargoyle on a wooden stool as if standing guard over the row of barred cages. His ribs jutted out, wrapped tautly in papery, jaundiced flesh; his cheeks sank like pits in his long, hollow face. He glanced up, his eyes glittering in the light, when they entered.

"You," he rasped, his voice every bit as papery as his skin. "You're not supposed to be out. You'll get a whipping."

"I'm looking for Davis," Jojo said. "Him or the magician. Where are they?"

The skeletal man jumped down from his perch, straightening out to his full height. He stretched out an arm and wiggled his bony fingers at Jojo.

"Come on, then. Back you go."

"Christ," Jojo growled. "What's he hearing, baby talk?"

The man scampered back suddenly, defensively displaying his palms.

"Whoa there, little fella," he said, eyeing Jojo cagily.

"I'd wager he's hearing you bark," Theodora ventured.

"Waste of time," he muttered as he turned back for the flaps.

"Wait!" the human skeleton cried. "No, stop!"

Jojo ducked to go back out when Theodora screamed, "Watch out!"

Instinctively he dropped to the sawdust, catching his weight on his hands and rolling away as the skeletal man's stool smashed against the ground and shattered. Theodora yelped as Jojo leapt up to a crouch and the man grabbed a splintered leg from the wreckage, which he jabbed at Jojo like a dagger.

"Back in your cage, you little puke!"

Jojo danced a circle with the man, shrugging out of his coat as they moved. The flame in the lantern flickered and the man lunged. Jojo met him halfway, quickly wrapping his coat around the sharp end of the stool leg and wrenching it out of the man's hands. He then sent an uppercut crashing into the guy's chin, snapping his head back and bowling him over. He collapsed on the sawdust, moaning pitifully.

Breathing hard, Jojo threw the coat and broken stool leg in a corner and bent down to take hold of the skeletal man's wrists. He dragged the man across the ground, from one end of the tent to the other, where the row of cages stood. There he paused for a moment, standing in front of the last one, the cage in which he was kept long ago. His stomach flipped and he tasted bile at the back of his throat. He shook it off, steeled himself and assumed a deep scowl as he dragged the man all the way into the cage and slammed the gate shut.

"You know that man?" Theodora asked.

"Probably."

He hooked an arm around the small of her back and led her toward the opening.

"This is a dead end," he said. "But I've got an idea where to go."

"The woods," she inferred.

Jojo touched the tip of his nose. "Bingo," he said.

※

Per the sheriff's instructions, Charles took the nozzle from the fuel pump and gave the handle a quick squeeze. Astringent gasoline spurted from the nozzle, dousing the section of bed sheet he'd affixed to the end of a table leg. He had three other makeshift torches at the ready, as well. He doused them in turn.

Across the street from the filling station, Ernie Rich struck a match and ignited his own torch, which erupted into a large bright flame. He was standing in front of the darkened windows of the Starlight Diner, one of which he promptly smashed in with the blunt end of the torch. Before the glass was done tinkling down to the floor inside and the sidewalk without, Rich hurled the burning torch into the diner. It landed behind the lunch counter, where its light was barely visible in the moments leading up to the sudden burst of grabbing flames that rapidly spread across the counter.

The heat took him by surprise, countering the frigidity of the night air and snapping at his face like wasp stings. He hurried to the middle of the street and watched as the fire quadrupled in size, filling the diner and melting the vinyl booths in seconds. He heard a distinct *whoomp* close by and turned to see Charles igniting his first torch, whereupon he touched it to the dry wooden siding of the city records office, which went up nicely. All the damn records were worthless anyway, fictions deserving of the flames that consumed them.

Rich sprinted back to the filling station to collect another torch. He took it back to the other side of the street before lighting it and carried it a block down to the Palace Theater.

))(

Barker Davis held the skull in the palm of one hand, blackened bits of flesh hanging in tatters like strips of rotted leather. He looked the skull over with detached interest like a jeweller examining a gem for imperfections. The nurse rolled her eyes and crossed her arms over her chest. Davis extended a forefinger and ran it around the edges of one of the skull's empty eye sockets, then brought it up to his nose and sniffed. Black dust wafted up from his fingertip and into his nostrils.

"Dust to dust," he said.

Margie watched intently, standing on the balls of her feet. Davis bent over the coffin to replace the skull, his back to her. She did not hesitate— Margie fell into a sprint, entirely unaware of which direction she was going. By the time she realized that she should have gone toward the smoke, rather than away from it as she had, it was too late to change her mind. She just needed to get away.

She flew through the woods, relying on instinct to avoid crashing into the trees she sped between. Dry twigs and brambles sliced at the bottoms of her feet, scraped the skin from her legs and sides. She did not care. She kept running.

Her mind reeled as it was, flitting across primitive, abstract concepts of terror and survival, and when she saw the distant, sputtering glimmer of firelight, she was sure she had gone full circle. The house fire had been behind her when she took off, and now it was flames that she spied ahead of her, dancing all Halloween orange at what had to be the edge of the forest. This meant to her that she'd thrown herself right back in danger's path, but also that her father's land was just seconds' running distance. A weird, involuntary giggle escaped her lips and she pumped her arms, willing herself to move faster for the open yard.

Voices filled the smoky night air: some laughing, some singing. Jangling music emanated from among the floating flames that she could see now were torches. And a figure stepped into her way, blocking her path—Margie could not slow down quickly enough and she collided with the coming shadow, shrieking as they fell together into a twisted heap of arms and legs.

"No!" she screamed, kicking at the figure with all her strength. "Get away! *Get away!*"

Arms reached for her, clawed at her shoulders. She spun away from them, scurrying over the cold dirt and crackly leaves and heaving herself back to her feet.

"Wait," said a woman's voice.

Margie did not think it was the nurse, but there was no sense in waiting around to confirm her suspicion. She swayed to the left and pointed herself at the torches, which by now symbolized a sort of salvation for her. Her plan permitted her to avoid the reaching arms of the figure she ran into—which was rising now—but did not account for the woman.

"Margie, stop," she said, and the woman embraced Margie in a tight bear hug that stopped her dead in her tracks.

She jerked and thrashed and let out a desperate cry. The woman squeezed her harder and the other one drew near, heavy footsteps crunching the undergrowth.

"Quiet, Margie," he said. "It's Jojo and Theodora."

"Wuh—what?"

"Shh," Theodora said. "Jojo, she hasn't got any clothes on."

"I think we're beyond propriety at the moment."

"They'll come after me," Margie stuttered, the sudden break inviting her tears. "They'll be coming."

Theodora released her and Margie stepped back, her nakedness only partially hidden with the moonlight streaming through the branches in thin, white shafts.

"We're finishing this," Jojo said. "Tonight. It's nearly over."

"Over? How?"

"Too much to explain," Theodora cut in. "But trust us: this ends tonight."

She reached for the girl's hand, and in that moment Margie blew a puff of air and her mouth went slack. Her head wobbled as if it were balanced on a spring and the skin around her neck split open, spraying blood in all directions. Margie said, "*Guh*" in the second before her neck snapped and her head shot away from it, leaving a spurting stump between her shoulders. Theodora screamed as the girl's decapitated body dropped to the ground. A crunching of leaves some yards distant signalled the landing of the severed head.

Jojo nearly dove to catch what was left of Margie before she hit the ground; some primordial impulse telling him to save her when it was much too late. Instead he grabbed fistfuls of his own hair and howled with despair. Between their combined cries of anguish, neither he nor Theodora heard the approach of the woman in the snug nurse costume. Only when the woman spoke did their cries turn to surprised gasps.

"No need for her anymore," she said, holding up a beheaded doll in her hand. "Or this."

She tossed the damaged doll into a tangle of brush and glanced disinterestedly at Margie's headless corpse.

"Goddamn you," Jojo growled.

"Helpful little things, poppets. And easy as pie."

Jojo roared with rage and sprang at the nurse, but his foot got caught in a tough root and he toppled over. The root then snapped out of the earth and whipped at him, cutting his face. He groaned and threw his hands up in defence. Two more gnarled roots shot up and wrapped around his wrists, pulling him to the ground and securing him there. He lashed his head from side to side and twisted at the waist, but the roots remained firm. A grumbling erupted from the ground beside him and he watched in terror as the forest floor opened up and swallowed Margie's body whole. In an instant she was gone and the ground was solid again; it was as though she'd never been there at all.

"Folk magic," Barker Davis said with a showman's flourish, emerging from the shadows into the moonlight. "Simple stuff, most of it. A little cheesecloth, the right mix of herbs—bones, if they are procured in just the right way—and anyone can make an effigy that kills surer than any weapon. Why, if our fighting men abroad had the likes of my poppets at their disposal, Hitler and Tojo would be reduced to minced meat like *that*."

He snapped his fingers and spread his arms, the performer even now.

"But why Margie?" Theodora sputtered, her voice wavering in her grief. "She was just a kid! What'd she ever do to you?"

"She lived too well," Davis said with mock-reverence, jutting out his lower lip and slowly shaking his head. "Though she died in terror, and that's what really matters, I think. I am a god here, in this place, and I am a god of chaos. But you—*you!*"

Instantly the showman's serenity turned to frothing rage. He sneered and assumed a wide, angry stance.

"You people, you *shut me out!* I made the world and put you in it, and you rotten shits went on with it as though it were all *real*."

"It was, to us."

"It *never* was. It was a cracked mirror and you simply stuck tape to the cracks and pretended it was never broken. You got married to one another and shat out babies and went to work. You could have had anything, you stupid fools. *Anything*. But you chose banality."

"So, what?" Jojo seethed from the impregnable prison of roots. "You brought all this because we were fucking boring you?"

Davis chortled through his teeth and swept his hand through the air, slicing it like a knife. The roots tightened and more sprang forth to wind about his chest. Jojo wheezed.

"I would not have come at all if I hadn't been invited, as you well know. And now that I'm here, I am looking forward to a fresh start. One that does not include either of you, naturally."

Another broad gesture and Theodora found herself yanked back until her spine smashed against a tree trunk. Her breath rushed out of her and didn't return for several agonizing seconds, while splintery ropes of wood clutched at her, binding her to the tree. When her breath returned it was weak and strained.

Jojo listened to her hissing breath and worried that the vines that bound her were only moments from squeezing the life out of her. He rasped her name, but it came out so weakly even he couldn't hear it. The nurse—Minerva—tittered at his plight, fuelling his already hot hatred for her. He squirmed, and the roots contracted even more. Barker Davis sauntered up to where he helplessly laid and rested a foot on the unbreakable bonds.

"Jojo, my boy, you were always meant to be contained. A beast like you should never be permitted to run free, not unless I allow it and I can only allow it if you're up to your eyes in malicious intent. But no matter how much I throw at you, your misery only simmers and never boils. A real shame."

"Goddamnit, Davis," Jojo hissed. "Why me?"

"Because you are a monstrosity, of course. A freak. And more than that, you are an *angry* freak. All I wanted was a circus of terror and rage, perhaps a liberal amount of depravity, and I counted on you to set it in motion. I consider myself a comparatively just god—I gave you, all of you, your free will to do with as you saw fit. But there was no imagination—hate, yes, and more than enough desire to carry that hate to its most interesting ends—but no imagination at all. I cannot begin to tell you how disappointed I am in you, Jojo. My heart weeps."

"Tough shit," Jojo said.

"Alas, it's tough shit for you, my boy. Goodnight."

He turned to bow at the waist to Minerva. She just grinned.

"Barker," Jojo grunted, his breathing more laboured than ever.

Davis glanced at him noncommittally.

"I'm going to kill you," Jojo said.

The magician jabbed his tongue into his cheek, jutting it out as he considered Jojo's threat. He opened his mouth wide, staring up at the sky, and said, "I wish you the best of luck."

He spun on his heel, dramatic as ever, and made a theatrical gesture to the nurse.

"Minerva."

She nodded as the ground between them opened up once again: a great, crumbling maw. Jojo stared, his heart thudding furiously in his breast, unable to know whether the hole was Minerva's magic or Davis's. The magician lifted his arms like a kid who needed help taking off his shirt, and leapt into the waiting mouth, vanishing down its blackness in an instant. In another instant, the earth sealed itself up again, no trace that it had opened at all.

Minerva sucked at the cool, fragrant air of the woods and exhaled it with a small moan. She then walked gradually, sensually to the tree against which Theodora was bound. Theodora whimpered, turning her head but keeping her eyes fixed to the nurse, who flicked her tongue at the captive which was a snake's tongue—long, thin, and forked. She drew up to her captive and for a brief moment the moonlight glinted in her eyes; her pupils long black slits and the rest marbled yellow and white. She hissed, her tongue thrashing wildly, and touched her hand to Theodora's cheek. The skin of her fingertips was dry and scaly.

Jojo went limp. He cried tears of rage. He heard Theodora yell out, and he knew Minerva was hurting her somehow. His throat constricted and his face burned hot. With the next sobbing scream he heard, Jojo opened his eyes to see Minerva pressed against Theodora, one leg hiked up and her reptile tongue whipping at the weeping woman's face. Minerva's head wobbled and her hair spun wildly out as her scalp split down the middle of her skull. She shook more violently then, her hair falling away like a wig as the skin tore further and sloughed to her shoulders. She was shedding.

Minerva had to undress to complete the metamorphosis, and she hissed and sniggered as she did so. Once the white nurse's blouse and skirt were discarded, she began to pull off her skin with equal ease. What emerged from beneath was a yellowish-green creature with slits for a nose and needle-like teeth that dripped slime from her gaping, unhinged mouth. Theodora was reduced to a low, keening moan, her mind breaking with terror.

The Snake Woman, Jojo thought. All she'd ever done in the Ten-in-One was gyrate on the platform in a tattered, revealing costume with a drugged, half-dead boa constrictor lounging on her shoulders. Barker Davis made her into something more literal than that, a construct of his Luciferian sorcery. And now, armed with his infernal gifts, Minerva was taking substantial delight in toying with her victim prior to ultimately killing her.

A plaintive wail rumbled out of Jojo's throat, blasting the treetops with his grief and rage. He dug his fingernails into the heels of his palms until they bled. Minerva dug her nails, which were actually something more akin to talons, into the trunk of the tree, raking them down to shower fragments of bark on Theodora's head. Jojo saw her squirm, trying in vain to avoid the sharp talons and flicking tongue. He filled his chest with air and released it with a deafening, animalistic roar. The sound shook the branches that hung above him and sparks burst among the twisted tangle of roots that bound him, crackling and erupting into flame.

The roots burned and so did his skin, but he pressed hard against them nonetheless, depending upon the fire to weaken their hold. It did, and as the wood blackened and hot, grey ash sprayed all around him, Jojo snapped the roots one by one until he was free. His shirt smouldered with sparkling orange pinpricks, so he tore it off and advanced, naked to the waist, toward the hissing creature that scraped at Theodora's face with its claws.

"Minerva!" he bellowed.

The creature twirled to face him, its mouth pulling back into a hideous display of sharp, crooked teeth. She arched her back and stepped out of the mound of ripped, pink skin. The segmented scales that covered her now gleamed like bits of glass in the sparse light of the moon.

"What the hell did he do to you?" Jojo said.

She lunged, bounded across the short distance to him, all teeth and claws as she fell upon him. Jojo threw a fast right jab that glanced off the side of her head, stunning her and sending her spinning away. She shrieked a sibilant scream and came clambering back at him. Jojo reared back for a second blow but she was faster, dragging talons across his hirsute chest that cut deep. The wounds burned worse than the flaming roots and he moaned, stumbling backward. She made another pass, stabbing three claws into the flesh of his right shoulder and sinking her teeth into his left bicep. Blood boiled up from the wounds. Jojo gritted his teeth until his jaw throbbed and thrust his head against hers, smashing against her left temple. Minerva whipped her head back, black blood hanging in ropes from her teeth. Jojo wrapped his red arm around her neck and squeezed. She withdrew her claws from his shoulder and swatted at his face as he tightened his hold, constricting her throat in the crook of his elbow. Her jaw crunched and jutted out at an awkward angle; her perfectly round eyes stared without emotion.

"Jesus, but you're an ugly bitch," he said as he jabbed a thumb into her right eye.

The orb caved against the pressure, bursting wetly. She bellowed in pain and wriggled in his grasp, but to no avail. Jojo only squeezed harder still and kept on squeezing until her thrashing grew weak and her screams quieted. He maintained his grip even when she stopped moving altogether, listening closely to the cracking of her windpipe and the last of her whistling breath until she was dead.

He released Minerva, and her body sagged, sliding down the length of him until it came to a rest on the ground. The sharp, rusty odour of blood wafted up to his face, and he saw that the corpse at his feet was that of a skinned woman, all corded muscles glistening red and white. He gagged and looked away. The magic died with her.

Theodora whimpered again, snapping Jojo back to reality. He staggered over to her, the fresh wounds in his chest, shoulder, and arm screaming at him to stop moving. He felt like the recipient of a knife attack and knew he would have fared no worse if he had been.

"Jojo," Theodora said quietly. "What . . . what was that?"

"An old friend," he said as he grabbed handfuls of vine and pulled with all his strength. They did not break, but they loosened enough for him to work them up and over her head. Some of her hair got caught in the knots and was yanked out with the rescue. She yelped and her shoulders jumped.

"I'm sorry," he said.

"It's all right."

"Careful not to trip."

"Is she dead?"

Jojo looked to the bloody body on the ground and then back at Theodora. "Yeah."

"Good."

She took his hand and raised her legs, one at a time, out of the loosened vines. She touched her face where Minerva had scratched her and winced.

"Is it bad?"

"You're worse."

"It's relative."

She screwed up her mouth to one side and sniffed at the air. "Smoke," she said.

"The preacher's house."

"More than that. I think it's from town."

"That's good. That means the boys are getting it done."

"Those roots," she added, her brow creased in thought. "They burned, too."

"They did, yeah."

"How'd you manage that?"

"I have no idea. And I'm not going to worry about it now. He's still out there, so we've still got work to do. Or at least I do. After all this—"

"I'm coming," she said sharply.

Jojo said, "All right," and left it at that.

"But what now? For us, I mean. Where do we go?"

He scratched his chin with one hand and patted his pockets with the other, looking for a packet of cigarettes that wasn't there.

"Where would you go if you were God?"

"You mean the church."

He nodded. She blinked, touched the deep scores on her face again and then started back the way they came. He caught up with her and together they navigated the dark woods until the border between forest and field came into view. The circus was gone and the night was silent, black. The church loomed in the middle distance, dark and lonesome-looking on the slight rise. They emerged from the trees and paused to look at it.

Theodora coughed, fought back a sob. "Margie," she said.

Jojo said, "Yeah."

They resumed walking and headed up the rise to the church.

CHAPTER TWENTY-SIX

The Palace burned, the blaze snapping and roaring. The roof caved in, and for a moment the screen would have been visible to anyone standing in the street.

But no one was. The streets and sidewalks were empty, the buildings all vacant and mostly dark until the fires reached them. As the flames spread, leaping from rooftop to rooftop and seeking easy purchase in the old, dry wood that comprised most of them, there was no one around to lament the loss of their town centre. The Starlight Diner had already collapsed into a smouldering heap of wood, brick, metal and glass. Tuck Arnold's hardware store went up in mere seconds, his substantial stock of lumber in the back providing additional fuel to help the inferno along. Finn's drugstore burned slow for an hour before exploding, hurling burning shrapnel every which way, which in turn ignited nearly everything it struck. Even the trees burned, and there were plenty of trees around Litchfield.

By the time the rolling hellfire reached the Litchfield Valley Hotel, the last guest was long gone. None of Barker Davis's roadshow company remained and all the staff were either dead or otherwise engaged. There had been a smattering of other people, travelling salesmen and drifters for the most part, but they simply burned up like morning mist in the sun before the fire came anywhere near the hotel. Had anyone been around to see them vanish, they would have thought it was as though they'd never been there at all. But no one had.

What people remained in Litchfield were the true locals, the people who had always been there from the very start or those who were born there. Nearly all of them were asleep in their beds in their homes which were beyond the reach of the inferno. Some were dead, however, their remains turned to ash in the conflagration. Russell Cavanaugh and Phyllis Gates, Finn and Jake and Hershal who sold shoes all cooked in the intense heat or beneath fallen debris. Tuck Arnold, too, burned in his storeroom and Betty Overturf froze to death in the Starlight's walk-in freezer before the diner burned down.

When the Palace's screen collapsed onto the seats, its frame cracked Ernie Rich's skull and sent him sprawling. He remained semi-conscious for the duration, wondering what had ever possessed him to enter the theatre after he set it aflame. His scalp trickled blood and his hands stuck to the hot, tacky floor. It occurred to him that the kids who worked for Russ Cavanaugh never did a very good job of cleaning the place up, and that was last coherent thought to pass through the sheriff's mind before he burned to death, trapped underneath the crushing weight of the aluminized screen upon which he'd seen dozens of pictures over the years.

One of the very last institutions of Litchfield's town centre to burn was Wade McMahon's filling station, the source for all the gasoline that fuelled the firestorm's first baby steps. Charles returned to it after torching Earl's tavern, which felt devilishly good considering how Earl would never let Charles enter the place on account of his colour. Upon returning to the filling station, he discovered that he had one torch left among those he'd doused with gas and left on the curb. He picked it up and glanced around in search of something else to burn. A smile played at his mouth; in spite of what was at stake, in spite of himself, he was having a grand old time. And upon realizing that the only place left to him was McMahon's pride and joy, and that he would have no need of torches anymore, his smile only broadened.

They were so gorgeous, those dancing flames. They surrounded him on all sides, swirling ever upward like dervishes. Only the castaway island of the filling station remained still, unmoving, unlit. So Charles unhooked the nozzle from the fuel pump and squeezed the handle, sprayed acerbic smelling gasoline at the gas-stained pavement at his feet. It splashed back at him, soaking his shoes and trousers. He hummed while he did this, a little hymn his grandmother taught him when he was just a boy. Something about racing against the Devil.

Charles let the nozzle fall from his hand and it hit the ground clattering, still spitting gas. He fished in his vest pocket for the book of matches, half of them torn out now. The back of the matchbook had LITCHFIELD VALLEY HOTEL—SINCE 1888 printed in gold lettering on it. He read this and chuckled, shaking his head.

He said, "1888 my foot." Then he tore a match out and struck it against the strip on the back. He dropped it.

The ground vomited flames that engulfed his feet and spread up his legs. He danced, kicking his legs like an Appalachian hillbilly, and let out a long and high-pitched wail when his trousers melted into his flesh. The pain was unbelievable, yet oddly satisfying. He laughed as he screamed.

And in the brief moments before the fire shot up the nozzle and the fuel pump exploded, Charles sang his grandmother's hymn at the top of his voice.

"I an' Satan had a race—
Hal-le-lu! Hal-le-lu!
I an' Satan had a race—
Hal-le-lu! Hal-le—"

The explosion rocked the town centre, shaking the earth and bringing the filling station down in a rumbling crumble of brick and mortar and roaring fire. An enormous column of flame shot into the sky, a screaming tower of light and heat at the nexus of Barker Davis's wonderland that could be seen for miles in any direction, had anyone been around to see it.

But no one was.

CHAPTER TWENTY-SEVEN

Jojo had only very rarely visited Litchfield's sole house of worship over the years, and typically only upon the occasions of birth, marriage and death. His own wedding to Beth, such as it was, had been conducted there, and she was now buried in the churchyard on the south side of the clapboard building. Regular Sunday services, however, were never his style and he avoided them like something catching, despite the countless, unwanted recommendations that came to him in the wake of his wife's suicide that "it might do him some good." The funeral was the last time he set foot in the church, until now.

It was a rectangular building, some fifty or sixty feet deep with white siding where the paint wasn't peeling off. There was a stumpy steeple over the eaves with a white wooden cross jutting out of it, and a short porch sagged before the two front doors. Over the doors was a hand-painted sign nailed to the façade, its three simple words crafted with care: *He Is Risen*.

Jojo gave a grunt at the sign and climbed the four creaking steps to the porch. Theodora came close behind.

"No lights in there," she observed.

"Well, if he's undoing his creation, I guess the light would be the last to go."

"How very ecumenical of you."

He snorted and grabbed the door handle. "Are you ready for this?"

"I don't even know what 'this' is."

"This, Theodora, is Little Big Horn."

She bunched her eyebrows into a tight knit and faintly smiled. "And I don't reckon we're the Indians, are we?"

"Not by a damn sight, no."

"Glad we cleared that up, then. Open the door already, would you?"

He did.

A blast of freezing air rushed out of the church, slamming into them and eliciting cries of shock from both. The unlikely Chinook was many times colder than the impossible winter that befell the town before, so cold that it stung their skin badly and stabbed at Jojo's wounds like daggers. Theodora jounced to the side, seeking protection behind the refuge of the open door. Jojo pressed on, his hands up to cover his face. A deafening, enraged roar shook out of the blast, a thousand voices in torment and dripping with hate. All of them belonged to Barker Davis.

The blast lessened but the chill remained. Jojo stepped into the chapel, the floorboards groaning beneath his weight. When another roar sounded he braced for it, but this time is was nowhere close. From the porch Theodora shouted, "Look!"

He turned to see a pillar of fire jet in the far distance in the general direction of town.

"He's in town?" she asked.

"I don't think so. I don't expect there's any town left by now."

"Maybe we should wait, then. For Charles and Sheriff Rich, I mean."

A low, throaty chortle sounded from the back of the pitch black chapel: a response to Theodora's suggestion. Jojo turned toward the awful laugh and peered into the chapel.

"They won't be joining you," Barker Davis said, his movements noisy but invisible in the shadows. "No one will come. Litchfield is gone, all but this church, which will be the rib from which I remake the world."

"But why, goddamn it?" Theodora yelled into the darkness. "What do you get out of something like that? Or do you just get your kicks from torturing innocent people?"

Davis laughed a steady, simmering laugh.

"Innocent? Not hardly. Innocence died the last time a deity wiped the slate clean. And as for why—well, I'm perfectly flabbergasted that you should ask. Here I am a god, and gods reign indefinitely."

Scraping steps shambled across the floor, drawing nearer. Theodora backed against the door and Jojo assumed a fighting stance. Davis approached the dim greyness of the outside light and came into it, his black, skinless skull grinning permanently at them.

Theodora gasped, covered her mouth with her hand. Jojo merely flashed a disgusted look at the walking corpse before him, all decked out in black tails, cummerbund and a sombre black bowtie. The corpse bowed slightly, extending skeletal hands out with gentlemanly flourish.

Jojo said, "Black Harry."

"Abracadabra," the dead magician rasped, a grey tongue, half eaten away, flopping behind rotten teeth.

"You know something, Harry?" Jojo said, sneering. "I never much cottoned to you."

And with that, Jojo charged Black Harry and tackled him. A cloud of foul-smelling dust burst from the magician's sleeves and collar. They fell into a heap, Jojo on top, and the skull leered up at him, wobbling as laughter continued to echo out of its gaping mouth. From floor level Jojo noticed the shape of a man lying still under the pews. He needed only a moment's glance to tell who it was. And in that moment Black Harry Ashford started to mutter in a strained, sandpapery voice.

"*Lucifero, Ouyar, Chameron, Aliseon, Mandousin,*" he intoned. "*Premy, Oreit, Naydrus, Esmony, Eparineson, Estiot . . .*"

"Ah, for Christ's sake," Jojo grumbled. He pinned the corpse's neck to the floor with one hand and landed a punch to its jaw with the other. The jaw crunched and jerked askew. Then the thing's entire body spasmed and the jaw righted itself.

"*Dumosson, Danochar, Casmiel, Hayras,*" it continued.

"Knock it *off!*" Jojo shouted as he planted both his hands on either side of the skull. The bone was slimy with rot and earth. He dug his thumbs into the small holes at the bottom of the temporal plates and squeezed. Sutures cracked under the pressure. Jojo then wrenched his arms upward, defying the burning pain in his shoulder, and pulled with every ounce of strength available to him.

The skull babbled even as the bones of its neck splintered and fractured.

"*Fabelleronthon, Sodirno, Peatham . . .*"

With an enormous groan, Jojo bared his teeth and pulled the head free of the body, severing the frail neck completely and silencing the putrid skull of Black Harry Ashford forever.

He hefted the skull up like some primitive, cultic offering, his chest rising and falling with gasping breaths. The panting breaths soon turned to panting cackles, a breathless sniggering that would have seemed insane to anyone who failed to grasp the circumstances.

"Is that all he had?" Jojo wheezed. "Is that all it took?"

He heaved himself up, first on one knee and then to his feet, still grasping the skull. He regarded the grisly thing for a moment, a dead and empty thing, and then hurled it at the nearest wall—against which the skull shattered like a vase, splitting into countless shards that dropped harmlessly to the floor in a clattering rain.

Next, Jojo returned his attention to the rest of Harry Ashford: the well-dressed headless corpse on the chapel floor. He raised his right foot over the cadaver's trunk and brought it down hard and fast, destroying the rib cage in a crunching burst of broken bone and grave dust. Unsatisfied with this, Jojo continued to stomp on the body, crushing the delicate old bones underfoot with each crushing step. In no time at all, he found himself merely grinding up dust, contained in a tattered magician's tuxedo.

"It's done," Jojo whispered. "It's finished."

He could not help but smile as he wiped the cold sweat from his brow. He straightened himself out, worked a kink out of his aching shoulder and turned back to the doorway. Theodora was not there. He called her name but received no answer. He went out to the porch, looked around the immediate environs of the church. He didn't see her anywhere.

Bewildered and not a little exhausted, he returned to the chapel and felt blindly along the wall for a light switch. It took some time and a fair amount of stumbling, but he found one and flipped it. A tacky fake chandelier with a dozen small bulbs made to look like candle flames flickered on above him. Its smoky yellow light glinted off a metallic object in the centre of the well-trodden aisle between the rows of pews. Jojo was astounded to discover it was Jim Shannon's Lucifer sigil.

"What in God's Jesus-green earth . . . ?"

Not two feet from the sigil the dead, paper white hand of Barker Davis sagged from beneath a pew. He saw the body when he was on top of Black Harry Ashford, and he knew then what it meant. Ashford abandoned the body, the young man who swept up the puke and popcorn and animal shit when he wasn't hurling invective at the gypsy with the monkey or trying desperately to get into Minerva the Snake Woman's pants. He'd grown old in it, waiting predatorily for his moment to strike and then, like the atrocity Minerva became at his behest, he had shed the skin of Barker Davis.

The hand seemed to point lazily at the gleaming metal of the sigil, which darkened under the approach of Theodora, who appeared from among the pews and walked slowly, seductively toward him. Jojo froze, staring stupidly at her red smile and pinched eyebrows.

"Come Lucifer, come," she said in a deep voice.

"What is this . . ." he mumbled, knowing but not believing.

"Come Lucifer, come," Theodora repeated. And then again. And again.

Jojo took several steps back, involuntarily shaking his head as the tears welled up in his eyes. "You son of a bitch," he said. "You rotten, goddamned son of a bitch."

"All I ever wanted was a mad, mad world," she said.

"You had it. It already was. For Christ's sakes there's a World War on."

Even as he said it, Jojo doubted its veracity—was there really a war sweeping the globe, or was that just another one of Barker's . . . of *Ashford's* lies? He guessed he'd never know. He backed up all the way to the porch.

"The fires were beautiful," she said, floating her delicate hands to the buttons of her blouse, which she began to undo, one by one. "I thank you for that."

The blouse fell away like paper ash in a breeze, and her stiff wire brassiere followed it. Jojo looked away, embarrassed to see what she'd never have wanted him to see, not like this. As if noting his shame, she shook her shoulder to make the full breasts bounce. Jojo stumbled off the porch and tripped down the stairs, landing on one knee and grunting in pain. Theodora laughed and shimmied out of her skirt and slip and underwear.

"I learned the magic, the real magic, and it's wonderful. It's life, you see, and it's forever. But that's all for me. Everything ought to be. That's how power works. But for a god, power is wholly dependent upon penitents, and you abandoned me, Jojo Walker. You left me up there on my Holy Mountain all alone, shut out, forbidden to come into my own world."

"I didn't do anything but live my shitty life," he grumbled, rising clumsily to his feet. He saw the fullness of her nakedness now, a spectacle he knew he'd longed to see under different circumstances that he also knew would never come to pass, now.

"It was not enough," she reprimanded him, her face registering anger.

"Ah, but I made mistakes. It was all marvellous in theory, on paper. Isn't that what poor Trotsky learned, too? Only you won't put a hatchet in *my* head, Dog-Boy. I'll simply start over, just me and Theodora. This time it will be a goddess instead of a god. This time it will be terrible and gorgeous, a world powered by the dichotomy of pain and those who inflict it, madness and monsters. The Ten-in-One writ large. A lunatic matinee that never ends."

Jojo wiped the dirt on his hands across the fur of his torso and felt his head swim. His muscles screamed at him to stop, to give up and lie the hell down already, and his conscious mind agreed. It only stood to reason that resistance was a joke at this point, that he'd lost the fight. The war was over and the bad guys won. Besides, what would he do even if he did prevail? Where would he go? Where *could* he go?

Either way—any way he sliced it—he lost.

He clenched his fists and hung his head. Theodora *tsked*, smacking her lips with a noisy scolding.

"Mercy me," she said. "You know something? I believe I miscounted."

Not understanding and only vaguely caring, Jojo looked up at her, hating himself for registering how lovely her body looked in the moonlight. The body that wasn't hers at all any longer.

"I didn't finish the incantation," she said. "Silly me."

Raising her thin, white arms into the night, Theodora focused on the smoky grey clouds blocking the stars and sucked in a deep breath to shout, "Come Lucifer—come!"

And in the next moment, Jojo knew without a doubt that the late Reverend Shannon had been wrong about the nature of Black Harry Ashford's magic. Horribly, egregiously wrong.

CHAPTER TWENTY-EIGHT

The skin at opposite sides of her hairline split and bled. Jagged nubs of bone press through. Horns. *Of course*, Jojo thought. Because the summoning was not symbolic at all, not as the reverend determined and believed. The black magic of Black Harry Ashford was as black as it came.

Theodora's breasts shrank like deflating balloons, the skin tightening against her chest as she jutted her shoulders forward and emitted a low, nasty growl. She jerked and hopped on one leg and then the other: a wicked Saint Vitus Dance. As she spread her lips impossibly wide and they tore at the corners like cooked beef to reveal sharpening, yellow teeth, Jojo thought back to all the friends and neighbours and old enemies and the uncharacteristic things they had done since Barker Davis came to town. He thought, *The Devil made them do it*.

And as if telling him to shut up his silent thoughts, Theodora—or at least the creature she was rapidly becoming—screeched like an angry hawk. Her eyes were now bulging orbs the colour of custard, her nose collapsed and shrivelled up: a rotten scrap of leather with flaring holes on either side of it. Gone was the Widow Cavanaugh's prior beauty, her melancholy elegance and sharp, stunning intelligence. Here before Jojo was a convulsing, shrieking thing straight out of Hell, a screaming demon, a dancing carcass with gnarled claws for hands and a face only a medieval painter's worst fever dreams could conceive.

The thing rolled its gummy yellow eyes and stuck out its crumpled chest while its hissed and bellowed. Disgusted and bereaved, Jojo closed his eyes as tears scored burrows through the dirt on his face. Theodora was effectively dead. Charles and his old boss Ernie Rich, too. Litchfield was ash and the show was almost over. Almost.

The hissing demon stretched its maw open wide, displaying long, needle-thin teeth. Jojo did not back away. He did not move at all. Somewhere the calliope started up again, cranking out a tinkling tune. From beneath the shrill music, a murmur of voices rose. The demon screeched terribly and performed a jerky pirouette. Behind it the church creaked noisily; dust spilled out from between the boards that held the old structure together.

Jojo looked over the simpering devil's shoulder and watched impassively as the church shuddered and its walls cracked. The steeple split apart and tumbled from the roof in pieces. The porch collapsed and the entire building gave a great, juddering sigh before Jojo realized that it was expanding, growing. Turning blood red.

The creature sniggered and swiped a clawed hand at him, missing his face by inches. The music grew louder, and so did the voices. By the time the church had fully transformed into Leroy Dunn's barn, it was already filled with people who milled about in their best going-to-meeting clothes. At the centre, lit by a circle of lanterns swaying gently from the rafters, a boy and girl slow-danced to the delight of every onlooker.

The devil hissed even as it grinned at Jojo, its yellow eyes wide and bulging. Jojo looked from the creature back to the kids dancing in the barn, the crowd giving them a wide berth. He recognized the girl first— Nancy Campbell, the girl who got knocked up and shuttled quickly out of town. The boy he knew, too—Eddie Campbell, who ran away to join the Army, never to be seen again. Both young people wore long, dour expressions as they moved in a slow circle, their movements awkward and stiff. Though they remained as young as ever, their haggard looks belied a weariness with life and the world that came with many more years than either Eddie or Nancy had between them.

"Fine," Jojo grunted. "I see them. What's your point?"

"*Go inside,*" the abomination hissed. "*She is waiting for you.*"

Jojo glanced down at his shoes and heaved a sigh.

He didn't know who the devil was talking about, not specifically, but all the same he said quietly, "I love her."

"*I know.*"

"I killed her, didn't I?"

"*Yessss.*"

"All of them."

"*Killed them, yessss. All of them.*"

"The whole fucking town."

"*Your loves. Your ladiessss.*"

With a sniff and a groan, Jojo raised his head and peered into the barn, wondering who it was, which blameless soul he'd condemned to this harlequin hell. Beth, Sarah, Theodora? Or somebody else entirely? It could have been nearly anyone, he knew. He'd damned them all.

"*Go to her.*"

The music had become so piercing, so horribly loud that it sounded like an air raid siren. Jojo winced, then stepped forward, snagging his foot on something—Theodora, or what remained of her. Just skin, hair, and a dress. A shell shed by the demon who was now tittering with glee. Jojo squeezed his eyes shut and walked over the awful thing in the grass. He went to the barn and walked inside.

People were chatting, but their voices were completely drowned out by the screaming siren. He cut through the throng, went to the centre of the hay-strewn dance floor where Eddie and Nancy continued to jerk about in awkward circles. The boy's face was ashen, his eyes puffy and red. Shouting above the din of the calliope he said, "I tried to leave, Mr. Walker. I tried to get out. He wouldn't let me. He wouldn't let me leave."

Jojo said, "I know, son," but he couldn't even hear himself.

The girl was still pregnant. Jojo could faintly make out small movements beneath the fabric of her dress—the forever unborn, illegitimate child just as imprisoned as the rest of them. Nancy grimaced. Still, they danced.

Momentarily, a man with paper-white skin dressed in nothing but a loin cloth placed a bony hand on Eddie's shoulder. Eddie immediately disengaged from Nancy and the skeletal man moved in to resume the dance. Jojo narrowed his eyes, thought, *Hal White, the Human Skeleton.* Eddie, meanwhile, took up with a chubby bearded woman. They kissed and spun around. Eddie said loudly, "I should be dead in France right now." The bearded woman laughed.

"I can't get out," he sobbed, his tears soaking the woman's beard. "I can't even leave just to get killed."

Nearby, Lion Jack hefted a massive barbell over his head and grinned madly. Betty Overturf watched him and swooned, nearly dropping the carafe of coffee in her hands. At Jojo's feet a small brown monkey scampered, a dull maroon fez strapped to its head. A squat man with a greasy moustache scrambled after the monkey, muttering in some language Jojo didn't understand. The calliope-siren had devolved into a strident ringing in his ears that made understanding all but impossible, anyway.

He shook his head and staggered back, away from the crowd and toward the open barn doors. He wanted fresh air, but he was frozen mid-step by the approach of the obsidian devil. It was prancing toward him on goat's feet, its awful mouth hanging open and slavering freely. As it came, the creature dug its pointed claws into the flesh of its own chest and raked its trunk open. Coal-black skin fell back in two great flaps that seemed to unravel the demon—in moments something else emerged from its skin and sinew, taking up the stride without missing a step.

"Hi, Jojo," Beth said.

She barely afforded him a glance as she floated by, her white dress sparkling like diamonds in the lantern light. She had never looked better, not even on the day of their wedding. Not their first date. Not even the very first time Jojo ever laid eyes on the freckle-faced brunette with eyes like chocolate drops and a smile that never stopped melting his heart until she stopped smiling altogether.

Beth was radiant. She was *alive*.

Nancy's grimace deepened at the sight of her. Beth swept past the barn doors, paused, and turned at the waist to look back at her husband.

"Are you coming?" she asked.

Jojo curled his hands into fists and barked, "No."

Beth's face fell. "Oh, Jojo," she said sorrowfully as she produced a small revolver from thin air.

Jojo whispered, "Beth." Then she raised the gun to her temple and fired a round into her brain—a scene he'd played out in his head a million times since it happened, and here it was happening again.

Beth slumped, collapsed to the ground. No one seemed to notice. Jojo whimpered and felt his eyes burn. He wiped them dry with his hairy knuckles and stepped over his wife's corpse, back to the middle of the makeshift dance floor. He scanned the sour faces, the slowly and clumsily moving dancers, and his eyes lit upon a pitchfork propped up against the same stack of hay bales he'd laid Theodora upon when she twisted her ankle. He retrieved it and lifted it up, snatching one of the lanterns with the tines. Jojo then took the lantern and dropped the pitchfork, and he made momentary eye contact with a pair of men who were framed in a sort of milky haze at the back of the barn. Black Harry Ashford and Barker Davis.

Jojo grinned.

"Go to hell," he snarled.

"We never left," the men said in unison.

"And neither have you," Ashford added in a low, raspy voice that sounded right next to Jojo's ear.

Jojo's grin melted away and he hurled the lantern at them. Ashford and Davis vanished before the lantern struck the wall and exploded in a ball of fire that rained down on the hay scattered across the floor. Someone screamed and the barn doors flew shut as the flames rapidly spread, igniting every strand of hay and climbing the walls. It climbed the dancers, too—great orange and yellow bursts flared as dresses and slacks and jackets and cummerbunds went up and burned brightly, sending the two dozen phantom revellers into a shrieking panic, banging on the barn doors and knocking one another down as they burned and screamed and died.

Jojo sat down on an upended copper tub and watched the people burn. Nancy was the first to turn into a column of black and grey ash that flew apart in the air. Others followed suit: the bearded woman and Phyllis Gates and Hal White the Human Skeleton. The inferno rose and in no time at all there was no one left in the barn but Jojo; all the rest were reduced to ashes. Not even the bones were left.

The heat stung his face and the smoke stopped up his lungs, and Jojo felt himself closing off, shutting down, even as he wondered if any of this was at all real. If anything was.

And when the flames at last overtook him, Jojo remembered that he had no cigarettes left, and he chuckled, thinking about when he had them but nothing to light them with.

"What a world," Jojo bellowed at the blaze that ate away at his suit and hair and skin. "What a goddamn circus!"

CHAPTER TWENTY-NINE

The forest went on forever, or at least that was the way it certainly seemed to Theodora Cavanaugh. She figured she'd be lost if she had much of destination in mind, but she hadn't. She had been walking for hours, well into the purple haze of dawn and past it, into the early morning sunrise that shot spears of white light through the dense, green treetops. Her shoes were abandoned ages ago, so now she walked barefoot through the twigs and dead leaves and cool, fine dirt of the forest's floor. There were no squirrels scampering among the branches, no birds singing from high nests or in the open sky above. Theodora was completely, utterly alone. It was strange, though not a tenth as strange as everything else she'd seen and done in the last day or so. And she was cautiously prepared for more strangeness, yet.

She had just stepped off the church porch when the woods closed in on her the night before. One second she was standing beside Jojo and the next she was alone in the wilderness. For the first stretch she'd tried to get back out again, back to Jojo. Now she figured it didn't much matter which way she went, so long as she kept going. If she stopped, she was afraid she would never get moving again. She'd just take root in the ground and become part of the lifeless scenery. So on Theodora walked.

In the mid-afternoon, the sun grew bright and she came upon a large clearing. A few dozen people milled silently around, dismantling tents and lifting big black trunks into carriages. A dwarf and an obese woman shared a cigarette and a flask beside one of the carriages, and there was a monkey leaping around, though it went largely ignored. Theodora stopped just shy of the clearing, hidden by the trees that ringed it, and watched as a tall, bearded figure emerged from the last standing tent, a leather-bound book held tight to his chest, and vanished into the woods on the other side. Like the monkey, he too went ignored by the toiling carnival folk.

The notion to join them startled Theodora, who gripped the rough bark of tree she hid behind and imagined running away with the circus—at her age! Maybe, she thought, *they* could leave. Maybe there were other towns, other Litchfields, other little hells in the middle of nowhere to which she could go and live and fear and weep and love and die. . . .

From amidst the throng of sweating carnies a small, dark form burst forth—a little boy, five or six years old, pumping his little arms and legs as hard as he could in his flight for the tree line. He was covered in hair from head to toe; apart from that, he was naked. Theodora gasped, dug her nails into the bark. The boy came hurtling toward her, his feet barely touching the ground, his hairy little arms pinwheeling crazily.

The boy wept plaintively as he ran, the hair on his face hanging heavy and damp.

Theodora braced herself for the inevitable, for the men who would come after him, yelling and swearing and all but foaming at the mouth to get their wicked hands on him. . . .

But no one came. The boy made it to the trees and bounded into the shaded forest, his every step crisp and crackly as he bounced over the dead brown leaves. Theodora waited, holding her breath and quietly crying. Then at last she gave chase.

)(

She found him shivering under a blanket of damp, mouldy leaves, hugging himself for warmth and kicking one leg. He was asleep, but still running. Her heart ached for him, but she came on slowly, cautiously. She did not want to frighten him off.

Upon touching the boy on the shoulder, he started. His eyes popped open and he yelped, scrabbling up and out of the leaves in which he'd buried himself. Theodora reached for him, said, "No, it's all right, it's all *right*."

The boy rose to his feet, his canny eyes jetting between Theodora and the endless expanse of forest behind her. She held out her hand and smiled slightly.

"It's all right, Jojo. I'm your friend. Really I am."

Jojo opened his mouth as if to speak, but he said nothing. His teeth were brown. His eyes spilled fresh tears.

Theodora waggled her fingers at him.

Jojo took her hand.

)(

They slept a short while after nightfall, Theodora leaned up against a thick oak and Jojo nestling his head in her lap. She awoke with a snap from a vivid dream, though the details washed away in an instant. The boy was looking up at her from her lap, his eyes glinting in the moonlight.

She stretched her arms and yawned, then told Jojo to wait for her while she found a private spot to relieve herself. He looked positively terrified when she returned, as if he thought she'd abandoned him.

She swept him into a tight hug and held him that way for several minutes.

Then they walked on.

)(

The chasm appeared in the weak, misty light at dawn. It was a good thing they hadn't found it earlier—they might have gone right over the edge in the pitch of night.

They stood together at the edge after emerging from the trees; what remained was a ledge no more than six feet from a sheer drop to nothing at all. The boy reached for her hand, and she squeezed it in hers. They took it all in, the vast open whiteness before them, and neither of them made a single sound.

The ledge extended as far as she could see in either direction. Below, the precipitous drop fell a mile before becoming obscured in a bluish white mist. The mist stretched out beyond the chasm indefinitely.

Theodora and Jojo had reached the end of the world.

In an instant she understood everything. There was Litchfield, then the drop. Then: nothing at all. She had never been to St. Louis, and Jojo never bet on any horses at Hot Springs or anywhere else. There was only Litchfield. It wasn't just that the magician *wouldn't* let them leave—they *couldn't*. There was nowhere they could possibly go.

Theodora had to laugh, and she did. For a long time. Jojo just sat down on the edge and dangled his hairy legs above the infinite void. After a while, he scooted away from it, stood up, and pointed at his stomach.

"Hungry?" she asked him, her voice raspy from the laughing. "Me too."

Once again she took his hand. Once again they set off into the forest.

)(

Sitting on a felled tree beside a bright green bush, they dined on handfuls of the red berries that grew there. Theodora's lips were stained with the juices. Jojo's fur was matted and sticky.

When he finished eating, he spoke to her for the first time.

"What am I?"

"A boy," she answered quickly. "You're just a boy."

"Mr. Ashford said—"

"Forget what Ashford said," she snapped. "You must forget about him."

They rested, silently, and resumed their journey in the cool gloom of the evening. Theodora spent this time turning philosophical questions over in her head—does St. Louis even exist, or is there any place else at all?—but she did not give them voice. Vaguely, she knew the answers already. In a strange sort of way, she supposed she always had. She kept expecting the boy to ask her what was beyond the chasm, but she guessed he knew, too. There was nothing more. Because Ashford hadn't made anything more.

)(

The light that glowed in the middle distance was all that kept her going; it was very late and she wanted nothing more than to sit down and sleep and maybe never wake up again. Besides, she'd been carrying the boy for the last hour, and she was nearly certain he weighed more by the minute—he was growing, she was sure of it, and at a very rapid pace.

Since she did not know what caused the light, Theodora gently laid the boy on a soft bed of moss, out of the moon's silvery reach, and tiptoed on ahead alone. As she drew near and the trees seemed to part for her, she sucked in a sharp breath. For there in the middle of the wilderness was a massive, shimmering movie screen.

Seated in a small, circular auditorium of chairs made from living roots was an audience of twenty or so people, their eyes collectively glued to the screen. Theodora could hardly look away herself—she was curious and afraid, and more than a little interested in the pulsing, full colour title card up there that read:

THE STORY OF LITCHFIELD

But then, the film burned up in a bubbling, black and orange mess. The screen went stark white and the audience groaned.

For her part, Theodora ducked behind a tree as she had at the devolving carnival sideshow and watched in silence. In twos and threes the audience rose, muttering and grousing, and wandered in every direction, vanishing into the inky shadows of the forest. The screen went dark. And someone touched Theodora on the shoulder, eliciting a sharp shriek.

She spun around the tree as if it was May Day and backed quickly away from Barker Davis, who stood with one arm behind his back and grinning ear to ear. He was back in old form—pressed blue suit, flouncy bowtie, his shellacked hair combed down on either side from the part in the middle. He raised the hand with which he'd touched Theodora's shoulder and gave a playful salute.

"No show tonight," he said softly. "It isn't finished yet, you see."

Theodora sneered.

"What more do you want? What more is there for you to do to us?"

Davis' grin retracted and he regarded his hand for a brief moment before twisting it quickly at the wrist and producing a long-stemmed rose from thin air. He chuckled lightly, poked the stem between his lips, and with another flourish of his hand it became a cigar.

"And for my last trick," he said in a sing-song way, and from the palm of his hand grew a long, thin flame from which he lit the cigar. He puffed away at it for a few seconds, the smoke trailing out of his mouth and nostrils, and then heaved a deep sigh.

"Some years ago," he said, his eyes on the burning ember at the tip of his smoke, "I saw a picture called *Battle of the Sexes*. Now this was a silent picture, must have been around, oh, 1914 or so. Not terribly memorable, apart from the fact that Griffith—he was the director, you understand—made the same picture again years later, around '28. Now why do you suppose Mr. Griffith did that?"

Theodora remained silent, watching the magician with weary eyes.

"We-ell," he drawled, taking another long puff from the cigar, "for one thing, this new version had sound—Movietone sound-on-film, they called it. Quite an innovation, it was. Had a little song in it and everything. 'Just a Sweetheart.' I still remember the words.

"I loved the pictures back then. Still do. A whole different sort of magic there. Illusion and trickery the likes of which crummy sideshows never reached. Never, Theodora. Not even . . . well, I digress.

"Things *change*, my dear. We learn from our imperfections, our mistakes. And, if we've got the mettle, we can always try again, can't we? Say, I think I've got an awful lot of mettle, don't you?"

His grin widened again, smoke seeping out of it. Theodora took another few steps back.

"I liked that second version much better, myself. An improvement on every count. And I think I shall like the second Litchfield much, much better, too."

"There's nothing left," she stammered, ashamed of the hitch in her voice. "No one."

"That's not true. I have you, Miss Cavanaugh. And the dog boy, of course."

With that, Davis turned on his heel and called into the darkness: "Come on, little one. Come into the light. I won't hurt you."

"Stay where you are, Jojo!" Theodora shouted. "He's a monster!"

Davis laughed. "*I'm* the monster? Have you seen the little beast? Sakes alive. . . ."

"He's just a boy!"

"And I'm just an entertainer, my dear."

Momentarily the boy emerged from the shadows, rubbing his tired eyes with his fists. He looked from one adult to the other, his face slack and expression puzzled.

"Hello there, Jojo," Davis cooed, bending over. "How would you like a proper place to live? A real house with a real bed in it?"

Theodora said: "We burned them all."

"No, not all. And you will rebuild. If people do anything at all, they destroy and rebuild. Destroy and rebuild. A new life, a new chance. A new Litchfield."

"A new lie," she put in.

Barker Davis whipped around and hissed at her, his eyes yellow and bright.

"It's all you've *got!*" he screeched.

Theodora jumped backwards and collided with a tree. She stumbled and fell over, then quickly scrambled away from Davis. But before he could return his attention to the boy, Jojo leapt into the air and fixed himself to Davis' back, scraping claws at the man's face and sinking his half-rotted teeth into the flesh of the neck. Davis screamed and slapped at the hairy child, but Jojo held on, scratching and biting, biting and scratching.

"Jojo!" Theodora yelled. "Jojo, no!"

"I won't let you," the boy bellowed, his voice breaking. Deepening. "You took everything from me. *Everything.*"

Before her petrified eyes Jojo was growing into a man, even as he dug in with nails and teeth and shredded Barker Davis' face and throat. Blood flowed freely from his cheeks and open neck. It was jet black.

Before long, Jojo's feet touched the ground; he was as tall as Davis now, if not an inch taller. He seized Davis by the shoulders and spun him round. Smoke roiled up from the leaves at their feet—the cigar had dropped into the detritus and ignited it. Neither man noticed, for one was in a savage frenzy and the other was in the process of being torn apart. Theodora cried as she watched.

"Beth!" Jojo screamed. "Sarah! My job! My friends! My whole goddamn life! You took it all!"

Davis opened his mouth to answer, but only wet, black bubbles passed his lips. Jojo howled madly, a wolf's howl, and brought his foaming jaws down upon the middle of Davis' face. He clamped down, growling as he wrenched his head from side to side, and tore away the man's nose and upper lip. Theodora yelped with fright.

Jojo chewed the skin and cartilage before spitting the whole gummy mess right back in Davis' annihilated face.

"You won't take her, too," Jojo said, and he lifted Barker Davis up in the air before hurling him at the nearest tree. Davis smashed into the sturdy trunk with his back, which snapped like a toothpick. The man dropped then to the ground, entirely motionless and twisted impossibly.

Leaves crunched close by and Jojo started at it. Theodora had fallen to her knees, trembling all over, her face a sagging mask of despair.

"Jojo . . ."

"Pardon the mess," he said, his broad, furry chest heaving.

"Is he—?"

"Dead? No way. Not him."

"Then . . . now what?"

He stretched his back, arching his neck to take in the night sky. He said, "We go back."

"Back? Back where?"

"To town. Home."

"We have no home! Don't you remember the chasm? There's nothing, Jojo! *Nothing!*"

"There's us," he said calmly as he walked over to her and extended his hand. "There's still us."

Theodora took his hand and Jojo lifted her up to her feet. She fell against him, buried her face in the hair of his chest and shoulder, and she sobbed.

"He'll come back, won't he?"

"He'll come back," Jojo agreed.

She reared back, wiped her eyes and face along her sleeve and then locked eyes with him.

"He won't let us be happy," she said. "He won't. He won't allow it."

"I'm not asking his permission."

"All this, it was to do it all over again, don't you see? He's going to make it *worse*, for god's sakes!"

"And he'll make the same mistake he made the first time, Theodora. He'll forget about things like love and the huge, stupid determination of people like me. I'll go through this a thousand times for you, damn it. A *million*. Because you're all I got. And all I want."

"Oh," she muttered, because it was all she could say. She wanted nothing more in the world than to kiss him, but his face was dripping with blood and bits of skin. *His* blood and *his* skin. It made her shudder.

"I'll shave, of course."

"Jojo."

"How about George this time around?"

"George."

"It's my name."

"I know."

"Just George."

"I like it."

※

Neither of them could have realized they'd gone the wrong way until they emerged at the ledge overlooking the great, yawning chasm again. Jojo—now just George—went cautiously to the edge and stood there in silence for several long minutes, breathing deeply of the thick, misty air that rolled up from the vast emptiness before him. A hollow sound, a sort of moaning wind, filled the void. After a time, Theodora went to him.

"It won't do any good to stare at it," she said. "We should go back the other way."

"Goes on forever, I guess."

"I guess it does."

"Do you suppose we're in hell?"

"Not with you. You wouldn't be in my hell."

He smiled, but it was a tense smile.

"She's right, you know," came a weak voice behind them. They both jerked around to see who had spoken. A man was shambling along the ledge, coming toward them from the east. He was small and thin, his clothes shabby, his face dirty and unshaved. His eyes were rimmed with red and his hands shook. When he was no more than a couple of yards away from them, he stopped. "You'll go mad looking down into that. I've been looking at it for weeks, and look at me."

"Who . . ." Theodora whispered.

"A trick," George said.

"No, not me," said the man. "You want tricks, try one of those—"

He pointed a trembling finger at the tree line. Theodora followed the finger to the trees with her eyes and yelped. George looked, too. A thin, obsidian-skinned devil was prancing amongst the trees there, flicking its grey tongue and waggling its arms theatrically.

"You won't see them for a while once you've started over," the man said sullenly. "You'll think they've gone away, that you're safe again. But you won't be. Nothing you can do will satisfy them—satisfy *him*. And he'll start tearing it all down again." His voice cracked and he placed a hand over his eyes. "It's worse every time."

"My God," Theodora said, keeping the devil in her line of sight until,

291

at last, it vanished. "You—you're the one who called me, aren't you. It was you who warned me about Barker Davis."

The man nodded.

"Fat lot of good it did, huh?"

George narrowed his eyes, said, "How many times . . . ?"

"Too many," said the man. "Too many. I won't do it again. I won't watch everyone go mad again, everybody die. I won't stand by and watch it all burn."

"Then help us. Help us make it right for once."

The man snorted and shook his head.

"Sorry," he said with a quivering grin. "But hey, best of luck. To both of you."

And with that he launched himself at the edge and leapt into the gaping expanse. Theodora cried out, and both she and George hurried to the edge in time to see the rumpled, tired little man get swallowed by the mist.

She screamed after him, and her voice echoed out infinitely. George swallowed hard and gazed at the swirling mist, wondering what the man would find down there, if anything at all. There would come a time, he knew now, when he would think of doing the same. He, too, would one day find himself standing where he now stood, comparing the dark carnival of Litchfield to the unknowable emptiness that surrounded it. Which would win out?

He narrowed his eyes and studied Theodora's tear-streaked face, which was getting brighter and shining in the gathering dawn. She also stared with wide eyes at the edge of the world and all the impossible oblivion beyond it, stretching on and on and on forever. She also considered the jump, the quick end. The escape.

Instead, she squeezed her eyes shut and turned away. And when she opened them again to look up at George Walker's dirty, shaggy, wolf-man face, she smiled sadly.

George smiled back at her.

She didn't look a damn thing like Irene Dunne.

ACKNOWLEDGEMENTS

Infinite gratitude is owed to Brett Savory and Sandra Kasturi for taking a chance on this novel, not to mention for bestowing upon it a far better title than originally it suffered (with great shame and mortification). Many warm thanks to Samantha Beiko for editing the manuscript, and to Erik Mohr for the gorgeous cover art. I am indescribably honoured to join the ChiZine family, and obliged to you all for making *Rib* a better book. Thank you.

ABOUT THE AUTHOR

Ed Kurtz is the author of *Nausea*, *A Wind of Knives*, and *Angel of the Abyss*, among other novels and novellas. His fiction has appeared in numerous magazines and anthologies like *Thuglit*, *Needle: A Magazine of Noir*, *Shotgun Honey*, and *Psychos: Serial Killers, Depraved Madmen, and the Criminally Insane*, and he was selected to appear in *The Best American Mystery Stories 2014*. Kurtz lives in Minnesota where he is at work on his next project. Visit Ed online at edkurtzbooks.com.

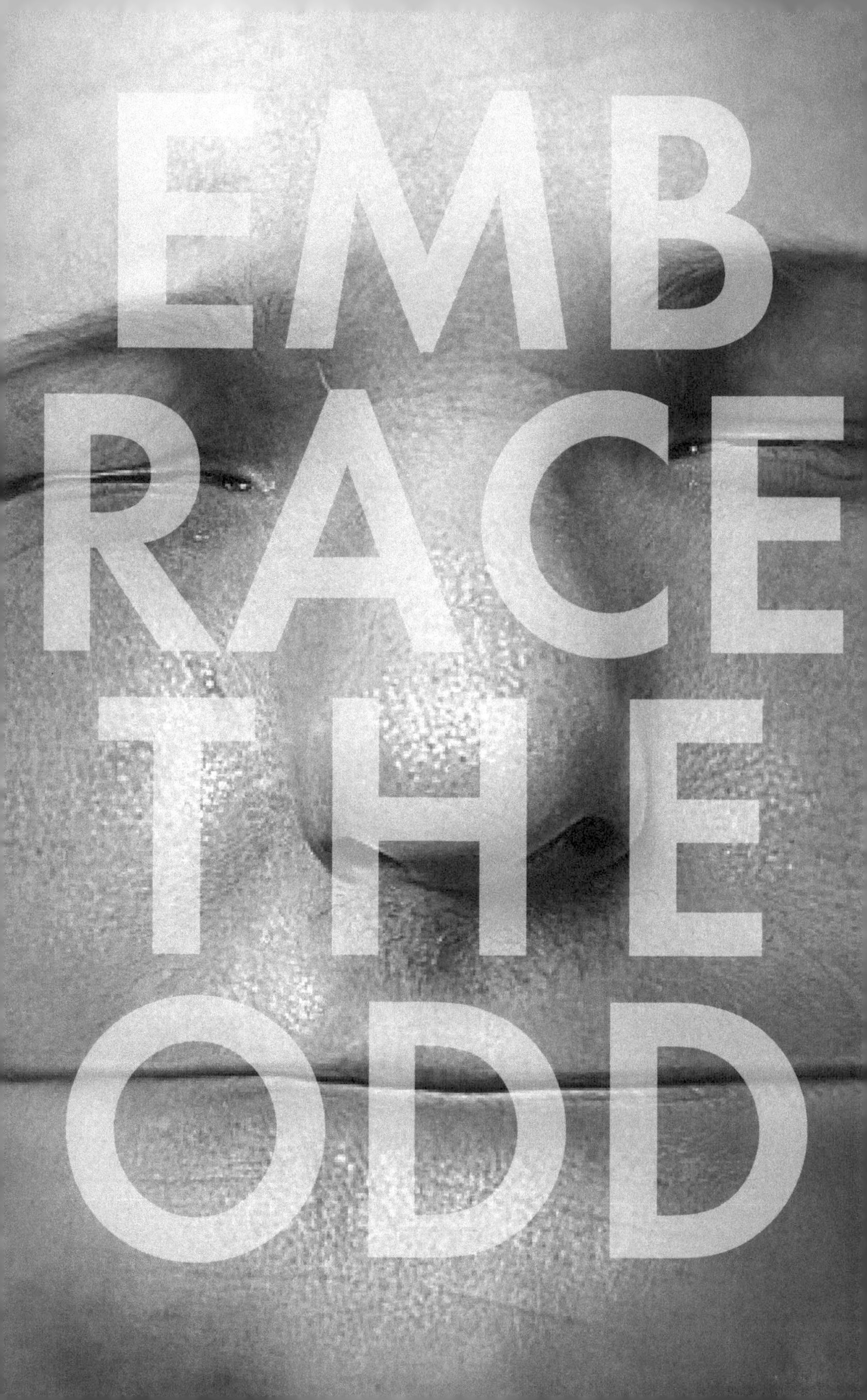
EMB
RACE
THE
ODD